PHANTOM DEATH

Sadie Montgomery's Phoenix of the Opera Series

The Phoenix of the Opera

Out of the Darkness: The Phantom's Journey

The Phantom's Opera

Phantom Death

PHANTOM DEATH

Sadie Montgomery

iUniverse, Inc.
New York Lincoln Shanghai

Phantom Death

iUniverse books may be ordered through booksellers or by contacting:

iUniverse
2021 Pine Lake Road, Suite 100
Lincoln, NE 68512
www.iuniverse.com
1-800-Authors (1-800-288-4677)

Because of the dynamic nature of the Internet, any Web addresses or links contained in this book may have changed since publication and may no longer be valid.

This is a work of fiction. All of the characters, names, incidents, places, organizations, and dialogue in this novel are either the products of the author's imagination or are used fictitiously.

ISBN: 978-0-595-48568-0 (pbk)
ISBN: 978-0-595-60663-4 (ebk)

Printed in the United States of America

To the Lovely Ladies of the Lair,
Gracious Gals,
Sweet Tarts and Tartans
Everywhere.

As always, with love, to Mom and Betty,
And to my men, Doug and Zach, for living with my obsessions.

And he arose, and came to his father. But when he was yet a great way off, his father saw him, and had compassion, and ran, and fell on his neck, and kissed him.

And the son said unto him, Father, I have sinned against heaven, and in thy sight, and am no more worthy to be called thy son.

But the father said to his servants, Bring forth the best robe, and put it on him; and put a ring on his hand, and shoes on his feet:

And bring hither the fatted calf, and kill it; and let us eat, and be merry:

For this my son was dead, and is alive again; he was lost, and is found. And they began to be merry.

—*King James Bible, Luke*

Prologue
The Phantom

He touched her nose lightly with his lips. His face was so close to hers when she woke that she was momentarily startled. His hair had fallen forward over the right-hand side of his face, but it did not disguise the uneven and roughened surface of his disfigurement. For just an instant his eyes narrowed, wary and intense. Before he could draw back, Meg brushed her fingers across his cheek and pushed the hair away from his mottled skin and smiled at him. She gently touched the twisted folds around his eye, the reddened expanse of tissue along his temple, as if to soothe a wound. In the green depths of his eyes she could see gentleness and warmth replace caution. He pressed his face against the pressure of the palm of her hand, seeking her caress, and then bent to graze her lips with his.

Erik lay warm and solid next to Meg. She rolled farther into his arms. Intimately close to him, she heard the steady beating of his heart. His large hand braced her lower back, urging her to mold her body to his. His finger gently lifted her chin, and he smiled down at her.

"My little canary, my light. Come closer," he whispered in a husky, warm exhalation as his lips trailed down the column of her neck. "My sweetness." His teeth grazed against her throat.

His hands threaded down her body, tickling across her ribs. She giggled and squirmed uselessly in his hold. He leaned back against the mattress and pulled her deftly across his body. They greeted the morning as two lovers.

Afterwards, they slept again. Meg watched him doze, quiet and safe, as the light spiraled through the curtains, warming their naked skin with its hope.

Eventually he stirred. He rose from the bed. As she watched sleepily, his broad form fill the room. He poured the water from the night before into the basin and splashed it over his face. Then methodically he washed the sweat from his body and dried himself before he went to dress.

Meg lay like a fat, lazy cat purring softly as she admired him. He was tall and strong, a beautiful man in spite of the face he hid behind a mask. His body hummed with a raw animal joy. His skin was the color of honey touched by sunshine, and his limbs were sculpted by a master's skill. Meg watched him dress and imagined that day at the Opera Populaire in Paris when she pursued him beyond his lair. There she had stolen her first glimpse of him naked and feverish as he waited for death.

Her heart contracted momentarily as she ran her eyes over the long slope of his back. The well shaped muscles were not disguised under the scars of the whip that his sojourn in the Paris prison had left him. Time had faded the raised ribbons the slash had painted, but their trace of pain would never go away. And the more recent evidence of a burn across his shoulders was a mute reminder of how close Meg had come to losing Erik forever. Although she grieved for the suffering he had endured, these scars were also a testament to the strength of their bond. He had survived; they had survived.

"Are you going to lie there the rest of the morning or are you going to get dressed and come with me to the theater?" Barely throwing a look her way, Erik sat at the small vanity in the corner of the room and combed his hair. He brushed it in such a way that it disguised the edges of his disfigurement. He didn't look at himself directly in the mirror. Instead he looked to the side or at a point just beyond his face, casting only a glance at the surface as he covered his features with the half mask he wore in the house. Although Meg encouraged him to go without the mask, he protested that Marcelo had too many servants any of whom could come across him at any moment in the rooms below. He simply would not put up with the possibility of their discomfort or stares.

Even so, at times, late in the afternoon or at night in the company of his family, when he was sure that the servants would not disturb them, he would wearily remove the mask and wipe the feel of it away from his skin. It had taken time, but he knew he could trust them.

At first, when Meg and he would make love, if her hand or her lips traveled to that part of his face which he insisted on hiding, he would pull gently away from her, turn his face, to direct her attention to the unscarred landscape of the other cheek. Then one night when he twisted in Meg's arms and buried that side of his face against the cotton cover of his pillow, she forced him to look at her. She would not let him hide.

"I want all of you," she had told him in a tone that would brook no argument. "I want your beauty, your ugliness, everything. All of you or nothing, Erik. I insist."

With a thinly veiled strain of doubt in his voice, he had protested, "Don't pretend to love something that you can only find hideous. You've learned to bear it, that's all."

Meg had understood that whatever answer she gave him at that moment would direct the course of their lives. She couldn't lie to him, but she knew she had to make him understand. With actions more than words, she soothed him. She ran her hands along both his cheeks and whispered close to his mouth, their sweet breath commingling, "I won't lie. You've had to live with it your whole life. Nothing can change that. It's a part of you, and somehow you wouldn't be you without it. When I touch you here and here and here," and she branded those strange features of his tortured face with kisses, "I feel such a tenderness for you."

Quietly he accused, "Tenderness or pity, Meg?"

"Why in the world would I pity you?" she chided. "You've fathered my children, and every time you touch me I'm incapable of speech. You're passionate, loyal, and tender. You had every reason to lie down and die like a dog, and you stood like a man. You write the music of heaven and hell. You're the most beautiful man I've ever known. Why would I pity such as you?"

He looked deeply into her eyes, daring her to retract her words or to turn away, until something, something ineffable, must have convinced him that she spoke the truth.

Unfortunately the rest of the world would never really know her Erik. They would only glimpse some of his genius. Marcelo Costanzi had given Erik the direction of the Teatro dell'Opera, and Erik found himself, finally, at home in the demimonde of artists and bohemians. No longer did he skulk among the dark shadows, behind the curtains, in the wings, enviously spying on the frenetic life of the stage. No longer did he write his compositions in the bowels of underground chambers and tunnels and dream of sharing his gift with the world above.

Here in their new home in Italy, Erik was no longer the Phantom of the Opera. He *was* Opera.

CHAPTER 1

To Dream

True, I talk of dreams,
Which are the children of an idle brain,
Begot of nothing but vain fantasy,
Which is as thin of substance as the air
And more inconstant than the wind, who woos
Even now the frozen bosom of the north,
And, being anger'd, puffs away from thence,
Turning his face to the dew-dropping south.

Romeo and Juliet, William Shakespeare

the smell of smoke acrid stings his nostrils, the crackle and hiss of wood splintering from the heat, and screams knifing through his ears and behind his eyes, piercing and bleeding him, dead people, dead eyes, crushed skulls, twisted limbs covered in crystal and fire, mea culpa, mea culpa, his voice strangled as he drops through the wooden floor of the theater, no, not the theater, not the trapdoor, not the escape, dropping, he drops, heavy, arms empty, heart scoured, into blackness, his body jarred by the abrupt stop, the pull on tendons and muscles and bones, the rope rough and coarse against his skin, burning and cutting into his throat, naked on cold stone, the taste of blood and bile on his tongue, sad animal groans leach from his mouth, he curls himself, a chrysalis of pain, his fingers, the broken keys on a piano, the man wears a mask, his features twisted and painted, an obscene smile under his black moustache, his officer's uniform a disguise, the notes from his mouth dissonant chords, demanding, refusing, condemning, behind the mask worms and clouts of death, behind the mask, black emptiness, horror, bars spring up and press hard against bloodied flesh, naked he hangs by the neck as strangers beat him with the long stems of thorny roses, the points tear him, blood sprinkles

5

the open grave below him, inside someone screams, nails splinter against dry wood, the smell of earth pungent fills his nostrils, he opens his mouth to call out and earth pours in drowning the sound, stopping his air

He woke violently from the dream. Meg shifted and moaned next to him, then spooned herself to his shape and settled immediately back into the sweet dream she must have been having. Erik wiped his hand across his forehead, pushing the cold sweat from his skin. His heart raced. He fought down the urge to retch from the lingering smell of decay in his nose and mouth. Meg lay soft and warm next to him, and he buried his face in her hair and breathed in the scent of lilac. Slowly, his heart took the rhythm of her pulse, and the images of the dream faded, receded to a safe distance.

The dream had not tortured him for many years. Recently, however, it had returned with a vehemence that made him dread the night. Fortunately Meg had been tired and was sleeping deeply. She didn't need to be reminded of those last months in Paris. They had left the past behind them and created a new life for themselves in Rome. Meg stirred in his arms. He kissed her on the side of the cheek, untangled their limbs, and carefully slipped out of bed.

Finding his clothes, he dressed quietly, taking care not to disturb Meg. He walked down the hallway to his children's rooms. First, he checked in on the two boys, François and Mario, then he went to Laurette's room. She didn't like sleeping in her own room, and Erik had wanted to argue with Madeleine and Meg when they insisted that the boys should have a separate room. Why would anyone choose to be alone? He had spent too many years alone, and his heart ached when they laid Laurette in the bed that was too large for her and she fussed for someone to stay. In spite of Madeleine's scolding, he lingered each night and waited for his baby girl to drop off to sleep before he was willing to leave her.

He bent and picked up the blanket that had slipped to the floor and covered her with it. As he turned to go, Laurette woke and called out to him to pick her up. She was almost four, but she still had the softness of a baby about her.

"Papa," she insisted, and without thinking twice, Erik picked her up and held her against his shoulder, rocking gently from side to side.

"Do you want me to sing to you, my petal?" he whispered.

He felt her tiny cheek nod against his, and he kissed her on the top of her head as she lay flat against him. He sang the lullaby he had composed for her. Her body relaxed, so calm, so trusting was she. She fell asleep before he finished the song, which was simply a listing of all the wonderful things she loved, but he continued for several more minutes to hold her and sing. Her calm flowed over him, too. Only when her hands fell heavy to her sides did Erik return her to the bed, cover her, and quietly back out of the room.

He knew he'd not sleep again this night. The images from the dream were too raw and painful, and they would spring immediately full-blown to his mind if he lay down to sleep. So instead of returning to his and Meg's bedroom, Erik went down the stairs to the music room. Although there was no fire and the room was cold, it didn't bother him. He had spent years in the cold damp of the underground tunnels of the Opera Populaire in Paris. It was only in the prison cell that Erik had known what it was like to suffer from the cold. In his underground refuge, Erik had worn cashmere and wool sweaters, coats, or vests, had thickly woven cotton shirts and heavy, lined trousers. In the prison, they had left him barely clothed, and the freezing temperatures of early morning often formed a layer of ice on the water in the basin left for his basic needs; his breath came out in harsh white puffs of crystallized vapor. The chill in the music room was nothing compared to the cold abandonment and hate that had hounded him in the Parisian jail. So he sat without a fire, lit the lamp at the piano, and ran his stiff fingers over the cold ivories of the piano. He didn't play at first but caressed the keys with ghostly pressure and stretched his fingers over imaginary scales and chords. Then his fingers lost their rigidity and danced across the surface, teasing out melodies known and unknown. A refrain tumbled round his mind, and Erik let it spill forth onto the keyboard, paused, repeated, adjusted the key, allowing his left hand to accompany the right one, paused again, and searched for his ink and jotted splotchy notes onto a blank sheet of staff paper. It was merely a simple song.

Months ago, he had finished an opera for the Teatro dell'Opera. Having satisfied that burning impulse to commit the sounds to paper, he had immersed himself in constant revisions and then the staging of the work itself. Now sated and calmed, he wondered if there were any more notes to write. Of sounds, melodies, cadences there were plenty, like the notes of a lone oboe or the steps of a single dancer on the stage, or the rending sigh of a violin, but he must wait. He must allow the music to swell and unfold. Its individual strains would eventually coalesce and demand release. Nothing yet. No driving desire to bring it forth. Not yet.

He was tired of strife, tired of drama. If only he could write a light operetta, one to make the audience laugh. His fingers ground to a stop, and he was forced to look at them. The police inspector had crushed them one by one—several on each hand. The man had known how important his fingers were to him, how without them he'd not be able to play his music, perhaps not be able to compose.

Erik flexed the digits. Several of the knuckles were enlarged. If one looked closely, one could see his fingers had healed bent and twisted. His index finger on the left hand would bend only partially, but he had learned to compensate for it. The pain at times was unbearable, but he forced them to work. Meg would massage them at night; she was the only one who had any idea how much they bothered him. It was a miracle he could play at all, but he could never play the way he once had.

She had come up behind him silently, and when she placed her hand on his shoulder, he immediately stiffened and turned.

"What are you doing up?" he asked, accusingly. He pulled her down to the piano bench next to him and looked into her face with a reproving scowl.

"I woke and found you gone. I could hear you playing."

"I'm sorry. I hadn't meant to wake you."

"I don't think it was the playing that woke me. I think it was the fact that you were missing. I kept backing up to find you. I nearly fell out of bed before I realized you hadn't simply rolled away from me," she complained, teasingly.

Erik squeezed her hand gently and then began to play a soft melody that she recognized as one she had sung in a recent production. It was not one of his own arias, and it surprised her that he played it. He rarely played any but his own compositions.

"I liked that one." Meg hummed along for a few bars with Erik's playing. "Why did you wake up?"

"Oh, just not sleepy, I suppose."

She knew he was lying. She could tell. He didn't realize how well she could read him. He was as clear to her as the notes on the music score were to him. "You had a bad dream, didn't you?" Her tone allowed for no denial.

His brows furrowed in a brief sign of annoyance. He felt petulant and considered not answering her. But she sat so patiently that he felt foolish. "Yes."

When he didn't elaborate, Meg felt a shiver run down her spine. What ghost was haunting him now? He had been through so much. The two of them had been through a great deal of torment. But the past year or more had been glorious. Never had she been happier. They had put to rest all the demons that had pursued them. She was convinced Erik finally accepted that he had a right to be happy, to be loved. The old tension between her and Christine had been resolved. She was absolutely sure Erik loved her and no other. Yet in the past weeks, Erik had awoken abruptly in obvious distress nearly every night. He was suffering from lack of sleep; great dark patches lined his eyes. When she asked him about the dream, at first he scoffed at its importance and said it was shadows from the past. He had even snapped at her that it was nothing. But it was clearly not "nothing."

Steeling herself against his anger, she took a deep breath and asked, "What was the dream about, Erik? And before you tell me 'nothing,' let me say that I don't believe you."

His fingers pressed angrily against the keys, but his lips were pursed solidly shut. Meg waited and watched him. She would not be denied this time. Sooner or later he would have to speak to her.

After nearly ten minutes had passed in which Erik insisted on ignoring her presence and continued to play more and more discordant and dramatic movements of a yet unwritten score, Meg could take it no longer.

"God in heaven, Erik! You are so stubborn."

Fingers crashed down once and twice and again on a jumble of notes, not music but the wail of a wounded lion. Meg's mouth gaped at the unexpected violence of her husband's reaction. Without a word he rose from the piano bench and paced belligerently between her and the fireplace. After several passes, he finally stopped and stared into the cold, dark hearth.

Meg resisted the shiver that clutched at the back of her neck. She hadn't expected him to react this way. She didn't know what fine line she had crossed. Usually she could scold him into opening up his heart to her. How was she to help him if she didn't know the problem?

When several moments passed and Erik continued to ignore her, Meg remarked, softly, addressing no one in particular but herself or the emptiness around her, "I'm cold."

"Then go back to the bedroom!" His tone was angry, and Meg felt it like a slap in the face.

She fought back the sudden burning sensation behind her eyes and nose, bit away at her lower lip, and then called up her own anger. How did he earn the right to speak to her like that? Hadn't she given him everything? Hadn't she risked everything for him? The selfish, selfish beast! When would she learn to see him as he really was? A beast, nothing but a beast who licks his wounds and bites the hand that tries to feed him.

Meg no longer felt the cold. Her temper had risen to such a pitch that she considered removing the robe she had put on over her night clothes. She stood in her best ballet pose, her spine painfully straight, the muscles along her entire body ready to move, and scolded him, "You have no right to speak to me that way! I am only concerned for…"

"You have no idea who I am!" His eyes sparked green fire in the darkness.

"Perhaps I don't," she answered, meeting anger with anger.

Meg could hear his breathing, deep and harsh, as if he barely could control his emotions. She knew she could not stop the tears if she stayed, and she feared what she might say if he spoke to her again in fury. So she turned and walked quickly to the door.

Just as she reached out toward the door, his large square hand descended heavily onto hers. He swept it from the knob and dragged her to the sofa. There he placed his hands squarely on her narrow shoulders and forced her down onto the cushion. She tried to rise only once, but she could swear she heard him growl as he pressed her down again.

Sensing no more resistance from his wife, Erik backed away to stand near the fireplace as he had before.

"Listen to me. Don't interrupt."

He waited to see some sign of compliance on her part. When she managed to nod her head only slightly, he began to speak again. His tone was terse and unpleasant, but it was steady and restrained.

"The dream I keep having is nothing but a reminder of who and what I am. Even now, even here with you, with the…children…" His words were suspended for a moment as he fought to keep his emotions from rising and choking them off. "I remember the fall. It gets all tangled in my dream with my escape that night in the opera, the night of the chandelier." He wasn't talking to Meg any longer. His voice, at first restrained, wavered and drifted as if he were unconsciously voicing his inner thoughts. "That fall turns into the other fall, the one on the hangman's scaffold. I sometimes think I've died, not once but many times."

Suddenly Erik shook himself as if he had emerged from the ocean and wished to shake the moisture from his skin. He looked at Meg, studied her, but didn't approach. When he spoke again, his voice was gentler. "I'm sorry I frightened you. I haven't slept well for several nights."

The anger Meg had felt dissipated. Erik sank to the chair near the cold hearth, and Meg dared to come to him. She sat on the stool at the foot of the chair and cautiously touched his knee.

His eyes moved from a vacant spot somewhere in the darkness to stare down at that slight, delicate hand. It almost seemed to glow in the faint light from the lamp by the piano. He barely touched her finger tips with his own.

"I want to go back, Meg." She had not moved away. He took her hand in both of his and held it tightly. Yearning filled his voice, softening its timber. "I want to go back to my rooms, the ones I built of props from the operas. I want to lie in my bed, the one I slept in all those years. I want to hear the sound of my native tongue around me. I…"

Meg couldn't believe what he was saying. How could he wish to turn back the clock and return to his solitary existence in the bowels of the Opera Populaire? Could he really regret their life together, their children? She could tell there were unspent tears in his plea, but she felt cold when she spoke to him. "I suppose that you wish for a simpler life, unencumbered. But you can't go back to those rooms."

He missed the point she wanted to make. Instead he addressed the practical obstacle she had raised, the warning that a return to Paris was impossible for him. "I can't go back because to do so would sign my death warrant. He'd be waiting for me."

So if not for the threat of death, he would abandon them! Meg looked away from him. She stared over her shoulder at the far dark corner of the room. She would not let him see that she was crying.

When he touched her hair, it startled her. Angry, she pulled away, dragging her hand from his grasp.

She didn't see the confusion in his eyes.

"Meg?" When she didn't answer, he called to her again, "Meg? Please look at me."

"No. I don't think I want to."

Erik could tell he had somehow hurt her. How could he avoid it, he who had done such ugly work in his lifetime?

"Very well," he said, annoyed with himself and with Meg.

She whirled on him then and accused him. "You say you'd prefer to go back to a time before us! How am I supposed to understand that, Erik?"

"No, no, you don't understand," he answered, unable to disguise his frustration. "How can I make you understand? I don't want to return to that life. I'm not mad. But it wasn't all loneliness, Meg. Those rooms under the opera house saved me. I was in control. I was powerful. I felt…safe. I had escaped. But now…There's no sanctuary for me. Even the subterranean rooms of the Teatro dell'Opera are gone, destroyed by the fire. Meg, I can't shake the feeling that I'm in danger again. I keep dreaming of the policeman who captured me, Leroux. I keep seeing his face, and he knows I didn't die that day at the end of that noose. He knows!"

"But it's only a dream, Erik. That was over ten years ago now. You have a new identity. You live in a foreign country where he can't touch you. Why are you afraid of him?"

Meg sensed his doubt. She knelt before him, pushed her body between his thighs, and wrapped her arms solidly around his shoulders. He accepted her effort to comfort him. Slowly his arms returned her embrace.

Yet it was impossible for him to escape the feeling that he was doomed. The dream had taken the form of a premonition for him. He was a hunted criminal. Leroux would find him and drag him back to Paris, to his execution. Erik had tempted fate. If he had been content to lead a quiet life, then this would not have happened. If he hadn't shown his masked face to the select enclave of society to which Marcelo belonged, then perhaps he could rest easy.

"When did you start to have this dream? What happened to bring it back to you?"

Erik tried to think of the first night he dreamed of Leroux, dreamed of the inspector crushing his fingers, relived the whippings and humiliations of prison, the torment of his public trial and execution. It was nearly a month ago. What had been unusual about that time? Nothing that he could think of offhand.

Meg had been glorious in his tragedy of a young woman who becomes obsessed with ballet. The heroine Amélie refuses even love, knowing that it will take her from the stage and destroy her chances for perfection. In the last scene as her lover begs her to marry him, Amélie is torn between her desire for him and her need to pursue her art. When he walks away, she performs her final dance. She gives a perfect performance, her feet are bleeding from the effort, and as she bows before the thunderous applause of the crowd, she sees her lover's face just before he turns away, and her heart simply stops.

The critics had been appalled by the cruel ending; they hounded him for days to comment on it. Marcelo paid several assistants at the opera house to deal with the journalists and to keep them at bay. But one very ambitious man had somehow gotten past the managers, past the ushers, past the performers themselves, and had cornered Erik in the wings.

He was a young man, energetic and driven. Erik nearly plowed into him as he turned to speak with the scene shifters. His name was Paolo Ricci, and he wanted to write a story, not a review of the play but a story about the mysterious musical director of the Teatro dell'Opera who took such risks with the tastes of the opera aficionados, the man who appeared out of nowhere many seasons ago and revolutionized Italian opera.

When Erik tried to get past the young man, the latter had blocked his way. Each time Erik turned, the young man darted in the same direction, effectively cutting off his retreat. Tightlipped, Erik had demanded that the intruder remove himself. To which the young journalist cocked his head to the side and remarked, "French? You are French, not Italian, are you not?"

Erik spoke little, but his Italian was flawless. How this young upstart could have detected the strains of his French under the fluid cadence of his Italian was more than Erik could imagine. He had fooled even the members of the aristocracy who dined on occasion with his patron, friend, and adopted father, Sig. Costanzi.

Erik abruptly called out. Two large beefy men rushed to his side. Before they could physically remove the reporter, the latter had blurted out one last question. "Why is it that you hide, Monsieur Costanzi, behind that mask?"

That was shortly before the dreams began. That was it. That was the chink in the wall he had constructed painstakingly around himself and his loved ones to keep the evil out, to keep the past at bay, to keep them all safe.

"I'm too well known here, Meg. This is not what I had expected. I thought to remain in the shadows, backstage." Marcelo had given him the chance to write and direct his own work, and Erik had grabbed at it. It wasn't enough to compose and instruct the orchestra and maestro. Soon he was involved with the actual staging itself, making decisions about sets and costumes, choosing the cast. "I thought it didn't matter if only the performers and technicians saw me, knew something about me. But they won't let one be. The opening night receptions, the journalists, the impresarios and directors from other theater companies, all of them demand to meet me. Marcelo has tried to keep it under control, but the last two seasons have been devastating. I saw a caricature of myself in one of the gazettes Jacopo was reading." Jacopo, a scene shifter at the Teatro dell'Opera, had folded the paper and stuck it in his back pocket as Erik came backstage. Unfortunately, the paper had fallen from Jacopo's pocket and had lain open at the cartoon. Erik felt sick when he recognized himself as the subject. "It was a drawing of a man in a mask and the caption asked, 'Who is this mysterious masked genius of the opera?'"

Meg couldn't quell the shiver that ran down her spine at the image and the name the cartoonist had penned for her husband. It recalled to her his former identities. "But surely no one outside Rome sees those?"

Erik scowled at her. "I wouldn't be so sure, Meg. Marcelo mentioned that the other day when he and Madeleine attended the soirée at Sig. Quomi's villa, he met a certain Maurice Chalmers recently arrived from Paris. He's a patron at the Opera National. He asked about me."

"What? About the Phantom?"

"No. He asked about Sig. Erik Costanzi, the mysterious composer who refuses to let anyone see his face. It appears that my reputation is reaching several of the capitals of Europe. How long before someone wonders about the coincidences, Meg? If Leroux thinks for a moment that I still live…"

Meg bit her lip until she tasted blood.

Raoul muttered to himself as he adjusted his sleeves and pushed his heel into the boot his valet held for him.

"My Lord?" offered the valet, thinking Raoul might be addressing him.

"Nothing, Georges. Pay me no mind." Raoul dismissed the valet and studied his reflection in the full length mirror. He was the epitome of a gentleman, tall and narrow hipped with a slender, but powerful build. He should strike an imposing figure, especially when confronting someone of Inspector Leroux's class. He refused to be cowed by the little bulldog of a man. Who the hell did he think he was, asking the same old questions year in and year out, poking his nose into the count's affairs?

Raoul had no patience with the inspector. It had been more than a decade since the case had been closed, and yet Leroux persisted in his mad obsession with the events of 1870 at the Opera Populaire, the strange events involving the Phantom of the Opera. The count, as always when Leroux chose to visit, wondered why the inspector had taken such an interest in the murders of the Opera Populaire. His particular zeal in pursuing Erik and bringing him to justice had been maniacal, almost personal.

Leroux had been shown to the front parlor. Raoul had purposefully tarried in his toilette, hoping to make his displeasure clear to the police inspector by making him wait for nearly an hour. But he could forestall the visit no longer.

"Dupré?" He called to the butler as he descended the central staircase to the foyer.

"My Lord?"

"Does our guest still wait in the front parlor?"

"Yes, My Lord, and may I say he seems rather impatient."

Raoul smiled roguishly. "Good. And my wife?"

"In the music room with master Victor and mistresses Elise and Erica."

"Be sure we are not disturbed. I don't want the inspector interrogating the countess and upsetting her."

The butler seemed well aware of the situation and bowed slightly in agreement. "I'll see to it that Madame is occupied."

"Good man."

After dismissing his servants, Raoul waited yet several more moments. Taking a restorative breath, he opened the door wide and ventured forth to greet the police officer, Inspector Leroux. The inspector was not a tall man, being several inches shorter than the count, but he had unusually long arms and a broad chest for his height. His dark hair was graying at the temples and thinning along the pate. His moustache was already chalky gray and grew thick and bristly over his narrow top lip. However it was his eyes that struck Raoul, small and dark and hard, two shiny orbs that seemed to lack the slightest hint of human warmth. The man smiled and bowed to the count, but his smile never made it to those two, unrelenting eyes.

Raoul ignored their penetrating stare and indicated the large overstuffed sofa near the fireplace. He himself chose a tall-backed chair at a perceptible distance from the seat the inspector occupied. The distance between the two men effectively suggested the count's attitude toward this worn intrusion into his private life. The count had considered standing without offering a seat to this annoying man, but the affront would have been too obvious and was not in Raoul's nature. There was something about Leroux that unsettled him, and although he didn't think he had anything to fear from the inspector, he didn't relish having the little man as an enemy either. For this reason, he convinced himself to stretch his patience even further although it was wearing dangerously thin.

"Inspector Leroux, it's always interesting to have you visit, but my butler says it's official business. What business could you possibly still have with me after all this time?"

Leroux sat forward eagerly on the edge of the damask cushion and considered the count. He could not come out and directly accuse the Count de Chagny of his obvious complicity in a crime committed ten years before.

"It puzzles me, sir." Leroux intentionally avoided using the proper honorific with the count. After all, why had they fought the Revolution and yet retained such vacuous titles? The only reason Chagny was more powerful than an appointed officer of the law was his money. Titles meant nothing to Leroux. "Why would you have dealt with the Phantom of the Opera in the manner you did?"

The small hairs along the back of Raoul's neck stood stiffly on end. He would not take the bait. If Leroux knew anything, he'd have to make clear exactly what it was. Raoul simply arched an eyebrow as if curious to hear more.

"After all, you paid for his advocate in court." Leroux's tone was falsely incredulous. "This monster had kidnapped your wife, and he had kept her in his rooms for nearly a week." Leroux's voice dropped as if referring to some indelicacy.

The insinuation did not escape Raoul, and the blood rose unbidden to his face. He was glad Christine was not present.

"M. Leroux, my wife assured me that nothing of the nature you are implying happened between the two of them. My wife was nearly catatonic, if you'll remember. We had just lost our son. The Phantom believed he could help her."

"But my dear Count, wasn't this man the same one who unleashed the chandelier, as a diversion, killing eleven innocent spectators in the audience in order to kidnap your wife, at that time your fiancée? How could you minimize the danger she was in with this fiend? Clearly he wanted your wife and had no intention of returning her to you willingly."

Raoul, exasperated by Leroux's insistence in going over and over the same ground, rose abruptly from his seat. "Inspector, if you'll excuse me, I've several pressing matters. I see no reason to go over a case that was closed years ago. How many times can the Phantom be tried and executed?"

Leroux had not risen from his seat. He stared intently at the count. Instead of accepting his dismissal, Leroux relaxed back against the sofa cushions as if settling in for the afternoon. "M. de Chagny, I don't believe the Phantom was ever executed."

Obviously, thought Raoul, *or you wouldn't come sniffing around here every so many months hoping to find a clue to his whereabouts.* But suspicions were not proof. The inspector could not hope to prove that Raoul had rigged a fake hanging and spirited Erik away across the border to begin a new life with Christine's best friend, Meg. He had ultimately been moved to pity his rival, and Christine had begged him to save her former teacher, the man she had confused with the spirit of her dead father.

The count tried to soften the edge their conversation had taken. "Surely, Inspector Leroux, his grave and the fact that hundreds of Parisians saw him dangle at the end of a rope would suggest that he was indeed executed and has paid for his crimes. If records at the cemetery weren't so lamentable, I'd suggest you exhume the body so you could verify with your own eyes the man's death."

"I have."

Raoul's pallor delighted the inspector, who explained, "It has taken me years to track down the location of the prisoner's grave. After all he was buried without ceremony or marker. Recently I found the plans to the cemetery, and with some satisfaction I can say we exhumed his coffin and found nothing but this." From his pocket he brought a rosary with large black beads. Raoul recognized it immediately. The Mother Superior of the Convent of St. Isidore had given it to Erik. He had held it during the trial, and it had been thrown into the coffin with his body. Of course the execution had been rigged, and later that day Raoul and his men had dug up the coffin, rescuing Erik from dying in earnest, buried alive in the county cemetery.

Clenching the muscle along his jaw in vexation, Raoul finally found a response. "My God, Leroux, do you suppose the rumors are true? Could he have been a ghost? A phantom like everyone was saying?"

Leroux could not believe the count was mocking him! He knew damn well that the prisoner whose sole name was Erik was flesh and blood, no magical creature or demon like the newspapers ranted. The count was toying with him, but he would rue the day he had not taken Pierre Leroux seriously. "You know as well as I that the man tricked everyone in the opera house into thinking he was some kind of ghost. They were all a bunch of superstitious idiots. He hid in that opera house because he was a hideous monster, disfigured and insane, and there was no other place where he could exist. He terrorized everyone, demanded money of the owners, and became obsessed with your wife when she was a student in the opera dormitories. I know, I know how human he is, though. I saw him bleed. I heard him cry out from the pain as I crushed his fingers. I nearly broke him. A few more sessions with me and he'd have lost that arrogant pretense. He was nothing but an insane freak."

Had Raoul once thought that, too? Listening to the inspector talk of Erik, some of what he said did indeed sound familiar, but it no longer rang true. It had been a long and gradual process, but Raoul had come to know Erik, perhaps better than any other man with whom he was acquainted. And as strange as it was, Raoul couldn't say what their relationship actually was any longer. They certainly were no longer rivals. Erik truly loved Meg and had extricated himself from his unhealthy and tragic obsession with Christine Daaé. They were not enemies. Raoul knew he could trust Erik with his life, and Erik could say the same of him. Surely they were friends, perhaps even more than friends.

Raoul cleared his throat and attempted to reason with Leroux. More and more he thought "obsession" was not an inappropriate term to apply to the inspector's inability to put the case of the Phantom of the Opera behind him. Why did he pursue him so doggedly?

"Inspector Leroux, I'm sure you know how public the Phantom's execution was. And there were many who had taken a prurient interest in his disfigurement. Would it be at all surprising to find that someone had bribed any of a host of workmen to tell him the location of the grave site of a specimen as unique as the Phantom? Grave robbers supply cadavers all the time to the medical schools—it's a well-known scandal. Or perhaps one might find his body preserved in some gypsy fair in formaldehyde and exhibited as one among a number of monstrosities. Or is it easier to imagine a hanged man rising from the dead and walking away from his grave? Please, Inspector Leroux, be reasonable." Raoul smiled amicably at the dark-eyed inspector, who sat still and listened.

"Perhaps. Perhaps."

"There, you see? Now if you'll excuse…"

"Except for other things that have come to light. I've been digging in more than the cemetery, and then again I've heard some interesting news from Italy. There are some coincidences that are quite striking."

Raoul knew Leroux was watching him carefully, but he steeled himself to avoid any and all reaction. However, inside he felt his heart drop to the pit of his stomach and wondered if he could dissemble his quickening pulse.

Given the count's silence, Leroux continued, "There's a new star of the opera scene whose fame is just now spreading to other capitals on the continent such as ours. Normally I could care less about artists and opera and theater, but something about the rumors caught my attention. This musical genius seems to be a mysterious figure, a man who wears a mask."

"Such affectations among the bohemians are frequent. You shouldn't put too much stock in it." Raoul waved his hand as if to shoo away an annoying insect, but he worried that Leroux could hear the heavy, rapid pounding of his heart.

"But he is also married to a young diva who hails from Paris itself, a former Mlle. Meg Giry. I believe you know her, do you not, Count? Was she not your wife's childhood friend and did she not visit with the two of you in your summer chateau a year or so ago?"

"Inspector," Raoul's tone had decidedly changed as he bit out the word, "I must ask you to leave." There was no room for argument. He turned his back on the policeman and went to the door.

"Very well, M. de Chagny. I'll call perhaps at another time, one more convenient for both of us."

CHAPTER 2

The Hangman's Noose

I am sorry for thee: thou art come to answer
A stony adversary, an inhuman wretch
uncapable of pity, void and empty
From any dram of mercy.

The Merchant of Venice, William Shakespeare

Christine watched the dreaded little man leave the portico and enter the waiting carriage. She had been fretting by the large veranda window for nearly an hour while Elise executed her piano lesson and Victor worked at his sums. On the floor, under the watchful eye of the nurse, Erica crawled in search of the retriever's tail. She squealed gleefully as the fur brushed against her face. Christine turned momentarily and scowled at the baby for pulling a few stray hairs from the patient dog's tail. "Erica, don't pull on Robespierre. You'll hurt him." She smiled as the golden haired child stared wide-eyed up at her and held out her chubby arms to be picked up.

She reached for Erica, bringing her up in a tender embrace and balancing the child on her left hip.

"Madame, you don't want to be picking her up any time she makes a squeal or she'll be spoiled." The nurse was one of those who preached against coddling, but in private lavished every possible sign of affection on the children. Christine knew how insincere the advice was and simply smiled knowingly at the young nursemaid.

Erica safely anchored on her hip, Christine returned to look past the veranda window where Leroux had been just minutes before. A detestable man, a true sadist, he had tortured Erik in prison purely for the pleasure of it. From the moment Erik had been betrayed and captured, he had made no pretense of trying to avoid punishment. He had resigned himself to pleading guilty and facing his execution. He had no false illusions. He had gone mad; his actions had led to the deaths of innocent spectators at the performance that night so long ago now that surely it could be forgotten. What vengeance, even righteous, should hound a man for eternity? It was at moments like these that Christine despaired over certain truths taught by her religion. Damnation and eternity were concepts commonly bandied about in any discussion of the just deserts for a sinner. During the course of the trial against the Phantom of the Opera, she had heard those around her say that he deserved just that: damnation for eternity. But they had not seen his soul! How could they know what God had in store for him? They had not lived as he had. They had not suffered what he had suffered.

She did not, for one moment, regret asking her husband to help Erik escape hanging. She'd do it all over again. Erik had saved her sanity. When her first child had accidentally drowned, Erik was the only one who shook her from her despair. She had simply stopped living. She was like the dead until he took her in hand and made her face her child's death. He forced her to turn again toward life. She had glimpsed more than Erik had wished to reveal in those days, locked away with him in his underground sanctuary. She had glimpsed yet another corner of his soul. He was not mad, and he was not evil. Those who whispered about him as the Opera Ghost or the Phantom of the Opera or simply the monster or murderer thought him a ghoul, a thing that lived off the dead, death itself. What she had seen when he forced her to face her child's death was a man desperate to live, a man pleading to be brought from the grave, to be allowed to stand for the briefest of moments in the light. She saw a man who had been locked away from all the joy and pleasure of the world, trapped in an illusionary simulacrum of shadow and light. And then Leroux captured him and took him to a prison of stone and bars and marched him to his public vilification and execution. She could not allow it. This man, the Phantom of the Opera, had brought her from the edge of grief, not once but twice, and had given her the freedom to follow her heart. He had given her music, and when she turned away from him, he had still loved her.

Erica pulled sweetly at the long curls that fell past Christine's shoulder. The little girl, named for Erik, had been born at a sad moment when they all thought Erik had perished in a fire in the Teatro dell'Opera. Fortunately this was not the case. But such a recent reminder of how dear her Angel of Music was to Christine was still fresh in her heart. She would not let anything or any-one harm him again. Leroux had to be stopped.

"Jeanne, please take the children out for some fresh air before lunch. I must speak with the count." Christine pulled her hair from Erica's clutched fist and plopped her solidly on the nursemaid's generous lap. The babe gave only a modest sign of displeasure, but found herself almost immediately engaged by the glossy round buttons on Jeanne's bodice.

"Maman, is there anything wrong?" asked Victor who was very sensitive to his mother's moods. Elise looked up worriedly at her young mother when she heard her brother's question. How much the children knew was something Christine couldn't tell. They roamed about like silent mice picking up crumbs of information as they fell from Raoul and Christine. She knew they both were fond of Erik's and Meg's children. Victor and François were as close as broth-ers after the months they had spent in Italy, and Elise doted on little Laurette. Mario, the young homeless boy Erik took in and adopted, had managed to find a spot among the children as well. Even though his life on the street troubled Christine—who knew what he might teach the other children—she had been touched by the obvious ties of affection between the boy and Erik.

"No, there's nothing wrong. Finish your work, Victor. Elise? Is that the music M. Costanzi wrote for you?"

"Yes, Maman. I nearly have it memorized! Listen!"

"Later, my love. I have to speak with your father right now."

"Doesn't sound as good as when he plays it, I can tell you," mumbled Victor grumpily.

"Victor," admonished his mother. "When you play the piano better than your sister, then you may voice an opinion about her rendering of the piece, but not before."

Christine left her children in the sunny room and went directly to the front parlor where she surmised her husband would still be.

When she opened the door, she was shocked to see the frown on Raoul's face. Normally, after Leroux's visits, they would come together and laugh about the officer's foolish obsession. He had seemed inept, especially to Raoul, who always calmed Christine's worries. Something was different about this time, though.

"Raoul?" she called anxiously. "What did he have to say?"

Raoul considered his wife. It was there, just under the skin, that invisible cord that knotted her to the Phantom. He mentally chastised himself for revert-ing to the "Phantom" after having slowly and painfully come to accept the man as Erik. The effect of Leroux's insidious hatred of Erik must have affected him more than he was willing to believe. To see Erik through the inspector's eyes was to bring back all the jealousy and terror of those first few months when Raoul came into contact with him at the Opera Populaire. He considered his wife again. Yes, it was inevitable. She'd always care for the man, and Raoul would always feel the twinge of jealousy when he recognized that another man had a claim to his wife's affection, even if it was simply concern, for Raoul was confident of Christine's love.

"He knows, Christine. I can't figure out how, but Leroux knows Erik didn't die on the scaffold."

"What? Well, we always knew Inspector Leroux was strange. He's never let on that he thought Erik somehow escaped. Why do you think he suspects he's alive now?"

"Yes, his previous visits were mostly macabre anniversaries of a sort, a rehashing of the case. Even so, I always had the feeling that Leroux didn't accept that Erik was dead, that he came looking for clues, anything that would tell him what really happened. But this time, Christine, it was different. He was very sure of himself."

"But he can't possibly know."

"He's opened the case again. He's had the grave exhumed."

Christine went white with shock and sank to the cushioned footstool by her side. "But there is no grave!"

"He found the plans of the cemetery. The graves of each executed prisoner are clearly set out. No names are registered, just the dates. From the date and the plans, Leroux found the site of the grave. He had the coffin brought out and opened. Of course, there was no body in the coffin. They knew that the moment they lifted it. But inside they found the rosary the Mother Superior had given to him. Leroux remembered the rosary. He must have thought it an irony that Erik had it in the first place."

"Then he knows that Erik…What else does he know?" Christine knew that Raoul could be in serious jeopardy if anyone were to discover his role in Erik's escape. Fortunately, Erik was far away and well beyond the inspector's grasp. Leroux might know that Erik wasn't in the grave, but he wouldn't have any idea of where he was. And if he did somehow suspect Erik had crossed the border to Italy, he had no power outside France. He certainly would not be able to convince his superiors of such a wild scheme as to set off searching for Erik.

"Leroux knows that he's Erik Costanzi, that he lives in Rome, and that he's married to Meg. He didn't come out and say as much, but he's implied the connections. Someone must have written to him. I can't think of why he'd know anything about the opera scene in Italy or why he'd have thought to follow Meg's career after all this time. It's been a decade. If he found nothing to go on in the first several years, why would he investigate Meg so many years later?"

"But what can he do?"

Raoul ran his hands through his dark blond hair, smoothing it back behind his ears, and grimaced. "I don't know. I don't know, Christine. But why come here to tell me all this if he can do nothing? If there's nothing that can be done, why wouldn't he simply drop it? I don't like the way he spoke to me. He's up to something."

"We have to write Erik. Or at least Meg. They might be in danger." Christine made as if to rise and leave the room to do just that, but Raoul called her back.

"No, Christine. No, we can't write them. Not just yet. If I know the man, he'll be expecting us to do something like that, to write or to go off to visit them. First of all we'd be confirming what might still be only a suspicion, and second of all we might lead him directly to Erik. If I were he, I'd be watching the estate and the mail very carefully for the next several weeks." He took Christine's hands in his and looked down into her frightened eyes. "We have to wait. But we will do something, my love. We won't let Leroux find him."

Leroux unfolded the rose tinted letter for the last of many times and ran his finger over the delicate, feminine hand. It was the first of several anonymous letters that had reached him from abroad. After so many years, finally, a door was opening.

M. L'Inspecteur Leroux,

You and I have not had the pleasure of meeting, and my identity is of little or no relevance to you; however, I have long watched your career and am in awe of your dedication and perseverance in the name of justice. I particularly followed from afar your most glorious success in bringing to an end the reign of terror of the infamous Phantom of the Teatro Populaire some years ago now.

Knowing that you would not rest until this monster was forever eradicated, I am convinced that certain information of which I am in possession cannot be silenced and must be disclosed to you as the only person who can act on it for the good of all. For is it not your sworn duty to protect your citizens——and any innocent wherever they may reside——and to fight evil?

You may have heard the stories of the opera ghost and how he was able to come and go as he pleased as if he were indeed supernatural? People would glimpse him, at which point he'd simply slip away through a solid wall! Then there were the strange incidents, a shredded costume in a locked dressing room minutes after the seamstress had finished her last modification or the cut ropes to the backdrop or a missing prop, the chair with broken legs and so on and so on. In short, M. Leroux, the Phantom was a master of disguise, a trickster, a magician, as well as an escape artist.

But no one could escape your diligence, you might remark. Yet M. Leroux, did you witness the Phantom's burial? Did you yourself cover his eyes with copper coins and hold a glass to his lips to check for the mist of living breath before they took him away from the scaffold?

Or perhaps now he is indeed a ghost! For I must confide in you that the Phantom walks. I have seen him.

An Admirer and most humble servant,

C.

Leroux hadn't foreseen his own reaction to the Phantom's execution. It had been too quick, too clean. He had vowed to break the monster's spirit, and he had nearly done so. The inspector had imagined climbing the stairs to the gallows with his broken prey, grasping the prisoner by his hair, and dragging him kicking and screaming to the hangman's noose. He would, if he had to, raise him to his feet himself and place the rope around his neck. He had imagined the Phantom trembling in his arms, had expected to revel in the anguish in his eyes, the fear, the pleading, the weeping. But then the legal wheels had ground inevitably along their course, taking the prisoner out of his hands. Not only had the Phantom faced his execution without begging for mercy, but he had struck a dignified pose on the scaffold. Leroux had gnashed his teeth impotently as he waited for the man to crumple to his knees and bellow his fear.

Irritated, Leroux rose and paced the width of his small study as he tried to wash the images from his mind. That was not how it had started. In the beginning he was doing his duty, coolly and professionally, in spite of the personal grief the Phantom had caused him. He was the inspector; the case had fallen to him. Day after day, he searched the dead carcass of the theater. Methodically he combed the neighborhood, interviewing the important and the insignificant among the survivors. Piece by piece the picture emerged of a monster who had existed, immune to prosecution, in the depths of the opera house, a fiend who was allowed to grow and strengthen to the point of apparent invincibility.

No one would disclose the Phantom's origins, and no one could explain his strange ability to navigate the world above and below, unhindered for so many years. It occurred to Leroux that this denizen of the underworld was responsible not only for the cataclysmic events in the Opera Populaire but for sundry violent crimes over the course of many years. Those atrocities that had not been explained were surely his work as well. Only in the fatal rage of madness had the Phantom killed in his own den! And Leroux had vowed to bring the fiend to justice. He would be God's instrument, His slayer. Leroux would not allow such an abomination to exist.

That was how it had begun. As the tool of justice, he had vowed not to allow his personal desire for vengeance to enter into it. God would work through him. But the Phantom had continued to escape him, to taunt him, to taunt God himself. The Phantom had even dared appear in the cemetery, at the top of the hill overlooking the burial of the Count and Countess de Chagny's child. The count himself had rushed up the grade to apprehend him, while the Phantom had arrogantly stood as if waiting. When Leroux's officers reached the apex of the hill, they had found nothing. As before, the Phantom had worked his magic and disappeared. But Leroux had resolved to prove that the Phantom was not supernatural, nor superior to man. Though his evil came directly from Hell itself, he was a man. He would bleed like any other man. He would suffer. How he would suffer!

The inspector had always suspected the Phantom had an accomplice. It puzzled him that it would be a woman of such grace and character as that of Mme. Madeleine Giry. She had been the one who brought the so-called ghost's notes to the owners of the Opera Populaire. It was her voice that often announced the Phantom's designs and demands. It was tedious, but Leroux had investigated the comings and goings of the mistress of the ballet to find that she was legally the administrator of large sums of money in various accounts throughout Europe. Mme. Giry had resisted Leroux's attempts to gather information about the monster. She had refused to admit her direct connections with him, but Leroux knew the truth. Of course, in the end, the Phantom himself had betrayed even this woman's loyalty.

When Leroux's clerk announced that Mme. Giry had come seeking an urgent interview with him, the inspector had already narrowly missed apprehending the Phantom on several occasions. Despite all his efforts to capture the monster, it was a woman who would finally deliver him to Leroux's justice!

He remembered his feeling of triumph as he anticipated Mme. Giry's confession. At last, she would surrender the Phantom to him. She sat at his desk, the color high in her cheeks, her breathing shallow, obviously still torn. He admired the rare vision of her naked collarbone in the simple dress she wore. Her hair was arranged in a long braid wrapped several times upon the back of her head and fixed with barrettes. She pulled the shawl around her as if she were cold in spite of the fact that the office was warm. She would not look him in the eyes until the end when she said she would take him to the fugitive's subterranean shelter. In that moment when her eyes met his, he knew she was as obsessed with the Phantom's capture as he was. What had turned her against the fiend, Leroux could only guess later when he saw how the daughter trembled and begged for mercy for the monster. Madeleine Giry would do anything to keep the Phantom from ravishing her daughter, the renowned diva of the Opera National, Meg Giry.

Once again a woman would bring the monster to his knees.

Leroux folded and unfolded the note, and the corners of his mouth rose in a sardonic smile. They had played him for a fool. He the instrument of God's righteous wrath had let the monster slip through his fingers. Not only had the Phantom disappeared, as he often had in the Opera house itself, but he had been living safely beyond Leroux's grasp in Italy. He enjoyed success and respect with his own theater and company, wrote his music and had it performed, and he held in thrall—how sickened Leroux felt when he imagined that beauty in the arms of that beast—the chanteuse that had once had Paris at her feet. This was not justice! This was a travesty worthy of the Devil himself.

Meg wiped the crumbs from Laurette's dress and lifted her down from the modest table in the breakfast nook. This was her favorite place to eat. Here the table was round and accommodated eight comfortably and a few more if need be. It sat in an alcove, surrounded on three sides by ceiling to floor windows, overlooking the gardens. Erik liked it, too, for the light was bright and cheerful in the mornings. He sipped at the tea after adding liberal amounts of honey and milk. Meg smiled to see his pleasure as he raised the cup to his lips. It was one of the small indulgences that he allowed himself that struck her as innocent and telling. Mario, as usual, was devouring the biscuits as if the servant would take the tray away from him at any moment.

"Mario." Her tone cautioned him.

The boy stopped, his cheeks bulging with uneaten biscuit, and looked up sheepishly at the beautiful, blond woman that his former master loved. He tried to swallow, sat up straighter in his chair after casting a general look around the room, and lowered the biscuit he clutched in his hand to the small plate before him. Meg smiled setting him at ease once more.

François had watched his mother as she dealt with the other boy. He was about to say something, to intercede for Mario, but his father laid his hand meaningfully on his knee. When François turned toward Erik, his father simply nodded his head almost imperceptibly. Then Erik took a biscuit from the platter himself and stuffed it whole into his mouth. Everyone including Laurette laughed riotously at his distended cheeks as he feigned difficulty swallowing the biscuit whole.

"Erik! I'm trying to teach the children a few table manners, and you're not helping."

Erik dabbed demurely at his lips with his napkin, gave Meg a sly look, and winked at Mario. "I just wanted to get my biscuit before Mario ate them all."

Mario blushed softly, understanding the point. He managed to eat the rest of his biscuit with more grace and even offered the platter around before indulging in a fifth one.

"These boys are growing so fast that I think they eat more than you now," Meg remarked to Erik.

Indeed François was growing like a weed. He would be tall like his father. Mario was somewhat older, but he had spent his first ten years on the streets, living by his wits. No one knew who his parents might be. Mario himself remembered nothing but life on the street. He was shorter than François, but not as slender. Since Erik had adopted him into the family, both he and Meg had seen Mario's color improve. He was growing, and what might have been a bowing of the knees was apparently correcting itself with fresh milk and good protein at each meal.

Laurette went directly to Mario's chair and tugged at his trousers. "Mario, will you build me a house in the garden for my dolls?"

Mario hesitated only long enough to ask to be excused, picked the little girl up, and started for the garden. He looked back over his shoulder at François, who turned to Erik. "Papa, can I go out with them?"

"I thought you wanted to come to the theater today?" Erik could see the battle on his son's face. Before he could help himself he raised his hand and lightly brushed the hair out of François's eyes. "I suppose you can. I will expect you to spend some time at the piano later today." He knew that his son needed no reminder; he would probably spend more than the designated time at his practice.

François ran out of the room to catch up with the others. Erik watched him long after he had disappeared.

Meg smiled to herself. Yes, it was time. She was sure that Erik would welcome another child. She didn't need to broach the subject. It would take care of itself, she was sure.

"How is it going with your personal assistant?"

Erik scowled. "I don't see why I need a personal assistant at the theater. There are more than enough hands around to run errands as they come up. He's in my way; I find him constantly under foot, looking over my shoulder, sneaking up behind me."

"Well, he's a young musician and comes highly recommended. All the other directors have assistants. Marcelo was quite impressed with him and says the young man idolizes your work."

The young man in question, Rinaldo Salvatore Jannicelli, was nearly twenty-eight and had studied at the conservatory of music. Evidently he was a son of a dear friend of Sig. Costanzi who had passed away some years ago. The son presented himself several months ago in hopes of finding a sponsor. The assistantship was a position that Marcelo thought appropriate for the son of a dear friend. Erik might benefit from having someone to copy scores, run errands, rehearse movements, act as messenger—in short, to carry out any of a number of tasks that Erik often spent long hours doing himself. Perhaps the young man would learn something from Erik too and eventually find a position of creative importance in the same theater or another company.

Meg knew that Erik didn't like the idea of a personal assistant, but he would never complain to Marcelo. If it hadn't been for the older gentleman, Meg would have lost Erik long ago. She recalled Marcelo's compassion when he found that Erik was hiding in the Teatro Argentina. At that time, her husband had been as forsaken and destitute as a man could be. But Marcelo Costanzi, too, was a man who knew suffering. He had lost everything, a wife and a grown son. Erik needed protection, and Marcelo needed to fill his life again. Meg would never be able to repay Marcelo's kindness toward her husband and her family. The Italian had taken Erik, her, and their children into his home, conferred on Erik his own family name, and adopted him as a son. Unfortunately, Marcelo too easily forgot how solitary Erik was by nature. Elevated to the status of gentleman literally over night, Erik had found himself in charge of an entire company of artists and technicians in the newly constructed Teatro dell'Opera. But Meg had tried to explain to Marcelo that Erik's position at the Teatro dell'Opera was a challenge as well as a gift.

During those dark spells when the expectations of his new life exceeded his ability to meet them, Erik withdrew from everyone except Meg. She was the only one who could approach him. He didn't want to rely on anyone else. He feared becoming dependent. He was deeply wary of others. In spite of Marcelo's good intentions, Meg understood her husband's reluctance to work closely with a complete stranger.

"He's competent enough." Erik licked the butter from his fingers and concentrated on the toast. He wanted to avoid returning Meg's gaze. "His ear is not bad," he added reluctantly.

"Have you discussed the next opera with him?"

Erik swallowed the bite he had taken, but dropped the unfinished slice of toast on his plate, his appetite gone. He felt on edge talking about the next opera. He wasn't sure there would be one.

Meg must have sensed his anxiety. As she was about to say something to him, her mother entered the room.

"Bonjour, mes petites!" she said brightly, kissing her daughter on the cheek and smiling at Erik. "Erik? Are you ever going to wear anything but black? I know it's elegant, and you are actually one of the few men I know who can pull it off no matter what, but there are other colors in the palette."

Erik lifted one brow at Madeleine's curious remark. She never spoke of his appearance. She was always reticent around him, but today she seemed empowered to say anything at all that popped into her head.

Seeing that Erik was not going to respond to her goading, she sat down beside her daughter and began to extol the virtues of the Italian climate.

"You must have slept well, Maman," ventured Meg, curious to see her mother so lively and expressive.

Erik sat with a look of pure concentration on his face. Madeleine's manner reminded him of a time long ago. He studied her carefully. She was older than he, and most people would say she was entering that period for women when they would be respected for their age and wisdom rather than sought for their beauty. But Madeleine had been a dancer and had spent her entire life in the theater. She knew the advantages of taking care of herself, and she knew how to present herself in the best possible light. She was striking, mature, vibrant, and still very attractive. Then he remembered what this reminded him of; it was the way she glowed just before she accepted her husband's proposal and left Erik alone in the depths of the Opera Populaire, a fugitive and an outcast.

"Madeleine? What's going on?" He couldn't very well ask her if there was a man in her life—not directly—but he damned well meant to find out who it was who had put that blush into her cheeks and that obvious spring in her step.

"What ever do you mean, Erik? Can't a body comment on the weather without there being something wrong?" She stared at him directly in the eye. She could tell he was suspicious, and she nearly blushed crimson to realize she was so transparent. "I'm just happy," she whispered, suddenly shy. "Can't you be happy for me?"

The dark look on Erik's face lifted slowly, and he eased the tension along his body. "I'm very pleased that you're happy, Madeleine. I would wish only to see you this way every day."

Madeleine felt a strange desire to weep in that moment. He was absolutely serious and absolutely sincere. It made her feel quite warm inside to know he cared for her happiness. They had come through many bad times, and she had thought perhaps she had lost her special place in his heart. The way he looked at her reminded her of other times, times before abandonment and before betrayal, when she had rescued him.

"Well, are you both done already?" she asked, returning to her cheerful tone of moments before.

Erik laid his napkin next to his plate and asked to be excused. "I should leave for the theater. Meg, are you coming now or later in the morning?"

"I'll follow later, if that's all right with you."

Erik came round the table and kissed Meg softly on the cheek before he left the room.

Meg waited until she heard the front door close, and then she turned to her mother. "Now what's going on? And don't tell me nothing. I can see it in your eyes."

Madeleine laughed a sweet chain of notes before she answered, "I'm in love."

She pushed the arthritic poodle from the stool and leaned against the man's knees. Lightly she ran her red nails along his thick thigh.

Piangi had gotten fatter over the past several years in spite of the fuss she made concerning his diet. He had always been a large, corpulent man; he said he needed the bulk to power the volume of his voice. He had been the leading tenor of the opera in Milan when she was a young singer in the chorus. Carlotta remembered hearing him on the stage so long ago and had to admit that his girth then had been an asset. He filled the amphitheater with his vibrato, and his body commanded the attention of the spectators as far as the back rows of the highest balcony. Next to him the divas seemed small and fragile, but that, too, lent charm to the spectacle, for when the diva sang, the contrast of such a powerful voice with her feminine delicacy always won the public's amazement and admiration. Piangi had picked her out from a bevy of potential leading ladies, and she had loved him from the beginning.

"Piangi," she cajoled, her hand circling higher and higher along his thigh muscle. "Let's take a turn around the fountains. We've been here for months, and we barely leave these rooms."

She would do anything to restore to him what had cruelly been taken. A silk cravat loosely tied about his neck covered all but a small swatch of the red scar. The memory of the moment the Phantom had wrapped the coarse rope around his throat and strangled him into unconsciousness was seared into his flesh. He had survived, but the injury to his vocal chords had never completely healed. Piangi spoke seldom, even though his voice was perfectly adequate to speech. It was laced with a scratchy quality that Carlotta did not find unpleasant. Anyone who had not known him as the star of the Opera Populaire or the rising talent of Milan even earlier would not remark on his voice. Even so, Piangi refused to come to terms with his loss. Even to Carlotta, he spoke only when necessary.

"Piangi, my love," she whined.

"No. I know your game. I'll have nothing to do with it."

Carlotta narrowed her eyes in frustration and anger. She stood and stared down at her lover, a man whom she now must tend and support, a man who used to be her companion but now weighed round her neck like a millstone. She had done everything to make his life whole again. For years after the madman at the opera, the one they called the Opera Ghost or the Phantom, had destroyed not only the opera house where Carlotta Giudicelli and Ubaldo Piangi reigned as stars but her lover's very manhood, she had taken him from physician to physician across the length and breadth of Europe, attempting to find the treatment to return his voice to its previous splendor. Piangi at first had been hopeful. Carlotta thought they would return to the stage. But when treatment after treatment failed to polish the irregularities or to restore the crystalline clarity of his voice, Piangi had insisted they stop wasting their time and resources. He encouraged Carlotta to find a position in one of many lesser known opera companies or to tour, until it became more and more embarrassing to find that the roles offered to her were for secondary characters, mere cameo roles. Bookings thinned; the remuneration diminished. The final straw had been in England where the impresario had indeed heard of Carlotta and respected her greatly, but he offered her a minor role as a nurse in a play composed by a young unknown by the name of Fournier. She read the score, searching for her arias, and found so little to recommend the role that her pride forced her to throw the score back into the surprised impresario's face.

After nearly eight years, she suggested they return to Milan where she decided to retire from the stage. Embarrassed to be known as the former diva of the Opera Populaire, Carlotta insisted on abandoning her stage name and took up once more her family name of Venedetti. Piangi had been removed from the opera scene already for so many years that he thought few would recognize his name. They still had resources from the days when they dominated the opera scene, and Carlotta immediately invested in a small opera house of some renown and courted several young composers. They lived modestly from the profits, and Carlotta at least felt that she was part of what she had always loved. However, the tranquility she had believed was hers dissipated many months ago when she read the article in the gazette.

"How can you sit there knowing he lives?" she hissed at Piangi. He sat like an invalid. "He meant to kill you! If I hadn't found you backstage and gotten you out, you'd have died in the fire."

Piangi stared out the window beyond her, as if she were transparent. He had heard this time and time again when Carlotta wanted him to admit he was indebted to her. She always wanted something. Why couldn't she just enjoy the fact that they were able to live respectably and enjoy retirement? He didn't miss the stage. He had known long before Carlotta, who was after all substantially younger than he, that their days at the Opera Populaire were dwindling. He had let her preen her feathers, strut about the stage, and bully the other singers and the owners of the company. She was still glorious, beautiful, but even then her voice was showing signs of stress. Though Piangi would never have told her so. There was no one else who could equal her range and presence on stage until Christine Daaé stepped forth. When Piangi heard the young girl perform Carlotta's aria, he mumbled a silent prayer that Carlotta was well out of earshot, locked away in her dressing room, pouting over a loose backdrop that had narrowly missed falling on her. If Carlotta had walked away, as she had threatened, the night Christine Daaé replaced her in the performance of *Hannibal*, then nothing tragic might have happened. Piangi and she would have returned to Milan and sung in one of the many venues available. Milan would have greeted them with open arms. At least for a few more years they would have held the stage against younger and better talents. But Carlotta didn't make anything easy. It was against her nature.

"Say something!" she screamed, and even now her voice was like a blow against his eardrum. He winced, but did not respond.

They should not have left Milan. They should not have come to Rome. They should not have come in search of the Phantom.

"Step out of my way!" Erik glared at the young man who had miraculously materialized in his path, his arms overflowing with sheets of music. They were nearly toe to toe when Erik drew up short and yelled at him. The young man was tall, but not as tall as Erik, and he held Erik's gaze for an uncomfortable moment before stepping back and mumbling his apologies.

Erik took several long strides down the passageway toward the orchestra pit. He wanted to speak with Sig. Bianchi, the maestro, about the finale. Something was missing, and he had just gotten a glimpse of it when his assistant had nearly collided with him, wiping everything else from his mind. What had it been? He clenched his jaw tight as he tried to recall the steps that might bring him back to the realization. It was after the fourteenth bar, very close to the beginning, where a new direction had to be taken.

"Sig. Costanzi?" Erik ignored the call from the young man and continued walking toward the pit. "Sig. Costanzi?" This time Erik knew that the young man had been calling to him, not to his adopted father, Don Marcelo. He had accepted Don Marcelo's family name, tremendously grateful for the legitimacy and respect it guaranteed him, but he was slow in accepting its use in his daily life. He was Erik. Nothing more. Those at the opera called him maestro or Don Erik. His legal name fit him badly, like secondhand shoes.

"What is it now?" he barked.

Rinaldo was not cowed by Erik's ill temper. He was beginning to find the rhythm of their relationship. It was painfully apparent that Erik saw him as little more than a nuisance, but Rinaldo was determined to find the chink in the man's armor. Rinaldo would find what he needed and would become the only one to supply it for him. "I hesitate to mention it, but the oboe didn't seem to work. It enters too soon. I thought perhaps it should be moved to the…"

Erik's eyes opened in recognition. That was it! That was exactly what had struck him. He stopped Rinaldo with a look and grudgingly admitted that he was correct. "It should go…Damn it, give me the score." Erik rummaged roughly through the sheaves of paper in Rinaldo's awkward grasp and pulled out the sheet he was looking for. The two men went to a nearby table and laid the score out before them. Rinaldo watched and waited while Erik glanced over the measures, the notes playing in his mind. Then when Rinaldo was about to suggest to the maestro that the motif should be placed after a particularly lyrical passage, Erik surprised him by discarding that obvious solution. Instead he jabbed his index finger at a point several measures later in the score. Rinaldo, annoyed and reluctant to consider that his own suggestion wasn't better, reviewed the measure leading up to the exact moment Erik had determined.

"Yes, I see," Rinaldo admitted, a note of consternation evident in his tone.

Erik considered the young man then for the first time without anger and frustration as if trying to second guess him. The corner of his mouth, near the half mask he wore in the theater, lifted slightly as he realized what Rinaldo would have done. "Of course, it might have gone here," he said moving his finger back several measures, "but that would have been rather obvious, don't you agree?"

Two dark brown eyes under thick, lush eyelashes, glared for a brief second up into Erik's deeply green eyes. Rinaldo reluctantly nodded. Still wanting to be useful, he thought to mention the cymbals. Erik listened attentively to Rinaldo's opinion. He crossed his arms in front of his chest, and then with great pleasure said, "Nonsense."

Without so much as a backward glance, Erik strode toward the stairs.

Piangi wondered what Carlotta had set in motion. Once more she had closed herself into the parlor. There she brought out the stationery she preferred, a delicately scented paper with a soft rose hue, and sat to write her regular missive.

The gazette lay open to the theater events for the week. A column running along the edge had this brief notice that Carlotta had read over and over again to Piangi.

The season would not be complete if not for the genius of the mysterious masked maestro whose touch, like that of Midas, turns all to gold. But of course the execution of such unusual and haunting scores would not perhaps call our attention so raptly if not for the beauty and talent of the diva, the incomparable Signora Costanzi, wife to that same masked gentleman. Why one might ask don a disguise? What indeed must the mask hide from us, the adoring patrons of the Teatro dell'Opera? Mystery upon mystery surrounds this talented couple. Sig. Costanzi gives us no hint as to his identity, but we certainly know that he was not born to the Costanzi family. Whispers are that he abandoned a lucrative career in some other clime, sweeping our diva off her feet and stealing her away from success on the stage at the Opera National in Paris, and has come to hide among us in the heart of opera itself. Paolo Ricci

How clumsy of the man to step into the light of celebrity. The mask ironically revealed his identity as effectively as if he had worn no disguise at all. Even Piangi had admitted to his lover that this could be none other than the murderer of the Opera Populaire, the madman that had plagued Carlotta for three seasons until he forced the owners to propel an unknown chorus girl into the role that was rightfully hers alone.

How could this have happened? For years, Carlotta and Piangi had journeyed through the European capitals. During that time, there had been no mention of the Phantom. The mob that had followed him to his underground lair had not found him. Rumors were that he had disappeared. Piangi had thought he had fled, perhaps he had even died down in the underground lakes and channels. Then news had circulated that the Phantom had been captured. Carlotta wanted to return to Paris for the trial and execution, but they were immersed in a treatment that Piangi dared not interrupt. Instead they avidly sought news from travelers and gazettes that weeks later made their way to the eastern slopes of Russia. The Phantom was dead. The last news they received was of his hanging. Piangi had despaired at the sight of Carlotta who wrinkled the paper in her hands as if it were the murderer's throat. He had hoped to see some calm, some relief in his lover's eyes, but her desire for blood was unappeased.

She said that she wanted revenge for what the Phantom had done to him, but Piangi was not fooled. She had always been and wanted always to be the darling of everyone's eye. She lived for the adoration. When it became clear to her that there was someone—and someone very powerful—who was not seduced by her charm, her beauty, and her talent, she grew petulant and angry. The Phantom had done something far worse than attack Piangi, he had wounded Carlotta's vanity. He had accepted her as the diva for two seasons, and then he had turned on her. He had preferred an inexperienced girl over her! If she couldn't make him adore her, she would seek his destruction.

M. L'Inspecteur Leroux,

I am appalled at your delay. I confess that I believed you would move mountains and oceans to apprehend the fiend that so easily hoodwinked you. Can it not fail to torture you to know that the Opera Ghost has not only escaped his punishment but has enjoyed a life of admiration and riches for more than a decade?

Where is your anger, your outrage? I have seen no sign of your resolve or courage—and I had thought you a match for the demon—no sign of even the simplest steps. It is not disguised that my first missive's origin is Rome, nor should it tax you unduly to think that the criminal would seek out safe harbor in the only world he has ever known, the theater. I grant you that Rome abounds in theaters dedicated to Opera, but even if your investigation hobbled along from theater to theater, eventually you would discover his tracks, eventually you would have to come upon him!

Then why do you tarry? Why do you remain behind, passively, in Paris? He will not come to you. The Opera Populaire is but the burned-out husk of a sanctuary. Where would he go?

Of course, you might delay because you wish to glean whatever information you may from those who so foully conspired with him to make a fool of you and of all Paris! And if you only followed the trail of those who had once come in contact with the Opera Ghost, you might easily find the magnet that should draw you. Indeed he cannot live without his obsessions, and since he seems to have released his former passion—whose name we need not mention here—he must have found another.

Ah, my dear Inspecteur, if only you were an opera fan! The whole world of artists has conspired against you, it would seem. Not only have they nourished him over the years—just think how complicit were the various owners of the Opera Populaire—but they revel in his genius. To demonstrate I enclose herein a small article of little intrinsic worth that any modestly intelligent person would understand immediately as the clearest signpost for your hunt.

As ever, your humble and supportive servant,

C.

"Carlotta, what have you done?"

She closed the door. The letter had been posted. Piangi lounged on the sofa near the fire, sighed, and shook his head. Carlotta pursed her lips, annoyed, and set her hands on her hips as she studied him.

"We can't let him get away with it! You read the notice. He lords it over us all, just like he wanted to do at the Teatro Populaire." She drew her skirts around her as she sat on the large cushioned chair across from her lover. Like him, she stared into the fire.

In a voice that could barely be heard, Piangi muttered, "The last time we tried to trap him, we lost our home and nearly lost our lives."

As if she hadn't heard him, Carlotta remarked, "I've set it in motion, but I'm not done with the Phantom yet. He'll rue the day he ever set eyes on me!"

CHAPTER 3

The Opera Ghost

Oh what a tangled web we weave
When first we practice to deceive.

Marmion, Sir Walter Scott

"Signorina Venedetti, your interest and support are most welcome. Please, please, do sit and enjoy the rehearsal." Don Marcelo smoothed the small gray moustache Madeleine had encouraged him to grow. He was impressed by the mysterious woman who had approached him on two separate occasions to discuss investing in the Teatro dell'Opera. As on the previous encounters, he was struck by her statuesque beauty. She was tall, for a woman, with an exquisite figure. She preferred the various hues of pink and rose, which contrasted with the red tint to her light brown hair. Today she wore a stylish gown of a deep pink edged with white and gold accents. She was clearly used to being the center of attention, yet curiously she veiled her face. Only the hint of honey in her large brown eyes and the scarlet of two full sensuous lips were perceptible behind the rose tinted gossamer of her veil. If this were not enough, she skillfully unfurled a white fan edged in gold that she demurely used to draw Don Marcelo's eye to those features she so temptingly hid.

"Oh, Don Marcelo, you are too kind," she whispered, her voice soft and melodious, but barely audible. She never spoke more than a whisper, her voice breathy, light, and intimate. Don Marcelo was irresistibly intrigued by this woman. Not only did she have a considerable sum at her disposal to invest in the company, but she knew opera. Her questions and comments demonstrated an insider's knowledge of the art and business of opera.

"Signorina Venedetti, you must let me introduce you to my son, the musical director of the company, Erik Costanzi. And if I could be so bold, we plan a small dinner party this evening at my estate. I would be honored if you could join us."

"Oh," Carlotta sighed in her softened and disguised voice. She waved the fan as if she were agitated. "I would like to meet the genius all of Rome is talking of. I must beg off your kind invitation, though, to dine with you this evening. Perhaps another time?"

She leaned forward in her chair so that Don Marcelo caught her scent of hyacinth laced with some exotic spice. He felt the wicked rustle of her skirt as it pressed against his knee. He cleared his throat nervously, and Carlotta smiled at the effect she was having on the older gentleman. He was a vigorous, handsome man, for one perhaps in his late sixties. Don Marcelo walked to the stage to speak with his son.

As they conferred, Carlotta dropped the fan to her lap and allowed herself the freedom to examine the man she had so long despised. Sig. Erik Costanzi turned to glance down at her in the amphitheater where Don Marcelo had settled her. As the younger man turned his eyes on her, she drew in a startled gasp of air. What if he recognized her? His eyes looked at her as if he could see to the roots of her soul! When the Phantom turned back to speak with his patron and adopted father, Carlotta realized he had not. Still she clutched her hand over her frantically beating heart. The acceleration of her pulse was not due solely to fear of discovery. In that moment when their eyes had locked, she had been overwhelmed by a disquieting attraction.

He had made her life impossible for three of her five years at the Opera Populaire. He had forever ruined Piangi's musical career. His madness had brought her Parisian success to an abrupt and tragic end. Yet she sat there admiring him.

She had seen the Phantom only in shadows until the night of the chandelier when the fire destroyed the premier opera house in Paris. Even then, she'd been reluctantly mesmerized by his magnetism. He had barely changed over the many years since that fatal performance. He was older, as was she, but he was no less virile, no less commanding than that night when he ruled the stage as Don Juan.

Now he wore a simple white mask over three quarters of his face. Having taken off his waistcoat, Erik Costanzi worked in simple attire. The first button of his white shirt had loosened. His cravat had been untied and lay askew at the opening of his collar. She found the view of his bared throat somehow shocking, unexpectedly intimate. She watched as his lips moved, his voice attenuated by the distance between them. She could see the lines of his shoulders, the power of his broad back. The dark trousers were creased and straight, displaying to advantage his narrow hips and long legs. She swallowed, her mouth awash in desire.

As she tried to recover her cold purpose, she saw Erik descend from the stage to follow Don Marcelo up the aisle in her direction. He called back over his shoulder to the cast to continue with the scene, his voice deep, like the purr of a lion. For a moment it occurred to her that she should like to anger him to hear him roar. A shiver of pure excitement coursed down her back. Her own reaction appalled her!

She knew as he approached she must be deathly pale as all the blood had fled from her face to the very soles of her feet. He stood only an arm's length away from her, her nemesis, her scourge. She thought for one moment that this light-headed rapture must be what that silly ingénue Daaé had felt when he sang on the stage with her.

Erik bowed his head only slightly, his dark green eyes clear and glinting seriously at her veil. "Signorina." His velvet voice swept over her. She imagined those lips soft and moist against her skin. They were beautiful, full and expressive, with no hint of the blemished skin the mask disguised. Instead of speaking, she managed to offer her gloved hand.

Erik took it lightly and made the customary gesture of kissing the cloth. Even though he had not actually done so, Carlotta imagined the weight of those lips on her hand. Summoning all her skills as an actress, she demurred. "Signore. I'm honored to meet the genius behind the success of the Teatro."

Erik's eyes furrowed at the compliment. Evidently he was uncomfortable with praise.

"So the rumors are correct. You prefer to hide behind a mask, too?" teased Signorina Venedetti.

Again the strange look of intent consideration darkened Erik's expression. How could a face be so expressive when covered by a mask? His eyes! They were alive, as if all that he was could be found there in those beautiful green spheres.

"It is no loss not to see my face." The question lay unspoken in his reply. She could see in his gaze the curiosity her own veil had aroused in him.

"Well, there is more than enough in your appearance to compensate for that loss," she whispered huskily.

Startled by her frankly flirtatious response, Erik glanced to see that Don Marcelo was engaged with one of the delivery men that had brought several crates of paint and powder for plaster. Carlotta, thrilled to see his discomfort, noted that Erik discreetly backed several inches away. To compensate, she leaned forward in her seat and added, "You must know the effect you have on those of us of the weaker sex?" She drew the sibilant out, a sensuous whip. She couldn't refrain from smiling in satisfaction as she saw his lips part and heard him clear his throat to disguise the effect of her words.

"Signorina…"

"Venedetti, my dear Signore Costanzi." She leaned back in the seat, allowing Erik the opportunity to run his eyes over her ample bosom to her narrow waist. She saw his eyes travel against his will. Then, with effort, he raised his chin and stared off into the distance.

"Please excuse me. I've much to do before opening night." Before she could protest, he turned and quickly walked back to the stage.

"Yes, signore. You've met your match, my dear Phantom." She chuckled gleefully to herself behind her fan. She would dog his every step, destroy whatever peace he thought was his, and do whatever she could to make his life a living torment.

"Rinaldo!" Erik could go nowhere in the opera house without tripping over his assistant except when he desperately wanted to find him. "Rinaldo, for God's sake!" he shouted down the wing for what seemed the tenth time.

"Yes, Don Erik?" came the voice from behind him.

Erik turned quickly round to face the assistant that he had never wanted. "Where is it?" he growled without explanation.

Rinaldo waited uncomfortably for Erik to explain to what he was referring. After several heart beats, the young musician and would-be composer shrugged his shoulders in defeat. As he started to open his mouth to ask, Erik interrupted. "You brought the scene from my office. There is a page missing! Where in the devil is it?"

Rinaldo reddened visibly. "I…I…I…"

"Yes? You?"

"I brought everything from the office, everything that was on the desk," he protested mildly.

"On the desk?" Erik's voice was gradually rising in volume.

"Yes."

Erik stared at the man as if he were daft. "The music was not on my desk. I had placed it in the right-hand drawer. I told you. I left nothing on my desk!"

Rinaldo had the sense not to contradict his employer, but Erik could see the denial in his flickering gaze.

Instead of arguing, Erik marched off to his office, Rinaldo close behind, and threw the door open. In three strides he was at the large oak desk and had opened the drawer. Nothing.

Quickly, his eyes darted round the room. The staff paper on the piano was unused. The notes he had transcribed earlier that day on several sheets of new paper were nowhere to be found. Several hours for nothing! He inspected the area near the piano to see if they had fluttered to the floor. There were scraps of paper he had consigned to oblivion, but the two sheets he had filled with great satisfaction were gone. Perturbed he looked at the assistant who stood, confused, watching Erik from the doorway.

Think! He remembered leaving the two sheets on the piano. They were ideas that he might incorporate into the final act. But he had placed the current scene, untouched, along with the rest of the score, in the drawer. There had been no papers left on the desk. Someone had taken the papers from the drawer, rifled through them, scattering them across the surface of the desk, and taken one of the sheets. Then the same person had absconded with the new material he had jotted down from where he had left it on the piano. It would not be the cleaning staff, for they were accustomed to him and never touched his papers. If someone had foolishly come to clean, they would also have removed the crumpled, rejected scraps that he had tossed to the floor.

"Is there anything I can do to help?" Rinaldo seemed genuinely worried by Erik's erratic behavior.

"No," he began, then changed his mind. "Yes, go to the maestro. Ask for the preceding and subsequent pages of the score. Come back immediately." Rinaldo rushed off to the orchestra pit.

The minute Rinaldo returned, Erik snatched the sheets from him and sat at the piano. He played through the preceding bars up to the missing notes.

"Transcribe what I play. Can you do that?"

"Yes. I think so."

Erik played from memory, the music softly present in his mind.

"You're going too quickly. I can't keep up," Rinaldo complained as he frantically scratched the notes on the staff paper.

"Damn it. Listen!" Erik played again, paused, and when he glanced at the transcription, barked out a correction. "Now the next part should go like…"

He played, stopped, dissatisfied, picked up the beginning from the transcription Rinaldo had made and then continued.

They worked like this, in halts and starts, for the next several hours until Erik sat back, rocking gently, his hands buried under his armpits.

"Are you all right?" Rinaldo asked as he saw the pain in the set of his employer's teeth, the way he cradled his swollen fingers in the warmth of his body.

"Give me a moment. We're almost done." Erik's voice had lost all its anger and was unusually quiet.

After several moments, Erik shook both his hands and laid them gently on the keys. Rinaldo waited, the pen ready to transcribe the sounds Erik teased and tormented from the piano. Erik stared at his silent fingers. Rinaldo could see the muscles in the man's jaw clench and release several times. Erik took a deep breath, studied the beginning of the notes on the subsequent page, and gritting his teeth willed his fingers to move.

"Is there a change in tempo here?" asked Rinaldo innocently, for the notes were not coming as quickly as they had.

"No," responded Erik impatiently. "The tempo's the same." He shook his hands once more, flexed the fingers carefully, and brought them down to the keys again. Rinaldo heard an unguarded gasp of pain as Erik played the last bars that led seamlessly into the next page of music.

The moment it was finished, Erik nestled his hands in his lap. They lay in soft fists close to his body. Pain roughened his voice. "Did you get that, Rinaldo? For God's sake, tell me you got it."

"Yes," answered the assistant as he read the notes he had scrawled. They were what Sig. Costanzi had played, but they should have been written in blood, he thought.

Afterwards, Erik had a chance to look over the recovered music. While Rinaldo put the score in order, Erik sat deadly still at the piano. Then slowly he rose and walked toward the door. Without looking at the young man, he said, "I would like you to transcribe the scene complete. Can you do that?"

"Yes, Sig. Costanzi. I can have it later tonight if you like."

"Then I want you to continue to the end of the opera, and then go back to the beginning and transcribe the rest. From now on, whatever I write, I wish it to be copied immediately. I want a copy that I can keep someplace safe. Is that clear?"

"Yes, sir."

The hand Erik lifted to pull the door open would not close over the knob. Rinaldo carefully edged near and opened the door for him.

Meg glanced out the window toward the garden on her way from the library. She had come to find something to read for later. Outside, among the roses, her mother sat. She was not alone. At first Meg thought perhaps Erik had returned early, for the man's tall, slender silhouette reminded her of her husband's. But when she looked more closely, she discovered that the man was Don Marcelo.

Don Marcelo and Madeleine were deep in conversation, and he had risen evidently to show Madeleine one of the newest buds on a nearby bush. Meg took a moment to study her mother's profile. Madeleine Giry had always been attractive, with well defined features. But Meg had not really looked at her for so long that at first it was as if she were seeing a stranger. The woman she saw was still handsome, mature, strong, and graceful. There was a sensuous curve to her body as she posed on the edge of the bench, as if she knew she were being observed. Her mother was always conscious of her body, of how she stood, the position of the hands, the angle of the toe, the tilt or the slight arch of the back, all these manipulations of line to give to the body the solidity of art and the impression of movement. She was beautiful, and Meg felt something catch in her heart, a sharp pain. Why would such an observation bring her pain?

Her mother laughed, throwing her head back; her body shook with the energy. The pose broken, Madeleine was momentarily without defenses. Then Don Marcelo bent over her parted lips and immobilized her with a kiss. Meg's legs felt weak. Her mother was in love, and Meg wondered at the sympathy of gestures and emotions between herself and her mother that brought her strangely closer to the older woman than mere blood ever had. This riotous celebration she had tried to describe to Madeleine when she had confessed that she loved Erik. Her mother must have felt something like this when she married Meg's father. Yet Madeleine had been appalled when she discovered that Meg and Erik had become lovers.

Suddenly Meg blushed crimson. Blood suffused her cheeks. Were her mother and Don Marcelo lovers? It shocked her, even the thought of it. She tried to erase the image that flashed across her mind. Then she recalled how, many years ago, her mother had not only found out that Erik and she had become lovers; she had stumbled across them in each other's embrace as they lay asleep, naked in Meg's rooms at the Opera National. Meg winced at the thought of her mother's discomfort.

But Meg would not react in a similar way. She would grant that her mother was mature and wise enough to know what she wanted. Don Marcelo was much older than Madeleine, but no one would know it to look at him. He seemed at least ten years younger than he was. He was also a wonderful man. He had been so good to Erik, so good to them all.

Don Marcelo had taken Madeleine by the hand and tenderly led her away from the garden. Meg craned her neck shamelessly to follow them but lost sight of the two almost immediately when they disappeared around a far corner.

"They seem content in each other's company."

Meg let out a startled cry as Erik spoke behind her left ear. She had no idea that he had entered the room. "You frightened me nearly to death!" she said, clutching her hand over her bosom as she tried to steady her racing pulse. Then she noticed that he had not touched her. He always touched her. Whenever they were in the same room, he would embrace her if they were alone, cup her chin in his hand and kiss her tenderly or passionately on the lips, or he would nuzzle close behind her pushing against her skirts in unambiguous desire for her. And if they were not alone, he would subtly graze his hand across hers or press his knee against her skirts. There was no one in the room, and yet he stood several inches back, leaving a cold gulf between them that she didn't understand.

"Yes," she answered. "I saw them kiss," she whispered naughtily.

The corner of Erik's mouth rose in mirth at Meg's glee. "It's good to see her with him. She's been alone for many years." Thinking perhaps Meg would mistake his statement, he hurried to add, "I mean she has not had the love of a man."

"I know what you meant. She had the love of hundreds of little girls, but it's not the same." Suddenly Meg wanted him to take her in his arms and make love to her. His eyes were warm and intense, but still he did not step forward or reach out to her.

She wondered if perhaps seeing Madeleine with Don Marcelo had disturbed Erik somehow. After all, Madeleine's relationship with Erik was a curious one. "Did you know my father, Erik?"

He raised his brow and replied, "You know you've never asked me that. You never speak of him."

"I didn't know him. He died when I was just a babe."

"Yes," Erik admitted, as if his memory had just been jarred. "I met him only a handful of times. Well, met is not exactly the right word. I saw him. I saw him and Madeleine together in the passageway outside the chapel once."

The skin on the back of Meg's neck prickled. Those passageways in the Opera Populaire were a popular site for trysts between lovers. They were narrow and dark, dotted with small alcoves where two people could easily be intimate. She noticed that Erik looked away, a shy reluctance seeming to take hold of him. "What was he like?"

Erik took a deep breath and sighed before he spoke. "I didn't like him."

"Why?" Meg couldn't avoid a hint of irritation in her question.

"I wanted Madeleine to myself," he confessed, his voice quiet yet unsure. He looked Meg directly in the eye. He wanted to see her reaction. "I was afraid she'd leave me." He couldn't sustain her gaze.

Meg reached across the narrow gap between them and took his hand. He groaned and pulled it away from her.

"What is it?" she asked. She sought his hand and tried to lift it gently with her own, but he moved beyond her reach.

"It's nothing, nothing serious. My hands are sore. I played too long today."

"What happened?" She insisted that he tell her. He was holding something back.

"A page in the score was lost. I had to reconstruct the music, fill the gap. By the time I finished working out the notes and Rinaldo managed to transcribe them accurately, I thought my hands were going to freeze up permanently. They're better already. See?" He lifted his right hand and flexed the fingers to prove to her that there was nothing the matter. Meg could see that the fingers did not unfurl completely.

"Let me rub them for you," she encouraged. Without waiting for a response from him, she led him by the elbow to the stairs, called to one of the servants to bring hot water with salts, and pulled him to their rooms. Once they were inside, all business, she helped him take off his coat and untie his cravat. She unbuttoned his shirt so that he was relaxed and made him sit on the stool by the basin where she pulled off his boots. She had him lay his hand in the palm of hers so that she could examine the reddened knuckles. The flesh was tender and swollen, and she could see that he was more worried than he had admitted.

A few moments passed before the maid brought the kettle of hot water to the room. She had thought to bring a pitcher of cool water for them as well. Meg laid out the towels while Erik watched her.

The moment the maid left, Meg went to Erik and removed his mask. He groaned audibly, and she rubbed her palms over his cheeks and back through his hair. He groaned again with the pleasure of her touch. She loved this moment in the day, when she wiped the tension away from his face. She could feel his muscles relax. She would often step into the space between his thighs to lean in against his chest as she massaged his temples. She loved the warmth of him through her dress. If she had thought of it, she might have changed into her robe. She enjoyed that even more. She would undo the sash, letting it hang open down the front. Then in his embrace, she was at his mercy as her hands worked the tension from his temples, down his neck, and across his shoulders. He would bury his face between her breasts. His hands would slip under her robe and glide, broad and strong, across her skin.

But tonight he needed other comforts.

She stepped back and examined his hands again. In the basin, she stirred the salts into a mixture of cold and hot water until she was satisfied with the temperature. Then she told him to rest his hands in the bath. To keep his mind off his discomfort, she stepped behind him to massage his shoulders.

"So," she said, as she listened to the soft sounds of pleasure he couldn't quiet. "Was my father handsome?"

"I suppose so," he answered in an offhanded way.

"Well, was he or wasn't he?" She slapped her hand playfully across his upper back.

"He was! All right, if you must know, he was handsome. He was perhaps in his mid twenties. Your mother was quite young. He was fair, slender, not very tall."

"No one strikes you as tall except yourself!"

"Well, he was more or less the height of most men. Is that better?"

"More accurate, anyway." Then in a serious tone, Meg asked, "Was she carrying me, do you think, when they married?"

Erik paused. "Perhaps."

"She must have loved him a great deal?"

"He made her laugh. I remember that."

Meg smiled. She liked that. Just a while ago in the garden, Don Marcelo had made her mother laugh. "That's good."

"Is that important?"

"What?"

"Nothing." Erik dismissed the question.

"Oh, I see. Are you thinking of yourself and me?"

When Erik remained still under her observation, she understood that he was indeed wondering whether Meg felt that something was missing. "You make me laugh, Erik," she said, trying to find a reassuring tone.

"Not intentionally!"

With that, Meg burst out with a wild, spontaneous laugh. At first Erik froze, then he chuckled lightly.

"You should laugh, yourself, more often. I love you, and I wish I could make you laugh everyday." She wrapped her arms tightly around his neck and kissed the side of his throat. He turned his face toward hers and kissed her tenderly.

"You make me smile even when I don't want to. Is that sufficient?"

"Yes, I suppose so. But to get back to what tied your muscles all in knots today. You're so careful with the scores. How in the world did you ever lose a page from the opera?"

He tensed just a little, as if in deep thought, and scowled. "I didn't. I know I put the score in the desk drawer in my office, the way I always do. But when Rinaldo went to collect the sheets for the maestro, he found them on top of my desk, he said. We both went to search for the missing page, but it wasn't there."

"That's strange."

"Not as strange as the fact that my notes from that morning were also gone. I had been playing for several hours and jotting down pieces of melody that I fancied. I left the sheets—there might have been four or five—on the piano. They, too, were gone."

"Who could have taken them?"

"I have no idea. I thought perhaps…" He started to formulate his suspicion and then hesitated. Meg encouraged him to continue. "Well, I thought perhaps Rinaldo had done it to vex me, but I'm sure he didn't. He seemed genuinely puzzled. It would have taken me days to work out the missing music from the score without his help. But the notes that I'd written down this morning, I'm afraid, are gone now, gone from the room and from my memory. By the time we finished, I was so exhausted I couldn't hear anything in my head but the notes we'd been working on."

"That's a shame," Meg commiserated. "How do your fingers feel now?"

Erik drew them from the lukewarm water and dried them on the towel. "Much, much better." He rose from the chair and went to lie down on the bed. "Do we have to dress for dinner?"

"We could ask for a tray. I'm sure Maman and Marcelo wouldn't mind having a nice dinner on their own together. The children have already eaten."

"Yes, please. Let's do that. I'm so tired." He lay back, stretched in such a way that his body occupied the entire bed, and closed his eyes.

Moments later, after Meg had instructed the maid and had changed into her night clothes, she tiptoed up to the bed where Erik lay on the edge of sleep. She loosened the cuffs of his shirt and unbuttoned his trousers. There was little more that she could manage to do without his cooperation. He stirred and rolled to the side into a sitting position. He quickly undressed, accepting the bedclothes and robe she had brought him.

"Meg?"

"Yes?"

"Have you felt anything strange lately when you've been at the teatro?" He tied the sash around the robe and went to sit in one of the wing chairs near the fireplace. Meg joined him, sitting in a large overstuffed chair across from his.

"No. What do you mean?"

He shook his head, as if trying to rid himself of an annoying insect. "I can't quite see what it is, but there is something different at the teatro. I feel there's a…presence."

Meg shivered involuntarily. "You're not saying that there's a ghost, are you?"

Erik understood her fears. They both had been haunted in one way or another by ghosts. "No. I don't know, but I don't think so. I have the feeling that someone is hiding in the teatro."

"We do seem to be having a run of bad luck, don't we?" Props had been damaged or missing, costumes ripped or soiled, music mislaid and never again found, instruments vandalized. Nasty smells backstage had led to a dead cat stuffed behind a stack of boxes, and several young chorus girls were afraid to be alone in the shadowy wings because of rumors of spectral beings roaming in the gloomy recesses of the teatro.

"Yes," Erik said, lost in thought. It all seemed uncannily familiar.

Shortly thereafter, the maid brought a tray of roasted meats, pasta mixed with butter and garlic, and various stewed vegetables. A carafe of wine and a basket of rolls were also on the tray.

As Meg rose to serve them, Erik grabbed her wrist and pulled her gently down to his lap.

"We can eat later," he suggested.

"There!" Carlotta raised the rose tinted sheet of paper gloriously in the air and waved it about like a semaphore. She placed a drop of cologne on the edge and readied the envelope and wax for the seal. Piangi sighed audibly. Carlotta had spoken of nothing else but the unfolding of her new scheme.

She rose from the chair, twirled, and danced to the hummed melody of a waltz until she playfully collapsed onto Piangi's lap, pushing aside the loose sheets of music that she'd stolen for him from the Teatro dell'Opera. "I've done it, my fat rooster!" Carlotta absently picked up one of the sheets and hummed the melody. "You were right, Piangi, my love. This is so much better, is it not? I should not have written the police officer. What use is he, eh? Outside Paris, he is like nothing. No one will listen to him rant about a dead man." Pointing a wickedly red fingernail at the sheet music, she asked distracted, "The tune, it is catchy, no?" Carlotta made as if to cast the sheet again to the floor, but instead she rose from Piangi's lap. She bent provocatively to retrieve the loose sheets and shuffled them carefully together to set at the piano. "This Leroux, he is probably thinking I am mad. And this letter I will send to him, and he will know that the others were simply a hoax."

"Carlotta, I think you need to reconsider this new scheme, too."

"Nonsense. It goes quite well. You must admit that I look wonderful with the veil, like a mysterious angel or a clever temptress. I already have the owner on his knees. He worships me!"

"What can you be thinking, Carlotta? The Phantom might recognize you at any moment. The man is dangerous!"

"My first thought, when we found out that he was here, was to try out for a part at the Teatro dell'Opera!" Carlotta saw the incredulous frown on her lover's face. "Oh, don't look at me that way! I can out act and out sing that weak-voiced blond sprite of his, Mag-Mig-Meg or whatever. His new whore! That's why she's the diva of the premier opera house in Rome. I have more talent in my fingernail than she has in her whole petite body!" Carlotta had squeezed the corner of her letter in her anger. She quickly smoothed out the wrinkled surface against the folds of her skirt. "Oh, Piangi," she pouted, plaintively. "I can't sing for them or even speak. I must disguise even my voice. He would recognize it! Who could forget my voice?"

Piangi smiled and patted her thigh. "No one, my dove, absolutely no one."

"No, no one! But Piangi, you should come see me. I strike a pose in my veil. I open my fan just so and flutter it before my face, hinting at my eyes simmering behind the gauze. And my voice, I lower it to a whisper, like a caress." She demonstrated for Piangi, pretending to wear the veil, fluttering the imaginary fan, and speaking in a low, husky whisper that made the fine hairs on the back of Piangi's neck stand erect. Then in her normal voice, she teased, "You see, eh? You see the effect I can have? Oh, the Phantom has no idea that two can play at his game. I'll be right behind him, on his heels, at his elbow, the entire time. I'll stalk him like he stalked me so long ago. We don't need old Inspector Leroux. We have our own ways, eh? Remember, Piangi, the horrid tricks the Phantom played on us?"

"Yes, my love," answered Piangi, resigned.

"Well, I have many tricks in mind for Signore Erik Costanzi and those who have taken him in and pretended he was not what he is—a monster. Oh, this is going to be such fun, Piangi, such, such fun!"

CHAPTER 4

The Fall

Now are thoughts thou shalt not banish,
Now are visions ne'er to vanish;
From thy spirit shall they pass
No more, like dew-drop from the grass.

Edgar Allan Poe, "Spirits of the Dead"

Meg watched as the backdrop came sweeping down as if it were in slow motion. She must have screamed just as she noticed the resolve on Erik's face. The weighted bucolic scene had been poised above the stage where directly in its path twirled a young student practicing the steps of the ballet for Act II. Erik roughly pushed the thirteen-year-old pupil out of the way. The girl safely fell outside the range of the backdrop, landing in a graceful position that might have been choreographed except for the look of sheer terror on her face. The weighted edge of the backdrop clipped Erik hard on the shoulder, and he crashed against the hard boards of the stage. Folds of painted canvas, flutters of greens, golds, and browns, shimmered and gathered about him like a closed fan.

"Erik!" Meg called out and ran to him.

Already he was pushing himself from the floor. He took one moment, with teeth clenched, to wave her back. He struggled painfully to his feet. Without so much as a second glance at Meg, Erik sought a glimpse of the young girl who had nearly been struck down. While Madeleine soothed the girl's nerves, several ballet pupils hovered round chattering excitedly. All seemed well. Relieved to see that the pupil was uninjured, Erik called up to the catwalks above.

"Check those damn riggings! I want to know how in the devil this could happen."

Several voices chimed in from various directions above the stage. None was in the vicinity of the catwalk nearest the rigging for the backdrop.

More softly Erik called Rinaldo over and whispered to him.

Meg would wait no longer and approached Erik, grabbing at his sleeve to turn him towards her. "Are you all right?" Her voice was even, but there was no mistaking the anxiety it barely restrained.

Erik was breathing hard. He softly stroked his hand along the side of his wife's face and looked into her eyes. The terrible image of Meg lying prostrate and broken on the floor of the stage would not leave him. Tenderly he reassured her. "I'm all right."

"Your shoulder?" Meg brought her hand to the shoulder that must have received the brunt of the impact. He brushed her hand away and forced a smile on his face, she knew, to placate her.

Then he was off shouting orders. The house was to be searched for any uninvited guests. The riggings were to be checked and rechecked. All employees hired within the past three months were to be assembled. Their credentials were to be reviewed. He wanted to know who hired them, what recommendations did they have. The current run of bad luck had started in the last two to three months.

As Meg watched her husband retreat through the wings, all purpose and determination, she felt curiously disoriented. It was as if she were a ballet student again at the Opera Populaire. She remembered the unexplained accidents—mostly nuisances, nothing horribly serious until Buquet. She shivered. Erik had been the author of the mayhem in the house. Everyone had thought him a ghost.

Whispers broke into her reverie, confusing her memories with her present. The young tittering of superstitious girls. "…ghost…shadows on the wall…the light just went off by itself…I felt a hand…it's haunted, I say, it is…since the fire they say it haunts…hideously burned…" Meg bit her lip in consternation. The young dancers around her were referring to the fire in the Teatro dell'Opera. Of course, they didn't even realize that there had been no deaths, thanks largely to her husband. Erik had nearly perished in that fire, but he had dragged to safety every other living soul, even Giovanni, the madman who had started it.

Meanwhile Erik had rushed backstage and quickly climbed to the flies above. Waiting for him was Jacopo, a scene shifter who had been with the company for years. The brawny man was rubbing the back of his neck as he looked down at the stage below.

"Well?" Erik's voice was curt, but not accusing. He knew he could trust Jacopo. They had worked together since Erik took over the directorship of the artistic program, and Erik knew Jacopo had worked for Don Marcelo at other venues before the Teatro dell'Opera was constructed.

"Didn't see anything, Don Erik. I was inspecting the rigging in the back and then went down to check on the scenes for Act III. Someone must have unfastened the side supports—he might have done so at anytime—and then unfastened this one."

"You mean he was up here at the time, watching, and intentionally dropped it at that moment?" Erik was not surprised. He had experience with riggings and had played havoc with them at the Opera Populaire. However, he had always taken care to avoid any serious injuries. But in this case, the person was either very clumsy or had meant to harm someone.

"Yes, signore. But the rope on the main rigging wasn't cut. It frayed and broke."

Erik turned his gaze on the man, intently interested in what he had deduced. "What does it mean?"

"Well, it might mean someone fiddled with the side supports alone and that over time—maybe a couple of hours, maybe more—the center knot couldn't bear the strain and broke from the weight."

Erik puzzled over the possibility. If that were true, the person might not be anywhere about at the moment of the collapse of the backdrop. Anyone who had access as much as the day before or only moments before the incident could have loosened the side supports. He was a fool, though, to have done it. He might have killed someone. It was of course the safest way to sabotage the set. Whoever it was could have chosen his moment and been long gone before anything happened, leaving himself plenty of time to establish a credible alibi. Perhaps he had misjudged the time the central support might fail. Or he had expected it to fall, early in the day, when no one was on the stage. In such a case, the incident would have been intended as one more annoyance to plague the rehearsal.

"Thank you, Jacopo. From now on I want someone on the catwalks watching."

"Yes, Don Erik."

As the man started down the wooden walk, Erik heard the crack of the slat. In a reflexive move, he grabbed for Jacopo who had lost his footing and was falling through the torn hole in the catwalk. The weight of the falling body pulled Erik down inexorably toward the plunge. If not for his grip on the side rope, the two of them would have crashed to the stage below, like fragile porcelain vases against a stone floor. With a torturous turn of his entire torso, Erik swung Jacopo within grasp of the riggings. The agile scene shifter managed to grab hold of a rope. As the man's body pulled away from him, Erik lost his hold above.

For one moment, he thought he was flying. And then it was done.

Meg had flinched as she heard the crack above her head. One look upwards suggested Erik and a man were struggling. In the next second, however, she saw the man clinging to a rope and Erik falling toward them. The hay wagon that had been brought to the stage broke Erik's fall, and he tumbled to the floor. Stunned she looked at the faintly familiar shape of her husband sprawled at her feet as if he were in their bed and had not yet woken.

"Don't touch him!" The sound slapped against them all. Madeleine rushed forward, pushing everyone else, including her daughter, out of her way. "Don't move him! You can make it worse."

Madeleine understood bones. She had had to bind broken arms, wrap twisted ankles, realign dislocated shoulders when she taught the ballet dancers in the Paris opera house. She had even seen one very serious accident when a dancer, too close to the edge of the platform, lost her balance, and careened off the stage into the orchestra pit. The unfortunate woman injured her spine, and her dancing days were over. It was a miracle that she eventually was able to walk again.

Madeleine had seen Erik fall. She watched him try to right himself, like a cat, in midair so as not to land head first. His body crashed against the wagon and toppled off. She judged the major impact most likely struck evenly along his back. If he survived the fall, he still might have permanently damaged his spine. He could be paralyzed. If they tried to move him, they could do more harm than good.

She knelt beside him, relieved to see his chest rise and fall. She studied his position. He was on his back. Not knowing what to examine first, she ran her hands lightly along his skull to check for a severe head wound. She found no blood, and the bones seemed solid. She called over her shoulder two brisk orders. One was to get the doctor; the other was to find Don Marcelo. She could see that Meg was near panic behind her.

"Meg, he's breathing. He's alive."

Something in her mother's tone did not reassure Meg. Madeleine had not said that he'd be fine. Erik might be injured—permanently. Meg felt her legs tremble. Rinaldo grabbed her hand and helped her to a nearby crate and had her sit down. Meg did not release his hand. Unconsciously, she squeezed it hard while she watched her mother slowly press along Erik's extremities.

Madeleine began at the arms and worked her way to the torso. Then she gingerly tried to straighten Erik's legs. Her hands were beginning to shake, and her eyes were filling with tears, making it difficult to examine him for obvious signs of worsening.

She recalled a fall he had taken only weeks after she had brought him, just a young boy, to the Parisian opera house to escape the police. He had been living—locked away in a cage barely large enough for a lion or panther—exhibited from town to town as the "Devil's Child." She had brought him to the underground tunnels, and he had disappeared in the dark underbelly of Paris to explore his new kingdom. Never had he had such an expanse of space in which to roam. So one day when Madeleine called to him to come for his supplies and he didn't answer, she was at a loss as to what to do. She dared not go down in search of him. She was sure she'd get lost. She thought perhaps he had run off. The next day he didn't come either. Nor the next. She had almost decided to give up when she heard a strange sound. He had pulled himself up the many flights of stairs, dragging his injured foot behind him. Several days before, he had fallen and hurt himself. He couldn't come when he heard her call to him, but he was afraid to cry for help, afraid someone else might hear him and come take him away. She wrapped his ankle and set his dislocated shoulder. He was in great pain, but he was stubbornly silent. Then Madeleine made the boy a makeshift bed at the top of one of the landings. There he stayed until he was able to support himself on his sprained foot.

Thinking of that day, Madeleine paused in her examination of Erik's injuries. She brushed aside the hair that had fallen across his mask. She imagined that dirty, haunted boy in this man. Then she noticed the skin along the edge of the mask. He was deathly pale, and his skin felt cool and damp.

"Bring a blanket," she called, and someone ran off in search of one.

Just as Madeleine thought she might examine Erik's neck, Don Marcelo and the new patroness of the opera came through the crowd.

"Oh, thank God, Marcelo! Erik fell." Madeleine stood to go to Marcelo when she noticed that he held the other woman by the hand. A look of guilt blazed across his face as he withdrew his fingers from Signorina Venedetti's gloved hand. Madeleine would not have thought much of it—she would have assumed he had simply tried to lead the signorina safely through the crowd—had it not been for the look on his face.

Recovering quickly and overwhelmed by worry over Erik's condition, Don Marcelo squeezed Madeleine's arm gently to reassure her and knelt beside Erik's prostrate form.

"Should we move him?" he asked.

"Here, signora, a blanket." Madeleine took the woolen blanket and spread it across Erik's still body.

Jacopo stood on the edge of the crowd. He was in shock over what had happened. He muttered over and over to himself. Snatches of what he was saying drifted toward the small circle huddled around Erik. "That should have been me. He grabbed me. He saved my life. That should be me lying there, not him!"

"I don't think we should move him, Marcelo." Madeleine bent close to Don Marcelo's ear and whispered, "He could have broken something along the back. We might damage it further."

"Here comes the doctor!" announced someone on the periphery. Then the crowd fell to either side to allow Dr. Pascuale access to the patient.

No one paid any attention to the beautiful veiled woman in a dark rose gown trimmed in black. She seemed to have come to a dead halt once she was near enough to see the figure on the ground. Her fan lay idle in her hand, and her eyes were fixed on the tragedy unfolding before her.

She watched as the doctor examined the Phantom, then she watched as several strong men brought to the stage a flat wooden platform approximately the width and length of a door. Slowly and carefully, the body was slid onto the straight boards. One man on each corner carefully lifted and carried the unconscious man back to his rooms. She heard the whispers around her about the ghost and how Erik had saved one of the scene shifters from certain death. She followed the patient back to the room that she knew was his office. Attached by an interior door was a private room with daybed and other conveniences in case Erik was forced to spend the night at the theater.

The men placed several boards under the mattress before they carefully transferred Erik to the daybed. His limbs were straightened out under the doctor's close supervision. Dr. Pascuale had him wrapped with other spreads and anchored effectively in one position for the night.

Was he all right? Would he live? Was his back permanently damaged by the fall? Would he ever be able to walk again? Carlotta looked from Madeleine to Meg to Don Marcelo. They were unaware that she had followed, so she slipped behind the screen in the corner of the room. She watched as they made him comfortable. Several hands came in and out with supplies. The doctor took

Meg's hand and patted it before he drew Don Marcelo out into the hallway to speak.

Madeleine suggested that Meg go home to get some rest and offered to stay with Erik until she came back. The three of them would take turns. Rinaldo offered to stay as well, but the two women exchanged an awkward look.

"Rinaldo, has Erik ever taken his mask off in front of you?" asked Madeleine directly.

Rinaldo was startled by the question and reluctantly confessed that he had not seen his employer without a mask of some sort.

"We want to have him as comfortable as we can. I don't think he'd like it if he woke without the mask and anyone but his family were here. But I appreciate your kindness and concern."

Rinaldo bowed slightly and asked if he could do anything else to help.

Madeleine responded immediately, "Take Meg home."

"No," insisted her daughter. "I'm not leaving. I'll stay with Erik, at least for a while."

Madeleine could see it would be useless to argue.

"I'll return in about three or four hours to relieve you. You must promise to rest. Rinaldo, there is a cot in the storage room. Could you bring it and some more covers and a pillow?"

The young assistant was pleased to have a task to accomplish.

Don Marcelo entered as Rinaldo left. His face was gray. Carlotta wondered if the doctor had been pessimistic.

In the next few minutes, Rinaldo set up the cot for Meg, after which Don Marcelo and Madeleine took their reluctant leave. Rinaldo offered to stay with Meg, but she said she preferred to be alone with her husband. Perhaps she'd sleep. The assistant was disappointed, but he didn't insist. He mentioned that he would be in one of the front offices if she needed anything, and although Meg rewarded him with a smile, for her it was as if he had already gone. Carlotta saw the young man slip sadly out of the door.

Behind the screen, Carlotta watched as Meg went to the side of the bed and bent over the unconscious man, near his face. When Carlotta saw the mask being set aside on a nearby table, she realized that Meg was trying to make her husband more comfortable. Then Carlotta watched Meg again bend over Erik. After several tender moments, Meg sat down on the cot next to the daybed.

From her hiding place, Carlotta could see mostly the unscathed side of his face and only a hint of the disfigurement. She wanted to gloat over the accident. It hadn't been what she had expected. She had given the man free rein to do what he wanted, but her instructions had been to cause problems. She had never meant to endanger any of the company.

Meg kept up a steady stream of conversation, and Carlotta was seriously tiring of waiting behind the screen, seated on the small footstool. She was about to risk sneaking out when she heard his moan.

"Erik? Can you hear me, love?" Meg's face was so near Erik's that it almost seemed to Carlotta that they were kissing. She was rhythmically stroking the hair back from his face as she listened.

He was trying to move, but he was tightly wrapped in the sheets and blankets. Carlotta could see the rise of his knee against the tight wraps, and he clearly moved his head. That must mean that he wasn't paralyzed.

Meg was unaware of the movement of his leg at first. But she searched under the covers for his hand and pulled it out. She held it to her breast tightly as she whispered to him. His movements grew agitated, and she tried to restrain him.

Carlotta saw her chance to leave. She edged out from behind the screen in the direction of the door. Once she reached it, she opened it quietly, prepared to leave through the adjoining office. Just as Carlotta was about to step over the threshold, Meg's voice stopped her.

"Please help me restrain him!" Meg called back over her shoulder. Having heard the door open, she had assumed it was her mother or Marcelo. Carlotta turned quickly as if she had entered rather than been on the verge of leaving.

"Oh, scuse. I thought this was Sig. Costanzi's office. I had hoped to speak for a moment with Don Marcelo." She apologized in her husky whisper.

Over the past weeks, Meg had seen the mysterious patroness several times. Erik had described her tersely, dismissing any importance to her presence. Don Marcelo had been curiously reticent to speak of her much but was often in her company.

"I need help. Please hold his legs down. He mustn't move." She knew it was risky to call the unknown woman over to help. Erik's mask was on the table, and Meg would not be able to hide his face. But when the tall woman approached and placed her hands on Erik's knees to force them down, she seemed unperturbed by what she saw.

Erik struggled against their restraint, groaning, his eyes closed. After a few moments of unsuccessful effort, he seemed to drift back into deep sleep. Meg whispered words of comfort without thinking of their meaning or the fact that a stranger was an arm's length away. Once Erik lay still, she loosened her pressure on his chest and sat back exhausted on the cot. The veiled woman released her hold as well and made as if she were about to withdraw when Meg called to her again.

"Please, signorina, could you stay for a few minutes?"

Carlotta wondered whether Meg would remember her well enough to recognize her through the light gauze of the veil. But it would be suspicious if she refused and rushed away.

"Of course." Carlotta carefully kept her voice to a whisper. She drew a chair near the bed and sat stiffly at a slight angle from which she could see both Meg and Erik. "I'm very sorry. Such an accident. He will recover, no?"

Meg smiled sadly and stared down at her husband. "He's very resilient. And strong. Strong as an ox. He'd have died long ago if he were not."

"Ah? But I thought Don Erik Costanzi was a musician, a composer? Hardly an active life for a man. You make him sound like a soldier or a laborer, one who uses his muscles."

Meg did not answer. She hesitated and glanced at the woman. "You weren't frightened by his face? I hope I can count on your discretion. He's already hounded by the curious."

Carlotta studied Erik. She'd seen him unmasked on stage that terrible night the Opera Populaire burned. But he had been at a distance from her. Now that she was able to study his disfigured face she felt overwhelmed by curiosity herself. "People can be cruel, no? He wears the mask always? With you?"

"No. Not with me. It has never mattered to me. He's terribly tormented by it." A violent blush rose in Meg's face. "Excuse me, Signorina Venedetti, he'd be so upset if he knew you were here and had seen him like this. I'm sorry I had to ask you to help, but I was worried he'd hurt himself. The doctor said he mustn't move until he regains consciousness and can tell us what he's feeling."

"My sweet, dear child, you should not worry. His face makes me sad. He must not worry that I've seen him."

Meg stretched uncomfortably and stifled a yawn.

"He's a remarkable man, you know. If people saw his face, they'd think ill of him or be repulsed. They'd never come to know him like I do." Meg's eyes began to tear up, and her voice caught in her throat as she continued, "I can't bear to see him so vulnerable."

Carlotta wondered what it would be like to have him at her mercy. If she could make Meg go, leaving her to watch over him for a few minutes…? She wanted to look down at him, knowing that she held him in her hands.

"Signora Costanzi, you need to get away for a few moments and walk about. I can stay with him. Put his mask on him and leave him with me. I will call for you immediately if he stirs."

"No! I can't leave him."

"You won't. You go out to the front and walk about the stage. He's deep in sleep. He won't wake for some time. There are plenty of people I can call, and they'll come find you."

Meg scowled down at Erik as if struggling to make a decision. She was very tired and tense. If she could walk about for ten to fifteen minutes, she'd be able to relax the knot at the back of her neck. She wouldn't go far. Signorina Venedetti was kind and seemed to be genuinely concerned for Erik. Don Marcelo must think highly of her to be so often in her company. After all, as one of the patrons of the opera, Erik's wellbeing should be very important to her.

"If he stirs, you will send for me without delay?"

"Of course."

Meg fixed the mask over her husband's features and left the room. The moment Meg disappeared down the corridor, Carlotta shut the door and drew up beside Erik. Hesitantly she took the edges of the mask that Meg had put back on the Phantom and lifted it from his face. She wanted him naked, exposed, at her mercy. She stared down at his strange face. Ugly. Hideous. Had he always been like this? She had heard the strange account of the boy who grew up in the bowels of the theater. She tried to imagine him as a boy, but the thought disturbed her. She wouldn't imagine him like that. He was not a boy. He was a grown man. When he had done those evil things to her and to those around her, he had been a grown man.

"You thought you were so much better than me! You, a monster!" But she had to admit that he was talented. And as Meg had said, he was certainly strong and resourceful. How could he have escaped not once but several times? She sat down next to him. She caught the light scent of his cologne mixed with the natural musk of his sweat. She listened to him breathe. His lips were slightly parted, and before she realized it she had brushed her fingers across them.

He stirred slightly. A soft purring moan came thick and rich from where she watched the muscles of his throat working. She couldn't make out his words, but she let the sounds rush over her. Pain or fear edged into his dream, and she sensed his disquiet. Without thinking, she whispered sweetly against his ear to calm him. "Shush…Rest." Then she started to sing to him a lullaby her mother had sung to her when she was a child. In a whisper Carlotta sang the words close to his cheek, and the tension on his face melted away.

At the end of the song, strangely moved by his response, she smiled. "And you used to not like my voice, eh? You tried to get me off the stage and put your own whore there, didn't you? A girl who didn't even want you! And now you like my voice? Now you want me to sing to you, to soothe your sleep?" She wanted to be angry but the intimacy of his closeness, the softening of his lips, even his smell called to her on a level that made it impossible to wish him harm.

But this man, this monster had ruined her world. For it had been her world, not his. She belonged on the stage. The Opera Populaire was not his world to rule like a despot. He should have come to her on his knees. He should have worshipped her as the queen of that realm. He should have written his wild, savage music for her to sing. What did that Daaé child know of passion? She ran in fear when this man reached out to her, when he showered her with his genius. *She, Carlotta Giudicelli, the reigning Diva of the Opera Populaire,* would have known how to respond to the Phantom's gifts. *She* would have tamed the beast and returned passion for passion. *She* would have sung his music the way he had meant it to be sung! Not the virgin rendering of the blood and fire that Christine Daaé had given.

But what was happening to her? She must get away from him. How could he exert his will even as he lay unconscious? For one moment Carlotta had thought she might kiss him, a being whose face was not human! This was the man who had destroyed her. And Piangi! Carlotta rushed to the door and called to a passing boy.

"Go for Signora Costanzi and be quick about it!"

While she waited, she heard Erik moan again. Deep in her womb, she felt the tug. She wanted to go to him. To go to him? For what? She clenched her fists and refused to look back at him.

Meg came running through the connecting door. "Is he all right?" she asked, frightened.

"Sí, sí. He was uncomfortable. I took off his mask. He was moaning. I thought perhaps you should be near."

"Oh, thank you so much, Signorina Venedetti, for staying with him. I feel quite refreshed now."

Carlotta was desperate to get out of the room, desperate to distance herself from the voice, his voice, his wordless sounds, the smell of his body, the pull of him. "Restored, yes. That is good. I will leave you now. I'm sure he will be fine. You'll see. He's too strong. Just as you said. He's a strong man." Carlotta smiled behind her veil and rushed from the room without glancing back at Erik, who was struggling to open his eyes.

"Madeleine, it's nothing." Marcelo's voice was rushed and urgent. But the moment Meg stepped out of Erik's room, pulling the door closed behind her, both Marcelo and Madeleine pursed their lips tightly shut.

Meg felt the tension immediately but assumed it was from concern over Erik's condition.

"He's better," she rushed to assure them. "He woke momentarily. He's resting now. He swears he's fine." When her news had little or no effect on her mother's gloomy expression or Marcelo's tight-lipped scowl, Meg understood that something else was the matter. "What is it?"

One corner of Madeleine's mouth lifted in a sarcastic grin. "Nothing, ma petite. We were just discussing the charming Signorina Venedetti."

"She was here just a while ago," said Meg, unsure of the reason for such sarcasm.

Madeleine grew curiously restive at the mention of the new patroness.

"She stayed with Erik while I took a brief moment to stretch. She's very strange, isn't she?" Meg didn't notice the glance Don Marcelo and Madeleine exchanged. "Do you suppose she is disfigured, too?"

Don Marcelo asked, "Why would you think so?"

Madeleine glared at Don Marcelo and inquired, "Has she granted you a look under that veil?"

Don Marcelo sighed heavily. "I told you, Madeleine, you're making too much of all this."

"I saw you!"

"What's the matter? Why are you two arguing? What did you see, Maman?" insisted Meg.

"It's nothing, ma jeune fille, nothing, nothing, nothing." Madeleine pulled her angry gaze away from Marcelo to stare at her daughter. Meg couldn't understand her mother's enigmatic reaction. The accusation spread to include Meg. "But tell me, Meg, what has the wonderful Signorina Venedetti done lately?"

Meg hesitated to explain, "It's just that she came in when Erik's mask was removed. She was very kind about it. And it occurred to me that perhaps she hides some disfigurement behind that veil. Her voice is strange, too. Perhaps her face and her voice were injured through mishap or disease."

"Well, she's not disfigured," replied Don Marcelo without further explanation. "She simply wants privacy."

"I'd say that's not all she wants!"

Meg was dumbfounded by her mother's anger. She raised her eyebrow in a questioning way at Don Marcelo, but he lowered his eyes, embarrassed, and followed Madeleine into the room to check on Erik.

Erik carefully stretched his body the length of the daybed until his feet stuck beyond the end. The pain was a dull ache along his back, and he desperately wanted to change his position, to find a way to ease the discomfort. Meg, Madeleine, and Don Marcelo had taken turns watching over him for more than forty-eight hours as he unwillingly drifted in and out of consciousness. But he woke this morning sick of sleep.

He had quickly grown irascible as they fussed over him. It annoyed and disquieted him that they treated him as if he were an invalid. He ordered them out. Meg had not eaten, and she needed to rest. Both Madeleine and Don Marcelo had suggested staying, but Erik refused their company. He irritably argued that he didn't need anyone to watch him sleep.

He didn't explain to them that he had no intention of sleeping. He meant to get up, but he wouldn't risk trying with Meg or anyone else there to witness his struggle. He wasn't paralyzed; he would heal. So there was no reason for them to hover over him and to treat him as if he were made of glass and might shatter at any moment. He had to get up to prove to himself that he was not seriously injured in spite of their long faces. And they were in his way. All of them were in his way!

He had other compelling reasons to speed his recovery. Something was seriously wrong in the opera house, and he could not lie in bed, waiting for everything to come crashing down around him. He could not let anyone or anything destroy his world again.

He rolled to the side, bending his knees and letting the weight of his legs bring him to a sitting position on the edge of the daybed. He pushed at the same time with his arms until his feet touched the floor and he was sitting stiffly straight. The muscles along his back threatened to spasm, but he willed them to relax, taking several deep, calming breaths of air. Feet and hands bore his weight, and he stood. A pleased grin began to spread across his lips when the first of the spasms clutched his lower back in a vice lock. He cried out with the sharp, deep, unrelenting pain of it and pitched forward onto the floor.

Chest heaving, he remained still, trying to figure out what would relieve the pain. He didn't want to move, but his current position on hands and knees brought him no relief either. Suddenly he saw a pink glove and satin-wrapped sleeve circle under his arm as if to pull him to his feet.

Barely able to breathe, he managed to plead with the silent intruder. "Don't. Please."

"What did you think you were going to do?" came a raspy whisper intimately close to his cheek.

Carefully he looked to examine the person's face. The veil mocked him, but as she inclined to help him, it fell slightly aslant, revealing a broad mouth with two full, dark sensual lips.

"I thought I dropped something," he lied lamely. "Please, don't pull," he requested again between teeth clenched against the pain.

"You can't stay like this. Come. You're too big for me to lift." Carlotta pulled at him in spite of the excruciating pain she felt assail him. He swallowed a cry as he came back to a standing position. She kept him close to her body, secretly enjoying his solid mass pressing against her. She helped him take a half step back until his legs were firmly against the daybed, and she forced him down again onto the mattress.

Erik tasted blood in his mouth as he bit into the tender flesh of his lip to stifle the scream his body insisted on releasing. He would have to be content with the fact that he had stood. He would eventually be up and about. The sweat pooled under his arms, along his forehead, across his upper lip, and along his throat. His mask felt as if it might slip down the dampness. He thought he might pass out, but he turned his eyes on the pink folds of her dress and let her help him recline on the bed.

"You are a very foolish man. It has to be your way, doesn't it? That's all you think. 'My way, my way, my way.' Well, you can't."

Erik listened closely to her voice. She was very near him, near enough for him to feel her warmth. Her perfume was strong, sweet, and flowery. It threatened to overwhelm his senses. She had been in his room before. He remembered the fragrance. She must have been here. She raised her voice slightly over the usual whisper, and he caught a note that seemed familiar. She spoke almost as if she were singing or performing a recitative. He wanted to hear her speak again.

"You think you know everything and the world must bend to your will. Isn't that so? Why should we listen to you? Why did Marcelo make you the director of the opera? What makes you capable of running an opera house like this one?" Erik listened, stunned by her insulting questions, her familiarity. He watched, puzzled, as she paced back and forth, like a caged panther, in front of him.

"Signorina, what gives you the right to be here in my private chambers?" He didn't like the fact that he was incapacitated, in his bedroom, while a woman he barely knew berated him. "If you want to expound further, perhaps you should seek Don Marcelo."

"Ah hah! Don Marcelo. You managed to fool him, too, didn't you?"

"What do you mean by that?"

The swirl of pink slowed and quieted. Several pregnant moments passed as she stared at him from behind the gauze of her veil. When she spoke again, her whisper had turned seductive and sweet.

"You must not pay me any heed. Your accident unsettled us all. After all, my entire fortune is invested in this enterprise, and it seems as if its success rests on the shoulders of a man who three or four years ago no one had even heard of."

Erik tasted the salty drip of sweat travel down and across the corner of his mouth. The pain was easing, but the new turn of conversation disquieted even more than the previous tirade.

Carlotta watched him carefully. Most of his face was invisible under his mask and yet those eyes, they shimmered and changed so easily. She could see confusion, annoyance, suspicion, and worry take their turns in the deep green of those surfaces. She resisted a foolish desire to take her handkerchief and wipe the sweat from his face. She imagined it was uncomfortable to wear the mask over his glistening skin.

"Where did you ever come from, Don Erik? Whatever was your life like before you came to the surface…here in Rome?" The question unfolded like a cobra from its den. She could see the shock of recognition in Erik's eyes. But there was doubt and confusion, too.

His lips parted slightly in an effort to respond that never succeeded. He lay very still watching Signorina Venedetti.

"Cat got your tongue? Well, we won't worry about that. Ah, do you sing, too, Don Erik? No answer? Rest. You want to rest after such an accident. But as we all know, these things do happen, eh?" And before she could stop herself, she stepped forward and placed her dark full lips on the blankness of his mask just above his eyes and kissed him through her veil.

Erik shivered from the strange intimacy and the threat it awakened. He stared after her wordlessly. Only when she had closed the door behind her, did he dare whisper her name.

"Carlotta?"

Erik had not touched his plate. He watched Carlotta exchange pleasantries with Meg who sat at her left. She took every opportunity to turn to her right where Don Marcelo, flushed with pleasure at her obvious interest in him, sat at the head of the table.

Thankfully Erik had worn his mask when he descended to the parlor and found that there was a guest for dinner. He had not run into the mysterious veiled lady since the day she caught him trying to rise from the daybed in the office. The next day he managed to convince Don Marcelo that with help he could make it to the coach. He left Rinaldo in charge, against his better thoughts, and insisted on completing his recovery at home, away from the teatro and from the veiled woman.

Could his senses have been playing tricks on him? Could this possibly be Carlotta Giudicelli, the diva from the Opera Populaire? They had tormented each other the last two or more years she had been at the Parisian opera house. He had plagued her constantly, disrupting her performances, ripping her costumes, sabotaging her in a thousand little, annoying ways in an attempt to force her to withdraw. She was proud and egotistical. Having grown complacent, she arrived late and left early, was concerned only with her own performance, sang the score in whatever way she wished at the time, heedless of the music or of M. Reyer's direction. Everyone had to bend to her will. And because she no longer saw the benefit of discipline, she had begun to lose some of her vocal range. She experienced difficulty with certain notes, and the strain was evident.

When Erik entered the parlor and his eyes lit on the imposing figure of Signorina Venedetti, he nearly lost the use of his legs. He had taken refuge at the estate to think his way through the threat, for surely her intrusion in the Teatro dell'Opera must pose a threat to him and everything he held dear. She knew who he was. She held his life in her hands.

Don Marcelo said something, but Erik could hear nothing louder than the pounding of his own startled heart in his ears. He pulled himself together when he saw their guest lift a black gloved hand for him to take. He forced his feet to obey and stepped forward to take Carlotta's hand. He brought it to his lips in a gesture of welcome he didn't feel.

Her whisper sank deeply into his mind, both familiar and strange, for he only remembered her voice as loud, grating, strident. The moment he looked into her face, he wondered how he had not recognized her before. Even behind the veil her eyes were intense, and the shape of her face was that of the famous diva. Her lips certainly now struck him as impossible not to recognize. Time and circumstances had lulled him into a false sense of security. He simply had thought that he had finally escaped his past.

"Don Erik," she whispered, her mouth turned up in a smile. "You are recovered? I'm amazed. How could a man survive such an accident unscathed? You must not be an ordinary man."

His lips thinned in a hard, long line. How was he to answer that? Everyone squirmed noticing his silence until Don Marcelo asked for the signorina's arm to lead her into the dining room.

"What's wrong with you, Erik? She was teasing you." Meg slipped up behind Erik and took his elbow to shake him from his distraction.

At the table, Erik had merely nodded as plates were set before him and removed untouched. He observed her as if they were all trapped on stage in a comedy of manners. She played her role as if she had written all the parts herself. She had completely enthralled Don Marcelo. He hung on her every word. Across from her, next to Erik, sat Madeleine. He saw her wilt before the radiance of Carlotta at her most predatory. Madeleine dourly cut her meat and pushed it around the plate, barely disguising her lack of appetite. She refused to look across at the woman who shamelessly flirted with Don Marcelo.

Although Carlotta was telling an amusing story about a young opera singer who had been having simultaneous affairs with the patron, her male lead, and the composer of the opera, Erik interrupted testily. "What interested you in our teatro, Signorina Venedetti?"

Don Marcelo coughed and protested Erik's lack of manners. "Really, Erik. You're usually not so rude. Signorina Venedetti…" But as he meant to continue, Carlotta placed her hand on Don Marcelo's sleeve and turned her attention on Erik. Madeleine's eyes were frozen on the other woman's hand, which had not moved from Don Marcelo's arm.

"Why, Don Erik, why wouldn't I be interested in the finest opera house in Rome?"

"What are you intentions, signorina?" he asked bluntly.

"Intentions?" Erik took note that, as usual, she was overacting. Her exaggerated confusion seemed to strike only him as parodic. "I have only the intention of encouraging real talent. Not the passing vogue for sensationalist excess. Don't you find, Don Erik, that the public unfortunately has a penchant for the bizarre?"

Meg tensed as she watched Erik absorb the patroness's unfortunate choice of words. "Surely," she interrupted, hoping to steer their guest in a slightly safer direction, "you understand the need to keep the arts alive and flourishing. And for that, it is always necessary to challenge the current forms, to look for something fresh."

Before Carlotta could respond, Erik remonstrated in an intense tone, "Nonsense, Meg. Art is art. The composer has no choice in what he creates. You make it sound as if what he writes is simply a correction to worn-out convention. The work comes. It is shaped by and shapes the composer. Whether the public understands it or not, it simply is."

Meg was stung by Erik's rebuke. She didn't understand the anger behind his words.

"Ah, Don Erik, that is so interesting. Then the composer is at the mercy of his art? And the art is shaped by the composer. Does this not seem a contradiction?"

"Just as we are victims of our own natures."

"So there seems little distinction between the art and the artist."

Erik held her gaze.

She continued when she realized he would not. "So what would your work suggest about you?"

Behind his mask, he knew he had turned scarlet. The accolades and diatribes the critics and spectators had hurled at him solidified and sharpened as if they were knives ripping away his mask, even his skin, leaving him bare and exposed.

"Madame, Erik's work speaks to us all. Anyone who has suffered understands his art. The music is the soul. It is angry, tormented, and yet it strives to escape its shackles. It reaches out for beauty itself. No one until Erik has had the courage, the strength, or the genius to be able to put that into form for the stage." Madeleine's voice grew in intensity as she spoke. A hush fell upon them all. Madeleine rose from her seat and dropped her napkin by her plate. "If you'll excuse me, I have a headache. I think I'll retire for the evening."

As she turned, she brushed her hand against Erik's arm. Once the dining room door was closed, Carlotta was the first to break the awkward silence. "Your mother-in-law mistook my intention. Please accept my apologies, Don Erik. I am a fervent admirer of genius, and I understand its demanding nature. I once had a modest career on the stage before it was…untimely…brought to an end."

Erik stiffened at her reference to their past. He nearly gave in to the urge to lecture her on exactly why her career had ended when Don Marcelo reacted in sympathetic reassurances.

"I can't express how unfortunate we are to have lost the opportunity to hear you sing, my dear. You must have dazzled."

Erik cringed as he saw Don Marcelo's hand cover Carlotta's so casually.

Meg took the moment to bring the conversation to an end. "Shall we retire to the parlor? The children will be waiting for us." She, too, had seen Don Marcelo's gesture and was uncomfortably reminded of the scene between him and her mother that she had witnessed weeks before. He had been so attentive to her, and now it was as if there were nothing but friendship or familial love between them.

Erik hung back watching Carlotta. She glided into the adjoining room, careful to brush frequently against Don Marcelo's sleeve. The older gentleman was smitten by her fawning, her presence, her mystery.

For a moment, Erik thought he could bear it no longer. He would unmask her and demand she tell him what she wanted. But what would the consequences of such a violent confrontation be? He must take his time. He would study her and find some way to disarm her. She wanted to revenge herself and her lover on him—of that he was certain—but how? To what lengths would she torment him? She meant to play with him, and until he knew the game, he must wait and watch. Her delight would be to see him squirm. Otherwise she would have struck more directly.

She had already threatened to destroy Madeleine's world. It was cruel, for Erik could tell Carlotta was only toying with Don Marcelo. But even so she would destroy the sweet ties that had tenderly bound Madeleine and Don Marcelo over the past years. These ties had just recently blossomed but were fragile and could easily wither.

François and Mario were bowing like little gentlemen before the imposing figure of his tormentor. Meg held the squirming Laurette in her arms as she spoke, unknowingly, to Carlotta, a woman who had ignored and despised the young girls like Meg and Christine that had lived and worked in the opera ballet.

Carlotta examined both boys intently. Erik didn't like the way she focused in particular on François. He could almost imagine her thoughts, her surprise. *This is the Phantom's son? This handsome child? How could he merit such a blessing as a child like this?*

"Two strong strapping sons, Don Erik. Unfortunately I can't say which favors you most." The subtle note of sarcasm was lost on all but Erik.

"*I* do." Seeing his chance to establish his privilege of being his father's only natural son, François immediately spoke up. "Maman and Grandmère both say I look like you, don't they, Father?"

Erik reluctantly nodded. He fought against the same old dull pain at the irony of his son's insistence.

Carlotta started to speak, and Erik tensed for the blow. Curiously she looked from the child to the man and reconsidered her remark. Instead of commenting on what must surely seem bizarre to her—for Erik knew that she had seen his face—she remained mercifully silent.

Mario had watched and listened to the conversation sensing that something dangerous lay just beneath the surface. He pulled at François who looked at him puzzled. Mario nodded toward their father, and François became aware of how silent and wary his father had become. The two boys went to Erik as if their presence might protect him. François slipped his hand into Erik's. The moment the child's hand touched him, Erik felt compelled to pull him closer. He dropped his son's hand and instead put his arm protectively around him, holding him tightly by his side. A moment later, he grabbed Mario as well.

"Mario is our adopted son," Meg explained. It was apparent that Signorina Venedetti was confused by his lack of resemblance to either parent.

Erik bent low and whispered to the two boys. "I want you to take your sister and excuse yourselves now."

"But, Papa, I wanted to play the gavotte for you."

"François, do as I say." His tone was unfortunately sharp, and he regretted it when he saw the disappointment on his son's face. But there was no help for it. He didn't want them near Carlotta. Mario, always trusting, went to obey without hesitation. Unlike François, Mario had experienced danger and trouble. He felt the currents of warning in Erik's demeanor far better than François did.

Laurette had forced Meg to let her down. She ran to her father and begged him to lift her up. Erik stooped and took Laurette for one moment in a warm hug and kissed her on the cheeks. Her hands went to his mask to remove it, as she always did whenever he wore it in her presence, but he stopped her before she managed to slip it up off his face.

"Non, ma petite," he whispered and kissed her again. "Go with your brothers. Ask your nurse for some pudding."

Mario took the disappointed little girl by the hand and pulled her toward the door. François lingered a moment longer before a severe look from Erik sent him along.

Carlotta had watched Erik closely as she pretended to listen to Don Marcelo talk of plans for the next season. Children? He had sired two children. The beast had mated. Why were they so beautiful? She had looked for signs on them of ugliness, violence, and madness, but all she had found were two beautiful, normal children.

She felt suddenly annoyed and out of place.

From the stage, he was uncomfortably aware of Carlotta's presence in box five. He tried not to look over at her. She sat like an Eastern potentate, her gown a deep red taffeta that contrasted teasingly with the reddish brown of her hair. A light black veil covered her face today just to the level of her upper lip, and Erik could see the sarcastic tilt of her lips as he directed Meg on the stage in the aria for the final act. In her hand, she held her black gloves clenched and poised on the ledge as she craned to watch Erik's every move.

He had largely recovered from the fall and wouldn't admit to the residual pain that plagued him after long hours of rehearsal. Today had been particularly long since several costumes had been found in shreds and several props sawed or broken. He spent useless time arguing with the stage hands over what they could do to prevent more interference in the next week before the opening night. And then when they were able to start the rehearsal, he was greeted by the unwelcome appearance of the veiled lady in box five.

Rinaldo cleared his throat to get Erik's attention. The assistant looked up in the direction of box five where Signorina Venedetti was waving her black glove yet again. Erik gritted his teeth and turned sharply toward her.

"What is it now, signorina?" he asked between clenched teeth.

The surprise was palpable. The chorus drew in a simultaneous gasp at Erik's angry tone. Even Meg seemed startled, but she had been expecting him to explode for the last hour. Signorina Venedetti could evidently not raise her voice over a whisper so whenever she wanted to communicate in the rehearsal— which was annoyingly frequently—she would find some way to catch Erik's attention and have him draw near her box.

Erik glared up at the woman, painfully aware that she was toying with him. He drew closer, his eyes fixed on her, his arms stiffly at his sides.

Carlotta smiled as she saw him obey her request. She watched him struggle with the impulse to refuse, and it thrilled her to see him lose. He stood at her feet. She smiled down at him. At last he would dance to her tune.

She whispered, "Don Erik, don't you think Meg's voice is straining to do the arpeggio? Perhaps the score needs to be simplified."

The green in his eyes flashed, and if she didn't know it was impossible, she'd swear they changed shades. His hands clenched shut. He didn't even acknowledge her suggestion. Instead, he marched over to the center of the stage and brusquely called to Meg.

"Sing the last five bars!" he barked.

Meg scowled at his unusually rough tone. He was not a patient man, but he was careful not to speak to her the way he sometimes spoke to the others. For a few seconds, she debated whether to walk off the stage in a huff, but she told herself that something the patroness had said must have goaded him.

She had barely begun to sing when Erik shouted, "Enough!"

He quickly went to the orchestra pit and demanded the score. He looked it over, his eyes rapidly surveying the notes. Then he turned toward Meg. As if he had always spoken to her impatiently, he called her over to look at the score.

"Is this what you think you were singing?" His finger struck angrily at the sheet.

Meg crossed her arms over her chest and stared at him instead of the musical score.

"Pay attention to the arpeggio, Meg. You're getting sloppy." He turned away from his wife and returned the music to the maestro.

The silence was deep and heavy. When he turned back to Meg, he knew he'd made a mistake.

She had gone from deathly white to crimson as she listened to Erik's harsh criticism. She waited only long enough for their eyes to meet, and then she turned and walked quickly off the stage toward her dressing room.

"Meg! Rehearsal is not over!"

"It is for me!" she shouted back over her shoulder as she disappeared.

Carlotta drew her hands to her mouth in glee. To anyone else her gesture might have looked like surprise or shock or even concern. She suppressed the laughter that bubbled up from her diaphragm. She saw Erik watch Meg leave. She saw the almost imperceptible hunch of his shoulders as he realized she had played him. He couldn't brook imperfection. All she had to do was listen and wait for Meg to be just a little less than perfect. She knew if she pointed it out, Erik wouldn't be able to ignore it. His music must be sung as he heard it in his mind—a perfect expression of the sublime.

Would he beg Meg to forgive him? Or would he insist that she had not been up to the challenge of his score?

Erik saw Carlotta from the corner of his eye. Yes, she'd been correct. Meg hadn't sung the arpeggio well. She was tired. He had noticed. Her voice was weakening. Once she could have sung for hours without the least problem. Now her voice thinned, eventually breaking after an intense session. Mornings were impossible. After a performance, she was often hoarse. He didn't want to admit that his canary was perhaps coming to the end of her career.

No, she needed a rest, that was all. The cold she'd gotten in late summer had attacked her vocal cords, and she'd not yet recovered. She would. She would recover.

He knew why this crisis would particularly please Carlotta. He had harassed her mainly because he found her voice lacking. She had to strain harshly and loudly to reach certain notes, certain registers. She could barely sing "pianissimo" toward the end of her career at the Opera Populaire. Every note had to be wrenched from her throat. She delighted in pointing out Meg's weakness. But Meg worked for her craft. Carlotta had not. In the safety of her fame and success, Carlotta had stopped trying, stopped struggling for perfection. She often missed rehearsals, saying they were for the novices. He had watched her from the wings go through the motions of rehearsal. Everyone around her was forced to compensate for her mistakes. She had even been known to forget the words to the arias and to make them up. She deserved his disapprobation. Not Meg, not Meg. She had bled for her art. She had suffered. He, after all, had been her scourge.

"We'll resume in an hour," he announced gruffly and went back toward the dressing rooms to find his wife.

The door was locked. His hand wrapped round the cold knob, and he rattled it loudly as he knocked yet again.

"Meg," he whispered harshly through the door. "Don't be silly. Open up!"

After a brief silence, he heard the lock click open.

He saw her red eyes reflected in the mirror as she sat back down to reapply powder to lighten the dark flush of her cheeks. He was annoyed that she was hurt. She must know that the music was the heart of it. One's personal pride was insignificant compared to the need to make the music. He thought she had understood what it meant to him. Yet she sat there in her robe—small and delicate, just like a fragile bird—and it was as if he held her in his hand and might so easily crush her. A tightness in his throat made it difficult for him to speak. Instead, he came behind her and reached out his hand to touch her. He feared she would balk, so he hovered over her shoulder. She refused to engage his eyes in the mirror. He went down on his knee next to her chair so that his head was on a level with her profile. She kept her face turned away from his, but he could see his nearness made her fidget. He cupped her chin in his hand and tenderly forced her to turn toward him. He placed his lips softly on hers.

He tasted salt tears. The pain of regret cut through him. He embraced her tightly, whispering against her mouth as he did, "Don't be sad, my canary. I spoke too harshly. Please, please, Meg, don't be sad."

She hated that she had cried. She wanted to yell at him, meet his anger with her own. She was tired. The stress since the accident, as well as other tensions, had robbed her of sleep. And he could be so unreasonable, so demanding. She knew she had not performed the piece well. She had every intention of doing it over until she had it correct.

"You're impossible, Erik," she complained, wiping her eyes with her handkerchief. She had managed to escape his arms and studied her puffy eyes in the mirror. "Everything has to be perfect with you. You expect too much."

Erik frowned at her accusation. It didn't strike him that his insistence on perfection was a flaw.

"You push and push and push, and you're never satisfied! You're inhuman!"

The minute she said it, she felt him rise to his feet and step back. She knew she'd said the wrong thing.

"Oh for God's sake, Erik. You know I didn't mean it that way," she hurried to say in frustration. "Don't look at me like that! I'm your wife, and you know I didn't mean what you're thinking."

Erik's shoulders lost some of their rigidity. He sat on the sofa against the opposite wall. "You're right. I'm not human, not when I'm out there in charge of the company. I drive everyone too hard. I shouldn't be the musical director. I don't know how…to cajole…to fawn and flatter. I'm sure it would be much more effective if I just let everyone do whatever the hell they wanted to do. After all, the music doesn't matter. We should all treat the score simply as a guide, a suggestion. So we sing flat! To whom does it really matter? There's barely an ear in the audience that would know a flat from a sharp!"

Meg knew better than to interrupt him while he was in such a black and sarcastic mood. His voice had begun contrite and calm, but as he spoke his anger had gotten hold of him again. He became more agitated and violent. Suddenly unable to hold himself back he rose and confronted Meg with a glint in his eyes and a killing edge to his voice. "But *I* would know, Meg! I can hear it! I hear every misstep, and every note that misses the mark hits me like a hammer here and here!" His fist pounded cruelly on his temple and chest. "I write…I write, I compose what I can't…can't have. It is music, and it must be perfect for that is the only perfection I can ever have!"

His words frightened Meg nearly as much as his passion. "You're scaring me, Erik," she said in a small voice. She pretended to a calm she didn't feel. "You sound like the only thing that truly matters to you is your precious music."

"Don't!" he growled, interrupting her. "Don't belittle my love for the music. It was the only thing that kept me alive in Paris…before…and after…Christine. It's the only thing I know I can trust."

"And me? What about me?! And our children?" She answered in kind, for now she, too, was desperate.

Erik's lips were an angry tight line. He stood over her, huge, panting from anger, silent, his eyes fixed on hers.

"I know we're not perfect, but we love you. So tell me this, Erik. What will you think of me when I can no longer sing? What will happen to us when I grow old and ugly? When I've lost my own measure of 'beauty'? And our children? What if we had a child that had your face, the one you hide?"

"God forbid!" he said before he could restrain himself. He had gone pale, and his lips trembled. "How could you throw that up to me?"

"You fear it, don't you? I confess it crossed my mind when I was carrying François." Though she could tell her honesty hurt him, she continued, "But when he was born and there was no blemish on him, I knew it wouldn't happen. Not to any of our children."

In a small voice, Erik asked, "And if he had…looked like this?"

"I was prepared for that, too, Erik. I would have loved him, and I would have done everything to give him a happy, normal life."

"Would you have covered his face so that the others wouldn't stare and taunt him?"

"No. I don't know. Maybe. But I don't think so. I would hope he'd grow up protected, and that people would come to know him as a child and love him as he was."

"Oh, Meg, you're so innocent."

"Well, what would you do?" she challenged him.

"I'd place him in a burlap bag and drown him in the river. Then I'd bury him with my own hands and cut my throat."

If he had said it in passion, she might have attributed it to the irrationality of the moment. But he had said it in a cold, even voice fraught with defeat.

She began to cry out loud, unable to look away from the man she had thought she knew. "Then, Erik, you *are* a monster."

She didn't see his look. She had turned away from him.

He hesitated for a moment to watch her cry. Then he left the room, pulling the door closed behind him noiselessly.

Rinaldo was coming down the passageway. "Don Erik, they're waiting."

Erik didn't answer. He walked slowly down the hallway to his office.

Rinaldo was surprised to hear the door close and the lock engage.

CHAPTER 5

It Is the Cause

O, beware, my lord, of jealousy;
It is the green-eyed monster which doth mock
The meat it feeds on; that cuckold lives in bliss
Who, certain of his fate, loves not his wronger;
But, O, what damned minutes tells he o'er
Who dotes, yet doubts, suspects, yet strongly loves!

Othello, William Shakespeare, 3.3

"That little stunt on the catwalk might have been serious. I want the opening night to fail. I want Erik to be the laughing stock of the opera season. I want him afraid to leave the teatro because something else will go wrong. I told you to cause problems, not to murder people. Steal the music, ruin the costumes, put live mice in the second soprano's vanity drawers, slash the backdrops, tear out the E string from the violins, loosen the piano keys, hide the maestro's sherry flask!"

"I thought the backdrop was going to fall sooner than it did. The rope was stronger than I calculated."

"And the board?"

"I only weakened it. I expected it to give slightly, but not to break through."

"Incompetent! Concentrate on the other plans we made. Are you making any progress with the other thing? Does he trust you? And Maggie? Is she responding yet?"

"Meg, you mean."

"I know the midget's stupid name!"

"Don Erik still looks at me sometimes as if he could just as soon step on me as speak to me. But I think he's beginning to rely on me in spite of himself."

"Yes, yes, yes, yes. And his whore? Does she warm to you? Has she gotten wet for you? Has she let you slide your tongue into her ugly little mouth?"

Rinaldo shifted awkwardly. He wanted to wash his hands of the whole thing, but Carlotta Giudicelli had given him good money, money he had desperately needed and had no way of repaying. And since the fiasco of the catwalk, she had told him in no uncertain terms that she would inform on him if he ever betrayed her. "I haven't gotten her to consider me as anything more than a friend."

"She considers you a friend? A friend?! A close friend? A carnal friend? A friend-to-warm-her-bed-at-night friend? Or a friend that she basically can ignore?"

"I'm sorry, Donna Carlotta. She seems blind to all my hints."

"You're supposed to have gotten her into your bed by this time! You had a reputation for being quite a Casanova in Milan. It would appear such reports were greatly exaggerated!"

"No, Donna Carlotta, but I have to be careful. If I proposition her directly, she'll go running to Erik. I had hoped to persuade her gently by my constant attentions, but…"

"But what, Rinaldo?"

"She loves him."

Carlotta paced back and forth in her apartment, annoyed. She was tiring of such indirect methods. She had succeeded only in annoying him. She wanted him destroyed. She wanted to see him suffer as she had, as Piangi had, even though Piangi had washed his hands of the whole plan. He wanted no revenge, he had told her when he packed his bags to return to Milan. She had yelled and pleaded with him to stay and watch the Phantom's world crash down around his ears. But when Piangi asked her to forsake her schemes and come home with him, she'd refused.

"Ah hah! I know what we can do. We have to arrange for her to see *him*, her loving monster, making love to the seductive patroness."

"But he can't stand you, Donna Carlotta. How can you manage to get him to make love to you?"

Carlotta glared at the impolitic young man. "If I had more time, he'd be eating out of my hand. But we are running out of time."

"Then how?"

She smiled and laughed completely captivated by her idea. "You be sure that Mag-Meg-Mug comes to Erik's office tomorrow night at half past nine."

"Go away!" shouted Erik after the third time someone came knocking on the office door. He wouldn't speak with anyone. He knew it wasn't Meg. He knew her knock. It was always followed by her voice, calling to him softly as if she didn't want any other ear to pick it up. Of course she would say it softly. It was embarrassing enough for the world to know she slept with a monster!

"Go away, damn it!" He stomped to the door and flung it open to see Rinaldo poised to knock once more. Erik's glare stopped him in mid-gesture or he might have pounded on Erik's chest. "What do you want with me? Can't you leave me alone? Dismiss the crew. Tell everyone the teatro is closed for the season! I'm done. I've washed my hands of it!"

Erik turned and retreated to the back of the room, leaving the door open for the stunned assistant.

"I told the staff and crew to break for the day. They won't be back until Monday."

Of course it was late in the day already. He had spent the night and had ignored the sounds of the teatro coming to life that morning. Meg must have gone home shortly after their fight. Would she be among the singers preparing for another day's rehearsal? He half wished she would come and rescue him from his dark mood. The fact that she didn't come and knock on the door, that she was content to let him wallow in his foul ravings, disturbed him almost as much as the nightmares that had plagued him throughout the night. She had meant it when she called him a monster. What he had said to her came back again and again to haunt him.

"They need not come back at all! It's finished. It's over." Erik slumped into the worn winged chair in the corner. He was half dressed, his boots astray in the pathway between the door and his desk, his waistcoat draped over the bust of Mozart on his desk, his cravat lay half submerged in a tankard of stale ale.

"I told them you thought that they needed the break and that they'd sing even better if they enjoyed a long weekend." Rinaldo stepped boldly into the room and closed the door behind him. He raked his fingers through his hair as he inspected the signs of Erik's temper. Besides the articles of clothing Erik had haphazardly strewn about the room, the floor was littered with staff music, individual sheets, some blank and others scrawled with notes. "Have you been working?"

Erik waved a hand noncommittally in the air as if uninterested in answering.

Rinaldo bent and lifted one of the sheets that was filled with tiny, exact black notes. He studied it intently, immediately catching the melodic thread.

He glanced over at Erik who ignored him. It was nothing short of beautiful. "Where's the rest of this one?" he asked but to no avail. He kicked the papers about with the toe of his shoe until he found another with similar marks and picked it up to examine. Soon he managed to find the third and fourth pages. The latter was filled to the last measure, but it was obviously not completed.

Erik raised an eyebrow as he watched the young man bending and rising and shuffling through his mess. He reminded him of a chicken in search of corn. The image struck him, and he laughed lightly with a deep rumble in his chest. Rinaldo stiffened and cast an inquiring look at his employer.

"This is beautiful!" he said, shaking the papers in his hand at Erik. "Have you finished it?"

The sigh that escaped Erik's lips was a mixture of pain and resignation. "You think so?" The question sounded more sarcastic than genuine to Rinaldo.

"Yes, I do. I know you don't much respect my opinion—or anyone else's opinion—but this is incredible. You must finish it."

"Must I?" The tone had turned decidedly dangerous. "Besides, you're wrong."

"What?"

"I do respect the opinion of some. Just not yours." Then in a much softer tone, he added, "Not always, anyway." He rose then and went to the piano. He sat and played the first measures of the piece from memory.

Rinaldo followed the music on the sheets and heard the painful longing in those first notes. He came behind Erik and placed the sheets on the piano before him. "Will you finish it?"

Erik's hands silenced the keys, and he paused considering. "I don't know if I can." The admission surprised Rinaldo. He had never heard Erik admit to possible failure. "Why are you here, Rinaldo? Don't you have some sweet young lady waiting for you somewhere? You're a handsome man."

From anyone else it would have sounded like a compliment. "Sometimes I'm more interested in the music than in any woman's caresses."

Erik looked at the young man seriously. "Do you have a love, Rinaldo?"

He wasn't here to talk about his feelings. He didn't relish what he had to do, so it should be done quickly. Instead of answering, he brought over a bottle of brandy he had set on the desk when he came in.

"I have a present to celebrate the upcoming opening night. I thought per-haps you might want to break into it early since you've decided to throw the whole show into the fire." Without waiting for Erik to agree, he opened the bottle. He emptied a glass he found on the table and another that had been left on a shelf. They seemed relatively clean, so he filled them both to the rim and handed one to Erik and kept one for himself.

"To what should we drink, Don Erik?"

Erik almost set the glass down without tasting its dark amber contents. He was not much for drink. The occasions when he had drunk too much had been linked to defeat and dejection, and the liquor had only increased his suffering. He tilted his head back and drained the glass. It tasted of opium dens and bordellos and pain. He wiped his mouth distastefully with the back of his shirt sleeve. Rinaldo quickly filled the glass again before Erik could resist.

"It's good, isn't it?" asked Rinaldo who had barely sipped at his first glass.

"Yes, I suppose it is." The liquor had traveled quickly on an empty stomach to his extremities, and the warmth was calming his disquiet.

"You've been locked away in here since yesterday. What happened?"

Erik scowled at the young man. What business did he have asking him about his intimate affairs? Intimate affairs? The phrase cut at him. He should have kept his mouth shut. He should never have been so blunt with his wife. He had damned himself by his honesty. It wasn't as if he didn't know how to lie. He had used deception to get what he wanted before. No, that hadn't been deception. When he had masked himself and sung to Christine in the Opera Populaire, it had been his attempt to transform reality. He had thought that he might become the angel she mistook him to be. Why not? He could mask the horrid ugliness. Was illusion always a lie?

He downed the contents of the second glass of brandy and patted the piano bench for Rinaldo to join him. The liquor was loosening his tongue, and he had no one else to talk to. "Do you see these fingers?" He held his hands up for Rinaldo to inspect. The assistant remembered having studied them before when Erik reconstructed the missing music. "See how they are turned slightly and twisted?"

Rinaldo didn't realize that Erik actually expected him to answer until the man turned his masked face and looked him dead in the eye. "Yes, I see."

"They used to be lovely. I liked looking at my hands. Sometimes I thought they didn't belong to me, but that I belonged to them. I was something they had to drag behind them in order to live the life they were meant to have. I used them to paint and draw as well as to play music. They were very agile. My reach is very broad, thus giving me an advantage over some musicians. Do you see?" And he placed his little finger on one key and spread across the ivories until he reached a far key with his thumb. "But reach is a small thing if the fingers won't move with precision." He demonstrated his agility by playing a few bars of a lively piece.

"What happened to them?"

"They were sacrificed to a god of retribution, a god with a tin ear, I'm afraid."

Rinaldo poured Erik another glass of brandy and slid it over toward him.

"I can't tell you what happened to them," he whispered as he took the brandy and downed it. "I have lived many lives, Rinaldo. But this recent one I had hoped might be the last."

"What did you and Meg argue about?"

Erik didn't like the familiar way in which the young man spoke of his wife. He knew they were closer in age than he and Meg were, but it seemed inappropriate to him for Rinaldo to call Meg by her Christian name.

"I don't want to talk about it," Erik said softly.

Rinaldo could tell the thought was painful to Erik. Suddenly he didn't want to be here in the office plying Erik Costanzi with strong liquor, trying to get him drunk so that the plan could proceed. He wished he could unburden his soul to the man. He truly admired his music even though he thought, as a person, Erik Costanzi was incredibly strange. When he considered the two of them—Erik and Meg—separately he couldn't understand why they were together. However, when he saw them together, he had to turn away, for their intimate love was too evident to be ignored.

Rinaldo took Erik's glass and rose to go to the desk where he had left the bottle. His back to the musician, he pulled out a folded piece of paper and opened it at one end. From it, he poured a few crystals into the glass. He folded the paper again and put it in his inside vest pocket before he poured the amber liquor and watched the crystals dissolve.

"I envy your talent, Don Erik." A few moments of honesty did nothing to assuage his guilt over his coming treachery.

Erik chuckled humorlessly. He continued to play, his fingers amazingly agile given their past injury. Pure determination and no small talent, thought Rinaldo, made the impossible possible. He held the glass out in front of his employer. At the completion of the phrase, Erik took it automatically and drained the contents yet again.

"Are you determined to get drunk, Don Erik?"

"Are you determined to help me?" Rinaldo was momentarily startled. "I don't like liquor, and I don't like getting drunk."

"Then why are you drinking the brandy like water?" he couldn't help but ask.

"Because I'm not very happy with myself right now."

Rinaldo let the silence sit between them as he waited for signs of the drug's effect to take hold.

"You shouldn't envy me, you know."

"Oh really?"

"Well, maybe just a little. But the cost is great. You think it comes without a price?" Erik lay his fingers on the keyboard. "Are you curious to see what I hide behind this mask?" He kept his eyes on the piano keys, uninterested in Rinaldo's true reaction. "I could show you things. I could tell you things. Things that would perhaps make you less envious." The fingers pressed slowly, softly on the minor chord, urging a plaintive moan from the instrument as if it were a part of his own body. "Maybe it was worth it, though. I had several years of paradise."

"Had?"

The fingers curled into fists, and the fists disappeared inside beneath Erik's folded arms. His body bent slightly toward the piano, his head lowered. His voice was soft when he spoke again.

"I don't feel well."

Rinaldo saw him totter slightly to the side and caught him before he fell. He was a large man, taller than Rinaldo by a few inches, broader in the chest. The young man grunted as he pulled Erik's weight from the piano bench and dragged him behind the desk. There he left him on the floor, hidden by the massive furniture. To make sure he was not visible from the door, Rinaldo threw the edge of the Persian rug over his legs. With luck, she'd never glance that way, and if she did she would not notice the irregular shape of the rug in the dim light of the room.

Meg saw movement through the slender gap in the office door. Rinaldo had mentioned that Erik and he were to finish reviewing the music for the dress rehearsal by nine o'clock. She had waited long enough for him to come to her. Resigned she had decided she needed to clear the air. They both had said horrible things to each other. Her mother had cautioned her to remember with whom she was bound. Erik could not be expected to conform to Meg's ideal. Wasn't it his strangeness, too, that had attracted her, that opened her heart to him? Did she not love him? Or did she sometimes love him?

Was it wrong that she had tried to change him? she asked her mother. Madeleine at first didn't answer. Instead she asked her own questions. Did her daughter wish to change Erik to ease his pain? Or did she wish to change him so that he would better match what she wanted him to be? Was he to change to make her happy? Or was he to change so that they could live together without violence, without tragedy dogging their steps?

Meg had spent the entire previous night thinking of him, hating him, desiring him, worrying about him, crying for him until, in the morning, she woke and knew that this emptiness was intolerable to her. Even if he could not accept himself, even if he was still a monster, she could not live without him.

So she stood there at the door, which was partially open, and took a deep breath to face her wild, wounded husband. Movement in the room made her pause. He wasn't alone. Very quietly she pushed the heavy door open so that she could see within.

He stood with his back to the door, a large man, dressed in his usual black. She saw no one else at first. As she thought to call his name, she saw his body was strangely bent forward, and then she saw naked fingers slide around the hard angle of his shoulder like a snake across a dark path in the woods. What had seemed motionless now moved in a tight erotic dance. Erik's body ground in minute circles against the hidden bulk. Her eyes traveled down his back, away from the sizzling fingers playing across his shoulder blades, to the subtle pulse of his hips and stopped as a woman's naked leg edged between his and lifted toward his groin. Then she heard her husband's low groan of pleasure.

No longer able to bear the intrusion of the woman's touch on her husband's landscape, Meg jerked her attention about the room to see the dark rose gown, the cream stockings, the corset, and twisted, abandoned undergarments, carelessly draped over one of the winged chairs.

She backed away, her hand clasped to her gaping mouth, the tears blinding her, making the two figures shimmer and undulate. She continued to back away until they melted and dissolved. Even so she saw him, her Erik, make love to Signorina Venedetti. She saw him in her mind's eye lead the naked woman to the private chamber beyond and lay her down across the daybed. She saw him drop to his knees beside her body and kiss her limbs, her breasts, her throat, her mouth. She saw him discard his clothes, reveal himself, and stand naked and unmasked before the woman. And she saw, to her chagrin, the harlot smile at him and raise her arms and accept his naked weight against her skin.

She hadn't thought he could go so easily to another woman. Only when they had been pulled apart had he sought someone else's touch. Only when he had thought he had lost her forever had he lain with other lovers. When he came back to her, he had pledged to be faithful, and she had believed him. Certain that only she held his heart, she had forgiven his carnal betrayals.

She stayed outside the door for several moments. She waited until her eyes cleared. She waited until she knew she could walk without crumpling to the floor. Then she left the teatro and walked down the dark street. She walked for a long time before she realized someone was walking behind her. She quickened her step and searched the street wildly for some lighted window, some open door, some business that yet was open. Finding none, she began to panic. She was far from the theater district. She had not paid attention to her path. Her heart was in her mouth, and she was walking so fast that it was nearly a run. She thought she might scream when a coach came round the corner. She darted into the middle of its path, nearly upsetting the horses, but the carriage stopped in time. She shouted to the man that she was being followed and quickly climbed by herself inside. It was fortunately empty, and the man flicked his whip sharply in the air over the horses and sped down the street. When they were in more familiar surroundings, Meg gave the driver her address and within minutes she was safely at home.

She raced to her room and closed the door. There the bed waited for her. It was too large for her body alone; it was too cold to warm her sorrow. She still smelled his cologne in the air. She still could make out the impression his body would have made in the mattress. It was as if he were still in the room. But as she turned in the bed and rubbed her hand across the cool sheet, she knew he was gone.

Even so, she felt his ghost brush her arm as even the memory of him rushed past her and away into the darkness. She pulled the covers to her chin, but there was no warmth left in the night. Only coldness embraced her.

He swore he'd never touch liquor again, not even wine. His head pulsed, expanded and contracted, threatening to squeeze his brain one moment and to explode the next. Opening his eyes hurt. He could hear his lids moving, grating across his irritated eyes. He lay still on the daybed and shifted slightly to retch over the edge of the mattress. Then he drifted back into an uneasy sleep.

Meg fled down the passageways in the depths of the Opera Populaire. She cast frightened glances over her shoulder as he ran after her. Even though he was panting from the exertion and pains were shooting up his legs from the effort to catch her, she was always just out of reach. She wore the ballet dress she had worn when practicing as a young dancer in the ballet school, a simple white skirt that came to mid calf, a slight bodice that left her long neck and arms exposed. Her legs were sheathed in white stockings, and her feet were in the ballet slippers he had brought her when she was little.

Why was she running from him? Perhaps something hideously fearsome was behind him. Was she looking at him or the thing behind him when she looked back in terror? He called to her, telling her to wait for him. He was winded, and she began to diminish in the distance as she outstripped him. He ground to a painful stop, and the lights in the tunnel went out leaving only an eerie blue-tinged phosphorescence. The silence was unnatural. Behind him the low dull thud of a heartbeat that could not be his own invaded the heavy stillness. The thing lived and scurried up behind him, but he was anchored to the stone by leaden feet he could not move! She had left him there alone to die.

If she had not left, there would be no thudding heart beat in the silence now. If she had turned and come back to him, the thing behind him would have stalked away back to its den. He didn't know how he knew this, but he did. She had promised to stay with him. She had brought him to the passageway and encouraged him to escape with her. The thing didn't want him to go. He would sleep deep down in the pit with it. They would close their eyes and breathe the dust of long forgotten bones in the church cemetery, and it would be as it had been before Meg came down to him.

Erik struggled to reach consciousness. A panicked "no" bubbled up his throat even as he understood that it was surely a dream, a nightmare, but too logical, too transparent. It was merely one of those dreams that torment the dreamer who skims the surface between sleep and wakefulness. He burst into daylight, dragging with him the thing that threatened him. A sinking dull sadness clung to his throat.

Around him the room was hostile. He didn't belong here. It said, "Go away. You have no place here."

He had not completely undressed; he still wore his linen shirt, the sleeves loose, the front flap carelessly opened. Nor had he removed his trousers. One foot was cold for the stocking was gone, but the other was warmly covered.

When he lifted his head, he thought someone must have struck him with a hammer for the pain was so intense. Slowly he rose. His mouth was dry and swollen. He eventually found his way to the basin of water in his office. He threw out the residual brandy from one of the glasses and filled it with the cool water. He drained this glass and several more before he went to dress.

There were only a few staff people in the backstage area. On another floor he could hear the girls who lived at the opera house laughing. Today was a day of rest.

He had not seen his children for days, and he was tired of feeling sorry for himself. He would go home and confront Meg. He couldn't allow the gap between them to persist or to widen.

Daylight proved more painful outside the theater than its filtered facsimile had within. He kept his head covered, using the hood of his cloak to shield his eyes, until he finally stepped inside the cool shade of the estate. Everything was unusually quiet. It was past noon, and the children must be in the playroom upstairs or outside on the grounds. Erik glanced through the veranda windows and didn't see them so he climbed the stairs to the playroom.

Mario and François were playing chess while Laurette tried to dress the cat in her own clothes. The little girl sat half naked on the floor scolding Puss for not holding still. Their delighted shouts were worth the pain their loud voices inflicted on him. Laurette wrapped herself around his legs and jumped up and down until he bent to pick her up, holding her warm, pudgy body close. François and Mario both came over and let him muss their hair and pat them firmly on their shoulders and back. Laurette would not surrender her father to her brothers so easily, so Erik sat and kept her on his lap while he studied the chess game.

He could tell François was anxious to ask him why he hadn't come home the past several nights, but Mario gave his companion a guarded look that kept him quiet. Erik appreciated the respite. He would have enough to discuss with Meg without having to explain to his children that sometimes adults had dis-agreements and fallings out as well as children did.

He lingered, watching them play and sometimes joining in. When he asked where their mother might be at that moment, they grew very quiet.

"Is she still angry with me, do you think?" he asked, as if he were a wayward child fearing scolding.

François smiled and answered, "Yes, Papa, I think she's in a foul mood. She won't come out."

Erik was surprised by that. He knew she had been angry and hurt when last they spoke. But it wasn't like Meg to sulk in her room for days. Surely she had gotten over some of her anger in two days' time. Why would she lock herself away when Erik wasn't even in the house?

"Well, I'll have to do something special to cheer her up, won't I?"

"She likes chocolates," suggested Mario because he liked chocolates even more.

"Of course she does. I'll find some chocolates for her. Shall I? And perhaps a few extra for Madeleine. And maybe a few more for Don Marcelo." He hesitated seeing the hopeful looks on his children's hungry faces. "Well, I suppose if I'm getting that many, I can find a handful or so for the three of you."

François was not fooled by Erik's playful tone. "Papa? Maman was crying this morning when I passed her room."

Erik's smile disappeared. This would be harder than he thought. Could words do this much harm? he wondered. He had spoken rashly. He couldn't say that he hadn't been honest. But it was a brutal admission that he wasn't sure was true. It was true or it felt true when he had said it. It didn't seem so true now, especially in the playroom, especially when he looked at his children. He was a monster to have hurt Meg this much.

"I'll speak to her," he assured them before he left.

He saw Madeleine come from his and Meg's bedroom, and he rushed to meet her in the passageway before she descended the stairs. He was about to speak when he saw her angry scowl.

"What are you doing here?" Madeleine's tone was unexpectedly belligerent. Erik stopped in his tracks at a loss for words. "I would never have thought it of you, Erik. I thought you understood what a miracle you'd been given in Meg."

Confused, he sputtered, "I do. I…I do understand. I came to apologize."

"I think it might not be a good time for apologies."

Before he could say more, Madeleine went brusquely down the stairs.

He knocked at the bedroom door softly and called out to Meg. From the other side came her voice, uneven from crying but forceful. "Go away, Erik. I don't want to see you. Not now. Maybe not ever."

"But Meg, don't be absurd. It was unfortunate, but we were both tired and upset. Open the door, and let me in."

"No! I said, go away. I mean it. I won't speak with you. I don't know who you are!"

Stunned, Erik heard Meg begin to cry unabashedly. He felt her sobs in the pit of his stomach. He wanted to go to her, hold her, and beg her forgiveness, anything to keep her from feeling such pain.

"Meg? Meg?" he insisted.

"Leave her alone!" Madeleine had returned with a tray upon which was a service of tea and biscuits. She glared at Erik as she never had before. Erik felt small and ashamed. But he couldn't think what he had done that he deserved to be treated so harshly by these two women.

"I just want…"

"I don't really care anymore what you want. I care that you've broken my daughter's heart. Just go, Erik." When Madeleine saw the crushed look on Erik's face, she relented slightly and spoke more kindly to him. "Maybe in a few days time. But not now, Erik. Not after what she saw the other day."

He looked back at the locked door behind which Meg still cried as if her heart would break. He felt the sting of tears at the back of his own eyes. But he couldn't beat down the door. If Madeleine had been more sympathetic, he would have enlisted her to speak with Meg on his behalf, but it was clear that Madeleine's loyalties were with Meg. So Erik slowly descended the stairs and asked the butler to hail a carriage for him. He had nowhere else to go but the teatro. He would go back for now and wait and hope that tomorrow would be better.

CHAPTER 6

Ex-Officio

*...there is nothing
either good or bad, but thinking makes it so*

Hamlet, Shakespeare

Raoul had gone over it and over it with Christine the past several months since Leroux had challenged him with news of Erik alive and well in Italy. Of course, if anyone seriously wanted to know information about Erik, he'd only have to be alert, ask the right questions, and look in the right places. But, for God's sake, Leroux had accompanied Erik to his execution and seen him hanged in the public square more than a decade ago. As far as Leroux had known, the Phantom of the Opera was dead. His continued obsession with Erik had seemed laughable to Raoul until that day the little man had thrown into his face the truth—that the Phantom's death had been staged and that he had fled to Italy.

Perhaps some strange twist of chance had brought Erik's existence to the inspector's notice. Or someone who considered Erik an enemy had informed Leroux. In either case Erik was in danger, although Raoul wasn't completely convinced Leroux would prove a great threat. The story of Erik's survival was so incredible that Raoul was certain Leroux's superiors would laugh in his face if he tried to pursue the case. However, if there was someone else involved who held Erik as an enemy, then there could be other dangers far worse than those the inspector presented.

All these thoughts and concerns Raoul had aired with his wife. He had tried to reassure her that they needn't believe the worst. Precipitous action could actually prove more dangerous to Erik. Yet Christine chafed at the silence her husband imposed on her. She had written to Meg several times, feeling horrid that she could not include any warnings. Raoul suspected Leroux would intercept the communications and read them. Whatever Meg would write they couldn't control, but he wanted Christine to avoid any reference to Erik or to the situation with the pesky police officer. Meg's missives were so natural in their tone that it would be hard to assume the husband she sometimes referred to had been Leroux's demon. And, as Christine assured Raoul, she rarely mentioned Erik. This puzzled Raoul. Christine blushed to explain that Meg still harbored some jealousy where she and Erik were concerned.

"She wishes to keep him only to herself," she added. "She's careful what she says to me in the letters."

Raoul pressed his lips tightly shut in an effort not to reply. Then he found himself asking the question he feared to put into words. "Should she be careful?"

Christine sighed audibly. She took her husband's hand and brought it to her breasts. "Not for the reasons she or you fear." Seeing his doubt, she continued to explain, "I don't care for him in that way. I love only you. But I think I'll always own a piece of his soul, even though I've tried to give it back to him time and time again. It's too deeply lodged somewhere in my heart."

"Is that supposed to reassure me?" he asked petulantly, but he didn't withdraw his hand.

She drew closer still and softly urged his lips to meet hers. He could feel her love, her yielding to him, in that touch. He knew when she leaned against him that she was his and only his. Softly and quietly, he whispered near her mouth, "I suppose I can leave him a small corner of your heart as long as you owe all else to me."

"All else, my love," she whispered back and kissed him deeply.

He twisted the scented sheet in his hand, filtered red instead of pink through brandy-steeped eyes. What game did this woman pretend to? If not for her anonymous missives, he'd have never known the direction the trail had taken. There was no going back now. She had not led him on a wild goose chase, of that he was certain. He had found the signs. There could not be any mistake. It was too much of a coincidence—a masked genius married to the former diva of the Opera National de Paris.

He opened the sheet yet again to read its lies.

Dear M. L'Inspecteur,

It is with great embarrassment that I write to you to dispel any false illusions I've unfortunately encouraged in my previous communications. I fear I can no longer be a party to the cruel joke your enemies have tried to perpetrate against you.

Indeed I have found that the masked musical director of the Teatro dell'Opera, the husband of the former Meg Giry, is actually a handsome and shrewd composer who, knowing the story of the Phantom of the Teatro Populaire, has used it to draw in the crowds to what—without such high theatrics—would be only modest successes. One only has to read the reviews of the last opera to realize that this Signore Costanzi, with his wife's aid, has stooped to sensationalism in an attempt to spark interest in his works. One can only imagine that the former Parisian diva has a flair for the dramatic and the macabre. Or we might speculate that she has sincerely tried to remake her pliable husband into the dangerous, yet charismatic, Phantom of the Teatro dell'Opera to satisfy some perverted obsession of her own. Such sick appetites must not surprise you; a man in your chosen profession unfortunately is no stranger to the dark illnesses of the human soul.

Whatever the case may be, I have, since my last letter to you, been privileged to break into the inner circle of friends of the Costanzis and have even dined with the charming and handsome Erik Costanzi at the ancestral home of his father. Whatever he might share in common with the monster that was executed so long ago is a consequence of smoke and mirrors I assure you.

I sincerely hope that you read this with relief for it would be an unfortunate waste of your time to pursue the line of inquiry that I formerly suggested and would only lead to your embarrassment.

Enclosed is a review from the gazette concerning a recent production. You will note that the artistic community sees through Signore Costanzi's shabby theatrics. Unfortunately bad opera may be an affront, but it is hardly a crime, even in Paris.

Your sincere admirer and most humble servant,

C.

The clipping enclosed was a harsh review of a recent work by the "enigmatic" Signore Costanzi. Leroux was not so much a fool as his correspondent thought him. The criticisms clearly revealed that the piece had been well received in other quarters. This reviewer also barely disguised his personal dislike of the composer, and his reference to the mask was a skeptical challenge for Costanzi to stop hiding behind it.

Leroux was not convinced that it was simply theatrics. He could not imagine Meg Giry lending herself to such tasteless mockery. As shocking as it seemed, he recalled how she'd nearly fainted in the courtroom when the Phantom was berated by the rowdy spectators. And if it were some sick fantasy she was living, what man would play such a thankless role even for the beautiful Meg Giry?

Besides, he had sought other sources and from these had gathered more information than the suggestive letters had afforded. Erik Costanzi had never been seen without the mask. He had appeared suddenly on the scene. A brief mention of the man's involvement with the Teatro Argentina had turned up as well as some indication that he had participated in the architectural designs for the opera house itself where he now reigned as artistic director. There were puzzling details such as the fact that Erik Costanzi didn't seem to exist before he was adopted by Don Marcelo Costanzi. Don Marcelo had lost a grown son, and in an unusual move he had adopted this stranger and given him his family name. Meg Giry had already resided in Italy for several years before this happened. Leroux was working on getting access to the records that might clarify Erik Costanzi's identity, but it seemed that it would require a trip to Italy itself if he wished to inspect the actual documents.

He didn't know exactly how the Phantom had managed to stage his own death, but he was also sure that he would not have been able to do so if not for someone else's help. And that someone had to be a powerful man. The only possibility that made sense was the Count de Chagny. Perhaps he had made a bargain with the devil himself to win his wife's undivided affection. Whatever the reason, Leroux was daily more certain that Raoul, Count de Chagny, had assisted in the Phantom's escape.

He crumpled the pink sheet of paper and threw it on the desk. He'd like nothing more than to embarrass the count who had always belittled him.

Leroux recalled the words of the letter warning that to pursue this trail would only lead to his embarrassment. Such was already the case. He had unwisely spoken to his superiors about the suspicions months before the letters began to arrive. The Chief Inspector had laughed in his face.

It was time to act on his own.

Within the hour he was in a coach and on his way to the Chagny estate. Whether he garnered more information or not, this would likely be the last visit to the count for some time. Next time they met, Leroux was determined to have evidence in his possession that the count had helped a criminal—a murderer—to escape punishment.

As the coach drew up to the gates, Leroux saw the young boy on the grounds playing with a stick and ball. He was alone. Leroux paid the driver and approached the door.

"I wish to speak with the Count de Chagny." Leroux felt no need to identify himself. The butler had admitted him on numerous occasions before. Surprisingly Dupré did not bow and beckon him in to the parlor as Leroux had expected.

"I'm afraid the Count and Countess are not receiving today." There was no apology in his tone, nor any hint of flexibility. Dupré had been told to dismiss Leroux in no uncertain terms. Before Leroux could remonstrate, the butler summarily closed the door in his face.

Leroux had difficulty controlling his anger. He stood facing the thick oak door as if he might be able to pierce it with his stare. Only gradually did he regain some composure and step back.

The count had not left him much choice.

Quickly he rounded the corner of the mansion and slipped unseen past the gardener who bent with pruning sheers over the flowering shrubs along the south wall. Eventually, Leroux spied Victor.

"You must be very good at games with a strong physique like yours."

The boy knew who the man was. He'd seen him come and go. His father had told Victor to keep out of the man's way for he was an officer and on serious business. The boy discerned that his father didn't much care for the little man. He considered walking off to the house, but it would be quite disrespectful to walk away from an adult—evidently an important man, too—without the proper etiquette.

Leroux beckoned for the boy to send him the ball. Victor gave the rubber ball a tremendous whack with the broad side of the stick. The ball went directly to Leroux who picked it up and rolled it accurately toward the boy who sent it speeding over the damp grass again. For several moments, Leroux and Victor played until the inspector saw the boy had relaxed and felt comfortable with him.

"Are you going back to Italy soon, young Chagny?"

Victor liked the way the older man used his father's title to address him.

"I wish I were. Perhaps in a couple of months."

"You liked it there?"

"Why, yes! There's loads of things to do. The city is beautiful, and the people are wild and loud. François and Mario and I have great fun together."

"Are they relatives of yours?"

"They're sort of cousins."

"How's that? How does one get a sort of cousin?"

"Well, they're children of my mother's best friend, Signora Meg Costanzi. So we've been encouraged to think of them as family. My mother and Signora Costanzi grew up together, you see."

"Is she, I mean Signora Costanzi, not the famous opera singer?"

"Oh yes. Although my father says no one sings better than Maman, Aunt Meg has a beautiful voice. Uncle Erik let us use his private box, and we often came to the theater to hear her sing."

"Are your father and Don Erik such good friends, too?"

"Sometimes they disagree and act like enemies, but mostly they're quite good friends."

"Have they come to visit you, your cousins and their parents?"

"Yes. When Maman was about to have my baby sister, Erica. Well…" The boy paused, a bit nervous talking about Erik. His father and mother had cautioned him that he should not speak of Erik to just anyone. But after all, this was a man of the law, a respectable man. Surely it couldn't be wrong to be truthful to him? "Uncle Erik couldn't come."

"Why not, do you suppose?" Leroux sensed the boy was becoming cautious. He asked the question as if it had no importance whatsoever and smiled as warmly as he could down at the child.

When the child didn't answer, Leroux knew he might balk at any moment. "I've heard of Signore Costanzi. He's quite famous, you know, and flamboyant. It's the mask. But of course he doesn't wear it when he's around you, does he?"

"Actually he usually does wear it around my sisters and me." Seeing Leroux's interest, he couldn't stop himself from adding with a certain dramatic tone, "I have seen him, though, without it." The initial excitement of sharing the forbidden secret disappeared quickly as he realized he shouldn't have said anything.

Leroux shifted his tactics slightly once more. "It's a shame that he was disfigured like that! Of course he doesn't wish to travel. The constant encounters on the road. People can be very curious, can't they?"

Victor warmed to Leroux's false note of sympathy. "Maman says the world has treated Uncle Erik quite cruelly and that only recently has he found peace. Aunt Meg and he love each other a great deal. He helped me and François and Mario build a fort at the estate. He showed me how to draw the plans. He's clever at all kinds of things."

So, Leroux thought, it is the Phantom. The boy accepted Leroux's reference to the disfigurement without protest or correction. A tight cramp rippled through his stomach as he thought how the monster had seduced even the innocence of childhood.

His next steps were clear.

"May I help you, M. Count?"

Raoul had waited barely minutes before the Chief Inspector greeted him personally and led the way back to his office. He quickly gauged the man, taking in at a glance the small personal items strewn about the office. A family man, the officer had a crocheted throw folded on a nearby chair, surely one his wife or daughter had made for him. A baby toy had fallen to the floor, one of those contraptions meant to make noise so the baby doesn't. It lay half hidden by the leg of the desk. The officer was an older man, so perhaps there was a grandchild.

The Chief Inspector studied Raoul as well, and with some curiosity motioned for him to take a seat on the other side of the messy litter of his desk.

"We're not often visited by men of your station, M. Count, unless there's been a serious crime. Have you come to make a declaration?"

"Well…" Raoul smiled broadly and tried to seem unconcerned. "Unfortunately, it is a rather awkward matter that brings me here."

"Yes?" he asked, intrigued by Raoul's strange opening gambit.

"Officer Leroux…"

"Forgive me for interrupting." He sighed audibly. "I believe I know now why you've come."

"I must insist that he be restrained from harassing me and my family. Just yesterday he accosted my son on our property. It's inappropriate for him to cross-examine my son without my presence."

"I quite understand." He grimaced. He opened a drawer and removed a thick bundle of papers organized within a hard cover file. He set them out for Raoul's inspection. They were reports and comments written in a small precise hand. Raoul was disturbed to see his own name repeated on the page as well as references to the criminal, Erik, known as the Opera Ghost, the Phantom of the Opera Populaire. Raoul glanced at the Chief Inspector and was relieved to see that he clearly thought them the ravings of an unbalanced man.

More confidently, Raoul pushed onward. "He's deluded into thinking the fiend is still alive and for some reason he thinks I can lead him to the man."

"Oh my. It's worse than that, I'm afraid. He came in the other day ranting that the Opera Spirit or Ghoul or whatever he was called is currently a popular and successful composer living in Rome. Can you believe that?" Raoul found it somewhat difficult to laugh along with the older man, but the latter didn't seem to notice. "He wanted us all to go hell bent to Rome to take a Monsieur…" Here he had to look among the papers. "…Ah yes, Costanzi, into custody. Well, it's all tragic really. We tried to placate him. We have no power outside the country. Of course, he suggested we enlist the local authorities, which we could have done, if there were any validity to the case." He smiled conspiratorially at Raoul who disguised his clutched fingers under his deer skin gloves. "But of course this is a ghost we're chasing, is it not, M. Count?"

"Yes, quite."

"I've only been in Paris for a few years, but I've been told the story. Evidently Leroux was once in line for this post, but his wild ravings had long brought him out of favor. Even before the trial, before the capture of the murderer in the opera district, he had been excessive in his dedication. He made his superiors nervous. You see, he had personal cause to hate the Specter of the Opera Populaire."

Raoul sat up, attentive to this unexpected turn in the conversation. He had always thought there must be something behind Leroux's obsession.

"What do you mean, Chief Inspector Renard?"

"Oh, I'm sorry. I thought you knew." He looked through the sheaves of papers, as if searching for some piece of information. "Well, it doesn't appear in the transcripts. You see it was not fresh enough, and the prosecutor told him he couldn't make the case. There was enough other evidence against the prisoner to convict without bringing into it the rape and murder of Leroux's ten-year-old niece."

Raoul shrugged out of his coat and left it with Dupré. He lifted the scowl the moment he saw Christine come down the stairs his way. She would be worried, and he didn't want her to be concerned. He didn't even want her to be thinking of Erik in the first place, and this would only complicate matters.

He greeted her warmly with a kiss and folded her into his arms to march her back up the stairs toward their bedchambers. His brisk step told her immediately that he wanted to be behind locked doors before he relayed the events at the police station.

Once he had locked the doors behind them, Christine asked, "Well? Won't they put a stop to his harassment? I hope you told them that he accosted our son?"

Raoul gave Christine a measured look but didn't answer her at first. The scowl, against his will, had returned to his face. Instead of answering her right away, he went to the side cabinet and opened a decanter of port and poured himself and her a modest amount.

Buying time. That was the expression that came to mind. He was buying time. But he didn't know what to say to Christine or how to start. There were several tangled threads that he had no hope of unraveling at the moment. Perhaps he never would.

All the way home he had thought about the information the Chief Inspector had casually given him. He had gone to complain about Leroux, to stop him. In the meantime, he had learned something about Erik that, if true, was disturbing. He warred with himself, unwilling to accept the incriminations without serious reflection. But the ride home hadn't been long enough for him to come to any firm resolution. To meet Christine with such dark thoughts about Erik was less than the best plan.

Christine accepted the glass and waited. Raoul was rarely at a loss. He was a man of quiet action; it was indeed one of several attributes that had attracted her to him. From the beginning, she had felt safe with him. It was nothing like the feelings Erik had inspired in her. When the world of the Opera Populaire had threatened to collapse around her, Raoul had taken charge of the situation and laid a clear path for her to follow. His current hesitation disturbed her.

Now that they were faced with a new, but related menace, she had expected him, as always, to set a confident course for them to follow. Even when she came to him with news of Leroux in the garden with Victor, he had met the challenge with a steely resolve. He outlined exactly what he would do, the consequences of such a plan, and set about to carry it out.

Then why did he seem so guarded?

"Raoul? What is it?"

He drank the port down in one very ungentlemanly gulp and set the empty glass next to the bottle. He crossed the space of the small parlor and sat by the fire as if he still might not answer her. Then he beckoned for her to come to his side. The chair was a large winged monstrosity, dearly beloved for its comfort more than its looks. It allowed the two of them to snuggle cozily together on the one cushion. She wrapped her arms around her husband, confident that he would soon begin to explain. He absentmindedly rubbed his broad hand along her arm as he stared out into the fire.

"I'm off to Italy."

"Italy? Why? Are you going to go to Erik?" She was puzzled because Raoul had all along suggested that any contact might actually draw Leroux's attention to Erik.

"Leroux won't be bothering us anymore. He's off to Italy to pursue Erik. On his own. Ex-officio. As a matter of fact his superiors think him quite mad. They have no idea that some of his rantings are true. He insisted the Phantom escaped the hangman's noose somehow and absconded to Italy. They have no interest in investigating."

"But then why is Leroux on his way to Italy?"

The concern in his wife's voice resembled his own, but it still vexed him that she was worried about another man. And after what Raoul had heard at the police station, perhaps it was naïve for both of them to have assumed that Erik had a right to live in peace. There were some crimes that had no pardon.

"He's gone after a ghost as far as the Chief Inspector is concerned. He thinks Leroux is on a mad chase and will either end up in an insane asylum or bury his ghosts and eventually come back, his tail between his legs."

"But you and I know that this is not a wild goose chase! What if he finds Erik? What will he do?"

"Well, he has no right to do anything, so we must assume, Christine, that there's no way to guess what he might do."

Though he studiously avoided doing so, if he had looked at Christine's face, he would have worried that she might faint. All the color had drained away but the deep honey of her eyes.

"Do you think he might harm Erik?"

He regretted the peevish reply but snapped, "And what if Erik does something to Leroux? Do you think that would be acceptable? What if Erik, feeling himself to be cornered, lashed out and killed Leroux?"

Christine pushed away from Raoul's chest in order to see him better. "Do you think Erik would try to kill the inspector?"

Suddenly Raoul was on his feet and pacing along the stone hearth before the fire. "Leroux beat him, Christine. Have you ever seen Erik's back? I have. And Leroux did more than that: He humiliated him. What you saw at the prison was the Phantom. He struggled to present a stoic acceptance. But I saw him unguarded; I saw behind the mask. Do I think Erik might try to kill Leroux? I think he would relish strangling the life out of him. I think, given the chance and with his back against the wall, Erik will do what he has always done—survive. He's killed before. And perhaps worse."

"You speak of him as you used to. I thought you and Erik were friends."

Raoul stopped pacing and kicked the edge of the rug that he had wrinkled. He leaned against the mantel and would not look at Christine. "I'm trying to be realistic. For God's sake, Christine, you can't be blind to what he's done."

There was a silence between them, sad and heavy. She knew that whatever defense she gave for Erik would strike Raoul as a betrayal. So she was silent and waited.

Raoul struggled with his own thoughts for several moments. He remembered the last time he and Erik had been in the fencing hall, just the day before he, Christine, and the children were to depart for Paris. They had taken each other's measure on several occasions and fought without regard one for the other. Of course they used blunted swords, and there was no chance that they would do each other any serious injury. But each one had fought to win.

At the end, they had embraced. Raoul remembered feeling that such warmth would be what he might have felt for a brother had he had one. How had the man found his way so deeply into Raoul's affections?

"No, I can't believe it." Raoul said it, without thinking. He said it to himself forgetting that Christine was an eager witness.

"What?"

Instead of answering, for he was still unsure, he asked his own question. "All those years in the opera, how can you be sure that Erik never harmed anyone?"

"Why are you asking me that?"

"No, seriously, Christine, I want you to think back on your childhood at the Opera Populaire. Why did he have such a hold on you?"

"I told you, he sang to me. He comforted me. I was lonely. I missed my father."

"How did he comfort you? Did he sit by your bed? Did he touch you? Did he hold you? How old would he have been? Nineteen? Maybe in his early twenties? He wasn't a child. He was a man. A lonely man. As far as we know, a normal man with…desires."

Christine sat still, her hand placed over her opened mouth, clearly shocked by Raoul's line of questioning.

"What are you asking? If he 'touched' me? You're trying to take something that was…beautiful…kind…and…and…and…make it…into…something… something ugly!"

Raoul held her gaze, his lips in a thin grimace.

"He never, never touched me! I didn't even see him until that night I sang in Carlotta Giudicelli's place."

"He never sat by your bed? You never recall him coming to your bed? It would not be your sin, Christine! You were an innocent. You might not even remember it correctly. You would not understand what was going on, I'm sure, and your memory might have transformed it into something else."

"No! I'm not a fool, Raoul. I know what you're saying. He never appeared to me. Meg caught sight of him in the dressing rooms picking through the costumes and the masks. But he didn't even know she saw him. He was a spirit, an angel to me. I only heard his voice. He never laid a hand on me!" Christine couldn't sit still in the chair any longer. She rose, as did her voice, when she spoke to her husband. "And if he had touched me? If he had come into the dormitory, he might have brushed my hair from my face or even kissed me chastely on the cheek, but nothing, nothing like what you're implying."

"So he did touch you!"

"I didn't say that! I said, if he had! I don't know if he ever came to my bedside. I was always asleep. He would sing to me, and his voice would lull me to sleep."

"Meg saw him? What did she say?"

"She told me once that she envied me. She mentioned that she caught a glimpse of him by my bedside. But he wasn't there to ravish my innocence. He was there to protect me!"

Christine's eyes were filled with tears of indignation, and Raoul regretted that he had sounded wicked and perverse. She was convinced that Erik had never abused her. Yet it nagged at him that she had been a child, and this man who was condemned to loneliness had come to her nightly and had sung to her. He thought of himself, as a young man, and wondered how he would have dealt with the extreme isolation that Erik had been forced to suffer.

"I'm sorry, my love. I know that he was your angel. I know that you were for him something pure and beautiful. I'm sure you're right. He would never have sullied you. But he was a man, ostracized and forbidden all the usual outlets a young man is allowed in our society."

"What did you find out at the police station?"

"It's just that Leroux was convinced that the Phantom had committed crimes, horrible crimes, even before the night he brought the chandelier down in the Opera Populaire. And it made me think of what his life was like for all those years, the things that he was denied, and the possible consequences. We know, for example, that the mirror in your dressing room was a doorway to his tunnels. We know that he could see you when you couldn't see him."

Christine turned scarlet as she understood his meaning. "I always dressed and undressed behind the screen."

"Well, that's a relief. But it still leaves the question as to why he used the mirror and what he might have hoped to see!"

"Don't! Don't! I won't go through this again!"

Raoul stared in shock as Christine screamed. She had folded her arms tightly around her chest and had slipped back until her legs grazed a small table toppling it to the ground. He rushed to her side as she bent to collect the broken pieces of the vase that had crashed to the floor. Her hands were trembling, and he took them into his and held them as if they were a wounded bird, its wings fluttering pathetically against his palms.

"Leave it, Christine. Leave it. You'll cut yourself."

He tried to raise her from the floor. Her voice came out small and tremulous. "I might have made a difference. If I had gone to him when he needed me. Perhaps none of those awful things would have happened."

Stunned, he looked to see if she were serious. She would not look at him. He forced her chin up and made her look into his eyes. Very quietly he told her, "None of what happened was your fault. Erik accepts that." Then, although he feared the answer, he asked, "Christine, you don't regret coming to me, do you?"

Oh to be split in two! That would have been the only way. Christine shook her head slowly from side to side and threw herself against Raoul's chest. She wrapped her arms fiercely around him. "No! Never!"

Raoul sighed with poorly masked relief and said a silent prayer of thanks. If she had said otherwise, he wasn't sure how he would have reacted.

Quietly she stepped away from Raoul, her tears now dried, her trembling now calmed. "Why are you condemning him?"

"I'm not."

"The questions?"

"I fear Leroux's madness is contagious. The things he accuses Erik of are shocking. I began to imagine Erik's life back then. How long had he lived in the vaults? It was unnatural. Then I wondered if we were naïve to think that he had not…done other things…before those final days."

Christine was not reassured by Raoul's vague explanation. It only reinforced for her the coincidence of Erik's moral disintegration with her own rejection of him. It only made her feel worse. But she held her tongue.

Suddenly Raoul seemed to shake some dark cloud from his mind. "I'm sorry. I forgot that I know the man. He's in danger, and I won't stand by idle."

"When do we leave?"

"Not we, my love. Just me. I don't want you anywhere near Leroux when all this comes crashing down around everyone's ears."

"I need to be there. For Meg!"

"Listen to me. If we all go off to Italy, we'll lead Leroux directly to Erik. He'll know where we are, and we won't have any idea of where he is or what he's doing. Let him stumble about looking for a few days. In the meantime, I'll go in disguise. I know where Leroux will eventually come. I can wait and watch for him, unbeknownst to him or Erik. Perhaps I can find out what he means to do and how. Armed with that knowledge, Erik and I can mount a more effective defense. I can't have you there. It will distract me."

"But it could be dangerous! I couldn't bear it if anything happened to you."

Raoul smiled and kissed his wife tenderly. He was heartened by her concern for him. "Nothing will happen to me. Leroux isn't after me, Christine."

She pressed her body firmly against his, so that he wouldn't see the look of concern that hadn't left her face.

CHAPTER 7

All the World's a Stage

And all the men and women merely players:
They have their exits and their entrances;
And one man in his time plays many parts

As You Like It, Shakespeare

He still felt absurd without his usual clothing. The fabric—coarse and poorly sewn—scratched at his neck. Dupré and Georges had assisted him in gathering clothes more appropriate to a bricklayer than a count. Georges had also suggested darkening his hair and even instructed him on an elementary use of cosmetics to darken his skin and create the illusion of a scar across one cheek bone. The eye patch was a last minute addition that Raoul particularly liked at the time, but soon he found it to be a nuisance. It was hot and limited his vision. So after wearing it for an hour or so before he arrived in Rome, he decided to forego its use. Surely Leroux wouldn't be expecting him, and the change in habit and darkening of his features would suffice to throw him off.

Raoul changed into his disguise at the final stop on the road to Rome. There he switched from the comfortable private coach that he'd hired to wait among the commoners for the public transportation that carried him the last twenty kilometers to the ancient city. In Rome, he rented a room in an inn of dubious reputation not far from the theater district. He needed to be close since he would mostly be walking.

Bone sore and smelling vaguely of chickens, Raoul installed himself in his room, washed cursorily, and then went down to the public rooms to dine. He ordered a fatty stew with bread and a cheap wine that he was barely able to stomach at first. It was already late, and he was tempted to postpone going to the Teatro dell'Opera, but then again this might be the best time to survey the area. He might even find Leroux skulking in the shadows.

Dupré had advised him to carry his money concealed in various pockets on his person and to use only small denominations. So Raoul pulled out a couple of coins and counted them out as if they might be his last. He dropped the money on the table and left.

It was a refreshing walk that brought him outside the theater at about half past nine. There was no performance yet—opening night was several nights away—and the streets were not crowded. Raoul saw several young women leaving with their beaux. They sauntered out, arguing good naturedly about their plans for the evening. Raoul steered clear of them and walked to the park on the other side of the street from which he could easily watch the comings and goings at the theater. He hid behind a large tree and leaned against the rough bark to watch.

He didn't notice a man hidden in the doorway of a tailor's shop right away because he was mostly in the shadows. He, too, seemed to be watching the theater entrance. It was not Leroux for this man was of medium height with a heavy, blocky build. Raoul was considering whether to approach the man directly or wait and follow him when another man exited from the side door of the theater and looked down the street in both directions. The man hidden in the doorway stepped forward and called to him, and the two went off together.

For this reason, Raoul nearly missed Meg as she came running from the Teatro dell'Opera. He expected to see Erik, but no one else came through the door. Instead of hailing a carriage, Meg took off walking at a fast clip down the street in what appeared to Raoul as decidedly the wrong way. The estate lay in the opposite direction and at quite a distance. Where was Erik? What was Meg doing alone on the street at this time of night? Raoul didn't think twice; he set out to follow Meg to make sure she was safe.

She was obviously distraught. She set off at a brisk pace, barely aware of the passing carriages or the few couples who walked arm in arm. Everyone turned to watch her as she sped past. It was unusual to see a woman unescorted on the street unless, of course, she was a prostitute. Meg's dress made it unlikely that anyone would think she was working the streets. But it also made her vulnerable to assault. What possessed her to run off like this on her own, and where the devil could she be headed?

Suddenly Raoul noticed Meg's gait pick up. Then she glanced once over her shoulder, and he quickly crossed the street. She knew she was being followed. Just as he was thinking he'd have to make his presence known to her, a carriage for hire came round a corner, and Meg stepped out into the road to wave it down. Raoul's heart was in his mouth for one second as he thought the driver might not have seen her and wouldn't stop in time. The carriage did stop, however, and Meg quickly stepped up into the cab. As she did so, her face came within the light of the lantern and Raoul could clearly see that she had been crying. Raoul watched the coach disappear in the opposite direction, back toward the theater or toward home. At any rate she would be safe in the coach, and it was headed toward a less dangerous area of the city.

The sausage pies were actually quite tasty, and Raoul ate them with relish, licking his fingers for lack of a napkin. He studied the regular customers at the bar and ordered what they ordered. He sat on a bench close enough to hear various discussions around him. Taking in the accents, he rehearsed the questions and waited for his opportunity. When he realized the theater was closed for the weekend, he made the rounds at the bars and restaurants in the area. Even so, he did pass by a couple of times each day to check out the building and to see if anything looked suspicious. At the bars and local establishments that catered to the working man, he hoped to hear something about a mad Frenchman asking questions. The conversations were singularly useless. They revolved around money problems, lack of work, complaints against hard-hearted bosses, randy talk about women, complaints about wives and children, and a good many tall tales about youthful adventures.

Then late Sunday night Raoul was nodding off at the bar after listening to a barrage of complaints about the rising price of cheeses and the poor quality of strong drink when his ears began to burn. Someone with a gravelly voice was laughing about a Frenchman. For a moment, he thought perhaps they were talking about him, but soon the description proved that they were talking about Leroux. They were speaking of him with some suspicion citing his military demeanor. The man with the gravelly voice vouched for Leroux saying he paid well and promptly for a little job he had done recently.

"Says he wants several men, men not afraid of a little rough stuff," the hoarse fellow was saying to a handful of men dressed much like himself.

"Why does he want to pay so much?" asked one, suspiciously. "Don't need any trouble with the law."

The figure the man had mentioned, Raoul realized, after a few days on the street among these people, was a substantial amount. Leroux's man whispered something to his listeners, but Raoul couldn't catch what was said.

The count threw a coin on the counter and walked over to the man, Piero, and asked, "Got some work for me? I've need of a job. Don't mind hard work."

Piero looked him over doubtfully and answered, "Well, I think we might have all the hands we need now. I'll let you know if we need any more."

Not willing to be so easily dismissed, Raoul asked, "Is the work around here? Or does a body have to go far?"

"Yeah, Piero, that's a good question the stranger be asking. My wife she won't let me go too far off."

Several men snickered, but Piero paid them no mind.

"The work's round here, so there's no reason for your wife to be pulling in the strings so tight, Egidio." Then turning to Raoul, he scowled. "You don't hear so well? We don't got no more openings."

Raoul knew he'd better back off, but at least it was clear whom he should be following in the next day or two.

Perhaps it was time to contact Erik.

Dearest Meg,

Forgive me that it has been several weeks since I last wrote. I have not been completely honest with you recently, and now I hope it is not too late for you to take precautions. Will the past never cease to haunt you and Erik?

The Chief Inspector who was in charge of the Phantom's case, M. Leroux, has regularly harassed us over the past years. I might have mentioned it to you once, and I believe we laughed over it. After all, what could he do? we thought. Recently his mad obsession has been given not only weight but a direction and purpose that heretofore it could not have had. We don't know who led him to the trail, but he knows, Meg. He knows that Erik lives. He's always suspected it, but now he has found out who Erik is, that he is your husband and lives and works successfully in Rome.

Please, take heart, my dearest sister. We have tried to stave off disaster. Raoul even went to complain to the police commissioner. They all believe Leroux is mad. This would be fair news indeed except that Leroux has taken a leave of absence and has left Paris. We have absolutely no doubt as to his destination. He is on his way, or perhaps he is already there. Raoul fears that he will do something horrid when he finds Erik. There is nothing legal he can achieve, for no one believes his crazy story. And Raoul assures me Leroux has no official power outside of Paris and its environs. But for this very reason, we fear he will do something drastic if he finds Erik.

Raoul has asked me to warn you. He has already left and should arrive in Rome even before this letter. But do not expect to see him. He has gone in disguise hoping to find Leroux's trail. He believes he will be able to help you and Erik better if Leroux doesn't know he is there.

You must tell Erik to leave, to hide. If Leroux finds him, I don't know what will happen. Although I cringe to imagine Leroux harming Erik, I think we both should also worry that Erik might be forced to do something unfortunate if he and the inspector come face to face.

I am making arrangements to come to Rome. In spite of Raoul's order that I stay here, I cannot leave you to face this alone.

Ever your sister and dearest friend,

Christine

Rinaldo had been kept waiting for several moments in the parlor. The household was in an uproar. Clearly Carlotta's little scene had had its effect. He blushed to think how far the woman was willing to go to get her revenge against Signore Costanzi.

The butler had shown him into the parlor and left to announce his visit to Signora Costanzi. He could tell that for anyone else but him the door would have been firmly closed.

When he heard the door open, he turned expecting to see Meg. It was not to be. Signore Costanzi, senior, stood majestically in the entrance, observing Rinaldo before he gently closed the door behind him and stepped forward into the room.

"Signore Jannicelli, please do have a seat. I regret that Meg is indisposed." Don Marcelo graciously motioned to a chair beside the windows overlooking the side garden.

Rinaldo had not expected to speak with Signore Costanzi. Indeed, he had half expected to be turned away at the door or perhaps Signora Giry might have approached him. It was imperative for him to be with Meg. He knew she would be terribly hurt, and he wanted to comfort her. He would not let her face her pain alone. After all, he had been a party to its cause!

Of course, Carlotta had demanded that he go to Meg for other reasons. Well, perhaps they coincided on some matters. Nothing could have kept him from trying to see Meg today, but it was not for the cold reasons that Carlotta had sent him. Yet might Meg's sorrow bring her to his arms? He hoped so. It was not the way he had wanted to win her heart, but he would not reject the chance to love her.

"I had hoped to speak with Meg about some details of the final rehearsal," he lied. He returned Don Marcelo's gaze, aware that his excuse for calling was weak.

"Did he send you?" Don Marcelo asked sternly.

"He? I'm sorry, Signore Costanzi, I don't understand." He shifted uncomfortably in his seat. Well, if Don Marcelo suspected one lie, let him believe this one instead. It made little difference.

"I can't believe that Erik would do such a pointless thing. If he sent you to make peace for him with his wife, he's more a fool than I thought. This is a serious matter, and it will demand his personal attention."

"Yes, I see."

Don Marcelo rose. The visit was at an end. He bowed his head slightly in dismissal and left the room.

Damn! The very opportunity to woo Meg was also the one that made her inaccessible. He twirled the brim of his hat in his fingers as he readied himself to leave the parlor. Something he saw out of the corner of his eye stopped him. Through the window, he had caught a flash of lavender and gold cloth.

It was not done. He went to the hall. Don Marcelo had expected him to let himself out. He had been a frequent visitor, and there was no call to rest on ceremony in this case. No one was very concerned about him or his presence. The air was heavy with sadness. Servants were keeping a wide berth, almost as if Meg had retired to a sick bed. But she was not too ill to spend an hour in the garden evidently.

Rinaldo glanced to see that the hallway was unoccupied, then rounded the corner to the library where the veranda doors opened onto the side garden. It was there he had caught the glimpse of Meg.

He stepped out and admired, as always, the lush, almost obscene, fecundity about him. A narrow cobbled path twisted and meandered through the flowering shrubs and opened unexpectedly on secret beds of tender buds. In the kiosk Meg sat, her lavender skirt spread like the petals of an exotic bloom.

A stab of remorse hit him as he saw her body tremble. She was crying. She was crying, and he had made her cry!

Meg didn't hear him approach. She was too overwhelmed by the pathetic catch in her throat, the whine that came through tautly stretched lips was like the unbidden cry of an abandoned child. She had stolen to the garden to give full vent to her tears. Curiously her mother's consolation had dried them. They clung painfully to the back of her eyes; her heart sank leaden and numb in her chest. Madeleine's outraged remarks berating Erik for seeking his pleasure in another woman's arms had given Meg no comfort. She had lain against her mother's breast, staked by a dead calm that insisted over and over that this could not be happening. Not to her. Not to her and Erik.

Yet she had seen him!

She jumped when she felt Rinaldo's hand on her shoulder. Her nose was a brilliant red, her eyes were nearly swollen shut, and her mouth was stretched in an ugly grimace of pain and despair. She brought her soggy handkerchief to shield her face from Rinaldo's obvious concern.

"I didn't mean to startle you, Meg," he said. And then he was seated next to her, and his body was so close she could feel his warmth. He leaned over her like the branches of an oak tree, and she feared his shadow, his hard body, his desire. She was wounded and in pain, and his presence was a dangerous harbor for her. It promised protection; it promised support. Her mind felt drawn, but her heart could not imagine any other home but the one it had lost.

She swallowed the staccato sighs her body still emitted; she wiped uselessly at her face and tried to smile at the young man. What was he? Twenty-four or twenty-five? She was a married woman of more than a decade and a mother.

"I'm…I'm…I should go in." She grasped at something to say.

"What has you so sad?" Her hand was resting on her skirts, and Rinaldo reached out and covered it gently with his own. She stared at the trapped hand as if trying to understand what it was. Very slowly she withdrew it from under his. To mask its escape, she rose in one fluid movement from the bench and walked over to the rose bushes.

Roses! The blood red violence of the buds made her reel with a dizzy sick feeling in the pit of her stomach. Had he ever truly loved her? Roses! He had given Christine roses, so crimson their edges were black! Red, sick and sweet, dried blood. She detested them! She took one bud in her hand and crushed it cruelly. The petals, velvet against her palm, fell lightly to the ground.

Oh she should not have done that! Poor, beautiful thing, she should not have destroyed it.

Rinaldo's hands were on her forearms. She felt him behind her, uncomfortably close, intimately close. She had no desire to feel another man's body this close to hers. It was his body, Erik's body, that she wanted behind her. She longed to smell his scent, a scent she knew was his alone, one she knew and missed!

"Please, I think you should leave, Rinaldo."

"Meg," he whispered, and his voice was husky and warm by her ear. His face was so close to hers. If she turned only slightly, his lips would be on hers.

"He doesn't love me," she complained, and the notes came flooding out on a wave of fresh tears, warm and heavy on her fevered cheeks!

"Oh Meg, he's a fool," he whispered, but he wasn't thinking of Erik. He was thinking of a young arrogant man who spent too freely, gamed too often, and whored too willingly. A young man from Milan who thought it a lark to be a has-been prima donna's instrument.

Did he pull her to him or did she fall into his arms? Her eyes were closed against the tears, and his lips were on her lips. She raised one hand to push him back, but she lacked the will. She imagined Erik's lips on hers. She heard him plead with her for forgiveness and felt his large hands take possession of her. She let him taste her, drink her tears, press his arousal against her.

It wasn't Erik. It was a tall, strong body, but it was not Erik's. The hands did not have the miraculous fingers that danced, crooked, creating a music that could only come from the depths of an old soul, a soul that had suffered, a soul that knew loneliness and abandonment. This was a supple young body of a man who had taken a fancy to a woman he couldn't have. She forced her arms between them and pushed away with all her might.

Rinaldo took a step toward her, but she held her palms up against his advance.

"No," was all she had to say. Her hand was at her mouth as if to wipe him away. That she did not do so was small comfort to Rinaldo. The barrier was painfully obvious. She would not accept his kisses. "Please, go."

Before he could protest, Meg disappeared around the path that led back into the house.

Carlotta had been wrong. Meg would not fall easily into sin with him. She was made of firmer stuff. Unlike him! Carlotta had insisted on the deception. She had dressed him like Erik, had staged the scene, had even stripped before his surprised eyes, and waited until they heard Meg's footfalls in the passage-way. Then she had come to him, without the least embarrassment, and wrapped her arms around him. She had kissed him as if they were truly lovers and had woven her bare leg round his, her thigh mercilessly gliding up toward his groin. And behind him Meg had watched!

It wasn't he and yet it was. It was Erik and yet it wasn't! It drove him mad to think that he could be Erik only in his betrayal of Meg and not in loving her!

He returned through the library. Watching for the servants, he slipped out into the hallway and was about to leave when he noticed the day's post on the table next to the door. There he saw the letter from Paris. No one was in the hallway. Rinaldo lifted the letter and examined the seal. Carlotta would want this. He slipped it into his pocket and left quietly by the front door.

He held out his handkerchief as if it were the end of a rope to which he clung for his very life.

Madeleine stared, unmoving, at the sight of the silk cloth limp in Don Marcelo's hand. Hesitantly she reached out and took it, but Don Marcelo took her hand in his before she could retire it.

"Madeleine, I've been a fool."

Her expression seemed to say that she fully agreed with him.

"Can you forgive me for the silly way I've acted lately?" He was old enough to know that certain hurts never healed and some left ragged, tender scars that always threatened to open and bleed.

Madeleine's downcast eyes suggested, as he feared, that she might forgive, but she'd never forget. She twisted as if she would escape past him to the sanctuary of the house.

"Madeleine, please stay with me and talk a while. I miss our talks."

"Marcelo, I've many things on my mind. You'll have to excuse me." Still she would not look him in the eye.

"Come and talk. Let me share your concerns." When she yet struggled to be free of him, he pulled her forcefully to the kiosk and sat her on the bench. "I'm not a young man, Madeleine. And God has tested me severely with the deaths of my wife and my son. But he's also blessed me with a strong constitution, and perhaps I'll live yet a good number of years."

The reference to his age and mortality wrenched Madeleine from her own wounded pride. She couldn't bear to think of Marcelo's death. He was certainly many years her senior and would most likely come to his rest before she would. Yet she felt giddy and happy when she was with him. She wasn't sure when it had happened, but she was hopelessly in love.

He could see she was not immune to his charms and resolved to use whatever he must to win back the place in her affections he had so cavalierly squandered for a frivolous flirtation.

"She means nothing to me. She's a shameless flirt, and I enjoyed her attention. I was oblivious to how it might affect us, I'm afraid. As much as you might doubt it, I always knew it for what it was. She enjoys twisting men round her finger. And I was flattered by her fleeting interest."

"Was it worth it?" she asked, her voice cold and biting.

Don Marcelo shivered unintentionally under Madeleine's unrelenting scrutiny. For the first time genuinely fearing defeat, he whispered contritely, "No."

"So she's thrown you over, has she?" she added with more than a touch of cruelty. She was a worldly woman. She understood the vanity of men. "You're all alike! You dally with whatever skirt you fancy and then expect us to be saints and to forgive and feel sorry for your disappointments."

"I did not dally with her, Madeleine. The most you can accuse me of is acting the fool and kissing her hand!"

Madeleine kept her lips squeezed tightly in a narrow line.

"I know that there are rumors that she has done far worse with Erik. Although I have no doubt that she would do such a thing, I can't believe Erik was fool enough to fall for her facile charms. He doesn't even like her!" he added.

"Well men seem to be able to separate their heart from their…bodily desires quite easily."

Suddenly the hardness softened. Madeleine leaned in against Don Marcelo's chest and allowed him to place his arm around her shoulders. "Oh Marcelo! I'm afraid Erik has hurt Meg so terribly that they'll never mend the rift in their marriage. They're both lost."

He soothed her for several moments, selfishly enjoying the comfortable intimacy that he had missed. In part because he wanted to console her and in part because he hoped it to be true, he offered, "They've come through too much to lose each other now. They're hurt, but they'll find their way back to each other."

Then softly, with hope, he added, "As will we."

She started to protest, but it felt too good, too natural to settle into his embrace to let the anger ruin it all. They didn't have the time to waste on foolish pride. They surely were wise enough to reach out and take what unexpected pleasures life had brought them. She only hoped that Erik and Meg would learn that lesson before it was too late.

CHAPTER 8

La Belle Dame San Merci

I dreamt my lady came and found me dead—
Strange dream, that gives a dead man leave to think!—
And breathed such life with kisses in my lips,
That I revived, and was an emperor.

Romeo and Juliet, Shakespeare

She was magnificent. All eyes were on her. She glowed as if lit from within by a thousand candles. Whereas he had slept fitfully, uncomfortably seated on the piano bench in his office, his chin and arms draped across the keys, she had slept the sleep of the blessed and was well rested. Whereas he had struggled with demons and heartache, she appeared blithely ignorant of suffering. Indeed she smiled and chatted with the tenor and the maestro who clearly were flattered by her attentions.

Erik hesitated before he came out onto the stage. The chorus was impatiently waiting. He adjusted his waistcoat and smoothed the hair along his temples and checked to make sure that his mask was snuggly in place. He would have to send to the estate for fresh clothes. He was woefully aware that his coat was becoming shabby, and there were stains on his breeches.

He stiffened his spine and walked purposefully out onto the stage, aware that the company had gleaned that he and Meg had fought. He would meet her disregard with fortitude as if it made no difference to him. There was a job to do. He was interested only in the music. In the cadences and melodies, he would grasp the true essence of beauty, not its mortal shadow. In the music, his music, he would take what was base and make it soar. He, an ugly beast, would create grand passion and eloquence. Meg's beauty was fleeting, an illusion. The beauty he sought in music was eternal. He would cling to that. He would seek his redemption in the music. It would fuel his life even if nothing else was his.

Meg slipped too easily out of his grasp. She no longer responded to his touch, his voice. He had no confidence that she would heed his instructions. Quite the contrary. But perhaps she would listen to the music.

He glimpsed over to his wife as she occupied center stage. She didn't so much as acknowledge his arrival. Pain made him wince. It threatened to weaken him. He could not show it. They waited to see him fail. *She* waited to see him fail.

"Maestro? From the top, Act III. Signora Costanzi, if you please?" He heard the mutters of surprise rippling among the company. No one was immune to the tension between the two spouses. Erik held his gaze down, fixed to the sheet music in his hand, waiting for the cue when Meg would begin her aria.

The cue came and went, but Meg was silent. The music died out haltingly without her.

Erik looked to her in surprise. She had purposefully missed the entrance.

She stood, a scowl on her face, as she observed him. For several seconds they simply took each other's measure, waiting for the challenge to be given. Then Meg unfolded her arms and nodded at the maestro to begin again.

Erik, once he had looked at her, could not lower his eyes. She sang as if transported beyond their time and space. Fascinated, he watched her transformation. Her eyes sparked with the emotion of her character, a woman torn by tragedy and yet desperate to hold on to a glimmer of hope.

Behind him and slightly above, he heard the unfortunate opening and closing of a door. Without turning to look, he knew it was Carlotta who had come to occupy her seat above them all, to sit in judgment, and to plot his destruction. His acute hearing perhaps picked up or only imagined the rustle of her skirts as they grazed the wooden legs of the chair when she sat or the snap of the fan as she flicked it open and fluttered it before her veiled face.

He forced his attention on Meg. She was in top form. The rest over the weekend had strengthened her voice. Without wavering, it held the notes like sharp crystal. She teased out nuances, deep rushes of despair and tender filaments of desire, from the complex weave of themes. Her masterly control of the dynamics wrung from the music and the words the emotion of unshed tears.

When Meg finished but before the warm resonance of her voice had dissipated, he could feel the waves of disappointment and annoyance beating against his back from Carlotta's box. He wanted to applaud for Meg, but as he stepped forward to compliment her, she spurned his praise and purposefully walked away. He thought he might stop breathing. Her coldness threatened to chill his soul.

Then he felt the fury rise hot and bitter from the pit of his stomach.

"The rehearsal is not finished, Madame!" Meg was startled to hear her husband revert to his native French. "The tenor would appreciate a partner for the duet, n'est-ce pas?"

Grimaldo, the tenor, shrugged his shoulders when Meg glanced his way. He was in no rush to become involved in the obvious discord between Don Erik and his wife.

"I will be with you momentarily, signore." She bowed to Grimaldo.

Erik had taken each slight with less and less composure. Her obvious scorn was not only insulting but threatened to undermine his position with the rest of the company. "Signora Costanzi," he began, but Meg turned sharply, her eyes flashing with an angry, dark light. She interrupted him.

"You may address me as Signorina Giry, monsieur!"

Under his breath, Erik muttered a curse he recalled from his childhood, an oath that he had heard only from the seediest of men. He saw Madeleine approaching from the wings, but he didn't plan to wait for her. He marched over stage right and took Meg forcefully by the wrist.

More in surprise than pain, she let out a sharp cry.

"I wish a word with my wife! Now!" Before Meg could refuse, Erik bent and grabbed her behind her knees and lifted her bodily over his shoulder and proceeded down the wings toward his rooms.

He could hear Madeleine crying after him to put her daughter down.

He yelled back, "My wife and I have something to discuss! Do not disturb us!"

Deny his name would she? Return to her maiden name as if to erase his very existence, his life with her, even the legitimacy of their children!

Meg didn't expect him to do more than rant under the circumstances. What could he do with the entire opera company standing as witnesses? Yet if she had thought more deeply, she might have realized that publicly humiliating him before the same company would force his hand.

She had wanted it to be clear that she could stand alone. She didn't need him. So if he thought she would meekly suffer his infidelities, he was wrong!

Once she regained her breath, she started to kick uselessly with her feet and to pound her fists upon his back. The moment she hit him, she heard him grunt with the unexpected pain. She bit her lip in regret. She had forgotten that it had only been a few weeks since his fall. She stopped struggling. By then they were at his rooms. He entered with her still across his shoulder and kicked the door shut behind them with the heel of his boot. Only then did he drop her brusquely to the sofa where she landed unceremoniously on her derrière.

This was where she had seen him making love to the Venedetti woman! How could he? It was even worse that he had chosen *her* with whom to dally! Don Marcelo was bewitched by the woman. Had Erik given any thought to how his affair with Signorina Venedetti might affect his adopted father?

"You have no right to treat me like this, Erik. We have to work together, at least for the time being. We have to make the best of it. I plan to quit the company after this opera. I'll look for a position somewhere else or perhaps I'll go home!" She peevishly smoothed her skirt out across her lap and avoided his eyes.

"Home?" The anger suddenly left him. How could she be so cruel to him? Yes, she could go home. She could take his children and return to Paris. There they would be grateful for her return to the Opera National. And he would never see them again.

"What did you expect?" she yelled at him, tears rising unbidden to her eyes.

Instead of answering, Erik sought the arm of the chair beside him and dropped heavily onto the seat. He wasn't sure he could speak. The muscles of his throat were so tightly knotted against the sorrow that threatened to engulf him. "You would do that to me?"

It was said with such innocent sadness that Meg felt guilty. She hadn't really looked at him in days. She did so now. She could swear that he had grown thin even in this short time. His clothes were barely presentable. He'd not changed in several days. She gnawed at the tender flesh along her lip holding back a question that would show her concern.

The knock at the door was followed by Madeleine's worried voice. She asked to be let in. She demanded to know what Erik was doing to her daughter.

When Erik didn't respond, didn't even move, Meg called out to calm her mother. "I'm all right, Maman. We're talking. Leave us alone."

That one glimmer of hope woke Erik from his despair. He wasn't angry anymore, and curiously he wasn't devastated by his wife's rejection. He was overwhelmed by confusion and the need to understand why she could be so cruel to him. What had he done that was so vile that it had destroyed not only the love she had had for him but even her compassion?

He came and knelt beside her knees, his hands braced on either side of her hips. He stared directly into her face and asked, "Why do you no longer love me?"

She tried to push him away, but he wouldn't budge. Instead he accused her. "You promised, Meg, that you would love me forever. Why have you broken your promise to me?"

"My promise to you? And what of yours to me?"

"I have kept that promise to you! You're everything to me! And yet you speak of returning to Paris, of taking our children away from me, for you know I can never go back there!"

"You should have thought about that before you made love to that woman!"

Erik stood abruptly and looked down at Meg as if she were mad. Even though he towered over her, Meg's anger made her feel invincible.

"I saw you! The two of you. She was in your arms, naked. In this very room!" As if she relived the scene she imagined his body covering Signorina Venedetti's and felt again the stab of betrayal. She had put up with so many troubles. She had remained constant through all their crises. But she would not be made a fool of!

"Who did you see, Meg?" he asked quietly.

"Oh, please! Must I say it again? I saw the two of you making love in this room last Thursday night. I came to talk, but you had other things on your mind evidently!"

"What did you see? Tell me, Meg."

"You!"

"What did you see?" He drew the words out slowly and carefully.

"Why are you doing this? You know very well what I saw! I saw what you did!"

"Was I naked?"

"No, not yet…"

"Was I lying on the couch?"

"No, you were standing." To demonstrate, Meg rose from the couch and went to the very spot where she had seen Erik that night.

"You were at the door? My back was to you?"

…

"Or did you see my face? Was I wearing my mask? Or was I without it?"

His even and emotionless tone was maddening to Meg. "I don't know if you were wearing your mask! I didn't see your face. You had your back to me!"

"What did you see?" Again he spoke the words as if she had never heard them before.

"Why do you keep asking me that? I told you. I saw you and that…that… that woman."

"And it was me? You're sure it was me, Meg?"

The question enraged her. Did he think she was an idiot? That she didn't know her own husband's…? She had only seen his back. "It was your office, and your clothes. The black waistcoat you used to wear."

Erik heard the creeping doubt in those words.

"The one I told you I couldn't find two months ago?"

Meg stopped. She thought back to one morning several months ago when Erik had torn through the wardrobe looking for his waistcoat. He tended to wear the same clothes over and over again unless Meg forced the issue. The waistcoat was old and worn, but Erik would not consider giving it up. So, after it was laundered, Meg had taken it to the teatro. There she had thrown it into one of the bins of costumes and odd bits of clothing. She had not told him because she knew he'd be angry with her and demand that she bring it back. Instead she had given him the new waistcoat that she had made for him.

Erik saw the ambivalence in her eyes. He had chipped away at the certainty she had held to. "You saw a man in my office. Was he my height? My build?"

Now she was unsure of what she had seen. Yes, he was taller than average. But Erik had wonderfully broad shoulders, narrow hips, and long, slender legs. She was not close to the man. She had been peeking in through the slit in the door. A door that was conveniently left open while a man and a woman made love?

Erik edged closer to Meg and tentatively reached out to her. She let him touch her. Then she let him pull her into his arms. Her body shivered with the joy of him. She closed her eyes and leaned her face against his breast. There she heard it, the sound of his heart, strong and steady and true. She felt his lips pressed against her hair. All it would have taken was this touch. If she had embraced him, she would have known that he could not have been that man.

Softly he explained, "Last Thursday, I was drinking, here in this very room. I must have passed out. I woke on the daybed in the other room. I couldn't have made love to anyone, Meg, especially to that woman."

Clearly it had been staged. One more attack, one more torment, but one more serious than all the annoying obstacles Carlotta had staged before. Except, perhaps, the sabotage of the catwalk. In that incident, someone might have died.

"We have to talk, Meg. I've been keeping something from you, and I see now that it was dangerous to keep you in the dark. If I had been more honest, this would never have happened."

They sat together on the couch, and Erik realized that he was relieved to be able to tell someone what had been going on in the opera house and who was behind it all.

"Signorina Venedetti is not who she pretends to be. Nor is her interest in the opera the reason she's here. She's here for revenge. You don't recognize her still?"

Perhaps she had sensed it from him, for the name came full blown into her mind. "Carlotta? Carlotta Giudicelli?"

Erik barely nodded.

"Why didn't you tell me?"

"I was reluctant to face the fact that I'd been discovered. Since she hadn't gone to the authorities, I understood that it was between her and me. It was her own private revenge she sought. I foolishly thought she'd tire of tormenting me. I thought I could bear it, as long as you and the children were safe. I reasoned that eventually it would have to come to an end."

"Oh my God, Erik. Did she mean to kill you that day on the catwalk?"

"I don't think so. I think it was an accident. Something got out of hand."

"You should never have kept this from me!"

"I know that now."

Meg sat up brusquely and asked, "Who was the man?"

Erik wondered if he should tell her everything he suspected, even though he didn't have the proof. Holding back his fears concerning Carlotta had almost cost him everything in life that was dear to him, so he decided he mustn't keep secrets from her.

"Rinaldo."

She remembered all the little comforts Erik's assistant had given her, his easy friendship, his fond devotion. Just a day ago she had cried in his arms in the garden at the estate after Erik had come and gone. That was the day she had refused to speak with her husband. Instead she had taunted him cruelly and told him to leave. Then she had gone to the garden to cry and think. Rinaldo had appeared out of nowhere. He spoke soothingly to her and looked at her with such compassion. She had never thought of him as anything more than a nice young man. He was several years younger than she, and he was her husband's assistant. It had never crossed her mind that he was wooing her—until the kiss. Seducing her would be more accurate.

The color rose in Meg's cheeks, and she brought her fingers to her burning lips. They stung where Rinaldo had kissed her. She had been awash in tears over Erik, yet she had let Rinaldo lift her face and place his lips on hers. She had allowed him to wrap his arms around her and to pull her into a tight, wild embrace of passion. She ached for Erik, but she had filled her arms with another man's body.

"Meg?" asked Erik. He was concerned by the devastation in his wife's eyes.

She rose from the couch and walked away from him. At the edge of the fireplace, she faced him. Her voice was tremulous, but she was firm of purpose as she spoke.

"I have to tell…to confess something to you."

Her lips trembled. Erik could not bear to see her cry, and he was at her side before she could protest. She vainly tried to move apart from him, but he resolutely held her pinned to his chest.

"What is it? If she has done anything to hurt you, I swear I'll…"

"No, it is my sin."

Erik paled at her use of the word. He feared the not knowing as much as the knowing, so he held her quietly and waited for her to continue.

"Rinaldo tried to comfort me in the garden the other day after you left."

She could feel his muscles tense under the fabric of his coat. She dug her fingers in deeply as if to hold him to her should he try to flee.

"I let him."

Erik struggled to get away from her. He struggled to move from her touch, fearing that he might hurt her. She pulled at his coat and cried for him to wait and listen to her.

He stilled, although everything in him screamed that he should run.

"He kissed me. That is all. But I didn't stop him. I let him kiss me. I was so heartbroken." She knew it was cowardly to try to excuse her behavior, but she hoped it would soften the pain for Erik as well.

It must have had such an effect, for Erik stopped pulling away from her. His eyes were glossy and bright with pain and confusion. His lips were parted as he tried to control his breathing. Gradually he came back to her arms, and they held each other tightly.

She was crying softly. "Don't cry, Meg. It was only a kiss in the garden. It does not compare to the thousands of kisses that I will give you."

They sat together on the couch and comforted each other for their past grievances. But time was passing, and Erik realized the company was still waiting for them to appear. They would be wondering what monstrous things he was doing to her.

"Meg? We need to talk. Carlotta wants to destroy us. We came quite close, it would appear, to granting her fondest wish. I say we let her think she has won."

"That way she won't continue to plot against us?"

"My thoughts exactly. If she believes you have forever rejected me, and thinks that I suffer, she won't need to invent some new stratagem to attack us. It would, at least, gain us some time."

"So, we are to pretend to hate each other?"

"Well, you can pretend to hate me. I can play the desperate and frustrated lover. I don't believe it would gratify her as much if she thought the hate was mutual. She wants me to suffer."

"But we should continue to argue? Oh, this could be fun."

"I suppose, in a twisted fashion, you're right. We'll treat it as our own opera with Carlotta our main audience. But to be effective, no one else must know it is only a show. Agreed?"

"The children? Can I at least tell them that it's a sham?"

Erik sighed, wondering if telling the children would be such a good idea. On the other hand, he couldn't bear thinking that they would be distressed by their parents' falling out. "I will trust to your judgment in that."

"So we should begin, don't you think? Everyone's been out there waiting for nearly an hour."

Meg stood and wiped her face and immediately started to yell at Erik. "You pig! You monster! You have no right to demand your husbandly rights of me!"

Erik winced to think of the role she had just forced him to play. Even so, he met her anger with his own loud, growling voice. "You're my wife, Meg Costanzi. I'll not have you make a fool of me!"

Meg opened the door, glanced around. No one was in the vicinity, so she yelled down the hall, "I despise you. I should never have married you. You are nothing but a tyrant!"

Then she blew a kiss at him and ran down the wings toward the stage. Madeleine was rushing toward her when Meg threw herself into her mother's arms and bawled, "He thinks he can force me to be obedient, Maman!"

Madeleine clucked soothingly and threw Erik a scathing look when he approached them.

"Madame, enough of your hysterics. We have a show to put on!" Without so much as a glance at Madeleine, Erik brushed past them and went to face an icy reception from the company.

I watch him watch her from the wings. He has stormed off the stage. She won't listen to him. She has gone to lock herself in her dressing room. I watch him, I glide past his shoulders, and breathe on his neck, and feel the pain radiate from his skin. It warms me and excites me. If I took him by the hand and led him to the dark corner and held his face—his masked face—against the silken bodice of my gown, against the swell of my bosom, his tears would course down my body, under taffeta, pink turned wet red, along the pathway down and down, deliciously against my skin, his warm salty tears. Such strength under my hands, I would hold him, and he would bend to me. I watch him, and I know his soul is shrinking, his soul is crying out, and I could swallow that cry deep inside me, it would grow and consume me, I would be that voice, and he would be inside me, captured, captured forever and for always. I watch him, and I know that he suffers. I feel that suffering as if it were rising from my own womb and straining against my heart. And I breathe ragged warm moist against his neck. My fingers rake through his hair, I push myself against his back. He falls into my arms, and he is mine. I watch him, I watch him

Carlotta was beside herself with glee. If she had been alone, she'd have clapped her hands, stomped her feet, and laughed out loud. The Phantom had lost his songbird. He had done nothing but complain and criticize the diva's singing even though to Carlotta's envious ear, Meg had never sounded better. Finally pushed beyond her endurance, Meg had, on the stage before the aghast expressions of the entire staff and theater company, slapped Erik soundly across the face. He clutched the side of his jaw wordlessly while Meg stormed off the stage in tears.

She almost felt sorry for the monster. He turned toward the wings, his face at an angle to her so that she could only barely make out the shocked expression in his eyes. The company visibly drew away from him as if by contagion they could catch some of his misfortune. Alone, Carlotta wanted him to be alone, forsaken. She'd only rest when she could see him slink miserably back into the sewer from whence he'd crawled.

Oh Piangi would have to admit now she had been right all along. This was so much more pleasing than standing by, a passive witness, while a wagon of police officers took him off in chains to a speedy and merciful death.

She flicked open the fan and fluttered it energetically before her face. She recognized Don Marcelo's solicitous voice behind her. Would she like him to call a carriage for her? She didn't turn so she missed the stern look on his face. She was tiring of his fondness. She congratulated herself that she had driven a wedge between him and the Giry woman that would be hard to dislodge, but she had no more need to string him along.

When she turned and smiled at him, Don Marcelo managed to hide his displeasure from her. Over the past several days the rumors had eventually made their way to his ears. He couldn't believe it of Erik, but he wasn't so sure about the enigmatic Signorina Venedetti.

Carlotta fluttered her fan and thanked Don Marcelo for his assistance. She added that the high tempers of the artists had worn her out and that she expected she'd retire for the evening. She smiled sweetly behind her veil and considered how best to let him down easily. Perhaps she would invent a lover, hire a muscular youth, and arrive on his arm for the next day's rehearsal. No explanations, no wearisome scenes would be required. Don Marcelo would recover as best he could.

His was not the admiration that she wanted. His lust was like ashes in her mouth. She resisted putting the thought into words. When Erik—the Phantom—strode off the stage, his hand protecting his face, the look of pain in his eyes—those eyes, those green verdant lush eyes—she could scarcely resist following after him. To what purpose? Surely to gloat! She knew she lied to herself the moment the thought formed itself in her mind. But the lie soothed, delayed the inevitable.

He had been the only man who had not crumpled at her feet! She wanted that strength, not its dissolution; she wanted it lying, throbbing, under her hand. She wanted that monster's chains firmly clutched in her fists.

She blushed at the image of Erik, naked and in pain, at her feet. She had never realized she was susceptible to such desires. She had never felt such an unnatural urge with Piangi. But the Phantom quickened her pulse. The violence made her shiver, not from fear, not from disgust, but from something else, something buried and dark and deliciously twisted.

The barmaid had filled his glass several times without his asking. He drank the dark brew slowly and watched her curiously from the corner of his eye. She was a young thing, perhaps not yet eighteen, and had that beauty that sits like dew on a maiden. Come her twenty-first birthday, such beauty might already have faded, but for now she was in her glory. She had dark hair loosely gathered under an unpleasant cotton cap. He could see some riotous curls that had escaped her endeavors.

Perhaps he was mistaken. He was uncomfortably aroused, much to his own dismay and annoyance. He had not been separated from Christine for more than a few days in the past many, many years. The only time of any duration had been after the death of their first-born, when despair and then Erik took her off to the underground tunnels. He didn't want to think about those days, the awful suspicions he had suffered. Each night she was gone he had imagined her in the Phantom's arms. It had nearly driven him to do something desperate. If Erik and he had met during those days, Raoul would have killed him with his bare hands or died in the attempt.

He sat stiffly on the barstool and reminded himself that he was not a green lad but a mature man, a gentleman, who had the moral fiber to resist a mild temptation. But a glance over his shoulder brought him unfortunately in contact with a dazzling pair of violet eyes, shaded by lush black lashes, and a red mouth turned up in a knowing smile.

Damn! The girl was by far too saucy for her years!

Raoul stood quickly hoping his arousal would not be evident in the loose fitting laborer's trousers. He dropped a coin on the counter, more than enough to cover the extra draughts the chit had brought him, and walked out into the refreshing coolness of the evening. The sooner this was all resolved, the sooner he could share his wife's bed again!

The weekend was behind him, and the work schedule had resumed at the opera house. He watched the comings and goings of the artists, the backstage workers, the delivery men. He was relieved to see Meg, safe and sound, arrive early on Monday. Puzzled that Erik was nowhere in sight, Raoul slipped into the theater to investigate. He managed to catch a quick glimpse of Erik in the wings talking with one of the scene shifters before his friend was distracted by a flamboyant woman, dressed in startling pink, who glided past him on the way to the stairs. She had a commanding presence as if she, instead of Meg, were the prima donna at the Teatro dell'Opera. A tall, young man with striking features followed her. He seemed intent on speaking with her alone.

"What you doing there? Hey, you!" The doorman had spied Raoul. It was too early to abandon his disguise. He'd be of more use watching from the shadows than revealed to Erik at this moment. As the doorman rushed forward, Raoul ducked behind the thick purple curtains and snuck back in the direction of one of the artists' exits. Before the doorman could reach him, he was safely in the narrow passageway between the Teatro and the neighboring business.

It wasn't until the next night that he saw Erik emerge from the theater. Meg had left hours before and returned to the Costanzi estate. More and more Raoul wondered why he never saw the two of them depart or arrive together. Even though the opening night was fast approaching and there were scores of last minute chores to be done, it was strange not to see Erik and Meg together, at the very least, in the morning. It was as if Erik were living at the opera house.

Raoul was about to approach Erik when he saw the shadow flit across the building in the same direction Erik had taken. The count stayed back and waited to see who had come out. The shadow soon gave way to the man himself, a large man. Raoul thought he recognized the man from the Boar and Bow, an inn and bar. The clientele were rather dangerous and none too particular about the work they did. The man and his friends had been discussing a crazy Frenchman who had come looking to hire some of the toughs. The one who seemed to be in charge, a man with a gravelly voice, short and stocky, was Piero. But there had been another whose name Raoul had overheard as well, a larger and beefier man with massive shoulders, called Edmundo or Egidio. The man who was following Erik was certainly the latter.

Raoul kept a safe distance behind both men. Erik was obviously in the mood to walk, for he had quickly set off taking large strides down the avenue toward the center of the city. Vaguely Raoul recognized the direction was toward the Costanzi estate. The three of them, like a reflection of a reflection, flitted in unison for some time until Erik suddenly verged off the path, apparently aware of being followed. The scoundrel in pursuit darted after in the general direction Erik had gone and found himself running between several buildings in an elaborate maze of back way alleys and small culs-de-sac. Raoul was confident Erik could handle the lout and reasoned that he'd be better off taking the chance and heading out toward the estate. He had walked along for several minutes when, much to his delight, he caught a glimpse of Erik's dark coat in the distance. Whatever had happened to Egidio, or whatever his name was, Raoul was sure that Erik had managed to shake the man off his trail.

Within another fifteen minutes—Raoul had never walked so much in his life as he had since he arrived in Rome—he saw Erik start up the path toward the door of the Costanzi residence. However, instead of going directly to the front entrance, he circled round behind and disappeared into the shadows of the large three story mansion. Careful to stay well hidden, Raoul tried to follow but the sound of a soft, but determined growl changed his mind. There were watch dogs on the grounds. They knew Erik's scent and had not made a sound when he had snuck round the building. Raoul's scent was another matter altogether. A large, black mastiff lit after him, but Raoul had not ventured that far onto the grounds that he couldn't easily reach safety.

Why the devil would Erik be sneaking into his own home?

The next day Raoul made it a point to drop by the Boar and Bow and within the hour a tall, broad shouldered man with a swollen, blackened eye came in and sat at one of the tables in the back. It was the same man, Raoul was sure. Obviously he had slipped and fallen in one of the alleyways or Erik had ambushed him, assuming that the man was after his purse. He didn't have anything worse than a black eye so Erik must have convinced him the pursuit wasn't worth it or he had knocked him out cold with the one punch. Raoul snickered to himself as he imagined the scene.

Piero came in a few minutes later along with several other hard looking men Raoul had seen the first night when he'd come to have a drink at the place. They sat and spoke quietly. Piero and Egidio exchanged a few angry words, the volume of their voices rising above the general din for only a moment before the others quieted them.

Raoul was eating his sausage pie very slowly since he was no longer hungry and had only ordered it so as to have a reason to linger at the counter and wait for the band of cutthroats to leave. Finally, when Raoul thought he'd be sick if he ate or drank another thing, Piero rose from the table and left.

In the street, it was already dark. Raoul stayed as far behind as he could without losing track of Piero. There were a fair number of people still out in the street, so it was easy to blend in with the general foot traffic. Piero stopped once to look back as if he guessed he was being followed. However, he must not have seen Raoul, who followed him to a small pension near the Tivoli fountains. Raoul shivered, recalling his encounter with Giovanni in a nearby plaza. His arm sometimes ached from the sword wound Giovanni had given him. It was Erik who had come to his aid that time. It seemed a lifetime ago, but it was actually only a little more than a year ago. Having arrived at his destination, Piero disappeared inside the inn.

An hour later, Piero finally emerged from the building and started back the way he had come. Raoul reasoned that Piero had met with the "crazy Frenchman," and Raoul had little doubt that it was Leroux he'd find if he went inside. There was no need to follow Piero. Raoul had found what he had come to Italy to find.

Erik had walked the entire way from the Teatro dell'Opera. He had slipped out after he was fairly sure that Carlotta had left. Rinaldo he had told to leave several hours earlier, but he had seen the assistant lingering around the wings until the last minute. When Carlotta left, Erik was certain that Rinaldo had accompanied her.

It was late when Erik locked the theater door behind him and walked out onto the street. It was foolish, but he needed the air to clear his head. Along the way he had heard footsteps behind him. Some ruffian was surely speculating that he'd have a heavy purse. He dealt with the man and within the hour made his way to the Costanzi estate.

At the back door, Erik knocked softly and waited.

He felt strange knowing that Rinaldo was working with Carlotta to bring him to ruin. He had not treated his assistant with much patience, but he had begun to trust him. Erik kept a purely professional relationship with most of the artists at the opera, including the maestro, whom he respected a great deal, for the man reminded him of M. Reyer. He had always had a fondness for M. Reyer at the Opera Populaire. After all, he had been Erik's unofficial tutor for years. As M. Reyer's shadow, Erik had learned to read and write music. He had always been able to pick up any instrument and play it by ear, but by watching and studying M. Reyer, Erik learned the secret language of music, the language that let him compose and preserve the music that was constantly playing in his mind.

Rinaldo at first had been nothing but a hindrance. Erik hadn't wanted anyone close to him. It was difficult to feel comfortable with others. He needed distance. It was the only way that he could come into contact with people on a day to day basis and remain sane. Yet Rinaldo had been invaluable the day a section of the musical score had disappeared. Erik had felt gratitude for the company and the work the young man had done with him that night. His hands had become claws by the end of the process, and he was aware that Rinaldo was witness to his pain. His silent companionship had broken down a wall in Erik's reserve.

How bitter it was to find that Rinaldo may well have been the one to misplace or destroy that section of the opera. That Rinaldo was helping Carlotta destroy Erik piece by piece saddened him more than he would have thought. He found it hard to look at Rinaldo and hide the anger and resentment he felt.

For the past two days, Meg and Erik had circled around each other like angry lions to the despair and annoyance of the entire cast and staff of the opera house. Madeleine watched warily, intruding between the two of them whenever she saw one take a step toward the other. Messages were relayed back and forth between them to avoid angry confrontations.

It had been a long two days, and Erik had not enjoyed pretending that they had stopped loving each other. It was hard to get work done efficiently when he had to talk through a third party. He genuinely felt angry with Meg on several occasions because she took the game a bit too far and was objecting to Erik's instructions. He wanted his old relationship back. Then, too, he felt the icy looks from the artists who, three to one, sided with his wife against him.

Only today had Meg realized the strain he was under. She had been playing the difficult artist and resisting his direction, enjoying the pretense. Then Erik noticed several of the chorus behind Meg were huddled together, speaking among themselves in hushed whispers. Although Erik had heard only bits and pieces of what they were saying, it made his blood run cold. Meg, too, had realized they were speaking about Erik, about his mask, about the disfigured face it must hide. They were complaining that someone like him couldn't possibly appreciate true art. Erik saw Meg turn, as if to snap at them, only to retrain herself at the last moment. It would not have gone well with her current role. The worst of it was that Erik knew that Meg's coldness was what had given rise to their snide remarks.

From that point on, Meg had tempered her responses to him, but the damage had already been done. Erik could feel the hostility coming from the chorus and even some of the staff when he addressed them. Once the major issues were worked out for the act, Erik had turned the stage over to Rinaldo. Meg, too, had finished for the day and had withdrawn, taking the opposite direction from Erik's. But as she was about to close her dressing room door, Erik grabbed the edge and slid furtively in through the gap.

He didn't wait for her to speak but grabbed her up in a fierce embrace and savagely kissed her. There was more than a little aggression in the kiss, his way of reminding her that she belonged to him in no uncertain terms. But there had also been need, a need to feel something other than her disdain and contempt, reassurance that she loved and respected him.

Breathlessly, they had broken the kiss, and yet he held her tightly against him as if he would never let her go again.

"Am I that good an actress?" she had whispered.

His eyes were sad, and she knew that she wouldn't tease him out of his fears.

"We're pretending, remember?" She had tried to soothe him. She caressed his hair, the line of his jaw, which was not covered by the mask. "You can't stay here. Maman may come at any moment."

Erik had nodded silently, but he kept searching her eyes for something.

"Go, Erik. You must go," she repeated, still whispering, but she regretted having to push him out.

"I have to be with you," he finally said.

"Erik, we agreed."

His hands on her were urgent and demanding. He kissed her breathlessly again, and repeated in a ragged growl at her ear, "I have to be with you!"

"Oh, Erik. Don't you think I feel it, too? But we agreed to pretend. She can't know we've made up."

"You're mine. Say it!"

"Oh God, Erik! I'm yours."

"I want you."

"Erik," she moaned as his mouth found its way along her neck and down the bodice of her gown.

"Tonight. I'll sneak away. Be at the servant's entrance at midnight. I'll knock twice, then three times, then twice."

"But it's not safe," she had pleaded one last time.

"I don't care!" He had released her then and peeked out the door to see if Madeleine was on her way. He turned quickly toward Meg and kissed her on the lips before he disappeared down the passageway.

Midnight had been slow in coming. He'd not wait any longer.

At the door, Erik gave the agreed-upon knock and listened. The heavy door slowly opened, and there stood Meg iridescent in a shower of light. Erik slipped inside. Meg took him by the hand to lead him to their room as if he might have forgotten the way during their brief separation. The servants were asleep, but Meg and Erik went cautiously. Going up the servants' stairway, they came out onto their floor at the far end of the hallway. They would have to pass Madeleine's room and the children's to reach theirs. In the hallway, one lamp remained lit through the night casting eerie shadows along the wall. Erik stooped and took off his boots so as not to make noise.

Inside their bedroom, Meg closed the door and set the lock. As she turned, she found herself trapped in Erik's arms. She leaned heavily against the door as he pinned her back with his entire weight. His hands seemed to be everywhere that his mouth wasn't. She wore only her nightgown and a robe so his hands felt as if they were on her skin. He was grabbing at the edges of her robe when finally she pushed him away. Reluctantly, he held himself in check as she slid the light material from her shoulders, allowing the robe to crumple at her feet. Then she pulled the gown over her head to stand naked.

He watched the silk float to the floor. He took the next moment to drink in the soft curves and swells of his wife's body. Then he eagerly worked at removing his own clothes. They fell onto the bed in a jumble of legs and desires.

There was no need for words. Although it had been little more than a week, the separation had seemed like years to both of them.

It wasn't only Meg's body that Erik ached for. He felt as if he had been spurned and tossed aside. The pretended slights had hurt as if they had been real. The rejection had also seemed real for the two of them had been separated and alone. Erik smothered her with his body, taking and giving eagerly, with an edge of desperation that neither had felt for some time. As if this moment were their last, they made love feverishly and repeatedly until they lay exhausted in the tangle of bedcovers that they had not even pulled to the side. Only then, was Erik able to hold Meg in his arms and speak.

"It's as though she has won," he said despondently. "We speak daggers at each other. We don't touch. We sleep alone. I don't think I can take this, Meg. It's as if we were still her puppets."

Meg couldn't answer him. She hadn't thought about it from that vantage point. There was some truth in what he said.

"But if we don't do this, then she might try to do something even more horrible to us."

"What can be more horrible than this? Not to touch you. Not to see you smile at me. Today, after the duet with Grimaldo, you looked at me as if you detested me. I know it wasn't true, but I felt it. Or perhaps it's the absence of the other that hurts. I need your smile, your kindness. I see only a monster reflected in your eyes when I look at you. And that's what she wants me to see. And you? What do you see?"

Meg's lips began to quiver. So he wasn't always pretending when he turned those sad eyes on her. "I see that you're angry or annoyed. The worst is when I see you're in pain. I thought, I hoped, it was an act."

"I tried. But I feel it as if it were real."

"What are we going to do?"

"Can she really do anything to us? Can she make you doubt me now?"

"No, not that. I swear to you that I will never doubt you again."

"Let's swear that we will always speak frankly to each other if there is ever a problem, a hint of discord between us. If we do that, then what can she do to us?"

"I don't know, Erik. I'm frightened. What if she tells the police? What if they believe her and carry you off to prison?"

"She doesn't want that."

"Yes, but if we thwart her in this, in her plan to come between us, might she do it or something worse as a last resort?"

Erik was quiet for a long while. Meg thought for a moment perhaps he had fallen asleep. Then he spoke again. "I have to confront her."

Meg lifted herself on her elbow to stare down at him. The light from a waning moon filtered through the curtains. It was barely enough to make out shadows, but she could see the glint in his eyes.

"No, Erik. No. We don't know what she'll do. It's too dangerous."

"Meg, *this* is too dangerous. We can't let her control us through fear. This is worse than being in prison, never knowing when the next accident will happen, wondering what she'll have Rinaldo do. What if part of her plan is to have Rinaldo seduce you?"

"And do you trust me so little?" In spite of the fact that she had let Rinaldo kiss her, she was insulted that Erik would think she was so easily swayed by another man's attentions. "If that's their plan, he doesn't stand a chance."

"And if you resist him, might he do something violent? What if he raped you, Meg?" She could tell that he was very serious.

"It won't happen, Erik. I don't think he's that evil."

Erik prayed that she was right. If he didn't confront Carlotta and find some way to appease her, then they would both be at her mercy. What if it came to violence? He would kill Carlotta if she harmed Meg. He would kill Rinaldo. Across his mind a million images flashed like the blade of a razor: He could see himself steeped in blood, running, hiding in the dark corners of the sewer. He didn't want to kill. He didn't want to live like a monster, like a phantom.

"Erik? Promise me you won't do anything foolish."

Foolish? Hadn't this game been that? Wasn't it foolish for him to have thought he could escape his destiny? Hadn't it been foolish to think they would let him live?

"I promise I'll wait and think about it before I do anything. But I can't let this go on interminably. I don't think Carlotta will tire of her games. I had hoped she would, but she stands by and watches us day after day, and still she's not satisfied."

Meg brushed her fingers purposefully over his lips to silence him. She would have this night without such thoughts. She would banish fears and worries. She lay across him, light as a sparrow. Their limbs joined, skin melded to skin. One desire. She kissed his face, his eyes, his wounded side and his beautiful side. Slowly, his hands rose and glided along the contours of her body until all thoughts were one.

CHAPTER 9

A Fan, a Veil, a Kiss

If music be the food of love, play on,
Give me excess of it; that, surfeiting,
The appetite may sicken and so die.

Shakespeare, Twelfth Night

"We have one more day before opening night. And from what I see, we might as well not raise the curtain!"

Meg blushed to hear Erik so angry. His complaint was not directed this time so much at her as at the entire company.

Erik paced before the orchestra pit, his hand pressing the mask hard against his forehead as if plagued by a migraine. His presence was never without effect on the company. Even in his silence, he drew all their eyes. They scanned him in an attempt to read his mood, to discern his secrets. His emotions clothed them, warm and comforting, or left them stripped and vulnerable. And they had begun to resent his power over them once they saw his songbird rebel.

Meg could see Erik pause and mutter to himself. She didn't remember him speaking so much to himself in the past but assumed it was an unfortunate result of the recent pressures he was under. She feared for him, for his peace of mind. She had wrung from him a promise to wait until after the opening night to confront Carlotta. And she made it clear that she, too, wished to be present at that meeting.

Erik seemed to recall suddenly where he was. The company waited, curious to see what he might do. He stared at Meg as if considering something involving her. He was truly perplexed. Then she saw the decision in his eyes. They took on a distanced and severe expression that disquieted her nearly as much as the previous distress.

He looked away from her to the entire stage company. Roving over the myriad people whose work came together to bring about the performance, he included everyone, from Jacopo, whose station on the catwalks had assured no more accidents of a dangerous nature from those heights, to the musicians behind him in the orchestra pit.

Finally he spoke. "It's clear to me that my presence is detrimental to the smooth functioning of the company. Rinaldo will see you through the final dress rehearsal. Perhaps you will find his leadership more pleasant. Everything is here. All one need do is let the music unfold, and all will be well."

The cold falling sensation in Meg's gut nearly forced her from the stage. She tried not to watch Erik walk off toward the wings, but she sensed he had been pushed to the wall. His surrender to Rinaldo was revenge against them all as well as his desperate attempt to escape the untenable situation in which he was trapped. Would he run away from her as well? She was about to slip away to find him when Rinaldo called to her to take center stage and sing with Grimaldo.

Erik would not approve of her coming after him. He would expect her to stay and follow Rinaldo's instructions. Her throat tightened against the music, and the sounds came out strained and alien to her ears.

she had lost him somewhere in the maze of the past days, he had called to her, had told her that he was falling, but she hadn't thought it would be such a precipitous and deep fall, he had told her with his eyes, the tentative touch of his fingers when no one was looking, the parted lips and woeful sigh, he was crashing against the stones at the bottom of his own chasm and the fall might break him this time this time there might not be a way back up, the demons were real this time not just effusions of a wounded spirit, a torn soul, a beaten heart, he had told her to watch out for him and she had turned her head for just a moment, just a brief moment, to smile at the girl in the lime-green tutu, to watch the dancer lift her leg high above her head and grimace from the aching inner thigh muscles rebelling against the unnatural effort, just a moment she had turned to congratulate the tenor on his vibrato, just a moment she had warmed in the appreciative glow of the chorus's approval, she had sung well today, sung with the grace and power and control that he had told her could be hers if she worked for it, the lessons she suffered through at his hand, beneath his steely gaze, under his iron will, the rules of the music, the rules of the voice, the limits of the vocal cords, the subjugation of the diaphragm, the timing of the blood, the blood, the whir of bodily sounds that he said she could harness, the pulse, the pulse that quickened when he drew near, that threatened to stop when he placed his hand, forbidden he should not touch her, not her the virgin, not her the desiring maiden, who lusted for him, who followed after him without shame to the very edge of madness, he put his hand on her diaphragm, his body so close behind her that she wasn't sure he was touching, wasn't sure he wasn't touching her, could imagine him touching her, and wanted him to press more than his hand against her diaphragm, he forced the air from her body, her soul rose through that gasp and begged him to trap it, to keep it forever in a gilded cage, in a scarlet prison, the scarlet prison of his heart, and she sang and just a brief moment she forgot him, her prison, her iron dwelling, her crimson love, and he was gone, and she had lost him somewhere in the maze of music and mayhem, somewhere trapped by the many arms of a past that would not die, she had not meant to look away, not even for that brief moment

Carlotta was perplexed by the turn of events. She was pleased to watch the problems escalate. The company was scared. No one seemed able to avoid the "accidents," and the superstitious ones blamed their ill fortune on Erik. She had laughed to see several of the silly chits cross themselves behind Erik's back when he passed. Recently one of the supporting singers, a soprano with a promising career, had withdrawn from the production. Rumors were that threatening notes foretelling dire events if she appeared in the production had shown up among her make-up and costumes, and a dead cat had been left in her wardrobe. Quite effective, thought Carlotta, perhaps Rinaldo was worth the sum she'd given him after all. Erik was forced to give try outs to several promising young women in the chorus and finally selected a replacement. Of course, this new girl had two days to memorize her part before opening night. It would be a miracle if she made it through without mishap.

Then there were the costumes that had to be replaced or repaired. Erik installed new locks on all the rooms, keeping the key himself and giving the doorman the only copy with instructions not to let it out of his sight.

The entire company was ill at ease, and most had lost confidence in Erik's ability to stem the destruction.

She should be so delighted, and she was. Truly she was. Yet there was a small corner of her heart that longed to see the production staged. The music, much to her surprise, was enchanting. After watching and listening to the rehearsals she had come to love the arias, the story, the duets, the overture, everything about the opera. It would, under ordinary circumstances, be a success, except that she'd done all she could to turn it into a debacle.

She had to admit that the Phantom was a remarkable musician, a unique composer. She could even admire his talent as director except that he was too rigid and too demanding with the cast. So she was surprised at today's turn of events. It was not very like him to walk off, defeated, to surrender his kingdom to a novice like Rinaldo.

The company was slowly switching their attention to Rinaldo, and Meg was singing the duet again with the tenor. Erik had disappeared. Carlotta listened for a few moments, but she was unable to sit still. Her thoughts kept returning to Erik, the way he pressed the palm of his hand against the stark white weave of his mask, his still body as he resigned his role as director before a hostile audience.

She was more and more convinced that he knew she was behind his problems. Whether or not he had guessed her true identity was unclear, but she saw in his eyes a wariness, a watchfulness not there before. He had no idea how she was orchestrating these nuisances. She was sure he didn't suspect Rinaldo or he'd not have left the show in his hands.

eyes, their eyes, their dead eyes threatened to drill behind his eyes, into his brain, digging and digging deep into the bloody matter, eyes without lids and ragged, sharpened teeth amassed on the stage and he held his mask firmly to his face, they must not see him, they must not, they should turn away, close their lidless eyes, put out the light, put out the light, darkness, cool and velvet falling over his burning skin like snow on moonless nights, what had seemed night no longer seemed so, then sounds had risen as if from one soul, his, now the ragged, jagged teeth, sharp, thick tongues spit out his blood, bite into his flesh and rip it from the bone and spew it out, music, notes chewed and spilling forth upon the stage, the blood seeps through the planks, limp and dying, his music, his children, his creations, unable to lift them in his arms, his children bleeding, crying in the dirt, the eyes stare without pity, without understanding, with hunger, with hunger and hate

The last person Erik expected to see at his door was Signorina Venedetti. She stood in the doorway as if posing for a painting, her head slightly tilted to one side, her hand gracefully poised at her breast, in the other a fan of rose and powder blue, partially closed and resting at the base of her neck against the swell of her bosom. Her powder blue veil edged in pink came just to the curve of her upper lip leaving her sensuous full mouth exposed.

How could he have not recognized her immediately?

Because he had thought he was safe. Because he had thought he had escaped. Because he had believed in hope.

He stood silent and expectant just inside the room, his hand still on the door as if he might indeed shut it in her face. So as not to give him such an opportunity, Carlotta stepped over the threshold. Since Erik didn't move aside, she brushed against him as she went to one of the chairs near the piano.

He remained still for a moment longer, his back to her. He could hear the swish of her skirts as she sat and knew she meant to stay. He left the door open and slowly turned to address her. He had to clench his fists against the desire to rush over and shake her. He wanted to rip the veil from her face and demand that she explain her purpose, make clear her plans, tell him what she would have of him!

But then what would she say? Would it be easier to know she wanted his failure, perhaps even his death?

"Signorina Venedetti?" He feared to say more.

She studied him. She should not have sat so quickly. He towered over her, and she felt vulnerable sitting as he approached. The sensation was not completely unpleasant, but she needed to be in control. To disguise her unease, not to mention the tingling sensation that coursed along her body even as she thought she hated him, she shifted slightly in her seat toward the desk, at an angle to Erik, and opened her fan completely to wave gently before her face.

"Signore Costanzi, I was surprised that you walked off leaving the production in the hands of an inexperienced young man." She carefully kept her voice low and sultry.

His eyes bore into her, and she felt her face flush with red swollen heat.

"Inexperienced?" Erik asked with meaning, but she pretended not to notice the sarcasm. "He fashions himself a composer, among other things. He should learn the business thoroughly. Besides all he needs to do is stand there and keep them on task. Everything that needs to be done has been done or it's too late at this point."

Why doesn't he sit down? Or come closer?

"You were very displeased with Signora Costanzi?"

"No, not at all," he answered her gravely.

"Then why the tantrum?"

He couldn't explain to her, not to her, never to her, the pain of standing on that stage when all their eyes were focused—demanding, distrustful—on him. To feel the resentment and the expectations of them all upon him. Their disapproval of his handling of Meg weighed heavy in the air.

"I'm through." He looked away as if embarrassed by his admission. He walked to the piano and sat down on the bench, his back to his guest, his uninvited guest. He softly picked out the melodic line of the overture.

In spite of herself she leaned back against the soft cushion of the chair and closed her eyes as she listened to the theme. He played it simply with a subtle accompaniment. There was nothing amazing about his playing yet the sounds swept over her like a thousand tiny kisses. So delicious she felt, listening to him, the Phantom, play for her. She could sit like this—the Phantom playing only for her, within reach of her hand—and listen to him forever.

"You sing, Signore Costanzi? I should very much like to hear you sing." She hadn't meant to make such a request, but as she sat, her eyes closed, she yearned to hear him. She remembered he had had a beautiful voice, but that was so, so long ago now.

"You wouldn't like my voice," came a breathy whisper that she sensed as if it were a touch.

"Nonsense, I loved it…" she stopped herself. "That is I find your speaking voice so pleasant, so rich, I can't imagine that your singing voice would be anything but lovely."

Erik cleared his throat and sang the first few bars of the lovers' song from the first act. He glanced at Carlotta. He could see her from the side. She lay against the fabric of the chair, her body at rest, the fan forgotten on her lap, her chest rising and falling with the rhythm of the music. She was caught in the wake of its cadence almost as completely as was he. His voice died, dry and brittle in his throat, as he imagined his music trapped inside her, suffocated by her embrace, drowned by her wicked laughter. She wanted it, but she wanted it so she could squeeze it in her fist and let it fall lifeless to the ground.

"What do you want, signorina?" he asked quietly as he continued to play the notes.

She didn't answer.

Erik's fingers quieted and lay still on the keyboard. He rose to go to her. There he knelt. She drew herself up stiffly and stared at him, her body tense.

She knew that if she looked at those eyes—those dark green surfaces—she'd be lost. They were so compelling, and he was so near, nearer than propriety would allow. Here he was—as she had fantasied—on his knees at her feet! His presence, always intimidating even from afar, shimmered with a reality never glimpsed in her daydreams. Real, solid, breathing, a quiet power, a dangerous power. He had held a theater full of dignitaries and nobles in thrall, this…man! He had killed.

He was so quiet, so still, Carlotta imagined she could hear his heartbeat. Or was it only her own? She fell into him, her eyes were on his mouth, full and sensuous lips swollen with meaning, pregnant with intentions. And then his sweet breath, her lips touched his, soft and supple, not hard and biting, as she'd have feared.

Erik drew back from her kiss. The lids of her eyes had closed heavily as she bent in toward him. He had knelt, fascinated by the waves of repulsion and attraction he sensed in her, and when her lips had sealed onto his, he was stunned. The light flick of a pink tongue on his mouth woke him from the spell, and he moved gently away from her.

He could see it in her eyes, the same stunned expression.

"Signorina," he whispered, puzzled by his enemy's touch. He had hoped to find some forgiveness possible. If he begged her for his release? Did she have a woman's soul? He had hoped to find some gentleness in her. He reminded himself that Christ had been betrayed by a kiss!

"Do you love opera, signorina? What do you feel when you hear my music? Does it move you? Or do you despise it?" *As you do me?*

"Quite the contrary. It is…beautiful."

Erik sighed heavily and bent his head. He remained that way for several moments before rising slowly. "I should want to die if I couldn't do this. If there were no music." He couldn't look her in the eye and make this confession.

The resentment and anger welled up unexpectedly in her breast. "Yet you think that would not be the same for anyone else? You think you are the only one who lives for the music?"

She momentarily lost control over her voice. For a second Erik could hear distinctly the Carlotta he had known.

Facing her, he rushed to admit, "No. You're right. If someone were to take my music from me, I would want to see him suffer. I'm sure that would be the same for anyone else who felt as strongly as I do about music."

"Quite," said Carlotta in a low, clipped voice. Recovering her composure, she rose and addressed him in her former concerned whisper. "Well, tomorrow is opening night. Surely everything will go without mishap. It would be terribly sad if the debut were a failure. I daresay, it might be the end of your career."

She swept out of the room.

Erik sank to the piano bench and cradled his face in the palms of his hands.

Erik was puzzled, dazed. He understood anger and revenge. He understood fear and loathing. He didn't understand Carlotta.

Her kiss had burned. It had disturbed him more than her petulant anger, more than her hysteric threats would have. She must be mad!

When Meg came up, almost imperceptibly, behind him, his head was bent over a strange melody he teased from the keyboard. His eyes closed, his ears were turned inside, obeying the sounds as the score unfolded upon the piano. Her fingers raked through the hairs at the back of his neck, and he involuntarily shivered. He grabbed her hand and pulled her forward to sit upon his lap. Pinned between his hardness and that of the wooden keyboard, she surrendered to his kiss.

"I was worried," she said when breathless he released her mouth.

He ran his fingers over her lips and brought the tips to his own in a suggestive gesture that made Meg tighten between her thighs. Instead of kissing her again, which Meg was hoping he would do, he gently lifted her to her feet and rose with her from the piano bench.

"Something had to change. They didn't want me there." He swept emotion from his voice, determined not to confirm her concerns.

"They're all wondering if you're ever coming back."

"No need. They're ready. It will be better without me."

"Erik?"

"Hush, Meg. Let's not talk of it. They're afraid. It's my fault. She wants to destroy me, but she'll destroy them, too, if that's the only way to get to me. She won't let me work, Meg."

"You're not giving in to her, are you?"

"Let it go, Meg. Please." Erik changed the subject. "Besides my absence today may save the company an unfortunate accident tomorrow. Perhaps distancing myself will keep her from doing something to the opening night production." He didn't sound convincing, not even to himself. He paused before continuing, hesitant to tell her but worried that keeping it from her could somehow play into Carlotta's scheme. "She kissed me."

Meg knew exactly whom he meant by his tone. His eyes were intently serious and watchful as she tried to think of a response.

When she remained silent, he added, "I'm as perplexed as you are. I asked her what she wanted."

"And?"

"She didn't or wouldn't answer me. She leaned forward and kissed me. Then she tried to act as if nothing had happened. I can't predict what she might do next."

"You think she might hurt someone?"

"Perhaps. No, not really. I still don't believe she's meant to imperil anyone's life. But…"

"Go on, Erik. I need to know."

"She…she blames me for the end of her career. I think she'll only leave me alone once I give all this up." His hand swept across the room, but it included much more than the theater. It embraced his entire world as a musician. Carlotta had orchestrated their separation. All that was left—short of Erik's life—was his music. He'd never survive without it.

"What can she do? The opera's ready. Opening night is tomorrow. You've managed to pull it together in spite of her attempts to ruin everything. She's lost, Erik. The opera is beautiful, perhaps your best work."

"Don't, Meg. Don't jinx it. She'll do something, I'm sure. She won't let the opera be a success. Somehow she'll do something to stop the production or to ruin it."

"Perhaps you should have confronted her."

"She could ruin me in a thousand ways. All she'd have to do is talk to that reporter, Paolo Ricci. He's already stirred people up with his talk about my mask. I couldn't bear it if they knew who I was, who I had been. I couldn't face anyone if she told Ricci about me, if he published the whole bloody saga. Even if the police couldn't do anything, I'd never be able to show myself in public. I'd have to go into hiding again. And what would happen to you? To the children? You'd be the Phantom's whore! The children would be the monster's seed. I'd go mad, Meg."

She had to grab him firmly by the shoulders to calm him. The panic simmered barely hidden under the surface. He was lost, teetering on an abyss, incapable of seeing his way clear of an imminent and inevitable tragedy. She remembered that look when they had fled Paris, and even before that when he'd gone deeper into the tunnels, seeking obliteration and death, and she had followed him.

"Erik!" She'd not let him spiral down into madness and despair, not again. "We won't let it happen. We'll face her together, after tomorrow night, and ask for her terms. Whatever she demands, we'll find a way to deal with it."

His hands slid up her arms to her neck and cradled her face lovingly. Slowly the panic receded. He focused on her eyes, so large and soft and tender, so full of hope and love. He leaned his forehead to hers and whispered, before taking her lips with his, "My light, Meg, you are my light."

Leroux had no use for masks or disguises. He was not ashamed of who he was. He was one of the righteous. In his person the law was made manifest. He would not hide or distort his face or hang back in the shadows to skulk like a criminal. If the Phantom were to see him, then so be it!

He understood he was on his own. The authorities had laughed in his face in Paris. It would be no different here in Italy. The people here were crazy anyway. They talked too loudly, drank and ate too much, and were always arguing and fighting. They were of no use to him. Of course they had embraced a murderer! What would they care if Leroux told them of the Phantom's history, his crimes? They wanted their opera, their sordid stories of passion and violence. It sickened him to the very bone.

So he walked outside the Teatro dell'Opera once he had tracked down the notices of the strange masked composer and director. He examined the building and watched as people came in and out. Then he followed some of the chorus girls into the back of the building. Immediately he was blinded by the lack of natural light. Inside was a world of nighttime. The ceilings were two to three stories high, cables and ropes hung about like wild vines in a tropical forest, curtains seemed to be hung everywhere and for no purpose other than to create a labyrinth through which the denizens of this immoral world passed. The noises around him were chaotic and distracting until the cacophony quieted. The voice of a man rang through the building with the authority of Jove himself.

It didn't take him more than a moment to recognize that voice! It was *his*— the Phantom's. For years he had heard it in his dreams. He had remembered the monster's voice from those days in which he held the Phantom at his mercy. It had been raised in anger and in pain. It had even whimpered on occasion from the violence it couldn't escape in spite of its foul bargain with the devil. It was his voice! His voice! And it struck Leroux with disgust for it rang out free and strong in this temple to vanity.

He listened to Erik give instructions to the chorus.

He worked his way round to the front hallway and climbed the gilt stairway to the special box seats that rose round the sides of the stage. From inside one of these private chambers, his back braced against the interior wall so that no one could spy him, Leroux stood and watched the rehearsal.

My God! It's him! Although he had always known it, he could not foresee the effect it would have on him to see the Phantom alive. It was as if time had not passed! Erik was speaking with one of the staff. He walked around in broad daylight just like the anonymous letter had said! He had created a new life for himself, one out among the rest of humanity, as if he were one of them. He hadn't aged. Perhaps there were a few wisps of gray about his temple. Perhaps the mask disguised the usual signs of age. But incredibly the Phantom seemed untouched by the passing of time.

Leroux was unaware that he was mumbling under his breath until he saw the puzzled expression on a tall, young man who stepped inside the dark space of the box seat from the passageway just beyond.

"May I help you?" The man had the dark eyes and hair of many Italians. He was quite handsome and dressed elegantly. Obviously he was not one of the workmen on the site, nor did he strike Leroux as one of the performers.

"I was hoping to purchase a ticket for tomorrow night's performance. Someone mentioned that I might pick one up inside." When the young man scowled but didn't respond, Leroux thought to explain his presence in the private box. "I was wandering about and heard the music."

Rinaldo looked suspiciously at the short man. He recognized something odd in the stranger's accent. Meg spoke with a hint of the same accent. Parisian? Rinaldo was certain the man wasn't telling the truth. He glanced in the direction the man had been staring moments before and noticed Erik speaking with Jacopo about the scene changes.

"Rehearsals are closed to the public, signore. You should drop by the ticket office later in the day, after five. I'm afraid I must ask you to leave."

Leroux didn't like the man's tone of voice. It was the same arrogance that he had found among most artists. They thought themselves to be superior to the rest of mankind. They lived their unconventional lives and made fun of men like himself who respected propriety and the law.

"Signore?" Rinaldo gestured for the short man to follow him out into the passageway and toward the exit.

Before he withdrew, Leroux threw one last look toward the Phantom.

Raoul had spent the better part of an hour trying to pick the lock on the stage door when suddenly it came flying open. He stepped back quickly into the shadows before he realized that the person who had come through the doorway was Meg. Before he could react, he was stopped by the strangeness of the situation. It was nearly two o'clock in the morning. What was Meg doing?

He was mistaken to think she was alone. Erik stepped halfway out onto the platform behind her and grabbed her by the hand and pulled her back into an intimate embrace. Erik was barefoot, and his shirt was hanging free from his breeches and unbuttoned. A closer look at Meg showed that her bodice was unevenly buttoned, and her hair had been carelessly gathered. Wisps of blond tresses were falling from the loose chignon. The kiss lasted several heartbeats longer than Raoul had expected.

He might have revealed himself to the two of them except that the embrace was too intimate, and he didn't want to confess he had observed them. When he thought perhaps Erik would urge Meg back inside the theater to continue their tryst, she disengaged herself with a grin on her face and admonished him to go back inside before someone came upon them.

He heard Erik say that he'd watch until she was safely in the coach. Standing half in and half out of the theater, Erik had his back to Raoul. Once Meg climbed into the waiting coach, Erik disappeared inside. At the last moment, Raoul stopped the door from clicking closed with his fingers, waited, and gradually opened it enough to slip inside. Before he ventured farther, he let his eyes adjust to the darkness. He could just make out the white of Erik's shirt as he retreated and finally disappeared at the end of the passageway.

The darkness was thick, and it took several minutes for Raoul to become accustomed enough to make his way safely back toward the offices. He was fairly confident he'd remember the way even though it had been some time since his last visit.

He was on his way down the passageway when an arm circled round his throat and tightened immediately against his windpipe. It cut off his air as well as his ability to cry for help. A hand grabbed one of his arms and tried to twist it sharply behind his back. Raoul reacted automatically with a jab backwards toward his assailant's torso with his elbow. The dull gasp confirmed he had hit his mark. The grip loosened just enough for Raoul to twist out of the other man's hold. But Raoul didn't calculate well his assailant's agility, and when Raoul lifted his fist to strike, he felt the other's fist bury itself deeply in his gut. Raoul doubled over. Two huge fists pounded mercilessly on the broad expanse of his back, forcing him to the floor to his hands and knees.

The light found him gasping to get his breath back. Expecting another blow, Raoul tucked his legs in and rolled to the side. That was when he saw Erik's startled face looking down at him.

"What the devil? Raoul?"

Erik bent and offered his hand to the count who reluctantly accepted the assistance to rise.

"You nearly killed me!" sputtered Raoul.

"It wouldn't be the first time!" growled Erik. "Seriously, I might have hurt you."

"Do you always attack first and ask questions later?" The count rubbed the tenderness where Erik had jammed his arm across his throat.

Erik examined the unusual clothes Raoul wore before he answered. "No one's supposed to be about at this hour. I think *you* have more to explain than I do."

Raoul dusted his work clothes off as if they were an elegant frock coat and trousers and followed Erik back to his office.

"Are you all right?" asked Erik as he poured them each a snifter of brandy and handed one to Raoul.

"You've got a strong arm. Have you been keeping up with the fencing?"

"Not as much as I would like." Erik sipped at his drink and waited for Raoul to explain himself. "Since you left, I don't have a steady partner."

Raoul was pleased to know Erik missed him.

"What are you and Meg up to?"

Erik wasn't wearing his mask. He hadn't expected to run into anyone this late in the theater. The color rose in his face as he realized Raoul must have witnessed his and Meg's leave-taking. That was why he had doubled back and attacked. He had heard the stage door close several moments too late.

"First you," Erik replied curtly. "You're the one trespassing."

"You've got me there," smiled Raoul, trying to set them both at ease. It was going to be hard enough to break the news of Leroux's pursuit to Erik. "I've been trying to find a way to speak with you."

"You might have dropped off your card at the estate or simply walked up and greeted me here during the day."

"I'm glad to know I'm welcome."

"Why the disguise? Why the cloak and dagger?"

Raoul could tell Erik understood that something was wrong. "I take it you haven't received Christine's letter yet?"

Erik rose from the chair alert and worried. "Is she all right? What is it?"

Raoul suppressed a momentary annoyance at Erik's concern for his wife. "Nothing with Christine. It's not we who have the problem. It's you. I've got some disturbing news."

Erik sat back down and gave Raoul his full attention.

"Leroux knows where you are."

For several moments, neither man spoke. Raoul saw that mention of the officer who had supervised the Phantom's arrest and imprisonment had hit Erik hard. He had not expected it. When Erik spoke again, his voice was very soft, almost a whisper. It was not a question. "He's coming for me."

Raoul sighed. "It's worse than that. He's already here."

Erik stiffened but didn't interrupt.

"That's why I'm dressed like this. I've been waiting for him to show himself. I thought it might help if we knew where he was. I believe he's staying in a rooming house by Tivoli Square, next to the fountain.

"Why hasn't he arrested me already?"

"He doesn't intend to arrest you, Erik."

"Oh. I see." Erik frowned. He got up and tossed the remaining brandy from his glass into the fire. The flames blazed and crackled as they vaporized the alcohol. "I'm relieved actually."

Surprised by Erik's reaction, Raoul explained, "He's mad, Erik. He's here for revenge."

"You wouldn't understand."

"Understand what?"

"I myself have unfinished business with the inspector. I can deal with revenge; I can't deal with imprisonment. I'd die before I'd let him take me back to prison."

Raoul avoided Erik's gaze. "He has no official authority here, and his superiors in Paris think him mad."

"Good."

"I don't think you fully appreciate the danger you're in."

"You don't think so? I spent several months as M. Leroux's guest. I think I know better than you what that man's capable of."

Raoul recalled the signs of torture and abuse he had witnessed on Erik's body. His eyes went inadvertently to Erik's once mangled hands. "And what about you, Erik?" He didn't want to ask him about the girl. "What are you capable of?"

The green of Erik's eyes was hard and cold as he looked at the count. The severe expression gave his disfigured face a diabolic cast. Raoul swallowed the last of his brandy and rubbed the glass back and forth between the palms of his hands. Yes, he wasn't sure what Erik was actually capable of. It unsettled him to think it.

"Now it's your turn, Erik," he said when it became obvious Erik was not going to say anything more about the inspector.

"Oh, my," he chuckled, but it was a mirthless sound that made the hairs on the back of Raoul's neck stand at attention. "I had thought we had problems enough until you brought me this little piece of news."

"You and Meg didn't seem to be having any serious problems," Raoul remarked, no longer so worried about having stumbled on Erik and his wife in a passionate embrace.

"There is no escape for the wicked, is there, Raoul?"

Raoul raised an eyebrow at the biblical resonance. Surely Erik didn't refer to himself. Yet, the sardonic expression on his face said it all.

"Then what has happened? Why are you here and Meg at the Costanzi estate?"

"I was so worried about ghosts that I forgot about the living. I have enough living enemies to torment me. I don't suppose it will ever be over. Maybe I don't deserve peace." Erik pulled up a chair and sat facing him. "You're not going to believe this."

When Erik finished telling him about Carlotta Giudicelli and the nuisance she had made of herself, Raoul couldn't help but sit back on the sofa and laugh out loud. Erik smiled indulgently and waited for Raoul to restrain himself.

"You're right to laugh. In comparison to Leroux, Carlotta is but a horsefly. Yet a well placed bite from a horsefly has been known to send an animal into a frenzy and unseat the best of horsemen. Carlotta nearly wrecked my marriage. So Meg and I have pretended that she has succeeded and thereby gained a bit of time."

"What are you going to do?"

Erik's smile was gone. Wearily he let his face fall into his upturned palms. His muffled reply came sadly forth. "I don't know, Raoul. I don't know." After a few moments, Erik lifted his face and continued, "I'll confront her after the opening. I just need to get through tomorrow night."

There was something disturbing about the way Erik had said it, but Raoul couldn't think of what to ask him. He had the strangest feeling that Erik spoke of the opening night as his last night on earth. It was as if it were the one thing he must accomplish. And then what?

"Do you think you'll get her to listen to reason?"

"Carlotta?" he chuckled. "Ironically, she's more likely to listen to reason than Leroux."

Raoul frowned at the point. Indeed, Erik was probably right.

The two men had conversed until nearly three in the morning when Raoul said he should best get back to his room. They decided between them that Raoul would stay in disguise for a while longer. He could help Erik more if Leroux didn't know he was in the city. The count would come to the opening night and watch the performance from a hidden seat near the wings, just at the edge of the stage itself. Don Marcelo, Madeleine, and the veiled Carlotta would enjoy the performance from Box 5, the one Erik traditionally reserved for himself and his family. From his more hidden position, Raoul would be an extra pair of eyes watching and waiting for Leroux to make his presence known.

Erik and Meg had already decided that the children would not be coming. He missed them sorely, having managed to sneak in to see them only a few times in the past week or so, but he would not have them at the theater on opening night. He expected something to happen. He just hoped it wouldn't be too serious.

It might have been their last night together the last night to touch her and to be touched without pain without horror without ugliness the last time for him and the rest of his life ahead perhaps if he were lucky it would be short and the pain would only brush past him briefly ever so briefly his soul protected wrapped in the warm memories of her touch, her touch so gentle ever more gentle than he had known existed how could a woman touch so gently and yet so deeply? for when Meg came to him in spite of his having told her to go home, go home and rest, love, you've sung your heart out today, and you will need your rest, you will need to be strong to raise my son, my sons, my daughter, to face the rest of your life, oh God let it be a long and happy one, let her find let her let her he couldn't think the words but surely the thought rose to heaven on his tears let her yes let her find love again don't let her live dry and lonely and he would not think of it his imagination running wild the soul not so strong, not as strong as he had imagined the anger roaring within at the thought of another man's touch on her, her body her arms her neck touched by another's lips he would banish the thought of that man's touch and cling to last night and her, golden in his arms, the brown mole that sat on the crème landscape of her body, the slope of her throat alive and trembling against the palm of his hand as he stroked her the rise of her bosom that he brushed his cheek against letting his lips taste her and the warm surge of her sigh as he took her again and again in the darkness of his rooms for she was always naughty she was always and always disobedient or she would never have gone down down down to the bowels of the opera house to face a demon to face him in his torment and it must have been destiny that she came when she did and with her spirit for he was a wounded animal licking the bloody stump of a heart he might have harmed her but she touched him with those hands those slight long slender smooth and live fingers and he felt them again last night on his face, along the ridge of his shoulders, down the roughened and scarred skin of his back down and down and down her fingers touched and held him until he quivered in her power last night it might have been for the last time that she accepted him that she pulled him deep deep inside her and held him captive to the humming in her blood until the world vanished into one whirling maelstrom of pleasure and he was pure joy and pure animal and pure soul and pure touch and mindless wanting and fullness the fullness of lying with her his golden angel his light his songbird as he heard her sing her passion to him and in him and it might have been the last time he would ever feel that joy that comfort that healing touch of her love and there would be no more joy, no more no more forever when he walked out tonight onto that stage it would be the end of something the end of him the end of them all for there were crimes to be paid there was retribution and Meg was a moment of paradise to test and taunt him and he must have failed somehow he had tried so hard to live among them he had tried he had but he must have failed she came to him but she had not been able to save him from what had already been, this respite was the moment between a whisper and a sigh and it was filled with happiness but it was too soon over it was over before it began since that moment he killed the man in desperation that had caged him, the man he would still not think of as father, since the moment he lost his soul to obsession, since the moment he destroyed the lives in the Opera Populaire, since those moments he had not been more than a phantom she had touched him and his body took on weight and substance and texture and taste and smell and it was real but only for a time and even though she might wish to hold on to him tightly to keep him real he was fading and had already faded into the shadows he would be the Phantom and the next touch he would feel would raise blood and cut flesh and sear his soul with suffering and last night might have been the last time a gentle touch would soothe him the last time he would touch his love it would wrap him with memories that the pain would try to cut away he must hold to that touch remember her hand on his brow, her lips on his mouth, her legs wrapped round his body sunk deep inside hers hold on to that touch the love the warmth against the fate the world had prepared for him against the dead arms reaching out to drag him down down down

CHAPTER 10

Opening Night

What would he do,
Had he the motive and the cue for passion
That I have? He would drown the stage with tears
And cleave the general ear with horrid speech,
Make mad the guilty and appal the free,
Confound the ignorant, and amaze indeed
The very faculties of eyes and ears.

Shakespeare, Hamlet

Damn Piangi! Hadn't she always sacrificed for him? Didn't she deserve his support now more than ever, now that her plans were coming to fruition? She might have continued her career. Several opera houses, including the Opera National in Paris, would have jumped at the chance to bill her as their leading soprano in those first months and years after the debacle at the Opera Populaire. The Phantom had no appreciation of true talent, mature talent like hers. He'd been swayed like so many foolish men by a young, pretty face with a sweet, but undistinguished, voice. Daaé had lacked her richness, her power, and the Phantom had been a fool!

Now she would see him grovel. Now was her moment of triumph, and she would see his humiliation.

The day she stormed out of the rehearsal and the Phantom's pupil was allowed to replace her had nearly been the worst day of her life. Daaé's success was like a knife in her heart, and she'd never, never, never forgive him! He'd see what it was like to be made a laughing stock. And she'd be there, in his favorite box seat, watching.

She pulled the dark red gloves up tightly over her elbows and placed several large gaudy rings on her fingers. She admired her reflection in the mirror. The gown had a scandalously low cut neck line, and the crimson made her skin glow with a cream and alabaster richness that she loved. The black veil and the red of her generous mouth struck her as deeply erotic and not a little wicked. It was appropriate after all, for she was after blood tonight.

She had destroyed his relationship with Meg. He was alone again, unloved. Tonight she'd take his music and his pride from him. If only she could get that song he'd played out of her mind. She knocked the heel of her hand sharply against her forehead and stamped her feet loudly in frustration. "Get out of my head!" she complained to a tall, dark figure dressed in red, wearing a black mask. Unbidden came the image of him the night he interrupted the Masque Ball at the Opera Populaire. He had appeared, as if by magic, at the top of the grand staircase dressed in crimson, the color of blood, the Red Death, and he had given them all his ultimatum. Such a violent, discordant music had appalled her as they rehearsed the opera he had written and forced upon them all. And yet the opening night she found herself overwhelmed, her palms sweating, her breath coming in shallow, rapid gulps, as she listened to him sing in Piangi's place. She had been hopelessly mesmerized, unable to draw her eyes away from the drama being played out before her on the stage.

This opera had none of the ugly violence of *Don Juan Triumphant*. In its stead there was a deep longing, a beautiful yearning and hope in it that tugged at Carlotta. God if she had been able to sing the part of the lover! Unfortunately, no one would ever hear the arias, the touching duet, the brilliant confrontation scene, none of it. It would all come crashing down moments after the overture. And it would be the last opera he'd ever write and produce. She'd see to that.

She selected a beautiful Valencian fan, black lace and red roses, and unfolded it with a flick of her wrist before the mirror. "Ah! You never understood how dangerous I could be, did you, Phantom?" She froze for a moment and studied herself carefully.

She was still attractive. The young man she had brought back to the apartment the other night had been very appreciative of her generous attributes, her eagerness, and her experience. Better not think of that now, she advised the scarlet woman in the mirror. She had found her passion spiraling out of control when she convinced the man to don the mask she'd taken from Erik's room. The moment he had placed it over his unremarkable beauty, she'd been swept away by a forbidden fantasy she barely realized she'd had.

"It was the power that drove you to distraction!" She told her image in the mirror. *Not the mask!* "And that little thing the ragazzo did so well with his fingers," she added with a sharp laugh that struck even her ears as hollow.

Well if Piangi refused to share her triumph, perhaps she would be better off remaining here in Rome. They'd begun to drift apart over the past several years. She was tired of living for both of them. Endlessly she pushed and cajoled him to get on with life.

"Look at the monster! Eh?" she said out loud as if Piangi could hear her even as far away as Milan. "Did he let a few murders and a fire and an execution keep him down?"

She stuck out her tongue at the woman in the mirror, pivoted on her black satin heels, and left the apartment.

The lords and ladies arriving at the opera house barely glanced in his direction as Piero waited. Furs and diamonds, sparkling tiaras and polished silver and gold buttons, fine tailored suits, crisp creases, silk cravats, an abundance of lace, fingers weighed down with stones of all the colors of the rainbow and necks choked by pearls and strands of gold chains, military colors and family crests. Such finery was distracting, and he considered for a moment brushing up against a couple of marks and lifting a purse or two, cutting a gold watch chain or unlatching a diamond choker.

The little Frenchman would have his hide if he didn't get a ticket for the performance so Piero kept his eye out for the disappointed lover or for the brash entrepreneur who would have an extra ticket to sell at the last minute. Finally he saw an old friend of his standing off to the side and quietly dealing with a dandy. It was Filippo, and he had obviously gotten hold of a few tickets and was making quite a profit on selling them to those who had unfortunately not already purchased a ticket to the gala opening of *La canzone di cuore* with the beautiful Meg Costanzi.

"Salve, Filippo. How many more of those tickets you need to palm off to break even?" If he got the ticket for less money, the Frenchman wouldn't have to know. He could certainly keep the difference.

"Piero, come stai? I haven't seen you since that row over the tailor's daughter. You must have gotten lucky. You aren't singing soprano yet!"

Piero grabbed his trousers in a lewd gesture to prove the point. "No complaints from the ragazza. It's fortunate I ran into you, Filippo. I might need one of those tickets. I could pay you a bit over the price." Piero grabbed several lira from his pocket and counted out a generous amount and pressed it into Filippo's hand before the man could balk.

"Che cosa! Dio, Piero. I can get double that on the street, and you know it."

"The crowds are thinning, my friend. You won't get anything for those pieces of paper once the curtain rises." Sighing histrionically, Piero pocketed the lira and made as if to leave.

"Aspetta, Piero. You're a friend. I can give it to you for half as much again."

Piero acted as if he were searching to see what he might have left. He brought out the original amount and added with a flourish another several coins. Then he pulled out the inside lining of his pocket to prove that he had given Filippo all that he had had.

"Per favore, Filippo. I have a thing for a friendly little cantante del coro. She thinks I'm well to do. I told her I'd be in the audience, watching tonight."

"Va bene." Filippo pulled off the ticket, handed it to Piero, and accepted the lira offered. He counted them rapidly before he pocketed them, tipped his hat, and looked on for other buyers.

Piero was satisfied. He'd made a bit of a profit on the ticket. The Frenchman would be happy to know the seat was in the middle range. Not so bad! He nodded to the shadowy figure across the road. Leroux stepped out from behind the fountain and crossed the street to take his seat among the wealthy patrons of the Teatro dell'Opera.

"Tie my laces, will you?"

"Where did my…?"

"What was the cue again, Margarita?"

"Watch where you put that pin!"

"Bring me the wig. The one over there by the feathers."

"That's my powder! Use your own."

"Ouch! Not so tight. I can't sing if I can't breathe."

"That dress fit her fine a month ago! Mark my words, she won't be here after another month or so."

"I'll be so glad when the first act is over! Look, I'm shaking all over."

"She's been spending time in the prop room with Lorenzo, that's who."

"At least you don't have to wear these shoes. Look at the heels on them."

"Will he marry her?"

"Oh, you look wonderful, signorina! You should always be a shepherdess."

"Help me pull the bodice down more, will you?"

"Pull it any lower and her breasts will explode during the performance."

"Already got a wife, that one does."

"Oh poor girl!"

"How much more time do we have?"

"Did you hear them arguing yesterday? I thought for sure he'd strike her, and she looked as if she were about to spit in his eye!"

"Twenty minutes at least."

"He's totally unreasonable. At the Teatro Argentina, they never start rehearsals before 2:00 p.m. It's barbaric the schedule he's kept us on. Slaves, he thinks we're slaves."

"Wouldn't mind being his slave for a couple of hours."

"I woke up singing the willow song in the middle of the night. Giacomo threatened to kick me out of bed if I didn't let him sleep."

"Well, he knows his craft. You can't say we're unprepared."

"Don't defend him. He thinks all he has to do is whistle and we jump."

"Well, it's true, isn't it?"

"Can I use your brush?"

"He's been sleeping here in the little room off his office. She kicked him out!"

"Good for her! She's the star after all."

"Damn, I broke the button off. Who's got the needle?"

"I'd like to see him up there doing what we have to do night after night."

"Oh my God. I just pictured him in my mind's eye dressed like Margarita!"

"My point is…"

"Oh for God's sake. We all know what your point is! He's impossible."

"But they pay us well."

"It's not *his* money. Don Marcelo's the one with the money."

"He's not like what you think! He gave my sister a job when I asked him to. He acts standoffish, but he's got the nicest eyes. He was real quiet when I asked him if she could come sing in the chorus with us. He didn't even ask to hear her. He took my word for it that she has a lovely voice."

"Your sister? Well I won't say she can't carry a tune, but really, Sophia, she's not an opera singer."

"Where's my other shoe? Has anyone seen it?"

"What color are they, anyway?"

"Is my eye shadow dark enough?"

"Green. As green as you can imagine!"

"I know he's demanding, but when he stands near me I break out in goose flesh all over. If it weren't for that mask, he'd be a…"

"I can't believe you're talking about him like that!"

"Pass me the rouge, please."

"You've got too much on the left eye. Here, let me."

"Well, he's got to have something or Donna Meg wouldn't have married him!"

"I like watching his…"

"Ouch! You're pulling my hair."

"He scares me. His eyes go straight through you. Rinaldo's much nicer."

"Rinaldo, is it?"

"Sig. Jannicelli let all kinds of errors pass the other day. He's nice, but he's too easy."

"Whatever you may say about Don Erik, if he hadn't pushed Fabiana out of the way the other day, she'd be dead now. And he himself almost died in that fall."

"Jacopo said he saved his life. That's why he fell. He pulled Jacopo to safety, but couldn't stop his own fall."

"How is it that he didn't die? Can you tell me that?"

"Any other man would have broken every bone in his body. Don Erik, not a one! Can you explain that?"

"Per favore, move over a little so I can see the mirror."

"There it is! I knew you had it!"

"What would I want with your shoes? They don't even fit. Your feet are as big as a man's!"

"I wouldn't mind him but for the mask. It makes me nervous."

"What do you think he looks like underneath it?"

"Has anyone ever seen him without it?"

"No, and I don't want to!"

"Ten minutes."

"Oh my God, oh my God, oh my God."

"Damn. I've got two left shoes here! Who's got the other one?"

"Where's the party going to be tonight?"

"At Il café di mondo. Don Marcelo has rented the entire place for the evening."

"I'm starved. I haven't eaten since this morning."

"Well don't pass out and land on me. Here, eat this."

"Hunger sharpens the senses."

"Do you think she's really mad at him?"

"If she's not, she's doing a good job of acting like she is. I actually felt a bit sorry for him when he left Rinaldo in charge and walked off."

"I've never seen him that upset before."

"She shouldn't really talk to him like that in front of others."

"Oh really? Is she just supposed to take his orders? Let him push her around?"

"He is the artistic director and the…"

"And what is it with that Venedetti woman? She walks around like she owns the theater."

"I think she has something to do with the row between Don Erik and…"

"Ladies, take your places. Curtain rises in ten minutes."

"Get off my hem! I nearly fell on my face!"

The audience hummed like a hive of unsettled bees. Flashing their colors, waving their feathers and fans, they flowed through the aisles and into their seats, craning necks to see and be seen. Hundreds of voices rumbled through the amphitheater, programs cracked, bodies shifted on leather and brocade cushions.

Behind the curtain, the staff set the props and checked and rechecked the pulleys. Slowly chorus and principals took their places on the stage. Nervous laughter punctuated the tap of heels on wood, soles of boots scraped, throats coughing and clearing the way for the notes. In the pit the woodwinds, strings, and percussion blew, vibrated, and clanged in a jumble of apparently meaningless sounds as the musicians readied their instruments. The reiteration and swell of a crystalline A became the shore against which all other sounds broke and merged.

"Jacopo, be sure you're up on the catwalk at all times. No one but you and those you trust."

"Sí, Don Erik. You can count on me."

"You examined the winches? The ropes are in good condition? You put in the extra lines?"

Jacopo vouched for all the gear, and only those workers who had been with him for several seasons would be up above the stage to guarantee that the backdrops were safely maneuvered into and out of place during the performance.

"Don Erik, rest assured. Everything's ready. You should join your guests and enjoy the performance."

Erik gave the man one more inquiring look but knew everything that could be done had been done to avoid problems. Jacopo had worked closely with Erik to simplify and limit the variations as much as possible without stripping the stage bare. They had installed extra supports, reinforced beams, replaced cables.

"Jacopo?"

"Yes, signore?"

"I want to thank you for all the work you've ever done for me."

Jacopo was surprised by the gravity with which Sig. Costanzi spoke. It was not said lightly. He had never been an effusive man. Indeed Jacopo liked the fact that Sig. Costanzi expected good work and took it for granted from those who were part of the company. It was a matter of respect.

"No need to thank me, Don Erik. It's been an honor to work with you."

Erik paused and considered the man for a moment. "Then let it begin. I'll leave it to you, Don Jacopo."

Erik walked down the narrow passageway toward the backstage dressing rooms. A steady flow of men and women was pouring out toward the stage. He waited for a lull and then slipped quietly, unobserved, into Meg's dressing room.

She was putting on the final touches of her make up. She smiled at his reflection in her mirror before rising and stepping toward him.

He would have liked to embrace her, but she was already in her costume. He didn't wish to spoil her efforts. She looked beautiful, amazing, almost magical. But Meg seemed not to care whether he mussed her hair or wrinkled the taffeta of her gown. She strung her fingers together around his back, hugging him tightly, and kissed him. Her lipstick left a rich red smear on his mouth, and she giggled at the mess as she wiped his mouth with her handkerchief.

He grabbed her hand before she could withdraw it and removed the handkerchief. He closed his fist on its softness and put it into his pocket. Then he raised her hand to his lips and kissed the soft and sensitive palm. He lingered in the warmth of her touch, his eyes closed, his mind resting, thinking of what might happen, what might be lost.

"Are you prepared?" he asked.

"Yes, I think so."

He saw the glow soften her honey brown eyes, felt her smile draw his own lips into a soft grin in spite of the dread and sadness that gnawed at him. How he loved her! How she moved him, brought out the deepest tenderness in him, a quiet, a stillness that healed and blessed.

"Meg, I love you." He wanted to say it as if he had never said it before, to make it seem as if it were the first time again that he had sworn himself to her.

She smiled and started to kiss him again, but he held her back for there were things he needed to say. "I have so much to thank you for. If not for you, I'd have died then, in that underworld. I know that. I had no reason to live and every reason to die. Instead you made me live. You gave me a life. It's been a sweet life, full of love and passion the likes of which I had never thought possible…for me."

"Erik?" She frowned in worry. "You're scaring me. Why are you saying these things to me now?"

He tried to smile to allay her fears. "No reason, my love. I should have told you last night. That was the moment for intimate confessions, was it not?" He would not tell her about Leroux, not moments before the performance. There was nothing she could do. Whatever happened, it was between him and the inspector. Leroux wouldn't harm innocent bystanders. But if Leroux were to attack, if things didn't go well tonight, Erik needed Meg to know how he felt. He might not ever have another chance to tell her what he deeply held inside.

"Last night was…wonderful, Erik. But tonight will be even better." She had decided that tonight, after the performance, she would share her news with him. "And then tomorrow we'll face Carlotta together." They were a family. Carlotta would have to be made to see reason. She couldn't destroy what they had struggled for and built over the past years.

Erik didn't wish to lie, but he had no intention of letting Meg accompany him when he stood before Carlotta. He'd confront her wrath alone. No one but he was responsible for the past. He kissed Meg softly on the forehead, almost a fatherly gesture, almost a benediction. Before she could say anything more, before she could see the yearning, the building wave of grief, the heavy resignation that weighed him down, Erik slipped out of the dressing room.

Slowly he made his way to the wings from which he'd watch the performance. He'd keep vigil from the dark passageway. Here he'd mourn the passing of this life.

"Don Erik, there's a gentleman who says you're expecting him?"

"Yes, take him to the side box over the pit."

"Yes, signore."

The lights were ready. The audience rumbled in anticipation, a rising and falling tide against the shore. Any moment and the orchestra would play the first notes of the overture and the performance would begin.

Grimaldo's room is around here somewhere. Yes, here it is!

The sound of another door opening startled her, and she retreated to the shadows of an alcove and waited for the person to leave. The footsteps receded down the corridor in the opposite direction, away from her and toward the wings. Carefully she poked her head around the corner to catch a last glimpse of Erik as he disappeared.

What were you doing backstage? She glanced at the series of doors. Besides the storage room, prop room, and Grimaldo's room, there was another dressing room. These were reserved for the principals. They were more private and quieter than those belonging to the chorus. She scowled to see that the only possible answer to her question was that he'd been in Meg's room. She leaned against the door, her ear to the wood, to listen for tears or angry ranting, any indication that Erik's visit had been unwelcome. Nothing but the soft sounds of rustling of skirts and soft footpads as Meg managed her last minute preparations.

So, you both are playing me for a fool! It is a game, eh? Or you've made up since yesterday?

She forced her jaw to relax. She had been grinding her teeth together in frustration. She wanted the Phantom and his whore separated, alone in their anger. They must not be together. He would be alone, abandoned, forsaken, destitute. She would find a way to come between them.

Once the opera fails, Meg will be less enamored of her monster!

Carlotta rapped softly on Grimaldo's door.

"Sí?"

"Don Grimaldo? I wish a moment of your time before the performance."

The tenor stood expectantly in the doorway. Signorina Venedetti, dressed in a seductive crimson gown, her head tilted coquettishly, held up a bottle of champagne and two glasses in her hand and smiled meaningfully at the man.

"A toast? Someone has left this bottle beside your door!"

"Please, signorina. Come in."

Raoul straightened his waistcoat, relieved to be dressed in his usual attire. Having warned Erik of Leroux's presence, he could forgo the disguise, donning it once again should he need to return to the inn.

The count leaned out over the edge of the private box seat. He was practically on a level with the stage and quite invisible to the audience. Even so, he had an unobstructed view of the ground floor and two thirds of the boxed seats and balcony in a sweep before him. Only those directly above and to his immediate left were outside his range of vision. Across the expanse on the opposite side of the stage, he saw movement in the box reserved for Erik's family and guests. Light flooded in as the door in the back of the dark interior opened permitting Don Marcelo and his guests to enter.

The count was curious to see the veiled lady dressed in an enticingly daring crimson grown edged in black make her appearance. Disregarding the peculiar looks given by Don Marcelo and Madeleine, she took the best seat in the box and sat down. Raoul momentarily turned his attention to the amphitheater, scanning the audience, when the entrance of a fourth, and unexpected, guest caught his eye. Don Marcelo held a seat for the young woman. Raoul nearly stood and shouted when he recognized his wife. She gracefully sat next to Madeleine and smiled in eager anticipation toward the center of the stage. Damn her for her stubbornness! Why wouldn't she stay put?

The first notes of the overture swept over them all, and the crowd immediately hushed. Raoul glared at Christine, despite knowing she'd not be able to make out his figure, he was so well hidden in Erik's special box. The crowd's faces were indistinguishable in the half light, but something told Raoul that Leroux had to be out there somewhere. How could the inspector bear to miss this opportunity to catch sight of his ghost?

The music swelled toward a hauntingly beautiful peak and just as suddenly stopped. Raoul jerked his attention to the orchestra pit over which his seat was suspended. He looked down into chaos. The maestro frantically fingered the score, flipping through page after page of the music. The musicians rested their instruments and stared from one to another. They, too, seemed obsessed with searching through the pages of the sheet music. Over the shoulder of a cellist, Raoul saw the reason for the confusion. Sheet after sheet of the staff paper was empty. The notes, the score, the music simply had disappeared!

"Get out of my way!" snarled Erik as he marched quickly toward the pit. In a glance he understood the problem. He frowned at the maestro in angry amazement, for one moment thinking that he had somehow meant to ruin the performance. Quickly the thought was dispelled. The maestro was appalled and baffled. The first three pages of the score were as they were meant to be. But once the maestro and the musicians turned to the fourth page, they were met with blank paper. The sheets had been loosely bound, and Erik could see that they had all been clumsily disassembled and reassembled. Someone had taken the score apart, leaving only the first three pages to give the impression that the score was complete. It must have been done between the previous afternoon, when Erik had abandoned the stage, and this evening's performance.

"Why did you stop?" he demanded of the maestro who flustered lifted his shoulders in a mute reply. "You know the damn music! They know it! Play the damn thing!"

"I can't. I can't direct such a complex piece without the score, Don Erik. I'm sorry." The regret and embarrassment on the older man's face reined in Erik's desire to snap at him. Perhaps he was right. It would take the merest miscalculation and the whole complex weave of counterpoint and balance would fall like a house of cards around them. What would be music would spiral down into cacophony, the worst of barnyard braying would not equal it for its ugliness. It was a true work of architectural beauty the opera he had written, but it was as delicate as an angel's sigh.

Erik didn't have to be told that Rinaldo had come down the stairs into the pit and was waiting behind him. He gritted his teeth to keep himself from attacking the young man both verbally and physically. Instead he whirled around and faced his assistant, eye to eye. And it was a terrible look that Rinaldo had to suffer! He knew. They both knew.

Even as he addressed the maestro, Erik stared at Rinaldo as if his words were truly meant for the young betrayer. He explained, his voice sharp and firm, "The performance will continue, maestro. I have secreted away a copy of the opera. Not even my bold assistant knew of its existence."

Rinaldo turned deathly pale. He held himself tense to avoid the trembling that threatened his knees. To his credit, he didn't look away from Erik's glare. He deserved to feel its heat.

Close to Rinaldo, Erik whispered, "I had much time on my hands when Meg banished me from her bed! I spent a good deal of it copying note for note the entire opera. A kind of insurance against disaster and wild thoughts. You will find it behind the Botticelli in the adjoining room. The key is under the bust of Mozart. I suppose I can trust you to bring it to me?"

Erik's breath was hot on Rinaldo's cheek. The scent of mint and fennel seemed incongruous to the young man who imagined in his mind the smell of charcoal and sulfur. He managed to nod his head, incapable of ungluing his tongue from the roof of his mouth. Shame was not a familiar companion to Rinaldo, but he understood that it would be a long time before he would be able to shuffle off this new sensation.

Erik watched the young Italian hasten toward the backstage. He saw one of the stage assistants above and motioned for him to bend down. "Tell the audience that after a brief pause of, say, five minutes, the performance will recommence. Be sure everyone is on their mark."

As the man stood to face the audience, Meg peeked out from the wings. Erik waved her back in spite of the concern he saw in her expression. He had no time to explain now. He turned his attention back to the silent musicians.

"You will be able to do it if you have the score? And the rest of you? Can you follow the maestro without the music? Have you committed it to memory as I demanded?"

He saw mostly agreement on their faces, yet one or two writhed uncomfortably in their seats. "Anyone who cannot perform under these circumstances had better say so now. You are free to leave. There will be no recriminations, and once the scores can be copied, you will be welcomed back."

A second violinist and one man on the flute slowly rose and began to pack their instruments. Erik's heart sank for a moment, fearing a mass exodus, but no one else moved. He waited until the two musicians vacated the pit, and he bowed his head just once to those who stayed. "I am pleased to know that you welcome the challenge."

The audience was fast losing its patience. The normal hum of voices carried an edge of worry and annoyance that threatened to unnerve everyone. Erik needed the performers to be steady and confident. Rinaldo should have returned by now! Unintentionally, he looked around, and his eyes collided with a vision in red. Carlotta's veil did little to disguise the delight she was feeling at his dilemma. She sat eagerly forward, and her body told him that she was staring down directly at him and at him alone. He cursed under his breath, but then he was sharply distracted by the familiar face and figure of another in the box. He realized to his dismay that Christine was sitting next to Madeleine at the opposite end of the box. As always her presence unsettled him. He willed himself not to look again at Carlotta, for she surely noticed his surprise and the object of it, and he did not wish to see her gloat over him. He directed his eyes back toward the wings, waiting, waiting, as the crowd became more incensed and bewildered, waiting for Rinaldo to pull the knife from his back. Just as Erik thought he might have to admit defeat, he saw the man coming purposefully forward, the leather bound scroll tightly held in his hands.

Wordlessly Rinaldo handed the scroll to Erik who did not hesitate to take it and set it on the podium before the maestro. He nodded to the stage assistant who understood immediately the signal to begin. The maestro crossed himself as if in prayer, raised the baton, and took charge of the orchestra. The overture rose like vapor on a morning lake. At first the audience was unaware that it had begun, but as it permeated the space about them, it seemed to charm them into silence.

Erik eased his way around the musicians and returned to the wings from which he could observe the performance and the audience. Against his better instincts, he risked glancing over to his private box at Carlotta. He expected to see his tormentor frustrated, fanning herself petulantly in annoyance that he had foiled her plan. Her calm regard struck him hard, like a physical blow, carving away at his but newly restored confidence. She didn't seem in the least disappointed. The nagging suspicion that there were other pitfalls to come clasped onto him, making it difficult for him to breathe.

The overture was ending. The curtain on cue fell away and revealed a woodland stream. An abundance of trees and vines graced the stage. Along the front of the proscenium strategically placed mirrors lay across the stage floor, and the fluttering ribbons of light blue and white silk cloth gave the illusion of a running stream in the forest. The chorus of women were huddled round with baskets of clothing to wash in the stream. Several draped their wet garments across the low bushes, across branches of the trees. Meg, dressed like a princess, walked arm in arm with a country lass.

Erik didn't realize he was holding his breath until Meg sang her first note and he finally exhaled. She sang a song about the simplicity of life among the common women and the desire to be one of them. She was to be married to a man she didn't love in order to end a war between her nation and a neighboring country of warlike people. Her notes took up the simple melodic line of the chorus and wove it into a complex and elegant song like the ripples across the stream itself. The chorus continued to anchor her to the setting, to the original folk song they sang as they worked, but for the princess the song became, inevitably more elaborate, tinged with sadness and longing, awareness that there was to be a loss of innocence—indeed the intuition that innocence was already lost.

Meg's companion offers to exchange roles with her for the afternoon, and the two women playfully run off stage and return in each other's costumes. Meg now sings the song of the washer women, but even though she sings as if she were one of them, the notes tease and resist the pull of conformity, creating delightful surprises and counterpoints. The friend wanders offstage with her swain to pretend at other games while Meg waits by the stream washing the sheets. Slowly the chorus retreats leaving her alone to sing her aria.

Erik was vaguely aware of the wrangler and several assistants helping the tenor, Grimaldo, onto the great white gelding for his martial entrance.

Unbeknownst to Elene, Meg's character, this handsome man was her intended, a powerful leader of his nation. He wished to travel the land of his bride's king-dom and to find out what he might of her before they married.

Evidently the staff was having some difficulty getting Grimaldo onto his mount. Just as Erik thought perhaps there was a serious problem, the gelding was led forward, and Grimaldo rode out onto the stage. The audience expressed their delight at the dramatic touch. Caspiano was a good horse, a very gentle one in spite of his proud stance. Erik was momentarily distracted from the stage and looked up at the box where his guests were seated. Carlotta leaned so far forward over the varnished banister of the box that she seemed poised to spring to the stage. The sound of a collective gasp from the audience and the heavy thud on wood brought Erik's attention back to the performance where he saw to his horror Grimaldo lying prone on the stage floor. Caspiano neighed in contempt at the man who had spoiled his effect by tumbling out of the sad-dle. Meg bent concernedly over the man's body.

Erik grabbed the stage manager by the sleeve and sent him for the doctor. Seeing no one else at hand, he pushed Rinaldo out to calm the audience and ask for their patience yet again. He signaled in the next moment for the curtain to be lowered and ran out onto the stage himself.

"What happened?" he asked Meg.

"He was swaying in the saddle, and then he toppled over."

Erik called back to the stage hands in the wings. "Did you notice anything?"

"He seemed…well…a bit tipsy, Don Erik."

It wasn't like Grimaldo to drink to excess before a performance. He was a professional. He might take a drink for courage, to calm his nerves, but not more than the one. Erik examined the man. He was out stone cold.

The doctor verified Erik's worst fears. Grimaldo was not going to come to in the next few minutes, perhaps not for several hours. "He's either very drunk or drugged."

Erik had several of the stage hands come forward. "Take him to his room. Find someone to stay with him."

In the wings, Rinaldo stood nervously watching Erik deal with the crisis.

Erik softly led Meg to the side and asked, "Are you all right?"

"I'm fine," she assured him.

"Did you have anything to drink before the performance? Did you accept anything from Rinaldo?"

Meg's eyes opened in surprise. "You don't think he's capable of…? Of course, you do. No. He's not had the nerve to approach me recently."

Erik sighed in relief. "Good. Good," he said with even more feeling. "If he'd done anything…I'd kill him and her, too!"

Meg squeezed Erik's arm tightly and whispered, "You must not think that way!"

Erik swallowed his reply, but Meg could see he was unrepentant.

The maestro and several of the assistants came forward all talking at once. Erik simply shook his head at their questions.

"What happened?"

"Is Don Grimaldo all right? Will he sing?"

"No, Grimaldo won't be back."

"He'll be fine in the morning."

"What should we tell the audience?"

"I've never been in such a situation."

"Are we going to proceed or do we cancel?"

"Cancel a performance at this point?"

"Someone should tell them that the performance will continue. They're becoming impatient."

"But how can we continue? How?"

"His understudy."

"Grimaldo's understudy, is he prepared to go on?"

"Find him and get him into costume immediately. Tell the audience we'll…"

"But he's not here."

"Where is he? What the hell do you mean he's not here?"

"Who is the understudy?"

"Bartolo."

"Yes, that's right. But where is he? Why isn't he here?"

"One of the chorines said he didn't show up today. Sent word that he was ill."

"That's it! There's no one to do it. We'll have to cancel."

"No." The roar silenced the cacophony of voices. Those present on the stage turned, as one, to face Don Erik.

"But, Signore Costanzi, be reasonable!" said Sig. Bianchi. "We've lost our lead tenor. Surely…"

"I won't cancel. I won't. It's my last…I won't. The opera will continue."

Meg's voice was by contrast quiet. She spoke to only one man, but something she said demanded the others' attention. "You're the only one who can do it."

Erik's shoulders stiffened as he stared down at his wife's upturned face. "I can't," he protested, pushing the words through gritted teeth.

Eagerly, the maestro took his place next to Meg and urged, "Don Erik, you have a wonderful voice. We can make some minor adjustments. You're not a true tenor."

Erik grimaced. He was appalled at the suggestion. "Don't be absurd. The two of you are mad! I'm the composer. I'm not a performer."

Meg winced at his choice of words. She knew the images such words evoked, images of a night of tragedy, of fire and madness. And perhaps behind that memory hid another more distant of a small child locked behind bars. She studied her husband. She saw him fighting to push the thoughts from his mind.

"You once took the stage, Erik." She knew her words pained him. She was asking him to risk everything.

"You know what happened that night, Meg," he whispered as if only she could hear him. "The world fell into a thousand pieces, and we're still paying for it now."

Meg reached out and touched the smooth white surface of his mask as the rumble of past memories drowned the voices around them.

"Erik, this has nothing to do with that night."

"Oh, doesn't it?"

Meg hesitated, then insisted, "You can do it."

Carlotta had not been able to restrain herself. She had to see his face! She excused herself from the box and found her way to the backstage. No one stopped her. She had enjoyed access to the entire theater since the beginning of her patronage. As she came around the corner and approached the back of the stage, she could overhear the conversation among them. Huddled around the figures of Meg and Erik were various members of the company. Carlotta immediately pulled back into the relative invisibility of the wings to listen to them.

Meg's voice quieted the others. She spoke solely to him—to the Phantom. *Take the stage?* Carlotta was, at first, stunned by Meg's suggestion, but quickly she realized that it made perfect sense. What a delicious prospect, too delicious to pass up. The chance to see the Phantom on the stage thrilled Carlotta. She remembered the scene of *Don Juan Triumphant* when he sang the duet with Daaé. Carlotta had never heard any voice as charged with passion or as darkly sensuous as his voice that night when he stole into Piangi's role. He who only faced the world from behind a mask had performed his seduction in front of hundreds of the most important people in Paris. It had been incredible. Yet she perceived now Erik's resistance to the notion of taking the stage. His hesitation actually touched her. And to think that his former protégée even now waited among the audience for his performance, the Daaé woman whose career had once been so promising, the woman for whom the Phantom had killed and killed for naught. *Over a puny-voiced upstart with less talent in her entire body than I, Carlotta Giudicelli, have in my little finger alone!* What shame must torment the Phantom to have to step out onto the stage and risk failure. Again.

This opportunity could not be missed.

Carlotta brazenly approached the Phantom from the side and intruded. "Signore Costanzi, forgive me for interrupting." She saw out of the corner of her eye the animosity on Meg's face. *Yes, they know who I am.* "I have heard you once on stage. You can do it."

The general murmurs of agreement and relief rushed over the men, but Erik was deadly silent as he searched Carlotta's eyes.

"But won't you have to take off the mask?" she added, incapable of retracting her claws completely.

"No! I won't remove my mask, and you damn well know why, Carlotta!" Erik would pretend no longer.

Carlotta's eyes flashed at the challenge. Arching her eyebrow, she gave him a sardonic smile. "Well, I suppose this might be interesting." With that, she turned—knowing that all eyes were upon her—and walked off the stage.

Erik waited for the red skirt to disappear completely from view before he dragged Meg aside and spoke in a mad panic to her. "You are to keep your distance from me, Meg. Do you hear?"

"Why?"

"I can't help but worry that this, too, is part of Carlotta's plan. I don't want you anywhere near me in case…"

"But Erik, we're lovers. I can't kiss you from across the stage, you know. Besides what more can Carlotta do?"

Of course he was no longer concerned about what Carlotta might or might not do. It was Leroux that concerned him. Raoul had said that the man was mad. If the inspector lashed out at him and harmed…? Surely he would not take the risk and squander the chance to catch his prey. No, thought Erik, it was much more likely that Leroux would bide his time until he could find Erik alone.

"Erik, is there something…?"

"No. Just please keep some distance. Do it, Meg, just to humor me."

Before she could argue, Erik urged her back to her spot on the stage. "Go. I'll do my best to find something appropriate in the wardrobe."

While the audience waited, Raoul made his way round the corridor past the front of the theater and to the opposite side. A few of the audience had risen in search of the water closet, but most kept their seats expecting any moment for the opera to begin.

The door to Box 5 was not locked, and Raoul had seen Carlotta leave just moments before. Quietly he opened the door and entered.

Madeleine gasped as she saw the dark-haired man approach from behind. Don Marcelo stood and sternly addressed him, "Signore, may I help you? This is a private box."

"Don Marcelo." Raoul bowed his head in greetings. Only then did Christine rise and come to him.

"Where have you been?" she scolded.

"Where have I…? I believe, my dear, that there are questions that I have that you must answer before you cross-examine me!"

Madeleine and Don Marcelo whispered softly as they watched Raoul and Christine.

"I hardly recognized you, my dear boy." Don Marcelo interrupted the count and countess.

Raoul had overlooked the fact that he had not been able to wash the dye from his hair. It had been sufficient to make his appearance strange. He turned to his hosts and replied tersely, "I can't explain at this moment, Don Marcelo. Time is of the essence. Hasn't Christine told you anything?"

"I thought it best to speak with Meg first," interrupted Christine. "She'd already left for the theater when I arrived."

"What is it?" asked Madeleine suddenly on her guard.

"Madame, I came to warn you." Raoul was not as patient with his wife as he had been with their hosts. "I told you to write a letter, but I expected you to remain safe at home."

"I did."

"It must have gone astray. Erik had no idea." Exasperated, Raoul released the tight grip he had on Christine's upper arm. If Don Marcelo and Madeleine had not been present, he would have demonstrated to his wife how much he had missed her as well as how frustrated he was with her. "It's more complicated here than we had thought, Christine."

"Excuse me, Count, does Erik know you're here?"

"Yes, Don Marcelo. I came because he's in danger." The look that passed between Madeleine and Don Marcelo suggested that they were already aware that something was awry. "I'm afraid that you've no idea how serious the situation actually is. It's not Venedetti that poses the greatest threat."

"What exactly do you know about this woman?" asked Don Marcelo.

"She's not what she seems. Erik and Meg know who she is." Raoul glanced at Christine out of the corner of his eye. It would be an unpleasant surprise for her. "The signorina is, in fact, Carlotta Giudicelli."

Don Marcelo recalled the name, but he was at a loss as to its significance in this case. Madeleine and Christine, however, knew the name well, and they also knew Carlotta's nature and why she would be a serious enemy.

"Meg hinted that she knew something about the woman, but she wouldn't say what," said Madeleine. She took Christine's hand and squeezed it when she saw how pale the young woman had grown. "I only understood that the witch was out to ruin everything. It all makes so much more sense—the accidents, the spitefulness, the overdone histrionics."

"She's an annoyance compared to the real threat. Leroux has tracked Erik down. He knows."

When she heard the name, Madeleine turned a ghostly white and collapsed heavily onto the chair. Her eyes darted over the auditorium as if to search out the inspector among the crowd. "He's here?" Her voice was thin and high in her throat. Don Marcelo went to her and placed his hand on her shoulder.

"I must go," said Raoul. "Christine, can you explain?"

Raoul waited for his wife to answer. She was obviously still reeling from the news that Carlotta had been sitting just a few inches away from her, watching as the production was dealt one blow after another. She gave a brief nod to assure her husband that she was recovered and turned to speak with Don Marcelo and Madeleine. Raoul stepped out into the gallery.

The count considered going backstage to see what was happening with the performance, but he wouldn't be of much help there. Just as he decided to trace his path and return to his special seat, he caught sight of Carlotta coming toward the box. Quickly he ducked out through one of the lateral exits until he saw her slip inside and shut the door behind her.

Changing his mind, he continued in the direction from which Carlotta had just come and found himself in the wings on the opposite side of the theater. The artists were returning to their marks as if preparing to start the scene again. Erik was nowhere to be seen. Rinaldo, across the space of the stage, off in the wings, leaned heavily against one of the walls. In a worried gesture he rubbed compulsively at his forehead and looked behind him toward the dressing rooms and forward to the stage. When he seemed to come to a decision, he turned his back on the performers and headed toward the dressing rooms. Raoul circled quickly around the other way, meaning to coincide eventually in the area of the rooms with the young Italian and perhaps to find Erik as well.

As Raoul had suspected, the young man came to an abrupt stop by Erik's office. Rinaldo knocked softly on the door and waited. When no one answered, he opened it and stepped inside. Within moments, he came out, a puzzled expression on his face. Raoul had just enough time to slip back in the doorway of one of the prop rooms before he saw Rinaldo knock at Grimaldo's door. Erik's voice answered impatiently telling him to go away.

"Would you like some help, Don Erik?" Rinaldo's voice was confident, but Raoul could see his troubled face.

After an uncomfortable pause, Erik himself opened the door and glared at the man.

Rinaldo's face turned a violent red. "You have every right…"

"Don't say anything now. Not now. We'll deal with this later. Go take my place in the wings."

Erik closed the door in the young man's face. Rinaldo took a deep breath to steady himself and walked back toward the stage.

Raoul waited for the young man to turn the corner and disappear before he moved from his hiding place. The count knocked quickly on the dressing room door. Without waiting for a response, he opened it and stepped inside.

Before the intruder could turn, Erik pushed him hard against the wall, his arm wedged under the man's chin and against his throat. The moment he realized it was Raoul, he released his hold.

"Damn! What do you mean coming in like that? I might have killed you."

Raoul sputtered and coughed several times in an effort to ease the choking he felt in his throat. "You could wait…just…a second…before…you try to…strangle a person to…death."

"I've no time for you." Erik sat back down at the table and added the minimal color to his face that he needed. He had darkened the area around his eyes to make them stand out starkly against the white of his mask. He stood and took the officer's jacket and squeezed one arm inside a sleeve. The moment he did he realized he was far larger than Grimaldo, a man of moderate height and narrow chest. The jacket would not accommodate Erik's shoulders.

"That won't fit."

Erik glared at Raoul's face reflected in the mirror. "Yes, I believe you're right."

Raoul ignored the sarcasm. "You're going on stage?"

Erik didn't answer. There was no need. The answer was obvious.

"Erik, I don't think this is a good idea. Leroux is out there."

"Have you seen him?" he asked, now intently focused on the count.

"Not yet, but I know he's there. If you go out onto the stage, Leroux might try something during the performance. You'd be a sitting target. In the confusion, it's likely Leroux might even get away with it."

Erik didn't answer immediately. He flung the military coat casually over his arm, opened a few inches of his white starched shirt, revealing his throat, as if he had decided to portray the officer in an unguarded and informal moment. Satisfied, he studied the effect in the mirror.

"I have no choice, Raoul. Carlotta wants the opera to fail. I can't allow it. It's my music, my work, my life. I have to take the risk. Leroux knows where I am. Whether I go out onto the stage tonight or not, Leroux will find me."

Raoul understood that there was no use in arguing with Erik.

"Did you see her?" he asked.

Erik's eyes searched his friend's face. They both knew to whom Raoul was referring. "Yes." He kept his tone carefully neutral.

"I told her not to come."

"She obeys as well as Meg does, I see."

Raoul gave him a half smile. "I wouldn't want her to see anything that would distress her. She's with child."

"Congratulations. You must insist that she be more sensible." He realized only after he spoke how intense his warning had sounded.

They were both quiet for a few moments. Then Erik started toward the door. "Go to her. There's nothing you can do. Events must take their natural course."

Erik beckoned for Raoul to precede him out of the room. In the hallway, they both embraced suddenly and spontaneously. Just as suddenly, they gruffly pushed away from each other as if overwhelmed by the unexpected intimacy and marched off in opposite directions, each toward his own destiny.

the sound of strangers their voices magpies cawing scraping their wooden feet against the floor, their bodies twisting and brushing against the fabric, impossible to silence the rapid beating of his own heart his body refuses to obey he stands next to Caspiano warm flanks flutter twitch the animal snorts his impatience nerves firing in anticipation his hand lies on the horse's velvet muscles caresses him tak-

ing pleasure comfort in the animal sensation guiltless timeless he has told them to begin he has ordered the curtain to rise he has committed himself to go out upon the stage he has given no explanations the crowd obeys the crowd waits the crowd will listen will listen to him to him as he comes out upon the stage in a costume that imperfectly fits with a voice that imperfectly plays with fear dread anger clutching his gut seething knowing who is waiting among the crowd who is listening who is remembering his pleas his tears his pain his suffering his curses his fury his refusal to die to lie down and die for him he catches a glimpse of Meg he would do anything for her not to be here between him and the man who wishes his pain to continue Meg a simple country lass a princess masquerading as a country maiden a princess no a queen she is Meg masquerading as the bride of a monster she sits by the stream enjoys the simple pleasures pleasures he is not supposed to experience a life out in the country under the infinite blue sky only here in this temple to illusion only the illusion of a life and this is act one but he knows it is unfortunately act three and the illusion will soon be dismantled for the moment there is magic for the moment he is Meg's handsome bridegroom stealing upon her unaware of who she is but mesmerized by her voice her beauty can he remember the cue? what was it? he won't remember he will panic it will all come crashing down but she is singing to her imagined lover and he mounts Caspiano and presses his knees and Caspiano trots forward onto the stage

The audience whirls and stares as they see him, a loud surprised rumbling, a general intake of air at the sight of a man, a tall imposing man, a man who wears a mask to disguise his features, a man on horseback. They buzz and screw their eyes into tight tiny slits to make out his features. He sits higher, taller on the horse than the tenor, yet he is slender, something majestic, something regal, something threatening in his stance, the way he overwhelms the stage. They nudge each other to quiet, to listen. He's about to sing…

he comes toward me and it is as if I've never seen him before this moment, his eyes never leave my face and I am mute, my heart is in my mouth, was this how Christine felt on the stage when the Phantom came out to sing to her? did she feel as if he were touching her with his voice, his eyes when he sang the role of Don Juan and she sang the song of the seduced maiden? he is strange and yet familiar to me, he teases me, he challenges me to meet him, to rise to his heights, to reach out for his glorious perfection with my own, to give myself to the music, his music, the music he writes with painful, twisted fingers, the music that comes from somewhere deep inside his soul, he sings to the simple maiden by the gentle waters, he an officer, a gentleman, a prince, unaware that I am his princess, his intended bride, his eyes laugh at me, his words barely veil the desire that possesses him, his voice began with the slightest hesitancy, the next notes he sings to me as if he had rehearsed this scene a million times and it thrills me to know that perhaps he has, each time Don Grimaldo performed, beside him, like a phantom, was Erik's voice, and I understand now hearing the words in his *voice how he has meant the song to be sung, what lay hidden in the playful sixteenth notes, the meaningful pauses, the subtle reiterated motifs, a man for whom war is life, death and violence and destruction, seeks a moment of peace with an innocent young girl on the bank of a foreign stream, a respite from the troubles and woes of his life, a man and a woman, outside of time, away from the enemy, he chases me, and I have never wanted to be caught so badly as I do now, and as we sing to each other, I let him catch hold of the hem of my peasant dress, he falls to one knee and kisses the roughly sewn fabric, he stretches the skirt out into a fan and I twirl and wrap round me the splayed breadth of cloth and gently fall into his arms, he lifts me when Grimaldo would have led me by the hand Erik lifts me the gentle warrior lifts me in his arms and carries me to the lilac bushes, we recline behind the paper and wire hedges among the eternally blossoming flowers and they hide us from the world*

"Who is he? Is his name in the program?"

"I don't know what it is about his voice. It's not exactly what one would expect for an opera, is it?"

"He's not a singer. Someone said he's the director, the composer, too."

"I found it…rather…rather…well…I did most certainly, if you know what I mean!"

"That's just what I felt!"

"I understand that the tenor was taken ill at the last moment."

"I'm quite excited! I came to hear the diva, Signora Costanzi, but this man is impressive. You'd think they really were attracted to one another."

"They should have announced the change in casting. After all, the tenor is one of the principals."

"Did you see how he grabbed her? I swear I don't think it was an act. I think he meant to ravish her before our very eyes!"

"His voice is too deep, too low for a tenor, is it not, Lord Galvagno?"

"I daresay he sounds damn good. The voice is nice, manly, strong, emotional. Not prissy in the least like some of them."

"Well I think he's a bit strange. Why the mask? The program explains that he is a prince, a warrior. His marriage to his enemy's daughter brings a war that has lasted for generations to an end. Is he, too, in disguise then?"

"I think of the mask as symbolic."

"Oh I suppose there's some deep meaning, but actually he's incognito so he's simply hiding his face. Maybe she would recognize him if it weren't for the mask."

"He's sneaking into the country to find out about his intended bride and to survey the kingdom their children will inherit."

"Oh so you think he'll take the mask off eventually?"

"I've heard he wears it all the time."

"Was the prince injured or something?"

"No, no, no, no. You've misunderstood, as usual. I'm not talking about the character. I mean the singer, Don Erik Costanzi."

"Isn't that strange? He's got the same family name as the diva."

"They're married."

"Oh."

"He never takes the mask off."

"How uncomfortable. Well, he must take it off from time to time. Doesn't he clean his face, for example? Or what if he needs to scratch his nose, for goodness sake? Or if he gets something in his…?"

"Oh for God's sake, Donna Rachele, in public he wears it always. Who knows what he does in private."

"Was he horribly burned in that fire, you remember the one, the fire that broke out in this very same opera theater a year or so ago?"

"No, he wore it even before the fire."

"Ah, Donna Bianca, it's so good to see you tonight. Is your husband not with you?"

"He's caught a touch of the rheumatism. My husband's associate, Signore Nespeca, was kind enough to escort me tonight."

"You've studied some of the fine arts, Donna Bianca. What do you think of the piece?"

"Why I don't believe I heard a note. I kept looking at his leg!"

"Oh, but you are wicked!"

"His shirt was open at the throat. Did you notice? Your seats are not as close as mine, but I think only the blind would have missed it."

"I confess I used my opera glasses. Quite lovely, my dear, simply exquisite."

"His voice is remarkable and such emotion. The walls were vibrating."

"From his voice or from your racing pulse, Donna Bianca?"

"You know that the diva is his wife, don't you?"

"Well that explains how...real...it seemed. Don't you agree Donna Rachele?"

look at them! cow-eyed and mouths gaping open like trout on a river bank! a man wearing a mask, a murderer with a flair for music and the dramatic steps out on the stage and they eat him with their eyes, they hang on every note he sings, and he's going to get away with it! the whole performance should have ground to a stop and crashed around his ears, after all my plans! the music was missing, the tenor was unable to perform, and so he does it himself, the nerve of the man, the bald nerve of him to act as if he can do it all, I never saw such pride, such overbearing pride as he has to attempt to save the performance at the last minute and he knows I'm watching him, daresay he knows I stole the music that I slipped the opium into the champagne Grimaldo drank in a toast to himself, the vain peacock, humph, he comes out on his white charger and he starts to sing and the whole house falls to its knees, how is it possible? just like the night he sang in Paris, the night he sang to that silly Daaé chit, but his voice isn't even right, he's not a tenor but a baritone for God's sake and the hero's a tenor, should be a tenor, not a baritone, and it's different, his voice has changed, there is a roughened edge to it, a low simmering growl that wasn't there that night in the Opera Populaire, but he delivers the song flawlessly with a dramatic flair Grimaldo never had even in his dreams, and all the women and half of the men have fallen in love with him! and even I, even I, I who have every cause to despise you, M. Opera Ghost, M. Phantom, even I cannot look away from you, even I try to steady the rapid beating of my heart, refuse to look to the side in case one of these fools notes the flush in my cheeks, the rapid rise and fall of my bosom as even I fall under your spell, the spell of your voice that comes from some dark and secret and wicked place to be able to affect me so, even I cannot resist the excitement of listening to him sing his desire and love, even I who have so many reasons to wish his failure, I who have plotted his downfall, I applaud, I applaud, my hands raw with clapping, in awe of his performance, in awe of him, and I curse that he turned away from me to hang his hopes on a silly, unbroken, twit of a girl when he should have recognized my gifts, my talent, my ferocious passion, was my passion not equal to his? he and I would have been magic, quicksilver together, he and I

Abomination! I brought him to his knees! I watched him reviled and condemned in a court of law. I saw him climb the scaffold to face his executioner! I witnessed him drop from the heights and dangle by the neck before a blood-lusting crowd! Abomination! He makes a travesty of justice. And they applaud. They can't drag their eyes from him. They have no idea what horror he hides behind that mask. What he is capable of. If the count had not aided him, his body would have rotted by now in the pauper's field. All that which they admire would have dissolved into an ooze and seeped through the planks of his coffin into the ground. They don't know what I know. I've seen him. I've seen him without that mask, without his illusions, without his lies, stripped, his body no less human than my own, his blood no less red than mine, his pain as inescapable. A weak, pathetic human just as miserable, as corrupt as any of us. But that pride of his, the depths of his resistance! I broke his precious fingers, one by one, and yet even though he howled in agony, those eyes glared at me with such ferocity, such unbending will! And now I find him, having defied death itself, living in Rome. Oh how he must have laughed at me over these years. The gall of him! I will cut him down. I will make him beg me for mercy. He will not escape my wrath. I will crush him. I will destroy him inch by inch. And if the count dares get in my way, I will cut him down, too, without a second thought!

Leroux walked among the spectators in the gallery who passed the time waiting for the next act to begin. No one paid him much attention, a foreigner, uncouthly dressed, they wondered how he had managed to purchase the ticket to attend the opening night gala. The tickets had been sold out well before the beginning of the month. Everyone who was anyone was adamant about not missing the opening of the new Costanzi opera. They were always the highlight of the season, always grist for the mill, daring and controversial, just like the composer himself.

Leroux, dressed in his finest coat, could see the tremendous gap between himself and the rich and aristocratic patrons of the Teatro dell'Opera. As he avoided their condescending glances, he heard wisps of conversation. Whenever the Phantom was on anyone's lips, Leroux felt himself inevitably drawn to their side to listen: "…brilliant…his portrayal…the composer…last season quite an interesting…yes, they're husband and…French some say or Russian…she's quite a tasty…magnificent profile in that m…is he not Costanzi's by-blow?… Erik…Danish…the mask…disfigured…pity, that…mesmerizing voice…" *Stupid, frivolous class of people, with no moral fiber at all.* Leroux scorned them all in their finery, not enough intelligence among them to fill a thimble. He slipped out into the street.

Down the street, in the shadows, he could just make out the form of Piero. He set off round the building toward the stage door. Piero followed discreetly.

"They'll be coming out this way. You wait until they do. You know which one I want—the one in the mask. Subdue him and bring him to the quarry. You have the manacles? Use them. Keep him there. Don't underestimate him. He's incredibly strong and quite clever. Bring as many men as possible and don't turn your back on him."

Piero listened carefully. Leroux had paid him handsomely and given him enough to pay a good seven or eight others. It was a good amount, and no one else knew how much Leroux had been willing to pay for services rendered. Of course Piero had no intention of hiring and paying out for as many men as Leroux had requested. They were kidnapping an opera composer. How dangerous could he be? He'd include a good two or three of his friends and pocket the difference. No one need know.

"How do you know he'll be coming out alone?"

"I don't. If he doesn't, we might have to find another way. They'll be anxious to celebrate. They're having a party at Il café di mondo. So after you wait a respectable amount of time, if he doesn't come out, you go in and get him. I want him tonight."

Leroux was about to return when he added as an after thought, "There's another man, a tall and slender man, more slender of build than Costanzi. He has unnaturally dark hair in contrast to his complexion. He, too, is French, and he's wearing a tawny coat of very expensive fabric and cut, his trousers are between burgundy and rust, a deep brown cravat, dark boots. If he accompanies Costanzi, stop him. I don't care what you do to him. He deserves whatever happens to him. Do you take my meaning?"

Piero shifted uncomfortably in his tracks. He certainly did understand. He wasn't a murderer, but then he was loath to have a witness who could later point an accusing finger his way. "Well, we might need to renegotiate the fee if the matter gets that serious, signore," he said slyly.

"Yes, I thought as much," sneered Leroux. He had a good deal of experience with the criminal mind. Piero's request had been anticipated. He was willing to pay and pay well to achieve justice in this matter. That was after all why he had pursued the case. He had seen the count as he made his way through the crowds. The darkened hair was not a very effective disguise. The hypocrite had known all along that the Phantom was here! He had come to warn him. His wife accompanied the Costanzi family in their private box. It was an abomination. Well if the foolish count had thrown his lot in with a criminal, he would pay the consequences. He was just as guilty as the Phantom and would have to suffer the righteous punishment of the law!

why did I write another tragedy why can I not write a love story that ends well a story that is full of light and tenderness in which no dark shadows mar the landscape where lovers twine fingers lips limbs and sigh and remind the audience of the grace of love the comfort of the pleasures of giving and receiving of harboring one's love in the bosom of one's body and soul why can't I write of passion that sings in joy and exultation at the attainment of one's deepest desire of the tremendous relief of looking at one's beloved and seeing love reflected in her eyes why did I write such sadness again and again I write I seem condemned to write the tragedy of love taken away of love thwarted of the gift destroyed or stolen and end each opera in a flood of tears with a kiss on cold dead lips on the absolute unforgiving loss of death? oh Meg, I hold you, Elene, but you are not the character that I wrote and mercilessly let die to touch strangers' hearts, the fantasy woman that I dreamed of loving and losing, a sacrifice upon the stage, you are my Meg, the treasure I was given and would keep safe forever and I hold you tonight in my arms and your counterfeit death wrings real tears from my eyes I feel as if I will die as I watch you mime the nothingness of death and I know my lips are trembling as I kiss you and I kiss you with my passion not the soldier's false passion not the paper passion of the libretto but my passion for I fear this might be my fate or yours I have no way to protect us from what I am what I have been for the danger is always inside me and the music has come to its climax and we have sung the notes and my lips are on yours and you stir I feel you respond to my kiss although your body does not break the illusion of your tragic death and I hear the silence after the last ringing note flies from us and the crowd has risen and they are stomping their boots against the floor and they are clapping their hands they have removed their gloves and violently clap their immaculate palms together flesh to flesh as they respond to our grief and I will not take my lips from yours I would I could never take my lips from yours and your hand rises you have risen from the grave and your hand poses gently on the back of my neck I feel it against my skin and they see that you have come back and our kiss is not for them but they don't understand this and they applaud even more loudly and call out bravos and bravas for our romantic touch they have no idea how much I need your touch how I wish to imprint it on my soul so that when I lie cold and dying I can call it forth and die in the memory of it and no other touch but yours

CHAPTER 11

The Beast

Tis now the very witching time of night,
When churchyards yawn and hell itself breathes out
Contagion to this world: now could I drink hot blood
And do such bitter business as the day
Would quake to look on.

Shakespeare, Hamlet

Rinaldo pulled at Erik. He took a handful of his shirt and dragged him back to the stage. Erik nearly struck out at the young man. The curtain rose, and he was blinded by the lights in the house. The roar was deafening. He turned to leave again, but the chorus flanked his retreat, and Meg's hand took his. He obediently followed her to the lip of the proscenium in the very center of the stage. She bowed gracefully, like the ballerina that she was. Below him the musicians tapped their hands and bows on their instruments in a respectful acknowledgement of the performance, their gaze trained upward toward him and Meg. Those seated in the front rows were so close Erik could see the jewels on the women's gloved hands sparkle as their mistresses struck their muffled praise.

They were too close, and even as they smiled at him he saw in their eyes the question, the puzzlement. The entire auditorium was standing. Erik did not wish to be on the stage. The opera was over. He had stepped out of character and stood unshielded, stunned, before a theater full of strangers. He looked away from them, did not want to look at them, to see how they observed him. They were out there, hidden among the spectators, the officers with their guns, the ghosts of that other night in which he lost control, the night when, maddened by her betrayal, he had descended into hell and had taken Christine with him.

Although Meg still had his hand, he reached out to her, tightening his grip, reminding himself that she was with him, he was not alone. He searched her eyes, desperate to anchor himself to the present, to fight off the panic. Her smile trembled as she looked up at him with obvious pride, oblivious to the stray tears that coursed down her cheeks. She mouthed a silent 'I love you,' and Erik squeezed her hand gently. He bowed his head slightly as the others did in response to the audience's exuberant applause.

At first no one heard the words, but ever so gradually a chant rose from the depths of the amphitheater. Erik heard it clearly before anyone else. He untangled his fingers from Meg's and stepped back several paces from the edge of the stage, his heart in his mouth, his body prepared to flee. "Mask. Take off the mask. Remove it. Let's see your face." It rumbled through the audience but never came to more than a slight ripple. The sound of applause silenced the few who called for Erik to reveal himself.

A young boy came from the wings, a huge bouquet of snapdragons, irises, and orchids in his arms, and presented the festive arrangement to Meg. She gestured to Erik, who had slipped away toward the back, and grabbed his hand and dragged him back to her side to enjoy the acclamation.

She nearly had to shout so he could hear. "No roses?"

He smiled, suddenly relaxed by her teasing and her evident enjoyment of the audience's attention. He couldn't help but look up to Box 5 to catch a glimpse of Christine. For her, he had selected one crimson rose, plucked off the thorns by hand, and left it for her on opening night. Roses were his gift for Christine, and Meg had lost her delight in them, for they would always be tied to Erik's obsessive love for another. For her, there were other blossoms, many and varied, hardy and fragile, and always abundant.

The applause continued, but Erik had had enough. He escaped Meg's grasp and walked briskly off stage. In the wings, he felt lightheaded and leaned against the wall until the feeling began to pass. He had done it! He had performed, and they had taken him seriously. For the time of the performance they had forgiven him his mask and had looked beyond his strangeness. Then, the curtain fell for the last time, and Meg flew to his side.

"Come to my dressing room," she urged as she raced ahead of him down the passageway. But Erik's mind was on other matters.

Where had Leroux been? Was he one of those who had challenged him to remove his mask? Was he that very moment making his way backstage to confront the "Phantom"? What would Leroux do when he found him? The former inspector couldn't arrest him and take him off to prison, so the only option Leroux had—if he were indeed mad as Raoul suspected—was to attempt to kill him. How would his tormentor do it? A blade slipped between the ribs? A gun shot directly to the chest?

As Erik watched, expecting at any moment to see Leroux approach, pistol drawn or knife clutched by his side, Raoul came into sight.

"Congratulations. You were…magnificent."

"Yes, I was."

"You are the most arrogant bastard I've ever met!"

"Did you see him?"

"I thought I saw him at one point, but I lost him in the crowd."

"So he's here."

Raoul stood silently by Erik's side as they wondered the same thing. When would he strike?

"Erik?" Meg called as the door opened, excitedly expecting it to be her husband. She didn't even try to hide her disappointment when she saw it was her mother.

Seeing her daughter's reaction, Madeleine stiffened her resolve. Meg wasn't going to like what she had been instructed to do. "Meg, you were absolutely wonderful!"

Meg smiled in appreciation. "You really think so, Maman? Wasn't it something to see? Erik and I together on the stage!"

"I have to admit that I was amazed."

"I expected Erik."

"I know, ma petite. But that's why I'm here."

"What?" Meg grew cautious at her mother's words. She sensed something was wrong.

"Erik wants me to take you directly home."

"Where is he?"

"He's with Raoul. There's something troubling him. He wants you safe at home."

"But I have news to tell him. And besides he promised that…"

Meg stopped herself before she complained that they had made a pact to speak with Carlotta together. She wasn't sure if her mother had guessed Signorina Venedetti's true identity.

Madeleine took Meg's hands and kissed them briefly with tender lips in anticipation of the news she thought her daughter had been keeping from her. "Tell me, ma petite, ma belle. How far along are you?"

"I don't already show, do I?" Meg asked, staring at her profile in the mirror. Indeed, she could barely notice the rounding of her abdomen through the material of her dressing robe.

"No, but I can tell. For several weeks, you were very ill some time each day, and lately your appetite has been quite wolfish."

"It's early, Maman. Perhaps I shouldn't tell Erik, in case something happens."

"You're several months, no doubt?"

"I guess a bit more than two. I've been trying to find the right time to tell him. I decided after the opening we could celebrate the opera's success and the baby."

"Well, perhaps at home, later," Madeleine hedged. She wasn't sure what the men were up to, but she prayed there would be time later for her daughter and Erik.

"I'm not going anywhere. Not without Erik."

"Meg, he asked Marcelo and me to be sure you returned home with us as soon as possible. I agree with him. We're not even going with the company to the café. There's more at stake here than you know."

"That tone won't work on me any longer, Maman. I'm not a child. I'm a grown woman with children of my own."

The door opened, and Erik slipped in quietly. When Madeleine hadn't reemerged from the dressing room, he concluded that Meg was refusing to listen to reason. He would have to explain how dangerous their situation—his situation—truly was. And then the risk was that she'd give no thought to her own safety. He would have to make her listen.

"Madeleine, I should never have sent you to explain what I should be telling her. Could Marcelo and you wait for her by the entrance? She'll be along directly." There was an edge of steel in his voice. He was determined she would go home.

When her mother left, Meg could contain her anger no longer. "She'll be along directly? What nerve, Erik. How dare you dictate to me. I'm not a child. I know Raoul and you are working together on something, but this situation with Carlotta is one you and I agreed we'd face together! If you plan to confront her without me, it's not going to happen. If it's tonight, I'm staying. Nothing you can say will convince me otherwise."

Erik watched her slip out of her robe, throw it to the ground, and dress hurriedly. He couldn't help but notice how anger brought a strange flush to her delicate complexion. He looked away from the brief glimpse of her taut rounded abdomen. He knew her body. He had told her once that it spoke to him, but he could not think of the next few months, only the next few hours.

By force of will, he distanced himself from her, dampening any hint of desire, as well as any longing to please her. He understood why she was angry and even considered her justified in being so. However he could see no way around it. He could not and would not jeopardize her health or her safety, no matter how much she resented his domineering treatment.

"We agreed we'd face Carlotta together, Erik," she repeated in an injured tone when he didn't respond. "You can't just send me home."

"Leroux has come to Rome to find the Phantom." He should have been prepared for it. She blanched, and if he hadn't stepped forward to catch her, she'd certainly have crumpled to the floor. He eased her onto the sofa, sat beside her, and clasped her tightly to his chest. She trembled silently in his arms. Her obvious fear distressed him. It brought his own anxiety dangerously close to the surface and made it tangible, real, substantial in a way that until that moment he'd been able to consider at one remove from himself. Now the possibility of his own death or exile weighed heavily on them both. Their life together, as they knew it, was coming to an end.

"I had news I wanted to share with you, but perhaps it should wait." Her voice sounded unnatural. It was flat, emotionless, the voice of a stranger.

"If that's what you wish." He tried to console her. His fingers became tangled in her silken hair. He kissed the top of her head and leaned his face against the soft blond tresses.

"Is that why Raoul has come?"

"Yes."

"What will we do?"

Erik swallowed hard to keep down the sorrow. "You will go home and stay with our children. You will keep them safe, and you will keep yourself safe."

"But…" Strong emotion flooded her voice, destroying the previous detached tone.

"No!" Erik interrupted sternly. His green eyes were demanding and unrelenting. "I will not put you at risk. Your presence would weaken me. I won't be able to do what needs to be done if I am worried about you, Meg. Please, the only way you can help me is to go home, now. If I can, I'll come to you tonight. If I can't, know that I had no choice."

His words terrified her, but the absolute devastation in his eyes threatened to strike her blind. She would obey him, but she could not just let him go. The implications behind his farewell were unbearable, and she wrapped her hands tightly around his neck and forced his mouth to hers. She didn't know where she found the strength, but she bent him to her, and her need was undeniable.

Their clothes were cast aside in desperate abandon, and their bodies wove together in the easy, familiar way of longtime lovers. He could feel her urgency, and his own awareness of possible loss would not let him linger or be tender. She, too, dug her fingers into his arms and pulled at him in her desire to feel him buried inside her. Still he trailed across her body with fevered lips, kissing and suckling at her tender breasts, nestling into the softness of her neck. He ran his fingers between her thighs teasing her until he knew she was desperate for him, then he wedged his legs between hers and cupped her buttocks firmly in his hands to drive her against him. She pleaded with him to take her, her legs wrapped aggressively around his hips, threatening never to release him again. He sank into her warmth, and they both knew it would only last moments. As Meg gasped and trembled in the last flush of desire fulfilled, he took her mouth and bruised her lips with his. She felt him shudder over her as he released his seed deep inside her, his moan wet against her cheek.

They lay, as if they would never move again, for several moments. Then Erik seemed to wake. Reluctantly they disentangled themselves, so sensitive and tender the pleasure and pain were inextricably tied together. He shifted so that she would rest more comfortably, but he couldn't yet let go of her. He lay with his head cradled against her breasts, mesmerized, listening to the beat of her heart.

Slowly, he rose. They dressed in silence. He walked her to the front entrance, his arm warm and tight round her waist. Just before she crossed the threshold, he could bear it no longer, and he pulled her back into the shadowy gallery and kissed her mouth again and again. One last tender taste of her and he guided her out into Marcelo and Madeleine's protection.

Carlotta's coach had hovered for nearly an hour outside the Café di mondo waiting for the diva and her hero to arrive for the post-performance celebration. The artists were giving vent to the tension of long hours and last-minute jitters, carousing and drinking with wild abandon. One of the older women from the chorus had kicked off her shoes and was dancing with animal pleasure for the delight of the crowd. Among the artists and significant patrons of the Teatro dell'Opera were several journalists who covered cultural events in Rome, including Paolo Ricci.

She had no intention of rubbing elbows with the company, and she would only enter the café if Erik and Meg or Don Marcelo were to show up. The lateness of the hour convinced her they had wisely decided not to attend. She was not planning a confrontation on such a public scale, not after the tremendous success of the evening. Everyone would most likely rally round the couple, and she would have no support. But if they had come, she was determined to be present so that they would not be able to relax and enjoy their moment of glory. She would at least have that! That is, she would have had that if Erik hadn't anticipated such a possibility and convinced Meg to forego the festivities.

She watched as Ricci came out of the café and hands in pocket searched the street. He kicked at some bit of trash on the walk and set off for his apartments. He, too, was disappointed by the absence of the principal stars of the night.

Tired and frustrated, she beat impatiently on the roof of the coach for the driver to continue on to her apartment.

No one was waiting for her. The rooms were dark and silent. Piangi had refused to return and no longer included a request for her to come to him. She sensed that somehow their relationship was over. She consoled herself that it had not really been much of a relationship in the last decade, not since the Phantom had ruined everything. The Phantom, Erik, she whispered the name, the latter being somehow more comfortable, more real to her now. Yet she shook her head and repeated over and over, the Phantom, the Phantom, the Phantom. He didn't deserve a name, a family, a life. He was a monster, wasn't he? Then why did his eyes keep appearing in her imagination? They were not the cold eyes of the monster. She imagined them soft and yearning, vulnerable, puzzled, so many emotions she had seen pass through those eyes as she had waged her silent war against him. A tender pain seized her as an uninvited thought struck her: He wants peace! He has found love and wants peace.

Surprised she wiped a stray tear from her cheek. Her breathing was not right. She screwed up her face in what she knew must be a hideous expression and an ugly cry came from her throat. She didn't know why she was crying, whether it was for herself or for…She sat in the dull light of the one gas lamp and stared into its flame. She wanted to be at the theater! Why had she left? She felt alive at the theater. Alive when she strolled backstage and spied on the dancers and the chorus girls as they put on their make-up. Alive when she caught a glimpse of Erik at the piano in his office. He often forgot to shut the door. She had spent many unguarded moments outside that office, listening to him.

She caught herself smiling. Smiling! Carlotta? Smiling like an idiot? What did she have to smile about? She had nothing, nothing, nothing, nothing. She stomped her foot in spite of the fact that the resident below her had already complained on several occasions of her temper tantrums.

Well if the Phantom thought it was over, he was very much mistaken. Tomorrow, bright and early, in her nicest rose gown, she would be there in the theater to dog his steps. No reason to use the veil, the cat was out of the bag, and its claws were exposed! She would walk into that theater like the prima donna she was! He would have to bear her presence until she tired of him, a poor bloodied mouse trapped in her paws.

She felt better once she determined that she would be at the theater the next day. It didn't even concern her that Rinaldo had quit her employ. She had threatened him, but he stood his ground like a stupid romantic hero in a bad play and refused to obey. Even that could not dampen her anticipation.

Tomorrow she would see *him* again. She would hear his voice, see those intensely green eyes. He would snarl at her, she was sure. It would be so delicious. She smiled and stared up at the dark ceiling. The moonlight cut a sharp line of gray across the mottled plaster of the low ceiling, and Carlotta imagined a half mask over a face that was looking down at her from above.

No one was left. Erik had sent them all away, even Raoul who had tried to insist that he'd stay with him. Finally Erik had convinced him that Leroux would wait to find him alone. Erik needed to draw him out. Leroux could strike anywhere and anytime. What if he struck when Meg or the children were nearby? He couldn't bear to think of it. Leroux would never have a better chance to attack than tonight, but he wouldn't come if he thought it was a trap. Reluctantly Raoul left.

The theater was eerily silent. It had been that way often in the Opera Populaire. Although there were dormitories for the young ballet dancers and chorus, the theater in the early hours of the morning was like a sleeping giant. Erik had wandered its halls and rooms in awe of the shadow kingdom he felt to be all his own. Here, now that all had gone, Erik was comforted by the silence. The evening had been too full of sound, teaming with life to the point that his nerves were raw. The constant worry that Leroux would strike had dulled, and he considered that he might welcome his enemy's assault if only to end the anxiety, the anticipation.

In part, Erik admitted to himself, he wanted Raoul to leave not solely because he wished to save his friend from a dangerous encounter. He feared the horror on Raoul's face if he witnessed Erik surrender to the deep anger inside him. Leroux had possessed his body and soul for months in the dank prison of Paris. He had tortured him and humiliated him to the point that Erik could not think of Leroux without feeling a madness threaten to overtake him. Raoul had once seen that mad creature in Erik, and it had taken a great deal for Raoul to see beyond it. But Erik sadly realized that the madness had not disappeared. It waited like a caged beast ready to pounce if the door were ever left unlocked. Leroux's presence dredged up every evil desire for blood and violence that Erik had studiously attempted to eradicate. He was ashamed that he was still a monster, yet he was no longer willing to struggle against this fact of his nature. It felt too powerful to refuse. He wanted to let the beast loose. He longed to exercise claws, fangs, naked strength and purpose. He chafed under the restraints of civilization.

Don Marcelo had lost his son to a meaningless illness in the prime of the young man's life. He had lingered at his son's sickbed, foolishly wishing to believe in the immortality of youth, in the continued vigor of the body, and the deluded optimism that all young men have. It had broken Don Marcelo's heart to hold his son's wan body in his arms and watch the strength slowly ebb away. Alone, he had looked down the narrowing tunnel of the last decades of his own life and understood with dread that it ended with his own death. There would be no son, no wife to his son, no grandchildren, only the emptiness of a barren life.

He had filled his days with the opera, his plans to build a temple to music, and the daily tedium of life. All that had changed when he happened upon the haunted man in the Teatro Argentina one night, well after the company had retired and the echoes had faded, who played a melody on the piano that was unknown to him yet touched the deep sadness of his mourning soul. Don Marcelo had stayed by the entrance and listened as the stranger, unaware of his presence, played.

The idea was mad, but for a moment Don Marcelo had stared at the stranger and thought perhaps his son had returned as a ghost. His son and this man were of a similar build. Had his son lived, would he have been nearly the same age as this man? The stranger's talent far outstripped that of Don Marcelo's son. Even though the latter had been a promising musician, his early compositions did not approach the genius of this simple improvisation.

Perhaps sensing his presence, the man had stopped playing. Unwilling to let the moment pass, Don Marcelo stepped forward and urged the stranger to continue.

"Please, don't stop on my account."

The stranger rose, the charm of the moment broken. Only then did Don Marcelo note the man's clothes. The fabric and cut suggested a man of means, a man of class, but the clothes were frayed and dirty. The condition of the garments bespoke some drastic change in fortune. Or perhaps this man had stolen the clothing? Taken them from his victim? But this, too, made no sense. A common thief or murderer could not have received the training this man must surely have gotten to play the way he did.

Don Marcelo came swiftly forward before the stranger could balk. As he rounded upon the man, he caught a glimpse of his face. The shock froze him to the spot, but it was not revulsion or fear that unnerved him. It was simply the sadness of such a fate, for he understood immediately why the stranger had excused himself and said that he would go away. He must have been accustomed to people reacting to him in such a way. He must have been spurned and chased from normal society. From that glimpse, Don Marcelo imagined his entire life. The man hid from the baleful gaze of human society, his only consolation the music he played. He came to this site above all others, seeking to be near artists and composers. Don Marcelo remembered the rumors of someone haunting the building. The unfortunate soul had not long been hidden in the theater.

The night he had come upon Erik, Don Marcelo knew that he would harbor him. At first he told himself that it was only his Christian duty, then he convinced himself that the man was a musical genius and that he must be protected for the sake of art itself. But he soon came to realize that somehow Erik had slipped into the soft and aching hole that the death of his son had left.

For Don Marcelo, Erik was a son. He could not bear to lose another.

He accompanied the women back to the estate and made sure that they were safely lodged in their rooms. Madeleine had followed him out to the hallway, somehow aware that he had decided to return to the theater. Wordlessly, she had laid her hand on his sleeve. For the first time in many weeks, he was sure that she was his. She didn't expect his kiss. Nor, if truth be told, did he expect to kiss her the way he did. He had thought those passions long dead. Without rational consideration, he gave in to the sudden impulse and took her roughly into his arms and burned her mouth with an unbridled kiss. He felt her stiffen momentarily from the assault and then warm and soften in his arms. And as his kiss deepened, he felt her body tense toward his with a responding need. The desires had lain smoldering and now burst into flame. A joy entered his heart knowing that the loneliness of his past was forever gone.

Reluctantly he broke their embrace and smiled ruefully at the small woman he still held in his arms.

He could see she was fearful, anxious for him. He steeled himself to insist, "Madeleine, I can't leave him to his fate. I sense that something horrid could happen tonight. He's my son. I must help him."

"I know. I would expect no less of you."

Christine accompanied Meg to the children's rooms. They both soothed the children's fitful slumber and kissed them softly before slipping out. Meg felt a gnawing guilt that the past many weeks had been so disruptive. Laurette sorely missed Erik, and the few occasions when he had slipped back to the house had only made his absence more difficult for the little girl. François and Mario were old enough to grasp that their father was unwillingly absent and that their patience and obedience were required for the present.

Mario and François could both tell that Meg was worried about Erik. François desperately wanted to go to the theater, even suggested that they sneak out and go to their father, but Mario cautioned him wisely that Erik would be furious with them both and that such an action might cause more harm than good.

Mario kept his own counsel about what he might do if it became clear that Erik were in danger. Unlike his brother, Mario understood the ugly side of life, had developed a repertoire of skills to protect himself, and was sure that he could safely come to Erik's side. However if he acted, he was sure François would be close on his heels, and he would never forgive himself if anything happened to François because of him. He knew that there were some in the household that thought him a bad influence and questioned the wisdom of Erik and Meg's having adopted him into the family. So he gritted his teeth and waited like the rest of them, hoping that the adults would be able to sort it all out and that Erik would soon be home.

François woke only briefly when Meg kissed his brow. He muttered something, calling for his father's kiss too, but he fell back asleep almost immediately. In the shadows, Meg could not discern the worried frown upon his face.

When Meg and Christine shut the door to Meg's room and sat on the bed together, they both gave in to their anxieties. Meg understood the ramifications of Leroux's presence as well as Christine did. She also sensed that Erik had already surrendered to despair. The moments before the performance when he had come to her dressing room now played over and over in her mind with the horrid weight of premonition. Now she reconsidered his words to her, their last embraces, as just that! He was preparing himself and her for the end.

What could they do? If Leroux planned to take Erik back to jail, that would mean his death. Meg knew that such an intention was unlikely. Leroux was acting on his own, but he still sought Erik's death. Careless of the consequences, Leroux would certainly find a way. In either case, Erik faced death. He must kill or be killed. If anything happened to Erik, how could she go on?

Selfishly he had told her to live! She had to care for their children, and now she carried another in her womb. And he didn't even know that he was to be a father yet again. She felt maddened by the thought of his loss. Without Erik she would not be herself. How would she be able to bring this child to term? How would she be able to soothe their children's grief when she would be overwhelmed by her own?

She clung to Christine and cried as she had not cried for years. How many times could she face losing him and not lose herself in the bargain? Madness and despair ate at her, gnawed her heart, ground away at her bones. She could not imagine anything but this pain except when she felt that it might be his pain that she was experiencing. No! Let him not suffer. She would take it on herself, just pray, God, that he not suffer! Torn between her own sadness and the unbearable thought of his pain, she could find no consolation in her friend's soft words and caresses.

Christine tried to comfort her, although she was frightened by the depth of Meg's feelings. She herself fought the urge to flee in the face of such pain. She did not want to imagine how she would react if Raoul were the object of Leroux's manhunt. But it was small comfort to think it was Erik who faced death. She would not like a world in which Erik did not live. He was her constant shadow and companion, a part of her that she had absorbed and kept treasured in a small, deep, warm part of her soul. He came to her on the undulations of a summer's melody. His voice sang beneath the strains of her own. If not for Erik, the world would be a silent place.

"How can we wait here? How can we sit with our hands folded and do nothing?" Meg's swollen eyes still streamed with tears.

"We have to wait. He'd never forgive us if we put your child in danger."

"And if he dies? Who will be there to hear his last gasp of air? Who will close his eyes? Who will hold him as he faces eternity?"

"Don't!" Christine cried. "Don't say that, Meg. He has to live. He will."

"He's so alone!"

"He's been alone, Meg. But he's not alone now. He's not."

"Leroux is mad! He's unpredictable! There's no way to protect oneself from a madman."

"Raoul hasn't come. I think he's waiting with Erik. Erik won't face Leroux alone."

"Do you think so? Do you really think Raoul is there?"

Christine shivered to think that he, too, would be in danger, but she managed to smile reassuringly for Meg. "Yes. He wouldn't leave him to face this alone."

"But Erik insisted that everyone leave."

"Raoul can be stubborn, too, Meg. He wouldn't leave a friend in such a situation. He will be there, somewhere in the theater, ready to fight side by side with Erik."

Meg's ragged breathing seemed to calm a bit, accepting the reassurance her friend had given. She held on to Christine tightly as if to let go would break the magic her words had woven. She whispered as if it were a chant, "He's not alone. He's not alone."

Erik woke with a start. The sharp, clear sensation that he was not alone raised the short hairs on the back of his neck. Someone was in the theater. He tensed and listened with his entire body for any sound to give the intruder's location away. Immediately he heard scuffling along the wooden floors coming from the area of the stage door. It was not one person but several. Sounds of a struggle confused him. He stirred at once, grabbed the gun that he had readied, and ran toward the noises.

As he approached the dull glow of the one light left burning, he was horrified to see Raoul doubled over and nearly motionless on the floor. Several men kicked and beat him with short, wooden clubs. He feebly held up one hand in a useless attempt to fend off the blows. Erik had no way of telling for how long Raoul had fought against the unequal odds, but he could tell that Raoul had managed to inflict injuries on his assailants.

Incredibly, Erik could not find Leroux among the attackers. This was not the way it was supposed to happen. Erik was enraged to see Raoul cruelly beset by five large and brawny cutthroats. Raoul no longer stirred, and Erik feared he had arrived too late to save his friend. The gun he had prepared to protect himself from Leroux was of little or no use against a gang of five men in such close quarters. He could easily miss and wound Raoul, so instead of firing, he rushed the men, throwing his bulk against the mass of flesh, in the same moment that he perceived the glint of a blade strike down at the crumpled body and rise to strike again.

Blood!

He let loose the monster inside and went for the man in whose fist gleamed a bloody blade. The man's wrist crunched in a loud and ugly way only made more sickening by the man's pathetic scream of pain. Erik heard the knife clatter to the floor and released the man's arm. At the same time, he lashed out with the barrel of the gun he still held tightly in his fist. The hard metal crashed into the face of a man standing over Raoul's still body. Erik raised his fist several times and clubbed him viciously across the mouth with the pistol. This one fell—blood gushing from his mouth—spewing broken teeth and spittle as he choked. Without a thought to the fallen man, Erik assailed each of the other attackers in rapid succession, giving none of them time to respond to his blows as he turned from one to another. A veil of red fell before his eyes as his fury rose uncontrolled. He was only vaguely aware that one or more of them managed to lash out and strike him; there was no pain, no sensation but the wash of adrenaline and the desire to inflict as much damage and as much agony as possible on anything that moved within his reach. He savaged several of the gang, bringing them to their knees in their own blood and vomit. They limped and crawled their way toward the stage door as Erik caught sight of a figure stepping out from the shadows.

Leroux's arm was bent, and his eyes were locked on Erik's. That arm—Erik understood, a second before it happened, the reason for its curious angle. In his enemy's hand, pointed at his chest, was a cold and dark metallic object whose use was well known to Erik. Leroux was about to fire on him. Without consciously thinking, Erik grabbed the nearest body, a man who had run toward him with murderous intent, and swung him in front of his chest. In the same instant, the gun fired, the bullet ripped through the man's chest, and Erik felt the dull impact against his own breast. They both fell to the ground. Erik fought the blackness that swam up dizzily over his eyes; his breath returned in a gush as he watched Leroux approach.

Hatred seized him, but the pain in his chest and the threatening waves of nausea and blackness in his mind would not permit him to rise. The dead man's blood seeped hot and wet down the sides of his own body, and the weight of the corpse pinned Erik to the floor. Defenseless, Erik watched as Leroux stepped nearer. *This* was the man who had gloated over his pain and his pleas for mercy in the prison. *This monster* had been his gaoler and tormentor. Erik wanted with all his soul to clamp his hands round Leroux's throat and squeeze until his face swelled and turned purple. Only then would he have released him. But even as the other man's body had shielded him, taking the direct impact of the gunshot, its dead weight now laid him out as an easy target for his enemy.

Leroux was grinning, the gun in his fist, the threat clear. He cocked the trigger and pointed the barrel down between Erik's eyes. But before he fired, he lowered his hand toward Erik's face. Erik squeezed his eyes shut, not certain of Leroux's intention, and he felt the cold air hit his exposed skin. He opened his eyes and stared up at Leroux who observed his unmasked face with a twisted look of triumph.

"Phantom. They said I was mad! You thought you could escape justice? You were condemned by a court of law to be hanged by the neck until dead! You and this worthless aristocrat, this count, thought you were above the law. You tried to make a laughing stock of us all. Well, he's had his punishment." Leroux jerked his chin in the direction of the still body on the floor. Erik groaned unintentionally as he noticed the spreading pool of blood under Raoul's body. He sought the darkness, asked for it to come, anything to blot out the red stream that crept toward him.

Leroux was still speaking, his pistol aimed just inches from Erik's brow. "You are a vicious murderer. A madman! Your very existence is a blasphemy. No one believed me, but I will rid the world of your evil."

Erik let the blackness rise and take him. He washed away the images of blood and pain and searched his memory for one golden moment. He found it among all the memories of his past—a heart-shaped face, a sweet red mouth, the warm golden honey of Meg's eyes. She was smiling at him. As he let go of this world, he heard a crash of thunder, a metallic clatter, the shudder of the beams below his back, and then nothing.

CHAPTER 12

Marigolds and Snapdragons

Dost thou love life? Then do not squander time, for that is the stuff life is made of.

Benjamin Franklin

Don Marcelo's hand did not tremble. He felt no remorse as he watched the small man plummet forward to the floor, the gun skidding across the planks to rest impotent beyond the dim glow of the light. His only thoughts were for Erik.

When he had arrived at the Teatro dell'Opera, he was surprised to see several dark figures running from the alleyway at the side of the theater. Quickly he and his servant Angelo rushed inside. It was too quiet, and Don Marcelo had feared that they had arrived too late. Shattering the silence came a gunshot that reverberated throughout the cavernous building. They hurried decisively backstage.

Don Marcelo felt momentarily paralyzed with fear. He was dead! He lay unmoving on the floor. Beside him only an arm's length away lay Raoul. But then Don Marcelo noticed a short man draw near and hover over Erik's body. In his hand a pistol that he now aimed at the still body. Don Marcelo's hand did not tremble. He felt no remorse as he fired upon the man who had killed Erik.

Leroux doubled over, fell to one knee, holding his injured arm, the gun forgotten where it had fallen. Angelo went to apprehend him, but Leroux rose jerkily from the floor and ran down one of the unlit passageways into the heart of the theater.

"Wait!" Don Marcelo called his servant back. Erik and Raoul had to be their first concern. Don Marcelo shoved the dead man from Erik's chest and bent to examine him closely. "See to the count, Angelo."

Erik was covered in blood. He must have been shot! However, the older man was relieved to see his chest rise and fall. He was alive! Next he thought to ask his servant about the other man. "Does he live?"

Angelo stared down at the count. He had turned him slightly in order to examine him. He nodded glumly. "His face, Don Marcelo, it's nothing but blood."

There was no time to give in to horror or despair, Don Marcelo and Angelo sent for the coachman and driver to help transport the wounded men to the coach. They would take them to the estate. Don Marcelo sent Angelo in search of the doctor. They would meet there as soon as it was humanly possible.

The ride to the estate seemed like the road to hell. Don Marcelo held Erik's head in his lap, while the coachman secured Raoul to the other bench. Conscious of each and every bump of the coach across the uneven cobblestones of the path, Don Marcelo watched the two men, thankful that they were both unconscious. At times he would hear Raoul moan in obvious pain, but mostly he was silent. As the lights along the way flashed inside the carriage, the coachman stole glances back and forth between the victims. Don Marcelo pursed his lips in disapproval as he realized the coachman was staring at Erik's unmasked face whenever the light would happen to fall across it. Gruffly he scolded the man, telling him to face forward and keep a steadying hand on Raoul.

Just as he suspected, Madeleine waited by the front window watching for his return. She slipped out of the house down to the street in time to see them carry the injured men into the house.

"Oh my God! They're not...?"

"No, they're alive. But I fear they are both quite seriously wounded. The doctor should be here any moment."

"Best take them both to the west chamber by the stairs. It has two beds."

Don Marcelo acquiesced and sent the men to the west chamber. It would do well since it was convenient to the stairs, and there were two modest-sized beds.

Madeleine struggled with her desire to stay with Erik and her need to prepare Meg for the news. She knocked lightly on her daughter's door. She was momentarily taken aback to find that Christine was in the room with Meg. She would have to face the two women at the same time.

"They've brought both of them home." Her expression was all Christine and Meg had to see to know that they were not well.

Strangely composed, Meg asked, "Where are they?"

Christine seemed frozen in shock.

"In the west chamber, the one with the two beds." Meg rushed past her toward the room. As Christine started to follow, Madeleine gently took her by the arm and stopped her. "Christine, I'm afraid Raoul is injured, too. There was a good deal of blood." She tightly clamped her teeth against her lower lip as she saw Christine's face dissolve into tears. Softly Madeleine held her, until Christine's need to see Raoul outweighed her need for comfort. Then Christine steadied herself, wiped her face, and went in search of Meg. Madeleine tarried only the time it took to compose herself and followed after.

he's alive, they've brought him home, he's alive, they've brought him home, if he were dead Maman would have said something else, she said they've brought them home, the two of them, Erik is home, he has come back to me, I will never let him go again, he is mine and I will keep him and he is home he is home oh my God, even if he is crippled, he is home if he loses the use of his limbs he is home he can look at me he can smile I can see him smile I can sing to him and play for him and he and I will talk and laugh, will we talk and laugh again someday? and if he is blind I will be his eyes and he will use his hands to find his way and we will sit in the garden and I will learn the language of poetry to fill his ears and we will hold each other at night and if he cannot move and cannot see I will live by his ear and whisper to him in day and in night and I will sing his music for him and he will sing to me, softly and quietly, and if he cannot hear...if he cannot hear...? oh my God let him be able to hear, I think he would rather die than not be able to hear, if he cannot hear how will he listen to his child's first cry? if he cannot hear what will happen to his music, if he cannot hear I cannot imagine the pain he will feel, but he is home I will not think about that, I will not think about his broken body I will not imagine him crippled, blind, or deaf, he is home and this is enough he is home my love my love has come home and I will make him whole

Christine sits by Raoul's side, her hand clamped over her mouth in horror at the blood spattered grimace. She cannot make out his features. Don Marcelo and Meg hover over Erik whose chest is awash in blood. The servant carefully cuts the fabric away from his torso. They have told the doctor to examine Raoul first, fearing his wounds to be more life-threatening. The doctor eases Christine to the side. Unconcerned by the bloodied face, he examines his patient's chest, listens to his heart, checks his pulse, allows the servant to undress him quickly. The chest is horribly bruised. Small abrasions and cuts lace the torso, but the doctor reassures her that these are nothing. Of concern is what we cannot see, he says gently, cautiously searching Christine's face to see how much he can and should say to this young matron, this fragile woman who stares in horror at her husband. Along one thigh is an ugly gash, narrowly missing the femoral artery. The doctor instructs a servant to wash the wound carefully and to flush it with warm water. He squeezes Christine's hand and turns away toward Erik.

She follows him for only a moment, her attention impossible to rip away from Raoul. He is breathing, she tells herself. He is not conscious, so he is not in pain. Unable to bear it, she takes one of the damp cloths and with trembling fingers she dabs away the blood on Raoul's face. At first she feels as if she is never to see his face again under the drying and dried blood, but eventually his features begin to emerge from the crimson gore. As she gently presses at the tissues, she sees the source of the blood along the left side of his face. Little by little she uncovers a long cut running from the temple, just centimeters from his eye, down across his cheek to stop just above his lip. A crescent shape, it angrily seeps.

"Doctor?" she calls weakly.

The physician speaks in low whispers to Don Marcelo and the servant attending Erik and turns toward Christine.

"My dear, you have been most helpful. A wonderful nurse, you've been. Now we see a nasty cut along his face which we must fix. This and the gash on the thigh are our first priority. We will have to stitch them both, I'm afraid."

"Will he be all right, Doctor? Will he live?" Christine is afraid how tremulous her voice is, but she can't avoid it. She is astounded that her voice works.

"We will be optimistic, won't we? The injuries on his body will mend. Until I can question him, we won't know if he has serious wounds inside. I have pressed along his abdomen. Here, my dear, look." Then the doctor takes the flat of his fingers and gently but firmly pushes down onto Raoul's abdomen. He does not stir, and the muscles rebound easily. "That is good. It would suggest there is no major internal bleeding. He has broken ribs. He is badly bruised, but I believe they are superficial. Not that they won't hurt like the devil and take their time to heal, but they are not deep. They are not bruised and bleeding organs. We will watch his emissions. Do you understand, my dear?"

Suddenly Christine feels like a child, silly and fragile. The doctor's patronizing manner would infuriate her at any other time, but at this moment she wishes to crawl into the doctor's embrace and let him comfort her like her father used to do when she was very small.

Christine is ushered to a corner by one of the servants assisting the doctor. From there she sees the needle, she sees the blood ooze in starts and stops, she sees the cat gut, sees the doctor's arm rise and fall over Raoul's thigh, then over his face. She feels like she is falling as she watches but she does not faint, she waits until the doctor washes his hands and turns toward Erik.

Raoul seems to be resting comfortably. He has been washed. Clean, white gauze bandages cover his wounds. Christine pulls the chair to his bed so that she can watch him and Erik across the room. Meg smiles back at her.

"Is he all right?" Christine feels guilty that Erik has waited for the doctor's care and that she has not asked before this moment.

Meg rises from the chair next to Don Marcelo, kisses Erik on the forehead, and comes to Christine. Madeleine occupies the seat that Meg has vacated.

"Erik's wound is not the source of all the blood we saw on his clothing. He is badly bruised by a bullet that was embedded just beneath the surface. It might have cracked his sternum the doctor says. He was able to remove it almost immediately with what looked like a pair of tweezers."

Christine throws Meg a puzzled look. "How is that possible?"

"Marcelo says he found Erik beneath another man, a dead man. It seems the bullet first went through this other man. By the time it reached Erik, its force was largely spent."

"Does he have any other wound?"

"Some cuts and bruises, but nothing as bad as Raoul."

"Why is he unconscious?"

"Because of the impact of the bullet and his fall, perhaps."

blood I taste blood it drips into my mouth I taste blood my eyes are heavy and I am buried under putrid flesh, dead bodies have been heaped upon me, their fish-white flesh cold and soft to my touch, their eyes filmed over with white jelly, their mouths open with stale breaths I am buried and I scream and struggle my hands grasp their limbs, my fingers sink into rotten flesh and the gob comes away from the bone dripping with sinew and gray skin and I scream in horror I swim up through the sea of excrement, blood, and rot I must get away from the dead away from the dead the breath wrenched from my chest aches, my chest aches with the pain of breathing with the pain of my heart beating and I ask am I dead? is that why I am buried under this sea of carnage? I ask and fear to hear the answer so I block my ears and squeeze my teeth and eyes shut and I struggle up instinctively knowing I cannot let myself sink farther down under the rotting mass of humanity oh God how can I ever reach the surface?

First there was the angry cry. It came unexpectedly from his body with the force of a blow. Madeleine rose so quickly that the chair she was sitting in tumbled backwards to the floor. The crash further agitated Erik who flailed his arms about as if fighting a host of assailants.

Don Marcelo grabbed his son's arms, and with the aid of Angelo the two of them forcefully restrained Erik. His eyes rolled wildly in his head, and his entire body arched off the bed in a vain attempt to rise and shake off those who held him down.

"Get off me!" he screamed at unseen enemies. "I'll kill you! I'll kill you!"

Meg came into the room, having heard the commotion down the hall. She ran to him, but Don Marcelo ordered her to stay back. Refusing to listen, she pushed her way forward and knelt beside Erik's face. She brought her mouth close to his ear and spoke in a soft whisper unintelligible to any but Erik. She calmly stroked his forehead with her hand as she continued speaking to him. He struggled, but the violence gradually abated. Panting, he finally lay still, but Don Marcelo and Angelo feared releasing him.

Meg reached over the brief distance between them and kissed Erik on the cheek. Her lips lingered, and she brought them slowly down to the corner of his mouth. There she kissed him sweetly and rested her forehead against his temple.

Don Marcelo could feel the fight drain from Erik's body. His breathing quieted. He gestured for Angelo to release him. "Meg, are you sure?"

She smiled up at Don Marcelo and nodded.

The two men stepped back for a moment. Erik's eyes fluttered and slowly opened. He stared round the room until his gaze fell on Don Marcelo. Then it seemed to relax ever so slightly. Immediately he turned his face toward Meg. His mouth partially brushed her lips, and he wrapped his arm around her as if to pull her to the bed.

"I think we might step out for a little while," Don Marcelo whispered to Meg as he indicated that Madeleine, Angelo, and the maid who sat vigil next to Raoul's bed while Christine rested should follow him out of the room.

"I had just gone to follow Christine to bed. We've been up most of the night with you both."

Erik's brow furrowed until he followed her gaze to the bed next to his. There he could make out Raoul's shape, his hair lay on the pillow, strangely black against the white muslin pillow case.

"Is he?" His voice, a moment ago harsh and ugly, was so quiet that Meg had to listen closely.

"He's been badly beaten and cut, but the doctor thinks he'll be all right."

He held her tightly at first, but as she noticed his eyes lose focus, his arm, too, relaxed its grip. She stroked him absently, gentling him back to sleep.

he's waiting somewhere he's in the dark in the shadows the light strikes the cold metal and flashes gray blinding me and he is aiming at my heart he waits inevitable he glowers over me his face in the shadows and he is aiming at my heart he will harm them he will kill them to get to me to put the bullet in my heart to wrap the noose around my neck to cut through my throat and drown me in the red gush of violence and retribution he thinks are his to wield he cut his face his beautiful unspoiled face he cut a moon along the side of Raoul's face disfiguring him with the mark of Cain so that they will shun him and it is my burden that he has done this to a man who became my friend my only true friend a man who hated me once and who now risks his life to protect me from the madness of justice the inhumanity of law he will punish my loved ones for the crime of loving me of accepting me of pitying me of allowing me to live he is the shadow and darkens my world the colors seep from the garden marigolds their bright sun fading into gray the royal hue of snapdragons blackens the purity of gardenia sullies into ash his shadow cuts the warmth of their embrace my soul grows heavy and cold waiting for punishment his shadow strips the world of love and pleasure leaving red rivers of blood the only hue that survives his devastation the ragged lunar scar upon the innocent's cheek the pain of guilt sucking the hope from my soul in spite of in spite of in spite of the flickering light of my love in spite of the touch of her hand the whispered words in my ear so hard to discern over the inevitable sound of his approach his footsteps walking in the darkness waiting and I am unable to resist his sentence a sentence laid upon my head at birth and sealed in the desperate rebellion of the cage my life a dream a sweet moment a candle fluttering out now the life she gave me as a gift a gift I should not have accepted a gift whose acceptance sullied the giver dragged her down into the gray and black depths of my lifeless existence into the charnel house into the grave into the rotting corpse itself

"Yes, the police did come. I met the officer in charge at the theater."

"What did you tell him?"

"Of Erik? Nothing. There was a break-in. I shot the intruder."

Don Marcelo drew Madeleine to his side and sat her next to him on the bench under the trellis. The garden was awash in sunlight, the afternoon rays spreading like a fan across the southern edge of the estate. A hummingbird hovered over the honeysuckle blossoms, and the breeze was warm and comforting. Madeleine touched the dark circles under the older man's eyes.

"You've not slept, have you?"

"No. There are things that must be done now. Later I can rest."

"Was the officer satisfied with your explanation?"

Don Marcelo hesitated. "I'm a wealthy and prominent man. He knows better than to question my testimony."

"So you think he was not convinced."

"He could tell that more than the one man were involved. I think he's puzzled that we didn't mention that. If need be, Jacopo and Angelo will come forth and testify that they fought off the other intruders. I will say that I thought it irrelevant to mention them."

Madeleine could tell he was not as confident as he wished to appear. He rubbed his thumb over the back of her hand nervously, unconscious of the gesture.

"We can't risk anyone investigating and finding out about Leroux. They'd be able to trace him back to Paris, and eventually they'd come across his connection to Erik."

"We will do what we must to protect him. The police will be reluctant to challenge my word." Don Marcelo shifted on the bench and faced Madeleine. His gaze was strangely intense. "Now I wish to talk of other matters, matters equally close to my heart."

Sensing the nature of his thoughts, Madeleine grew apprehensive. "Perhaps this is not the time, Marcelo."

"Are you still…angry with me about…?"

She tried to hide the blush that rose in her cheeks. Was she? Yes, a bit. His interest in Carlotta had wounded her pride if nothing else. But this wasn't the main reason she drew away from him. She had been alone most of her life, an independent woman. The recent debacle with Carlotta unsteadied her. Love brought with it heartache and demands that she wasn't sure she was able to bear. There were too many other concerns that drained her energy. Her daughter was pregnant again at a point when she might lose Erik. Perhaps it was better not to feel than to risk such pain!

"I've much on my mind. My daughter's happiness must be my first concern."

"You might be right," Don Marcelo answered softly as if he considered dropping the subject. Just as Madeleine believed he would remain quiet, he cleared his throat and addressed her in a firm tone. "Even so, I'm unwilling to put this off, Madeleine. I fear losing you. I've grown fond of you. No, that is not true. I've come to love you. I'm tired of being alone. I love you, and I plan to marry you as soon as we can decently do so."

Madeleine was momentarily taken off guard. He had not asked her so much as informed her that they would marry.

Before she could protest, Don Marcelo continued, "It may be that I have mistaken your...fondness and respect for me for something it is not. Perhaps I'm foolish to think I might have inspired other feelings in you. You're much younger than I. It's possible that you are misled as to the nature of the marriage that I offer you. I've been a widower for many years, but I have not been celibate. Until you came to live with us, I had discreetly kept a mistress. But shortly after we met—you and I—I found I'd lost all interest in this other woman. I have come to feel that you are...necessary to me. And although I cherish our friendship, I fear it is no longer enough. It has been a long time since I wooed a lady, and I have a poor memory for verse, but do not mistake my lack of poetry as a lack of passion. I want you, Madeleine. I will make you an attentive and ardent husband if you accept me."

Madeleine could feel the intensity of his desire. It swept over her, taking her by surprise. She had locked those feelings away so long ago, she thought she was beyond them. She felt the flush of her face and lowered her eyes to her hand. He had taken it and entwined their fingers tightly. "Oh Marcelo. I would be proud to..."

She didn't have a chance to finish her thought. With unexpected vigor, Marcelo embraced her. His mouth, both soft and intimate, dared her to respond with like passion. She was small in his arms, and for the first time in many, many years she was perfectly content to be swept away.

He bound the wound. The bullet had perforated the fleshy part of his arm and torn clean through the tissue. Fortunately it had not hit the bone. Most of the bleeding had finally stopped although the wound still wept, threatening at any moment to open again. He pulled the cloth tight using his teeth and his left hand to secure the knot just above the gaping hole. He lay back, exhausted, on the dirty bed linen. He thought to sleep, but the moment his eyes closed he saw the Phantom at his feet. The monster stared up at him with an evil fury.

He had nearly succeeded! From his place in the shadows, he had enjoyed watching Piero and his hired thugs mete out the punishment the Count de Chagny deserved for his interference with justice. The beating was brutal, and the man eventually collapsed to the floor unable to withstand the onslaught of the five men Leroux had paid. The one called Egidio drew his knife and slashed at the prostrate man. Leroux was about to come forward to watch Raoul die when he saw a madman leap into the fray. The Phantom rushed heedless of danger into the midst of the gang, striking out with his entire body. Within moments, the men panicked and scattered. Only Egidio remained, a surprised expression on his face.

Leroux knew this was the moment, his only moment to act. He stepped out, the pistol raised to fire at the Phantom. At this distance, death was inevitable. The madman's eyes latched onto Leroux's just in the instant that the latter tensed his finger. With a speed that defied logic, the fiend pulled the stunned Egidio and held him before his own body. Leroux could not stay the shot! The gun fired, and Leroux saw a blossom of scarlet spread across the hapless Italian's chest. The force of the bullet sent both men backward to the ground.

This, too, was the Phantom's crime! He had used the man shamelessly to save his own skin. Leroux was no more guilty than the gun itself. No one else remained. The others had fled, clutching their broken bones, wiping the blood from their faces. Cowards! All of them were cowards! Only he had the strength of character to face the evil thing that hid behind the mask. Only he was pure of heart and would vanquish the monster.

The Phantom lay buried under the massive body of the Italian. One look was sufficient for Leroux to know that Egidio was dead. Blood spread out from the bodies. Yet the Phantom did not rise. Leroux stared down at his prey. The eyes were out of focus. Perhaps he had not escaped the bullet? Suddenly elated, Leroux took the time to examine the man who had been executed before his very eyes more than a decade ago. It disgusted him to think the fugitive had enjoyed this respite. The thought of him with the Giry woman, the young chanteuse, the idea of their having had children turned his stomach. If he were strong enough he would punish her, too!

He had waited a long time to bring this man to justice. Everyone had thought him mad. Before him was the proof that he was more sane than any of the gullible and complacent officers in Paris. He aimed the gun, prepared for the moment of execution. He spoke to the Phantom, the way he had spoken to him in the prison. He had always been careful to use a calm voice while his deputy turned the screws on the contraption that broke the prisoner's bones, one by one. He waited for the Phantom to cry out or to pass out. His calm voice was the proof of the rational nature of the law; the inevitable use of pain was required to punish and purify. The Phantom had not understood. He had not understood that Leroux's mission was to purify, to wipe away the evil. If he had been able to break the prisoner's will, there might have been hope for the man. But stubbornly the Phantom took the pain, his eyes never acquiescing. Even when the Phantom had been unable to stop his cries of agony, his eyes defied Leroux.

He must face his executioner naked! Leroux bent and pulled the mask from the hideous creature at his feet. Yes! He remembered that face, and he saw recognition, too, in the monster's eyes. The Phantom saw his death! He knew he was about to die, and this time there would be no assistance from the count. Leroux couldn't repress the exultation of power that surged through his body as he cocked the pistol and lowered it to within inches of the Phantom's face. The monster's eyes dimmed, and Leroux cursed aloud that the animal might even then mean to escape him into unconsciousness.

And then the shock of the blast. The pain ripped through his arm. The pistol skittered across the wooden floor. The owner of the opera, the man who had harbored the Phantom all these years, stepped out of the shadows, the smoking gun still in his hand. Leroux's only thought was to flee. Anger drove him with a strength he knew he should not have. Don Marcelo Costanzi didn't follow him. He had remained to attend the monster.

Leroux drifted in and out of sleep, tortured by images of the Phantom towering over him, laughing at him, aiming the pistol in his face, and pulling the trigger. He woke with a start in the gray light of morning.

He must get out of Rome. They would look for him. He had changed his rooms several times, but the men he had hired were unreliable. One of them, Egidio, had been killed. At whose door would that death be laid? Leroux had no power in Italy. He was a foreigner. Don Marcelo was wealthy and respected.

But how could he leave his mission unfinished? He was sure that the Phantom had not been mortally wounded. How could he leave when the Phantom yet lived?

Leroux painfully rose from the twisted sheets and packed the few possessions he had. With care he pulled on his coat. The blood had dried a black stain against the black of the coat. The hole rent in the fabric could not be disguised. He would keep moving until he found somewhere to rest and wait. He would leave Rome. Perhaps he should return to France, wait until everything calmed, but he would come back. The Phantom would die.

"Where is everyone? Eh? What does this mean? Why is the performance cancelled?" Carlotta marched up onto the stage, her hands defiantly placed on her hips. She had spent the better part of the day selecting her gown, a deep forest green with gold and brown accents, a fleur de lis pattern along the edging on the sleeves and hem and the thick belt that cinched her waist. She had tired of disguise. She would face the Phantom, make him look upon her face, and accept his doom. He would have to recognize her beauty and his foolish squandering of her talent.

Several of the chorus readied themselves for a brief, informal rehearsal. The maestro scowled at the loud woman.

"Signorina?" he called to get her attention.

"Signorina Carlotta Venedetti, stage name Carlotta Giudicelli. You know it, do you not?" She smiled, proudly, at the maestro.

Indeed he had heard the name. She had been an important diva in Milan many years ago. He wondered at her reason for coming incognito to the opera house over the past several months. "Yes, I do. It is a pleasure to meet you. I recall a performance of yours…Was it in 1865?"

At his reference to the length of time past, Carlotta pursed her lips, furrowed her brow, and stomped her feet. "I was but a child when I starred on the stage in Milan. In Paris, I was the prima donna at the Opera Populaire. I have appeared on the stage of all the major capitals in Europe." It was an exaggeration that she was sure the maestro could not challenge. "I've sung in more opera houses than you have whiskers, Signore Maestro," she said snidely.

"Humph."

"Where is he? He! Where, eh?"

Rinaldo watched her from the wings. Sooner or later he'd have to come out onto the stage. He had returned that morning, intent on asking Erik to forgive him and to allow him to continue working as his assistant at the Teatro dell'Opera. He had washed his hands of Carlotta.

But when he arrived he had come upon the police and Don Marcelo in intense discussion. He gleaned the basics of the incident as told to the officer, but something wasn't right. He could tell that Don Marcelo was holding back information. After the officers left, Don Marcelo announced the temporary suspension of performances.

As the owner was about to depart, Rinaldo had taken a chance.

"I hope Don Erik is not gravely wounded."

Don Marcelo had stared at the young man, as if amazed that Rinaldo was present. He seemed reluctant to answer, "He's convalescing. I imagine we won't be able to keep him at home for more than a few days."

Rinaldo had been relieved.

Now Carlotta stood on the stage bellowing for Erik. Rinaldo assumed that she was the one responsible for the attack. But Carlotta glared at the company, waiting for an answer, obviously puzzled. She stared out toward the empty amphitheater, no doubt imagining herself singing to a packed house. Rinaldo was about to sneak back to Erik's office to continue copying the music, when her voice squealed out his name. "You! Rinaldo! What is the meaning of this?"

He was not going to escape. She would follow him to the gates of hell to get the answers she demanded, and he knew it.

Reluctantly Rinaldo approached the diva, for that was what she resembled now more than ever in the striking green gown, the view of her face unimpeded. Unexpectedly, Rinaldo felt himself stir when he looked at her. She was regal and passionate. Her eyes pierced through him. He found himself staring foolishly at her large provocative mouth. He couldn't tell whether he wanted to gag it with his hand or stop it with his lips. The image of his seizing her violently round the waist and pulling her to him and trapping her mouth—that full, wide, red, lush mouth—with his own caught him off guard. He stopped in his tracks.

"Yes, you! Come!" She wagged her bejeweled finger at him impudently, expecting him to come to her.

"Carlotta," he whispered, trying to sort out the confused reaction he was having to this diva, this force of nature, this unbridled and tempestuous woman.

He told himself it was merely the lust of the body. The night he had tricked Meg into coming to the office, Carlotta had stripped naked before him and held him, kissed him, rubbed her thigh enticingly along his groin. Even though he knew it was only an act, her naked breasts had been pressed against his chest, her moist lips had unblushingly demanded his partly opened mouth. After Meg had left, she turned from him as if nothing had happened between them and dressed. All the while she gloated over their success, he tried to calm the quickening of his body.

"You! Eh? Have you lost your tongue as well as your wits? Where is he, he, he, he, he?"

Instead of answering, Rinaldo asked, "Why are you here? And why aren't you wearing the veil?"

"Ah! It's useless. He knows! They all know. But it doesn't matter. Come here, bambino mio."

Her seductive and playful tone irked him. He hated it when she drew attention to the fact that he was younger than she. The gap between them was not significant. She was a mature woman, yes. But she was still vital and intriguing. She was no silly virgin, but a woman whose desires were perhaps somewhat daunting to most men. But not to him. He tried to focus on what she wanted instead of how she was trying to get it.

"He thinks he can be rid of me! This will not happen. I am the thorn in his side." With a wicked twisting of her fingers, she imitated a thorn or screw digging deeper and deeper into a wound. "I will be like this to him. Eh?"

"He's not here."

"Why? Why is this? He is always here! He cannot think of not being here! This is where he is always." She thought the idea ludicrous.

"There was an assault last night."

"What is it that you are saying, eh? Assault? Who assaults in a theater?" Then she laughed as if she had thought of some private joke. "Assault? So now someone assaults…him? In his own theater? Who is it who does this to…him?"

Rinaldo drew even closer to look down upon her face and watch her eyes. "I thought perhaps you hired someone to attack Erik."

"You are serious about this attack?" she asked, suddenly attentive for the first time. "And Costanzi? Erik? Is he…? Is it serious?"

"Then you truly didn't have anything to do with the assault last night?" Rinaldo could see she was concerned.

At first, she had thought he was joking or lying. Then it became apparent that he was serious. She wrung her hands in an unconscious expression of worry.

"Where is he? Is he badly hurt?"

"Do you care?"

Carlotta raised an eyebrow provocatively and stiffened her spine at Rinaldo's questioning tone. "Care? Care? Why should I care? I hope they cut out his liver! I hope they blinded his eyes! I hope they cut him into a million pieces." Her voice rose dangerously, drawing the chorus's attention downstage toward them.

At each statement she looked into Rinaldo's eyes. He had the peculiar sensation that she was checking to see if any of her curses had hit the mark. It was all an act! He was suddenly convinced that Carlotta, as much as she had ranted and raved over the past months, as much as she had protested that she wanted Erik's destruction, she would be appalled if anything horrid had happened to him. She did care! But it was important that she not seem to care. Rinaldo would allow her the subterfuge.

"Unfortunately for you, it appears he narrowly escaped major injury."

Something relaxed in Carlotta's stance. The quiet was a blessed relief. The rest of the company went back to their rehearsal. Rinaldo waited.

"Well," she said softly. "We will have to find other ways of making him miserable if we can't have his liver cut out." Without another word, Carlotta grabbed the edge of her wide skirt and strutted majestically off the stage.

Rinaldo watched her until she disappeared. He was glad that she had not decided to leave Rome. He wondered at the strange feelings he was having. She was a monster, a selfish and self-centered and vain woman. And yet he would be curiously sad if she were not there.

CHAPTER 13

Scars

He jests at scars that never felt a wound.

Shakespeare, Romeo and Juliet

Erik woke, his mouth dry as dust, and reached out for Meg. Not finding her beside him, he startled awake to blackness, the impression of other presences in the darkened room inescapable. A thrill of fear rushed through him. He rose quickly from the bed, naked except for the light fabric round his lower extremities. The night air was cold on his chest. Bandages were woven round his ribs, across his breast; otherwise his skin was bare. He wrapped the blanket tightly round him. A dull ache registered in his newly awakened mind on each expansion of his ribcage. The vague recollection of a fight, of animal pain and savagery, teased at the corners of his memory.

His eyes soon discerned shapes in the darkness. A maid slept, snoring rhythmically, undisturbed in the soft winged chair by the door. Besides the sleeping girl, Erik made out the solid masses of furniture, and eventually the bulk in a nearby bed. Raoul. Erik stood over the sleeping man, listened for his even breathing, traced the form of his body, and studied him. He had thought Raoul dead. He had lain so still, the river of blood too rich, too abundant to mean anything less than death. Briefly Erik thought he might have awoken sometime back. He recalled the echo of Meg's reassuring words, how a calm relief had flooded over him. Perhaps Meg had told him Raoul was wounded?

Erik shivered as he made out the light color of Raoul's face in the wan moonlight from the open window. The breeze was brisk now that the warmth of day had long vanished. He carefully, silently trod the length of the bed and rounded the corner on his path to the window. He eased the window shut, listening for only a moment to the cadence of night, the soft percussion of crickets, the lonely baritone of an owl in the nearby copse of trees, the rustling tinkle of wind through leaves like the low rush across the reed of a flute. He smiled to imagine plotting the notes to this natural symphony. A low groan distracted him from his fancy. He returned to Raoul's bed and bent closer to look at his friend.

A huge blotch of white struck his eyes as unnatural and out of place. For a moment he almost reached out to touch it, to brush it from Raoul's cheek. Then he recognized it for what it was, a large gauze bandage the length of the man's face. A flash of steel, a whirl of blood, Erik tensed in anger as the image assaulted his senses. The attack. There had been many men, many rough fists, short and thick clubs, a knife blade.

The realization tore at Erik. Cut? They had sliced his face? No mortal wound this, as he had feared. But a wicked, nasty blow it was. He forced his own hand down from his disfigured temple. *No, not like me! He can never be like me! One has to be born with this shame to feel it as I do!* But nevertheless the horrid sorrow of it threatened to wrench a sob from Erik.

Compassion and pity turned to anger as he gritted his teeth in frustration.

Why? Why didn't you leave like I told you to? I didn't want your sacrifice. I can't bear the weight of this pain, your pain. I didn't ask for it, for any of it. Why didn't you call out to me?

Perhaps he had. Erik had awoken suddenly at the desk. Might he have heard Raoul shout out for him? Had he called before? Had Erik not heard, not come? The thought troubled him even more than his anger with Raoul. He would not want Raoul to think he had ignored his cries for help. He came as soon as he understood the danger. He threw himself into the fray in a desperate attempt to avenge if not avert Raoul's death.

Erik sighed audibly. The girl stopped snoring and shifted momentarily in her chair but did not wake.

He returned to the bed, found the glass of tepid water, and drained it. He wrapped the blanket more firmly in place and stepped lightly to the door. Meg. He had to find Meg. His chest ached violently, not solely from the impact of the shot but mostly from the deep emptiness Meg's absence had left. She would have gone to bed. She was in their room, asleep, twisted in the white sheets, for she could not rest without him by her side. He would slip in and find the shape of her body and mold his to hers until she knew she was cradled in his embrace. He would warm her, and she would deepen her sleep until she found that place where they always met, the place before the nightmares, the place where he tried to stay, locked in the safety of their love. The nightmares always found him eventually and tore him from her side, but he would weave a spell so that she rested and dreamed he was with her. He would lie and hold her and tomorrow would not come.

Erik found his way easily to their room. Thankfully the door was not locked. His hand gently and quietly turned the knob and pushed the heavy door open just enough to slip along the ray of dim light from the hallway lamp. In that instant he saw where she lay, a small bundle amid the massive waves of sheets and blankets. His heart beat anxiously as if it might explode in his chest if he didn't draw near her soon. He didn't understand his desperation to be with her, whether it was for him or for her that he needed to caress her. He did not want her to wake. Waking would mean words, and he wanted only touch, the deep intense feel of her, the solid reality of her in his arms. And then to slip down into unconsciousness.

He dropped the blanket to the floor and slipped between the sheets. She tumbled softly toward him as he settled behind her, a soft moan erupted from between her half parted lips. His body enveloped hers which seemed to disappear in the massive shelter of his torso and limbs. Immediately he felt the warmth seep into him and along with it a blessed calm. No one, no one but Meg, could touch him this way. He knew with everything in him that she was his, that she loved him. Only Meg cradled herself, all trust, in his arms. Meg never saw the blood on his hands, the darkened stains even the sunlight did not lighten, the madness just behind his eyes, the misery and the ugliness. She kissed them away, she smiled and they meant nothing, she spoke to him and he was not a beast.

Meg twisted, sliding her body easily across his skin to nestle her head at the soft flesh of his throat. He felt her warm exhalation flow down his chest. Her hand rested soft and limp against his cheek. Her knee bent, and her leg fell across his hip bringing their bodies intimately close in a lover's pose. He drank in the scent of lilac soap in her hair, on her skin. His lips sank into the soft curls above her ear. He splayed his fingers across her back and her hip to ease her closer, closer still to his heart.

He must have dozed, for her words woke him. She whispered them, concern in the breathy voice. "Are you in pain?"

He barely shook his head, preferring to kiss her upturned mouth.

"You were moaning. It sounded as if you were in pain."

He didn't remember. Had he dreamed again? Was it yet again a nightmare? If so, he had fortunately awoken without any memory of it. He shifted slightly and felt the dull ache in his chest. Nothing else.

"Go to sleep," he urged her.

"But I have something to tell you," she insisted quietly.

"Mmmm," he exhaled, overcome by drowsiness.

She stroked his cheek and watched him. He could sense her eyes on him, but his lids were heavy, and he no longer had the energy to be attentive. He sank down deep into sleep again until the morning light.

"Erik," she whispered.

He groaned and pressed her more tightly in his arms. He hid his face deep in a pocket of warmth between the pillow and her neck. Strands of blond hair tickled his nose and mouth, and he kissed her softly behind the ear.

"I'm so glad you slipped into bed last night." She hugged him fiercely. Their limbs were a confusing knot between the two bodies, flesh on flesh taking up any space between the two of them.

Erik's dreams released him unwillingly to the daylight, and he tried to put in order the jumble of images knocking around in his mind. It seemed a silly thing for Meg to say. Didn't he always share her bed? Then a dull pain woke with him, and he realized what she had meant. He had been convalescing from Leroux's attack.

He pushed away from his safe and warm hiding place against her body just enough to look into her doe-brown eyes, wide and shiny with the pleasure of waking with him.

"I have something that I've been desperate to tell you for the past several weeks. It simply cannot wait!" She smiled at him teasingly.

He couldn't resist kissing her soft blossom of a mouth. The pain would wait. The fears would wait. He focused his attention on Meg.

"I'm with child." She earnestly watched for his reaction. Although she had pushed it to the back of her mind, she was tormented by the possibility that he would not be pleased by her news.

Erik could see her anxiety just below the surface of her happiness. He recalled their argument, how badly his brash and stark words had hurt her. His doubts, his fears, he had allowed them to seethe up from the darkness inside him, threatening to spread and taint everything in his world. Lying with her in the bright light of morning, he could not imagine why he had been so foolish to risk drowning them both in his desperate doubts. How could Meg have anything but beautiful, healthy children? Her joy touched him, warmed him.

"Why don't you say something?" She tried not to sound annoyed, but it was there inevitably in the question.

"I'm sorry, my canary. I was just wondering why you waited so long to tell me?" Indeed Erik had been expecting her news for quite some time.

"You already knew, didn't you? Of course," she said as she flopped back with an annoyed sigh onto her back. "You watch me, don't you? You keep track of things."

He stared at her quizzically. Why did it surprise her? Her body fascinated and intrigued him. He was amazed by its strange difference, its incredible changes, its magic. There was nothing about her body that she could hide from him. He slept with her. He knew when she was indisposed. At first it had horrified him to see her bleed, unable to separate the red stains from the threat of violence and injury. But now it simply intrigued him. He enjoyed her fluctuations, could tell when she was nervous and ill tempered, was sensitive to her bodily discomforts, stood in awe of her fecundity.

"I had noticed that you missed your courses," he answered simply.

"Are you happy?"

Instead of answering, he leaned over her carefully and caressed the small protuberance on her abdomen with his hand. It was hard and solid, alive. Magically things were happening inside her tiny body. She would swell and grow and change, and then she would open like a blossom and bring forth another child, a child of his body and hers. He kissed the cradle of life and encircled Meg in his arms and drew her close.

"You must take care of yourself and the child. Promise me that you won't be foolish and do anything to put you and the child in danger."

Meg promised. She felt a cold shiver crawl up her spine at his request. Erik was not safe, and as long as he was not safe, no one he loved was either.

he sleeps he mends the angry rictus of a wound across his face seems alive it writhes as the dream plays behind closed eyes he sleeps and dreams fitfully of being ambushed fists strike away and yet he doesn't call out, he didn't call out to me, he sleeps now safe if anyone can be safe in my world like a contagion the scar lives and grows on his face to cover the entire side leaving only an eye immune to its ravagement he sleeps while his face is taken from him the plague has come I am the plague that sows discord I am mayhem I spread the violence the madness the one who is two the flesh that rejects itself the condemned angel the penitent devil it is I who has taken your face from you the one you have known and left this lunatic vision to war with its double the mirror will always be your foe it will deceive in the language of contradiction you are not who you are you will misrecognize yourself and try to flee but you are still beautiful the scar will heal and calm its red rough complaint it will leave a dry furrow along the map of your face you will never be the same but you are still handsome a handsome man loved by an angel I have seen her touch you from my half dreams I have awoken and seen her touch your face draw back the hairs run gently across your fevered brow and lightly trace a companion route along that wound that will surely devastate you when first you mark its residence upon your skin such tenderness such love it has not changed her desire for you she brings your sleeping hand to her breast she sighs and leans against your side with more than pity my friend you will wake and find her there you are still loved you are still handsome she steals a glance my way and I know looks upon my disfigurement with what thoughts I dare not speculate I will not think that she compares your injured cheek to my monstrous visage I do not care to know that it fills her with relief that you are still fair when I never was I shy from imagining that she wonders if others will draw away from you because of a crescent shaped mark along the side of your face I quell my jealousy you are bruised and cut because you came to my aid it is for my crimes that you are marked and I beg your forgiveness I would gladly take your scar on the untouched side of my face and wear it proudly if it would bring you back to yourself but you are still handsome! you must look at me Raoul and know that your scar is but a scratch it is not who you are you were not born with it it has a meaning in its tender torn ridge is writ loyalty honor courage you must not despair my friend for Christine will be your glass and this but makes you look fierce and brave I am the monster you the warrior

Raoul had come in and out of consciousness. How many days had it been? It seemed as if time had sped up around him and that only he was unmoving, frozen in some chrysalis as life went on without him. He remembered Christine in her light blue chiffon, but next he saw her in a pale rust. Once he caught sight of her in the darkened room, barely able to make out the colors, in what appeared to be her night gown, a silk gold and amber robe loosely tied about the waist. She hovered so close he could see the red of her lips. Others came and went in the room or in his dreams, he was never really sure which was which. He knew he must be sick or injured. He was oblivious to pain. He wasn't sure where he was. The room did not remind him of any room at the Chagny mansion. Could it be the summer house? Had Christine redecorated? He gave in to the heaviness that closed his eyes. Somehow intuitively he understood he must go into the protective arms of sleep to heal.

Questions, questions, questions, over and over and over again someone droned the same questions. He couldn't make them out for a long time, but eventually the words ripped through his sweet oblivion and as they named his body parts he became aware of excruciating pain. A glancing pain in his leg forced his eyes wide open. The glare from the window blinded him, and he squeezed them tightly shut again.

"Signore Conte di Chagny. Does this hurt?"

"Mon dieu, qu'est-ce-qu'il m'a passé? Quelle douleur!"

"Dottore, can't you give him something for the pain?"

"Mia cara, I must examine him. For that, he must not be drugged." The doctor turned his attention to Raoul. The sooner he finished his examination, the sooner he would be able to give the patient something to calm the pain. "Signore Conte, tell me when it hurts."

Raoul had the presence of mind to realize that the doctor was searching for severe problems such as injured organs, internal bleeding. He stifled his reaction to the unexpected discomfort in order to listen to the doctor's instructions. The pain was not unbearable. It had shocked him. He had not felt much before this particular moment. Even during the fight he had been aware that the men were beating him mercilessly, but somehow this awareness was divorced from the actual pain, at least in his memory.

At first, he had simply been keeping vigil. Erik had told him to leave. He had argued uselessly and had finally agreed to go. But there was something ominous about the way Erik sat at the desk that disturbed Raoul. Something he had said about Meg. It came sharply into focus for Raoul the moment he started down the passageway toward the exit. Erik had no intention of surviving the night. He was preparing to meet Leroux and expected that he would be killed.

Angry with himself for agreeing to leave, Raoul decided he would wait and keep watch. The two of them together would have a chance, even if Leroux used underhanded means to attack, which is exactly what the vicious little man had done. Before Raoul could warn Erik, the thugs were in the passageway and on their way to the office.

Without much forethought, Raoul stepped out into the passageway and gave the first man a sharp upper cut to the chin. The man's teeth rattled from the blow, and he went down on his knees. In the close quarters of the passageway Raoul hadn't room to draw his weapon. Instead he relied on his fists. He managed to push back the cutthroats several yards and was on the verge of yelling out to Erik when someone hit him a glancing blow from behind. Stunned he momentarily saw nothing but blackness. The next blow hit him squarely in the gut, effectively making speech impossible. He recovered and forced himself to stand and lash out wildly to keep the men at bay. If he didn't, he knew he was done for.

A voice in the back of his mind chastised him for his brashness. He should have waited for them to pass him, to see how many there were. Then he might have come up behind them. He might have yelled to Erik, who would have met them on the other end, effectively bottling them in the narrow passageway. Between himself and the madman that Erik could be, they would have made short work of the thugs. But that was not what he had done. The little voice without the least hint of regret or sadness told him he was about to die. The blows came relentlessly now, since he was the one who was trapped, surrounded by the toughs. Hands and clubs rained down on him, and he knew all was lost when he sank to the floor.

Christine was the last thought he could remember. That and the faint sound of someone coming toward them. Just as everything went black he wondered if Erik had come. Would they kill Erik, too?

The doctor sat back pleased with himself and his patient. Raoul felt much better than he had when he first woke. Christine smiled broadly at him from the foot of the bed. Then he saw Erik from the corner of his eye. He was alive. His face was expressionless as he stood and watched. Had Erik found him bleeding to death in the corridor? Had the toughs been frightened off? Erik didn't look as if he had been touched.

Christine saw Raoul's questioning gaze and called Erik over to the bed. Hesitantly at first, Erik complied and drew near. The same frozen expression was on his face. The eyes were intense, waiting, expectant, but Raoul couldn't imagine why Erik was wary.

"He's going to be all right. Right, dottore?"

"Si, Signora. He will have battle scars, though. But scars just prove our mettle, do they not, Signore Conte?" The doctor didn't notice the rapid look Erik gave him as he gathered his professional tools about him and prepared to depart. Raoul noticed.

Christine's eyes, saddened for just an instant, went unintentionally to Raoul's face, not to his eyes, but to his cheek. The presence of a large amount of cotton and gauze along his left side awoke in him the dull throb of a wound. Erik's eyes answered his doubt eloquently. He had been cut, slashed. The wound was along the side of his face. Quickly Raoul tested his vision by blinking one then the other eye closed. He was relieved to know that his eyes had not been affected.

"So is it bad?" he asked Erik, not his wife. "Will I look as bad as you?" He attempted to sound wry, but he wasn't sure that a slight desperation didn't color his tone.

Erik's lips curled gratefully into a half smile, and he visibly relaxed. "Unfortunately, you're still going to be handsome. But you will have a large and obvious scar."

Christine hastened to reassure Raoul, which had just the opposite effect. She was too fervent, too eager to console him for a loss that she pretended did not matter. For the truth of it, he looked again to Erik.

Erik understood Raoul's need and edged closer to the man. He placed a hand on his arm, and without taking his eyes from Raoul's he described the wound. "They sliced you with a blade from the temple to just above the mouth. It's a curved slash that reminds one of a crescent moon. It will never look as bad as it does now. In time it will fade, but it will not go away. People will be drawn to it before they see anything else about your face. People who have known you will lament the sad maiming. Those of us who are close to you will not see it as anything but a part of you. It will loom as large as you wish or it will be as insignificant as you demand. But it will not go away."

Raoul swallowed several times. His eyes never left Erik's. Christine's hand nervously worried his palm. Erik's eyes darted once toward her and back to Raoul. Though not a word passed between them, it was as if Raoul could hear him say, "She is beside herself with worry. Say something to her."

Turning from Erik, Raoul smiled at his wife. Her eyes immediately brightened, but the worried rubbing of his palm continued. "Well, I just want to know if it will make me look dashing!"

Christine released a tight, nervous laugh and broke out into a genuine smile. Erik's hand squeezed Raoul's arm gently and then was gone.

Within moments, Raoul drifted back into sleep, only to wake nearly twenty-four hours later much more alert and with a gnawing hunger. Everyone was relieved to see him on the mend. After he had eaten the carefully selected meal Cook had supplied, Raoul asked to see Erik.

Within the hour, Erik was seated beside the bed.

"You must have found me unconscious. What happened? Did something frighten them away?"

Erik realized that Raoul had no memory and wasn't aware of what had happened. He didn't even know that Erik had been injured and had spent the first day in the small bed next to his. His wounds had been nothing compared to Raoul's, of course.

"I had fallen asleep. Something woke me. I came out and found them beating you to death. You were already on the floor, unconscious or nearly so. I fought. Leroux stepped out of the shadows and tried to shoot me. But instead, Marcelo shot Leroux, wounding him."

"Where is he?"

"We don't know. He got away. Marcelo doesn't believe the wound was mortal."

The two of them were quiet for several minutes. Nothing had changed, it seemed. Leroux was still a threat. He would be back. They didn't voice the obvious. Instead they spoke of other things.

Raoul was talking about the need to rise and exercise his limbs. Unable to contain it any longer, Erik blurted out, "I told you not to stay!"

Raoul was somewhat surprised at the vehemence of Erik's accusation.

"I came out as soon as I heard anything," Erik added. His tone was distinctly annoyed. But Raoul could hear the self-recrimination.

"I did nothing more than you would have done for me."

"Well," Erik answered, lamely. "At least I don't have your death on my conscience."

"Oh? You have a conscience?" Raoul teased.

"A very small one, but yes," Erik answered. "I thought you were dead. And now you have that wound."

Raoul did not respond. The silence was uncomfortable for them both. The count cleared his throat and whispered, "I would like you here when they remove the bandage."

Erik frowned. Clearly it was bothering Raoul. He was apprehensive about the scar. "Of course. Whatever you wish."

"I know that I can learn from you what it will be like."

"Raoul, it is not something that I can help you with. I have always been deformed. But your scar has not robbed you of a face, my friend. It will be bearable. Unless you make it out to be more than it is."

"Erik, why did you assemble the household?" Meg whispered the question on everyone's mind. "Was this a good idea? Raoul is just coming to terms with his scar."

The count appeared at the top of the landing, supported on one side by Angelo, on the other by Christine. They were helping him to the side parlor where the morning light was cheerful and full. He had tired of the sick room and wished to sit up and read. As he realized that the staff was assembled at the foot of the stairs in the long hallway, he hesitated. Erik could see the puzzled expression on his wounded face. The bandages had been permanently removed. The stitches were blackening. They would not be removed for at least another week. The swollen tissue was beginning to shrink back to its normal size, but the wound was still angry and prominent. All eyes were drawn to the handsome face ravaged by a knife.

Erik looked once at Raoul and then at the assembly. He cleared his throat, and most lowered their impertinent eyes to focus once more on Don Marcelo's son. Suddenly he seemed to have lost track of his purpose. Erik shifted nervously from one foot to the other for just a moment before finding his resolve once again.

Don Marcelo and Madeleine stood by, the children in front of them. Mario held Laurette back with a gentle arm around her shoulders. Raoul and Christine's children fidgeted, wanting to return to the breakfast room for more Italian pastries and anxious to spend some time with their father in the parlor. Erik studiously avoided looking at them, his attention fixed on the shadow people in his world.

He knew the names of the staff. Had they realized, they'd have been surprised. But they couldn't have because he interacted only marginally with most of them. He accepted their services indirectly, never allowing them access to his rooms whenever he was present. They watched him, studied him from their positions as servants in the house. His silence struck them as coldness, haughtiness, pride, yet they also caught glimpses of him with the children, with Donna Meg, and at times were even startled to hear him laugh. They knew he was not a monster. Yet it unsettled them that he would sometimes come into the kitchen when no one was around and serve himself a slice of smoked ham or that he scrounged around the larder for an apple, leaving quickly if he should hear Cook's footsteps, or that his shadow would often retreat soundlessly across the wall as they entered a room to clean.

Meg was his voice. They touched his things, cleaned and pressed his clothes, and laid out his boots each day; his coat they brushed and hung for his use should he mean to leave. They stocked the kitchen and the parlors with things he liked, the books recently ordered from the bookstore, the wine from Bordeaux, the cheeses and the fruits of which he never seemed to tire, the woolen blanket in the sitting room. Young Mariana always placed the dark honey and cream close to his place at the morning table because he liked his tea sweet and white.

She pretended not to watch his pleasure when he sat facing the sun, warmed his hands against the delicate steaming porcelain cup of tea, and took that first sweet taste.

They knew him to be gentle most of the time. But when there were loud voices raised in anger between him and the mistress, it frightened them. Unlike most gentlemen he made no effort to quiet his voice in those infrequent fits of rage. There was something uncontrolled about him that disturbed them. Stay away! they whispered among themselves. They feared his wrath. It was especially necessary to be cautious in the music room. No one cared to clean in this most precious of rooms for fear of upsetting his papers. He had snapped at one of them one day when she had collected the torn and wadded scraps from the floor to dispose of and then thought to tidy the piano by arranging the scattered pages into several neat piles. He ranted and raved at the poor girl. Just as suddenly as he had begun, he stopped. She was trembling and wiping frantically at the tears that were rolling in wide wet swatches down her face. Without a word of apology or dismissal, he left her crying in the middle of the room. For days afterward, he slipped in and out of rooms like a ghost; no one seemed to know where he was.

Cook liked to argue that he was shy. She made him special dishes, ones she knew he could not resist. She soon found he preferred simple meals to all the fancy ones she prepared. At the dinner parties for Don Marcelo and his guests, Cook would fix stuffed partridge in raisin sauce and jellied eggs and highly peppered sausages, but she always made sure that there were trays of simple cut meats, cheeses, bits of apple, grapes, a variety of olives, breads and sweet rolls drizzled with honey. She knew he ate to his fill on these, avoiding the smoked sturgeon, the pickled meats, the fancy pies she was praised for by the aristocratic friends of Don Marcelo.

They stood anxious and curious now, for don Erik never addressed them directly, yet here he had called them himself to assemble in the great hall without explanation.

Erik studied them, their curiosity barely disguised. Once he took this step, it would be irrevocable. The illusion would never be in his grasp again unless they dismissed every one of the staff and started afresh with new servants. These people were accustomed to his ways, had formed whatever ideas they might of him. There was no need to disrupt that comfortable balance of intimacy and distance. But Raoul stood at the head of the stairs, naked, exposed, his new face like a heavy yoke on his shoulders.

"I apologize for taking you away from your duties. I shan't keep you long. You've known me now for several years. But I daresay that I have kept mostly to myself." Erik paused as if not quite sure how to proceed. "With my mask, I strike some of you as odd if not frightening. I don't wear it when I'm with my family. But I have felt the need to do so when I come in contact with you. I must be constantly vigilant, and hence I'm aware of your comings and goings, because only when you are gone can I take this off." Erik pointed at the mask, the one he usually wore at home, the one the staff was used to as well.

Don Marcelo, Meg, and Madeleine understood now what he planned to do. Madeleine held Meg gently back to keep her from going to Erik.

"I would like to come home and know that I do not have to think of how someone might react if they were to see my real face. I need to be able to move about freely without worry that I will…frighten any of you." Again he paused, uncomfortable. He cleared his throat and cast a look around the room. He had never had to explain himself before. He had avoided it by hiding, ignoring the eyes of strangers, pretending to be immune to their curiosity, to be cold, aloof, and uninterested in others. It came to him that he had been living in Don Marcelo's estate much in the same way he had lived at the Opera Populaire, as if he were a ghost. He couldn't avoid all contact, but he pretended to be invisible to the staff. To a very large extent he managed to avoid running into them.

"Behind this," he tapped his mask with a finger, "is a disfigured face. It has been mine since my first memories. I believe I was born with it. I have no family that can tell me otherwise. People who look like me hide or cover themselves, as I do with this mask."

Erik stopped. He turned quickly to the children. He had forgotten they were present. His heart felt compressed and pained as he wondered how his son was taking this in. François was listening in rapt attention to his father's description of himself. Erik could not tell if the boy was ashamed. Would he understand why he was doing this?

Erik addressed the servants once more. "Perhaps a few of you have caught glimpses of me when I was unaware. Those of you who haven't may be… shocked at first. I hope that you might eventually become inured to the sight. My family appears to see beyond it. But I cannot count on that from you. Don Marcelo must forgive me if this proves to be too uncomfortable for some and they request to leave his employ. I have decided that I would like to call this home. To do so means that I must be able to walk about without this." Erik's hand traveled to the simple mask that covered most of his face. He lifted the edge with his thumb and index finger and casually removed it.

For one moment only, he looked away, at an oblique angle. Then he looked at each member of the household, one by one. They were deadly silent as they stared at him. No one moved or spoke. Gradually Erik noticed many of them relaxed their stance, shoulders lowered an infinitesimal degree, taut facial muscles released their edge. Erik felt as if a breeze rippled through the hall, as if they had all let out a collective sigh.

Some of the staff had at first been shocked. A few were repulsed but trained well enough to disguise their initial desire to frown or to back away. Many had indeed been prepared by brief glimpses they had stolen of him unawares. But none of them openly drew back in horror or disgust.

As he told them that they could go, Erik disguised a slight tremor to his voice, a silent prayer of thanks in his heart, that they had not called him a monster or fled shrieking.

As several began to drift away, Cook, a tall corpulent woman with sharp eyes and crooked teeth, called out to Erik, "Don Erik, would you like me to make the custard for you tonight? I thought we would have roasted lamb with mint jelly. Is there anything else that you would like?"

Erik didn't remember exchanging but a handful of words with the woman in the several years she had cooked his meals. He stuttered slightly over his response, but eventually he made a tentative request. "I like the herbed bread you made last Sunday. I would be content with that and the lamb."

"And the custard?" She smiled at him as if she had caught him in a lie.

"By all means, Cook. Yes, I should—indeed the children would also—greatly enjoy some custard." Out of the corner of his eye, he saw the delighted smiles on his children's faces.

The other servants who had lingered in the hall were touched by Erik's obvious gratitude to the cook. In turn, each of those who had not already returned to their chores, tipped their heads at Erik and addressed him, "With your leave, Signore." "Good day to you, Don Erik." "Your pardon, Signore." "At your orders, young master."

As Erik shyly acknowledged each departure, Raoul descended the stairs. No one marked his appearance. No one noticed the livid crescent along the side of his face. All attention had been on Erik. In contrast, Raoul's wound was but a crinkle in a sheet of fine paper, a streak across a crystal window pane, the blighted edge of an otherwise perfect blossom.

CHAPTER 14

Lady Macbeth

Hie thee hither,
That I may pour my spirits in thine ear;
And chastise with the valour of my tongue
All that impedes thee from the golden round,
Which fate and metaphysical aid doth seem
To have thee crown'd withal.

Macbeth, William Shakespeare

"This goes on too long," Carlotta fumed as she stood in the doorway of the empty office. It had been a fortnight. No sign of the Phantom. She stepped inside and crossed the room to stand opposite the Phantom's empty chair. Strewn across the dark wood surface of the desk were piles of receipts and bills, a ledger on which figures and names were scrawled. Someone had been working. Season suspended until further notice. Teatro dell'Opera Closed. She scanned Paolo Ricci's editorial in an old copy of the gazette that had been casually left on the desk.

> *In a season plagued with mishap, the current production of* La canzone di cuore *opened last night to a mixture of mayhem and applause. The reader will not be forced to read a tedious review of this latest opera composed by the mysterious masked genius of Rome—need I say his name?—Signore Erik Costanzi. Give me leave to admit that, as in other productions, the composer-director has succeeded in surprising and challenging our expectations. Those of you who faithfully follow this humble reporter's reviews will know that Sig. Costanzi continues to set precedents. We have long known his jealous control of the Teatro dell'Opera. Not only does he compose the majority of the operas staged at that venue, but in the recent seasons he has even taken charge of the*

artistic direction of the works. Now it seems he intends to star in his own com-
positions! Lest the reader ascribe this new turn of events to megalomania, we
must confess that the unfortunate collapse of the tenor, Sig. Grimaldo Tessari,
required that someone step forth on the boards. But are we to think that there
is no understudy for such an important role? Whatever the circumstances, Sig.
Costanzi evidently did not trust anyone but himself to adequately interpret the
role of the hero. Of course, he managed to do a respectably good job on the stage,
in spite of his insistence on wearing the mask. Ah, such showmanship! Is there
no end to this man's talent? Indeed it appears he would suggest there is not!

She crumpled the paper, annoyed by the obvious sarcasm of the article. Paolo Ricci had once delighted her with his acerbic commentaries. Now she found him too glib, too self important himself!

Every afternoon for more than a week, Carlotta had gone directly to confront the Phantom in his office only to find it vacant or occupied by Rinaldo Salvatore Jannicelli. Today was no different. So she had grabbed the first person she could find and sent him scurrying to find the young assistant. She wanted answers. Now.

In her reticule, folded into a small square of paper, was the article Ricci had written more recently, this one focusing on the mysterious circumstances of a theater company under siege by unknown, malevolent forces. In it, Ricci revealed the investigation into the recent death of an intruder at the Teatro dell'Opera. Supposition after supposition followed. Why had the company suspended the play when the tenor Grimaldo had apparently revived completely the day after his collapse on the stage? The cancellation of several weeks of performances and the loss of their revenue were not due to his inability to perform, according to an interview Ricci had had with the tenor. Then there were references to other accidents and problems, most of which could be ascribed to Carlotta and her assistant although the pesky reporter had not managed to find that fact out!

Rinaldo reluctantly entered Erik's office. While left in charge of matters, he had taken the office as his own. He took the responsibility as his only means to prove to Erik that he regretted his complicity in Carlotta's sabotage. She was the last person he wanted to see. Even as he wished she'd desist and leave the Teatro dell'Opera and Rome itself, he was uncomfortably aware of the strange effect she had recently had on him. He wiped his sweaty palm along the weave of his trousers and took his seat behind the desk.

"Signorina Giudicelli? I thought we'd settled matters a few days ago."

He referred to a loud and belligerent confrontation Carlotta had forced on him over her continued desire for revenge. He had made it clear that he would no longer assist her, and even worse, he would aid Erik in whatever strategies he proposed to employ in order fight back. She had gone pale with fury. She had ranted and raved in this very office, telling him he was ungrateful. Alternately, she had played on his sympathies repeating the story of past grievances—even when she kept these fairly vague. When this seemed to have little or no effect, she had threatened him, warning him that he still owed her a vast sum of money, that he had been the actual agent in most of the incidents that had plagued the company. And so on and so on.

He had held his ground.

"I want to know what this is about! Who attacked him? You have not told me. When does he return, eh? This you will tell me!"

"Carlotta, I couldn't say. I've already told you everything I know."

He leaned forward, his fists braced on the smooth, polished surface of the oak desk, his temper barely in check. Neither of them was aware that someone had approached until they heard the voice.

"I'm touched by your concern, Signorina Giudicelli."

Erik filled the doorway, his cool green eyes surveying his enemies in his own lair.

Carlotta's smile turned up at one corner of her wide, full mouth. She examined the man and found no hint that he had been injured in any way.

"You decide to take a holiday, eh? Or were you running away from me, M. Phantom?"

Erik stiffened and glanced quickly at Rinaldo. "I prefer you call me by my name, mademoiselle," he warned in French.

"Erik?"

"Signore Costanzi," he corrected her without apology for the formality.

"Erik, you have been a naughty boy." She ignored his aloofness. "You think that you can escape me?"

"You can't possibly be unaware that a man was killed here in the theater the night of the opening." He returned to Italian since Carlotta had not referred to him again as the Phantom.

"Ah hah! You think that I hired someone to assassinate you? You? The...? You fear me so much that you run away and hide? And the whole theater is closed?" She said triumphantly. "You can *not* blame that on me!"

Erik examined her for several moments without speaking. Raoul had mentioned that someone must have led Leroux to Italy. Erik suspected that it was

Carlotta, but it didn't seem logical. She was after her own revenge, had worked assiduously to achieve it, and hardly seemed generous enough to invite another enemy to share in her triumph over the Phantom. Surely she understood the risk of bringing Leroux into her plan? Unless she desired Erik's death?

"I assure you, signorina, that it was not your presence that kept me away from the theater for the past week. It was unavoidable. Performances will resume shortly."

"Why did this happen? I don't understand. This man who was killed, did he want money?"

She seemed genuinely curious. He considered telling her about Leroux, but for what purpose? She obviously had no idea that the inspector had found him.

"Signorina Giudicelli, we need to talk."

Carlotta threw back her head and laughed in delight. Rinaldo turned uncomfortably red as he watched Erik's reaction. He had never seen him so cold, so still, as if he might strike the woman a mortal blow.

"Oh, dear me, oh my, you must forgive me! That was just too precious to miss. You," she pointed at Erik and emphasized the word with her outstretched hand, "want to speak with me? What can we possibly have to talk about?"

"Rinaldo, leave us." The young man understood the ominous tone and dared not refuse. He rounded the desk, brushing past Erik who stepped aside to allow him to leave. After the young man passed over the threshold, Erik quietly closed the door.

In a movement that took Carlotta completely off guard, Erik grabbed her and lifted her from her seat. He held her roughly by the arms and shook her briskly. He was only inches from her astonished face, and she could smell the almond soap on his skin. His eyes, so compelling at a distance, were impossible to disregard so close to her own. She felt that he was holding her up and if he released her she would crumple like a rag doll to the ground.

"Carlotta, I stand on the edge of a chasm. I have tried to persevere despite your attacks, your threats. I have hoped that you would…understand…see that I'm…not what I was. I have tried, but you are pushing me beyond my power to control myself! We must talk! We must come to some…mutual agreement. If we do not end this, I cannot speak for what I might do."

She was speechless, dead weight in his hold. He gritted his teeth in an effort to curb the powerful desire to throw her against the wall, to shake her until her teeth rattled. Instead, he took a deep breath and set her down in the chair near his desk.

It took her only a moment to straighten her twisted sleeves. In the process, she recovered her former composure and managed to stare up at him archly. But she knew better than to say anything. She waited for him to speak.

"What will it take for you to let me go?"

"Let you go? Why would I do that?"

"What do you intend to do to me, Carlotta? Worry me to death? Annoy me until I put a gun to my head?" he shouted, exasperated by the petulant, self-satisfied expression on her face.

"Don't push me, Phantom!"

"I'm not the Phantom!"

He saw that she was unconvinced. She folded her arms across her bosom as if she dared him to continue. When he said it, he had believed it. But the sneer on Carlotta's face brought back every angry thought and fantasy that the Phantom had ever harbored regarding the egotistical Carlotta Giudicelli, prima donna of the Opera Populaire. It was as if he stood again in the shadows of the Parisian opera house and cringed at the diva's self-satisfied performance.

"I am not…that creature anymore." He fought the sharp spur of shame, for part of him felt he was betraying himself. What more would he be asked to give up to live in peace? "I've made a new life for myself."

Carlotta didn't blink.

He sighed deeply, frustrated and at a loss as to how to touch her cold, vengeful heart. He sat in the chair across from her. His agitation had revived the dull ache in his chest, the spot where he had been shot still sore and tender. He stopped his hand, forced it to his side, before it rose to soothe the discomfort.

"What do you want?" he whispered, trying to calm his breathing. "Do you want my death?" he asked, careful to cull any hint of emotion from his voice. For once, he was consoled by the requirement of the mask. It protected him from Carlotta's invasive gaze.

She frowned, but said nothing.

Anger stirred. He felt it rise like a belch of hellfire. It burned his throat. He tamped it down.

"What will satisfy you?" He dug his fingers into the palms of his hands. He would choke the answer from her if she refused to respond. There must be something that she wanted more than the continuation of this cruel, endless game.

"I want you to dismiss that whore of yours."

He rose so violently that his chair toppled noisily to the floor. He towered over her. In order to refrain from striking her, he kept his fists lowered, tightly braced against his body. Between clenched teeth, he growled at her, "Don't! Don't ever speak of my wife again!"

Just as angry as he, she stood and tried to push him away, both her hands flat against his chest. An involuntary sound of pain escaped Erik's tightly pressed lips. His reaction surprised her so much that she immediately brought her hands to her throat in a protective gesture. She had not budged him. Undaunted by the pain, he grabbed her hands and clasped them tightly in his.

"I accept that you have cause to hate me, even to seek my destruction, but if you threaten my family, I will finish, I promise you, what I started so many years ago in the Opera Populaire."

Carlotta understood the threat. Even though he didn't say the words, she sensed danger in his barely controlled strength.

"I can destroy you, Phantom!" She could threaten, too.

"How?" he asked with a hint of skepticism. He had seen what she was willing to do. And he had also understood that there were limits past which, for all her blustering, she would not go. He dropped her hands and backed away, waiting for her answer.

"What if I told Ricci who you really were?"

"Then your fun would be over, wouldn't it?"

"Do you think so?" She hated his smug confidence! "Wouldn't I enjoy watching them tar and feather you? Or perhaps they would finish what the Parisian police were so inept at doing. I would be there watching you hang, Signore Erik Costanzi!"

Yes, she could do it. She could send him to his death. If they believed her. And why wouldn't they? The Italian police could easily communicate with the authorities in Paris. The details Carlotta might furnish would prove true. The conclusive bit of evidence would be easy to obtain. They would simply need to see him without his mask. His face would be the final proof. Yes, it was within her power to see him put to death.

"So, is that what you want, Carlotta? To see me hang?" he asked, genuinely curious to know just how deep was her anger, just how cruel could she be.

"Yes!" she responded without hesitation. She spit the word at him as if it were a weapon, and Erik was ashamed to realize that he had visibly winced.

Several moments passed between them in silence. She waited for his next attack, looked forward to it, craved it. She wanted to see fire in his eyes! Instead he turned his back to her. When he spoke, it was without anger. She could not read his tone.

"And there is nothing else that you want? There is nothing that will satisfy you short of my death?"

Carlotta shifted nervously in the chair. Erik stepped back and studied her. There was something! He could see her mind working out the details, negotiating the pros and cons of her next move.

Finally she began, "I told you what I wanted. That is, I started to tell you. But you will not listen! You are impossible!"

"I will not dismiss Meg. She is the diva of this company. That is not negotiable."

"Humph! You see? You see? You are the Phantom! Everything has to be your way! You want your…wife…on the stage to sing your music. You want to stay at home, so there are no performances. It is always your will!"

"What good would it do you for me to remove Meg? How does that give you your revenge?"

"I want her off the stage! I want you to put me in her place!" Carlotta rose dramatically from the chair. She wagged her index finger angrily at Erik. "You took it away from me. I want it back!"

Erik was stunned. His mouth opened, his chin slackened, as he observed the demented woman. It had been years since she had graced a stage. She was far too old to play the ingénue. He wasn't even sure what was left of her voice. Certainly she had lacked discipline even as far back as her final tragic years at the Opera Populaire. Did she really expect that he would place her on the stage as the prima donna of the Teatro dell'Opera in Meg's place?

"You can't be serious!"

Carlotta pursed her lips angrily together as she realized he planned to refuse her demand. "You think I have no power? You think I won't go to the police. Well, maybe you are right, eh? But I can cause you pain, M. Phantom. There are others that do not know your true identity. I could make sure they find out."

Erik remained silent. He frowned at her vague threat, waiting for her to speak more plainly.

"You have a family. You have two beautiful sons. They are old enough, perhaps, to know who you really are? They know what murder is, do they not?"

When she saw the look in his eyes, she almost regretted having made the threat. She would have gloried in his anger, but the panicked despair that she glimpsed in those expressive eyes for the one moment before he veiled it made her ashamed of herself. He took one step backwards as if about to retreat. She could tell he was overwhelmed. But then he stopped. He squared his shoulders and considered her.

"I cannot give you everything you want, Carlotta, but I will do something better than what you've asked of me."

Carlotta scowled at the calm, reasonable sound of his voice. There was a note of surrender in it, but she knew he was a clever man. She listened to him intently. She would not let him manipulate her.

"You wish more than anything to be on the stage. I can see it in your eyes every time we rehearse. You yearn to be one of the singers on the stage, to sing before a packed and appreciative audience."

"Not just any singer! No, no, no, no, no! I was the star! You ended my career with your madness and your domineering will to have Christine Daaé on the stage in my place!"

Quickly before she lost control and said something insulting about Christine, Erik interrupted, "You are not a young woman, Carlotta."

As if this were a shock, Carlotta reddened to a deep scarlet. Erik raised an eyebrow, amazed by the extent to which the woman could delude herself.

Quickly, before she could recover, Erik drew close to her and whispered seductively, "You are a mature woman, a powerful woman, a desirable woman." The effect was what he wanted. She softened, drinking in his compliments. "You would be wasted on such roles as the innocent princess, a silly milkmaid."

"Why? I am twice the woman Giry is! I had audiences eating out of my hand!"

"Carlotta, you would be crushed if they laughed at you."

He hesitated, watching her carefully. He was dangerously close to ripping off the veil. He needed her to recognize the realities of her situation, but he also had to convince her that there was a way for her to come back to the stage.

His nearness stilled her. He walked slowly around her, his lips close to her cheek. She held her breath, following his movements out of the corner of her eye.

"You are at the point in your career where you are finally ready for some of the best roles for women." His voice, velvet, gathered itself about her shoulders and caressed her throat. "You, Carlotta, are not a simpering damsel. You are a Medea, a Cleopatra, a Lady Macbeth! Those are the roles that only someone of your presence and maturity can play to effect on the stage." Erik cringed inwardly at the necessary betrayal as he added, "Meg doesn't have the strength, the presence to portray those women. You do!"

In her mind's eye, she saw herself decked out in gold lamé, her eyes painted black like the hieroglyphic figures on Egyptian ruins, reclining on a litter, a viper clutched dangerously at her breast! She was a woman of experience, not a silly virgin to be manipulated by a handsome hero. The Phantom was right! It was all a matter of the proper role. She could be Cleopatra. She could urge her husband on to do the dirty deed in the Scottish castle and wring her hands in the light of a candle and sing of the blood that would not go away. She saw her clothes rent, her hair wild and black, the blood of her children on her robes as she accused Jason, her faithless husband, of betrayal and abandonment!

"You would cast me? You would direct me in these operas?"

Erik struggled with his doubts, with the monstrous absurdity of a pact between him and Carlotta Giudicelli. Oh he could certainly train her to rise to the demands of such roles. But not if she refused to put in the necessary work. Of course, he wasn't sure about her voice. It was possible that it was irretrievably lost. Yet he had no choice but to try.

Close to her ear, he asked, "If I agree to cast you in the role of Lady Macbeth, will you submit yourself entirely to my will?"

It was almost as if he had stroked her cheek. A frisson of indescribable pleasure ran up Carlotta's spine. She understood that he didn't necessarily mean the same thing she wished to understand when he spoke thus. Nevertheless it felt delicious to think that he would be devoting all his efforts to her success on the stage.

"Yes, I agree." She held out her hand for him to take and kiss in sign of their pact.

"No, it is not done." He ignored her raised hand. "You must give me some assurance in return."

"I owe you nothing! You are the one who owes me!"

He ignored her accusations. "You must promise me that you will not torment me or mine ever again. You must promise that you will absolve me of further guilt."

Reluctantly, Carlotta nodded.

"I must hear you say it, Carlotta."

"If you make me a success on the stage in this opera, I will forgive you what you did to me."

Erik frowned. He heard the careful phrasing. "And what of Piangi?"

"Do you think you can ever be forgiven for that?"

"No, you are quite right, but it is not your place to punish me for what I did to him. Has he been party to this?"

"You meant to kill him!"

"Yes, I suppose I did."

"Suppose?"

"I wasn't thinking clearly! I was being hunted down!"

"For killing that scene shifter!"

"I won't discuss my crimes with you!"

"And you dropped the chandelier in an auditorium full of…"

Erik flinched visibly at the charge, the only charge that yet tormented him. "Yes, yes, yes, a thousand times, yes! But I can't change the past. Not for you and not for myself."

Again she regretted her angry words. What if he decided he wouldn't put on the *Macbeth*? This was an opportunity that she hadn't even dreamed of! And he would be her director. They would work together day in and day out! Even so, he was the Phantom. He could not so easily brush that fact aside. And she would not let him.

"You are a murderer. You can't blame me for speaking the truth!"

…

"And you've had it all! You are a famous composer. You live in a beautiful mansion. You have everything you want!"

…

"You should pay for your crimes, shouldn't you? It's only right that you suffer!"

…

"Why don't you say something?" she shouted in exasperation, shaking her fists in the air at his silence.

He kept his face averted, his eyes cast down toward some insignificant spot near the floor. "There's nothing to say that hasn't already been said." His voice was low. "But you're wrong when you think I have everything. Every night I go to sleep I wonder if it will all disappear the next morning. Every stranger that passes me is my enemy, another tormentor."

"Am I to pity you?"

"No!" He whirled on her. "I don't want your pity! I don't want anything from you!" But before he looked away, Carlotta had glimpsed something besides scorn in his eyes. The next time he spoke, his voice was carefully controlled. "I'll expect you on stage tomorrow at nine in the morning. Rinaldo will give you the score. Review it tonight."

"I don't rise before noon."

"Well, signorina," he tossed over his shoulder, his hand on the knob, "from now on, you will go to bed early and rise early. Don't disappoint me, Carlotta. We have struck a bargain, you and I, and it will not be I who breaks it."

As he abandoned her in the office, she stomped her foot several times in anger.

"What is *she* doing here?"

"She works here, Carlotta, just like you."

Carlotta sneered openly at Meg, who shocked at the open hostility and bad manners, looked to Erik to say something. Instead he went to the orchestra pit and whispered instructions to the maestro as if nothing had happened.

When Erik returned, he took Meg gently by the forearm and guided her back to a corner of the stage.

Carlotta waited impatiently, stifling a huge yawn. She hadn't gone to bed early, and she had had no intention of rising early either. Erik had judged as much and sent Rinaldo at seven thirty to get her to the theater whatever the cost. The servant, frightened out of her wits at the mere thought of waking her mistress before noon, at first refused to admit Rinaldo. Little did she realize that he was as loath to disappoint Erik as she was her mistress, so after trying to reason with her, Rinaldo pushed her easily aside and marched directly to the main bedroom. He did hesitate, his hand on the door knob, but then he reminded himself that he had already seen Carlotta naked under even more inappropriate circumstances than the present ones. He almost retreated when he tried to imagine her anger. Between the two—Erik and Carlotta—there was little chance of surviving unscathed. So he bravely faced the tiger in her den.

He nearly laughed to see the imposing lady sprawled across the bed, one lovely naked thigh poking out from the twisted covers. Her face was completely relaxed, without make-up, and he noticed with a wry smile that not only did she have several light freckles on the bridge of her nose but that she had also drooled lightly onto her pillow case. When she slept, she was not frightening. She seemed smaller, too, than she was in all her glory, and Rinaldo was surprised at the healthy, fresh glow of her skin. Without the make-up and finery she always wore, she looked almost sweet.

How was he to wake her? He said her name out loud to no avail. She didn't even stir. When he approached the bed, he couldn't resist observing her even more closely. Her hair had spread softly across the pillow as if it were part of it, and she rested her face in its silky strands. Her long lashes cast a deep shadow on her cheeks. Her slightly parted lips allowed him to catch just a hint of a deep pink tongue and the barest edge of even white teeth. His eye trailed naturally down the line of her jaw to her throat. Her nightgown was open to the swell of her ample bosom.

Rinaldo shook the excitement from his mind, but his body was not so easily convinced. He must get out of her bedroom as expeditiously as possible. So he gently shook her shoulder, not once but three times, before she finally roused. At first, she simply stared at him. Then she threw back the covers and rose furiously from the bed.

"Francesca!" she shouted. "Who told you to let…?"

"I forced my way in, Carlotta. The poor girl is hiding in the kitchen."

His eyes couldn't help but take in her figure. She was voluptuous. Yet there was no delicacy about her; she was sleek and muscular like a panther, every inch of her made to enjoy.

The annoyance she felt faded as she noticed his eyes roaming over her. It pleased her to be watched, admired. His appreciation was obvious, much to his discomfort and her delight. She didn't move to cover herself. Instead she approached him with the confidence of a hunter. The poor boy was sweating, a light film beading his upper lip as he tried to find somewhere safe to rest his eyes.

"Don Erik sent me to escort you to the theater. He expects…"

"He expects? He? What time is it?" Suddenly all thought of spending the next hour with the young man in bed was shattered by the realization that she had been summoned by the Phantom!

"It's quarter of eight, and I'm to have you on stage by…"

"Eight? Impossible! Get out! Go tell the Phan…him…that no one tells me what to do." She grabbed the closest object, which happened to be a cushion from the chair, and threw it at Rinaldo.

Catching it easily, Rinaldo rushed to add, "Do you wish me to tell him you've changed your mind?"

Carlotta held the slipper she had picked up from the floor high over her shoulder, ready to pitch. She lowered it, annoyed. "Changed my mind? What do you mean by this? Do you think that he can squirm out of our agreement that easily? He promised me!"

"Then I suggest we get you dressed quickly, and we can be on our way. You must be excited to begin training."

"Excited?" she scoffed. But if truth be told, she realized she was indeed anxious to get dressed and arrive at the theater. "You go out to the parlor. Send my silly girl to help me dress. Wait until I call you!" She shooed Rinaldo through the door and closed it after him.

They had not arrived on time. Rinaldo was frazzled and apprehensive as he escorted Carlotta to the stage. Erik scowled at them both.

"It is half past nine," was all he said.

Rinaldo knew it was a miracle it wasn't later. He had watched as Carlotta modeled gown after gown before finally choosing the burgundy she now wore. He breathed a sigh of relief once Carlotta took her place on the stage and Erik began to speak with her about the music.

"Why do I start with scales? I have no need to do scales. I will start with the aria." Carlotta opened to the aria where Lady Macbeth sang of her plans for her husband's rise in power.

Before she could begin, Erik plucked the music from her hands.

"I see that it is dangerous to give you the score too quickly. 'A' major scale, two octaves." When there was only silence, he returned and took his place in front of her.

Standing a good head above her, he didn't intimidate her, she told herself. She might be impressed, but not intimidated. She held his gaze for several heartbeats until she realized she was thinking only of how beautiful and green his eyes were. She almost said as much to him, but his ego was already too big for him!

"Signorina, we will begin with the scales. Unless you have forgotten?"

"If you insist!" As he retreated, she grumbled, "It is a waste of time this singing of scales." She easily found the note and began. As she continued to sing, she examined her long, crimson nails as if bored.

"Signorina," Erik interrupted. "You are flat. Pay attention."

"How dare you! I have perfect pitch, and you know it!"

"Again, Signorina Giudicelli."

As if each note were a blow launched against him, Carlotta repeated the scale, ascending and descending.

"That is better," he said without enthusiasm.

"I can do it better," she protested. Raising her arms from her torso and throwing out her chest, she sang to the empty amphitheater.

"Proceed with the next scale." He put her through her paces. First he needed to find her weaknesses. Unfortunately there were many. Second he needed to train her voice and to stretch it. Third he was determined that she would follow his instructions even if he asked her to bray like a donkey!

"Again. Again from the beginning," he barked.

Carlotta frowned and squinted at him, but she didn't complain. Instead she sang the measures flawlessly.

Erik pulled at his collar to loosen it. They had been working for hours, but there was still something wrong.

It was not the voice, not this time. Over the past weeks, they'd sharpened her notes, polished out the roughness; she was singing beyond her original range, hitting both high and low notes that she had not reached for years. He had also adjusted the score, making modifications only a handful would notice and of which Carlotta would be blissfully ignorant. He resisted improving on the score—after all it wasn't his—but the temptation to go beyond the necessary to enhance it was almost too painful to resist.

No, it was not the voice. It was Carlotta. Regardless of the role she played, Carlotta was always Carlotta. Instead of tragically driven, she came across as petulant and spoiled.

"Enough!" She might have been singing the aria from any of a number of worn-out operas. It didn't matter. It all sounded the same.

His unexpectedly annoyed tone infuriated her.

"What? What? I sang it just the way you told me to! It was perfect!"

"Yes, you sang the notes, but an opera is more than a string of notes!" Erik fought to restrain himself. He lowered his voice which had begun to rise in volume. He took a deep breath in an effort to remain detached. "You are Lady Macbeth. Your husband would be content to enjoy the unexpected honors heaped upon him by fate. He lacks the killer's instinct. But as a woman you must work through the man. You see men, many of whom are unworthy of the power and position they hold, most of whom are your inferiors, and the only way you can climb is through one of them—your husband."

"But I love him, don't I? I want him to be King!"

"No! That's the problem! If not for your sex, it is you who has the mettle to triumph, to do what is necessary. But in this world a woman is only as strong as the man who owns her. *You* want to be King! It is *you* who should be Thane of Cawdor and King of Scotland."

Carlotta frowned and considered. "If I am so strong, then why do I go mad?"

"Your desire for power pushes you to commit horrors. You ask to be unsexed. You ask to be a monster! Power has its cost, Carlotta, a cost of which you are only dimly aware. You wish to transcend your sex, but you are a woman. You create a monster—Macbeth. You do all that is necessary, but who has the power? Not you. Not even Macbeth eventually. All you have is monstrosity."

"You would know about that, wouldn't you, eh?"

He blanched.

She quickly looked about the stage. No one was paying them any heed. A few of the principals for *La canzone di cuore* were reviewing sections for that evening. The theater had resumed performances of Erik's opera while the company simultaneously rehearsed and prepared for Carlotta's return to the stage.

Erik turned away from her and toward the pit. He stared blankly at the notes on the paper. When he spoke to her again, his voice was strangely breathy. "I think that will be all for today."

"Wait," she called out to him, but he kept walking.

Carlotta stomped her foot and bit at the nail on her finger. She wasn't sure what she should do. She didn't like the way he sounded when he walked away from her. She had insulted him on a daily basis. Why was this time so different? She marched off after him. No one walked out on Carlotta Giudicelli! She was done when she said she was done. He had an obligation to fulfill!

"Wait! Costanzi! Erik! Wait! M. Phantom, you will stop and listen to me!"

Her insistence on calling him the Phantom stopped him in his tracks. Didn't she understand the danger she put him in? Did she even care? What if others began to ask questions? To look into his past? Would it never end? Would there ever be hope of peace again?

Unable to restrain his anger, he turned on the woman.

"You are cruel and selfish, Carlotta," he snarled at her, incapable of stopping his mouth. "You care for no one and nothing but your own vanity! Your carelessness will surely lead to my death, and it will mean nothing to you! Nothing!"

He stormed off towards his office while she remained fixed to the spot. She had wanted to anger him. She had meant to do it! She knew he detested it when she reminded him of what he had been. What he still was, as far as she knew. Such airs! He acted as if his past could just be ignored. As if he hadn't done horrible things. He was the Phantom of the Opera, the Opera Ghost. He had been convicted of murder and had escaped just punishment. How dare he act as if he were not who he was!

She hurried to his office, and in spite of the fact that the door was closed to her, she flung it open and stepped inside. She was not prepared for what she saw. She was stunned. The mask lay abandoned on the floor where he had flung it. He sat on the sofa, leaning forward, his face in his hands. The sound of her entrance forced him to look up at her, the evidence of her havoc writ large upon his woeful face. His distress was only surpassed by his shame as he recognized her intrusion.

He rose as if to escape to his private room, but she ran forward and grabbed at his arm. He twisted away from her, his face turned so that she could not see his disfigurement.

"Erik." The word sounded strangled as she spoke it.

Not permitted escape, Erik was beside himself with shame, the shame of allowing her to see him without the mask, to see how successfully she had penetrated his defenses. Anyone but his enemies. Not her, not Leroux.

He felt stripped. Anger rose hot and wild. It made the shame bearable. "Can't you leave me some dignity?" His body trembled at the outrage of her invasion.

"I…I didn't mean to…" Her voice trailed uselessly away.

"I should have died on the scaffold. Well, don't worry, Carlotta, there is someone who will likely rid the world of me soon enough." He straightened visibly before her eyes and faced her with grim resolve.

She stepped out in front of him, barring his way to the private chamber. Before he could shrink away, she planted her hand on the smooth, perfect skin of his cheek. "You have such eyes!" she whispered, as if no one, not even he, could hear her.

Her touch was tender. He wanted to believe it was real. But he could as soon trust a viper as Carlotta Giudicelli.

"What is it like between you and your little blond fairy?"

Erik brushed her hand from his face. His silence was biting.

"No, I mean it. I want to know what happened to your great love for the Daaé girl? Didn't you burn for her?" She watched him closely. She noticed his hands closing into tight fists. The muscles along his shoulders were taut as his posture stiffened. He seemed to grow inches taller. His eyes were angry and intense.

Why did she push him so? Even now, after she had felt a momentary regret at having hounded him to exasperation, she wanted to see him angry, never cool or calm, never indifferent. She must inspire some strong emotion in him.

"How did you end up with Giry's daughter? Such a sweet, innocuous, little blond thing she always was."

"I won't discuss my relationship to my wife with you."

"Ah hah! I see. You don't really love her! She is warm, pliable, willing. That is all."

"That's a lie! I love her! She's everything to me." He hated that she had gotten him to speak of his feelings for Meg.

"And Christine Daaé?"

"It's none of your concern, Carlotta."

Something in his voice intrigued her.

The knock startled both of them. Rinaldo opened the door and stuck his head inside. "The count is asking for you, Don Erik."

Erik gestured to Carlotta. "Signorina Giudicelli, the rehearsal is over for the day. I will arrange for you to be escorted back to your apartments."

"I'd be happy to escort Carlotta home," the young man offered.

"That's settled then. Make sure she goes straight home, Rinaldo. She needs to be in bed early."

After Erik left, Carlotta grinned at the young man suggestively and chuckled, "You heard what the maestro said? You should get me to bed early."

Rinaldo watched her as she swayed seductively down the hall toward the exit. He had every intention of doing just that.

CHAPTER 15

Prima Donna, Prima Donna

Art thou afeard
To be the same in thine own act and valour
As thou art in desire? Wouldst thou have that
Which thou esteem'st the ornament of life,
And live a coward in thine own esteem,
Letting 'I dare not' wait upon 'I would,'
Like the poor cat i' the adage?

Shakespeare, Macbeth

Erik leaned against the soft curtain and buried his face in its plush folds. He breathed in the dust and sweat clinging to its fibers. It was warm and dark. He felt himself calm in response to its caress.

How was he to survive Carlotta's thoughtless cruelty? The longer he was around her, the more he recalled his experience with her at the Opera Populaire. But he also realized that she was a victim of her own petulance, her own willful self-destructive tendencies. She had talent. There was a reason she had risen so high in the world of opera. He caught glimpses of it sometimes in a particular way she sang, in a fortunate attitude struck, in the careful phrasing of a measure of the music. And it pained him to see her struggling to bring it together. She had wasted so much, for so long. How was he to help her recover what she had lost? And how could he listen to her revile him day after day? He could take the insults, but he could not bear the way she drew him constantly back to look at what he had been. He bled, the wound never healing, because she buried her sharp claws and ripped and savaged him daily.

He drew back from the curtain and consciously settled his body and mind to the task at hand. Raoul had finally left the safety of the estate and had come to the theater. It was a step long delayed and significant.

As he approached the count, Erik gave no indication of his previous distress. Raoul had taken his place in the secret box off the side of the stage. Christine was seated next to him. Her hand rested on Raoul's sleeve as she smiled up at Erik. He nodded a modest greeting to his former pupil, his former obsession.

"I see you've decided to come out of hiding."

Raoul gave him a sarcastic half smile but refused to satisfy him with an answer. "I've been busy even while convalescing. Angelo has made some inquiries and managed to speak with one of the men Leroux hired, a Piero. From Angelo's description, I think I remember seeing him."

"Has he found out where Leroux is?" Erik carefully controlled his expression. He knew Raoul and Christine were watching him. They would be appalled to know Erik's true feelings in this case.

"He's left Rome," Raoul said as if this meant all was well in the world again. He even smiled.

Erik remained unmoved. His expression did not change, or if it did, it was not joyful. In point of fact, Erik was sorely disappointed by the news.

"No one knows where he's gone?"

"No. I would like to assume he's simply returned to Paris." Even as he said it, Raoul knew it was fanciful at best. Leroux was not the type to give up.

"Marcelo wounded him. Is there any information on how gravely he was injured?"

"Angelo did trace him to several boarding houses. In one there was evidence of blood, enough to suggest a serious wound. But it doesn't appear that it was fatal or crippling. The innkeeper remembered Leroux leaving on his own two feet. He wasn't even aware that he was injured until later in the day when they went to prepare the room for a new occupant."

"So we can't fool ourselves that he's lying dead somewhere on the road. And we can't pretend that he will have washed his hands of his obsession with my capture or death."

"You are sure that he wants you dead?" Neither man had expected Christine to be so blunt.

Erik's eyes flashed with renewed anger. "Oh, yes. I can safely say that he means my death." Erik remembered lying crushed under the weight of the dead man. He remembered Leroux's delight at finding Erik at his mercy. He would not easily forget the sight of the weapon leveled at his face.

"You believe he is that determined to see this through?" Christine insisted, clutching at false hope. "You don't think his wound will deter him? Or that he'll change his mind now that he sees it won't be so easy?"

Raoul gripped Christine's hand in his as he put into words what Erik and he had both concluded. "Leroux won't have given up."

"Then he'll be back," she whispered.

Suddenly uncomfortable that they were speaking of blood and death in Christine's presence, Erik fixed his eyes on the stage beyond.

"It's worse than that, I'm afraid. We have no idea where he is and when he'll strike again." Raoul added what they were all thinking.

"What will we do?" asked Christine.

Raoul was about to answer, but Erik spoke first. "The question is what will *I* do? Both of you are to return to Paris as soon as possible."

"Excuse me?" protested Raoul, as if he hadn't heard.

"This is my fate, not yours. I won't have anyone else putting themselves in harm's way."

Christine shivered, knowing that Erik had every intention of killing Leroux. That was the only way that the nightmare would end.

"I don't think you understand, Erik. You are suffering again from delusions of grandeur if you think you can order me to leave," answered Raoul, grimly.

"You were nearly killed, Raoul. I won't…"

"It is not your decision, my friend."

The scar was still a vivid red slash across what had been a flawless face. It lent Raoul a dangerous edge Erik had never noticed until this moment.

"My friend?" Erik repeated.

Raoul's grim expression softened. His eyes darted away. Unexpectedly embarrassed, he gave a short deprecating laugh. "Well, strange things do happen, don't they?"

For a moment, Erik hesitated. He felt Christine's eyes on them both. He glanced in her direction and saw that she awaited his response. The hint of a smile on her lips. Then he nodded slightly at Raoul. "Yes, who would have imagined?"

"You're well?" he asked Christine as he escorted her outside to the waiting carriage to take her to Don Marcelo's.

"Yes, I'm quite well. I feel strong." She absently stroked the rounded swell of her body where the child waited. "I don't believe that the birth will be a problem."

"Raoul must be furious with you for traveling at this time in your condition." He tried to temper his concern with a flat tone. He looked away when Christine tried to engage his eyes.

"I couldn't let him come without me. I would worry too much." She slowed her gait, wanting to prolong their exchange. They so infrequently spoke nowadays, and it was suddenly comfortable to be with Erik in a way that it hadn't been before. "He can sometimes be rather rash."

"He forgets to think of his own safety." He smirked, recalling past encounters with Raoul in which the count had engaged him without considering the consequences. He wondered if Raoul knew how close he had come to death on several of those occasions? Erik had no doubt that he could have killed Raoul several times over. Something had always held him back. At first it had been Christine. He couldn't kill the count because Christine so fervently loved him. He couldn't take Raoul away from her. Later, he wasn't sure if that alone had restrained his hand.

"I'm pleased that you and Meg are expecting again. It seems as if the two of us are in some sort of pattern."

Erik feared speaking of the child that he might never hold. He banished the thought from his mind.

"I wish I could convince Raoul to return to Paris, Christine. This situation does not involve the two of you. It's my fate, not yours. I can't make him see reason. He's too…honorable, I suppose. He needs to be more selfish."

"Erik, you need to protect yourself. If we can help, you must let us try. It's not only your fate but Meg's and your children's that are at stake."

Erik tried to look away as a darkness crossed his gaze. He feared Christine would read what lay behind it. He must not let anyone know what he planned to do, what must be done. They might try to stop him. They might be appalled by him.

He had once said that he had tired of death. He had meant it. He still meant it. He didn't want to kill. And yet the thought of Leroux drove a white heat through his mind and heart that enraged him. He wanted to see the man destroyed. Would Christine sense it? He must not let her.

"I'm worried about you, Erik."

He froze as if she had read his very thoughts.

"I would hope that you could live in peace at last." She stood close to him, so close that the intimacy was apparent to both of them.

"It has always been my most fervent desire, Christine."

They had arrived at the carriage, and Erik handed her in. She leaned across the window and brushed his hand with hers.

The gesture was so tender that Erik looked up at her. Their eyes met, and he knew that Christine had foreseen the inevitable course of their lives. Before he could check himself, he touched her lips with his fingers. It was a simple touch, a gesture of gratitude and affection.

Quickly he stepped back and nodded to the driver. As the carriage disappeared down the street, Erik walked back to the theater, the dark thought of Leroux held safely in check for the time being.

Rinaldo sat uncomfortably close to Carlotta in the barouche. The day was beautiful, and Carlotta insisted that they take a turn through the parks and around the fountains before returning to her apartments.

"So, you think I'm ready? Is this not true? I don't know why we can't open early." She smoothed the taffeta skirt along her thigh. Rinaldo swallowed hard as he imagined his own hand doing the same.

"The opening is just a few days away. And yes, I think you'll be wonderful, Carlotta."

The diva smiled warmly turning her face away from the young man. She heard the huskiness in his voice. He wanted her! She had been more and more aware of his attraction to her over the past weeks. She pretended not to notice. She fanned his desires, enjoying the glow of his arousal. It made up for the fact that only a cold wind blew her way from Erik. Cold, cold, cold. How could he be so passionate with the others and not spark to her talent?

Yet there were moments. When she forgot herself and fell deeply into the role, when she woke realizing she had become Lady Macbeth, she saw the fervor in his regard! He wanted her to lose herself in the opera. She was exhausted by his intensity! She sometimes returned to her dressing room, wringing her hands as if still acting Lady Macbeth, and crumpled in nervous weeping for she knew not what. She wasn't sure she liked drowning in her role. Not even for the Phantom's praise!

"We've arrived." Rinaldo interrupted her thoughts.

Brought back to the present moment, Carlotta examined the young man. Yes, she could see it. He had been a Casanova in Milan, had broken many a heart, and had enjoyed himself immensely until his bad luck at cards caught up with him. She had doubted him when he couldn't bring Meg to his bed, but not now when she looked into his dark, dark eyes. He had a beautiful face, warm and full sensuous lips, a mouth she felt she wanted to explore thoroughly, his

hair a mass of loose black curls framed his face, bringing out his wickedly striking cheekbones. Even at this early hour of the evening, a heavy beard threatened to darken his jaw and chin. He was impressive, too. She liked her men big!
She wanted to feel small in their embrace. Oh, he didn't have Piangi's girth.
Like Erik, he was deceptively slender for his height and build. But he was powerful looking, pure male, pure animal somewhere lurking under his patrician
demeanor.

"You'll come up for a drink?" She smiled wickedly at him.

Rinaldo lay exhausted, the sweat a drying layer of salt on his skin. Next to
him, Carlotta slept the sleep of the innocent, but how that was possible Rinaldo
had not a clue. They had fallen into bed, wrapped in each other's arms, like two
drowning people. He dragged his arm from underneath Carlotta's shoulders,
the movement sending small fires of pain throughout his body. He felt as if he
had been beaten. The memory brought his hand to the side of his neck where
she had bitten him. There were bruises along her shoulder where he, too, had
given into a fierceness he'd never felt in any of his other couplings, and he had
been with women of wild spirit on more than one occasion. A tiger was tame
by comparison to the demon lying beside him, though now her features were
relaxed and soft, almost childlike in her surrender to oblivion.

He twisted his body to cradle her from behind. She moaned sweetly and gen-
tled herself back in his embrace. He buried his face in her rich red-tinged hair,
catching the strange citrus of her perfume. He could almost hear her purr!

His arms were strong and wrapped round her. He wanted, needed, to protect
her. Why that would occur to him, he couldn't guess. Carlotta didn't give anyone the impression that she needed protection. Rather, on many an occasion he
had thought that others would be well to look to their own defenses against a
voracious will like Carlotta's. Even so, after their wild and savage lovemaking,
she had sighed and gasped and then had cried just a little. He had struggled to
catch his breath and held her tightly as she shuddered against him. They didn't
speak of it, and in a very short time they had both fallen into a deep, deep
sleep.

Now the chill of early morning was on them both, and Rinaldo pulled at the
covers and brought them round the two of them.

Carlotta stirred and twisted in the circle of his arms to come face to face
with her young lover. Her eyes fluttered open, and she smiled at him. In a soft
whisper, she greeted him. "You're far too old for me," she teased.

His laugh rumbled deep in his throat, and Carlotta felt it ripple against her mouth as she kissed the bruises, the love marks, she had left him.

"You may be right," he said. "But I hope you'll be kind and make allowances for me."

She frowned for a moment thinking that she had better be careful with this young man. She was quite a bit older than he, and eventually the difference in their ages would outshine her dramatic appeal. She was not so much a fool that she didn't think his attraction was mere infatuation. She wanted to enjoy it while she could, but she would have to be very careful not to fall in love with him! But when she thought of last night, she wondered if it were already too late.

"Carlotta, for God's sake, tomorrow is opening night! We have gone over this a thousand times. Stop waving your arms around as if you were a windmill in *Don Quixote*!"

"You devil! You monster! You cannot speak to me, Carlotta Giudicelli, like that! Who are you anyway?"

Erik had been standing near the orchestra pit. But the moment Carlotta opened her mouth to berate him, he stormed across the stage and engulfed her. He did not lay a finger on her, but he stood so ominously silent, hovering over her, that she stopped and stared up into his glassy eyes.

"I was trying to emphasize the emotions!" she explained lamely, the fire having gone out of her.

Very softly he whispered to her, but the pent-up emotion in his voice was undeniable. "The music, the words are sufficient unto themselves, Mlle. Giudicelli, for the audience to feel your despair. Despair does not come in big swinging arms, but in the quiet devastation of the body that cannot move, cannot exert its will against insurmountable odds. Despair is not being able to change the horror that threatens to annihilate you. There is no hope in despair; there is no flight possible. And there are certainly no flailing arms."

Carlotta swallowed deeply as she listened. He was speaking of more than the role, she was sure. He was describing what he had himself experienced. She took one step away, feeling the intensity of him as if it were her own pain. She straightened her back defiantly in an attempt to save face.

"What if I just raise my arm like this?" she asked as she demonstrated a gesture of supplication toward the heavens.

Erik sighed and looked away. "Take it from the top of the scene again, signorina."

Carlotta had spent so much time with the man that she couldn't help but think she knew him. She saw the disapproval in his stance, the way he kept his back to her as she began the scene. She wanted him to turn and watch her. She thought of the song, her final aria in the opera, her tragic end as Lady Macbeth, as *she* prepares to end her life. She began to sing. The theater faded, the stones of a castle keep rose about her, the thought of her beloved in disgrace and in pain filled her mind, the ignominy of capture and treason. She imagined Macbeth's death, her own failure, her horrid cruelty. She sank to the stage, gasping in tears.

Strong hands grasped her by the shoulders and dragged her up from the floor. She felt the fibers of the coat brush against her wet cheeks and felt enveloped by a powerful warmth. The sounds slowly broke through into her consciousness, the voice a deep and rough demand. She leaned, giving over her will and strength to the wall that braced her so that she would not fall. The white mask, the green eyes, worry evident in their earnest gaze filled her vision.

"Stand up, Carlotta. Can you stand?" his voice demanded, and she found herself balanced on two feet.

She could not drag her eyes from his, from his concern...was it approval? But she nodded, "Yes, yes, yes, sí, sí, sí, I'm...I'm fine."

Erik held his breath through Act I. He found himself wringing his hands and pacing like a maniac during Act II. It wasn't until Act III that he was convinced that she had done it. They had done it! All the pain of working with her, the frustration, the anger and ranting and raving, the slow and tedious training of her voice, the repetition of advice, the flattery and the scolding had paid off. She was good. She was more than good. Her flaws seemed to enhance the character of the role. The singing was technically good. The voice served. The acting was better than anything she had ever delivered before. The audience was impressed, moved by her performance.

He had fulfilled his part of their bargain. God only knew if she would fulfill hers!

Meg came rushing off the stage after the final curtain and threw herself into Erik's arms. He grunted slightly from the impact. It had been a considerable time since the attack, but Erik's sternum had been severely bruised. It was still sore on occasion.

"It was wonderful, wasn't it? The audience seemed to really enjoy Carlotta's performance, don't you think?" She kept looking for his reaction.

"Yes, they did," he answered noncommittally.

"What is it?" she asked, apprehensive.

"Nothing, my sweet," he lied.

She pushed away from him but held his hands in hers. "What is it?" she asked again, more forcefully.

"You should have been the star, not the supporting singer, not Lady Macduff. We should have put on the opera we had planned, and you should be taking those bows."

"It's all right, Erik. I'm actually pleased for Carlotta."

He pursed his lips together in disapproval. "Well, we've had no choice."

"Do you think she'll be satisfied? You've made her a success. She's on the stage. We're free now, aren't we?"

She saw the answer in his eyes. He pulled his hands from hers and went forward to meet Carlotta as the curtain closed for the final time and she came off the stage.

"Erik!" she squealed in delight. She grabbed him round the waist for one brief moment, then as if she remembered herself, she backed away and hit him with a balled-up fist on the shoulder hard. "I told you! Didn't I tell you? I am a star! This is what you took from me!"

Meg couldn't believe the woman was berating her husband, the man who had put her on the stage and made her a success. Erik waved his wife back when he saw her step forward, an angry scowl on her face.

"Well?" Carlotta insisted.

"What do you expect me to say?" asked Erik in a tense whisper. Around them the rest of the cast filed off the stage. As they retreated toward their dressing rooms, some looked back, curious, over their shoulders at the artistic director and the diva.

Carlotta lowered her arms from her hips and folded them across her chest in an unexpected gesture of vulnerability. "How was I?" The former anger had completely gone. She anxiously waited for his approval.

"You were wonder…"

"Ahhhh! I knew it! I knew it!" Carlotta grabbed him and squeezed him hard as she screamed in delight. She had done it! She was a star!

With some difficulty, Erik extricated himself from Carlotta's grasp. "Yes, Signorina Giudicelli, you are a star. But I would think it more important for you to be an artist."

"What is this that you mean? What is this 'artist' instead of 'star'? What are you trying to say to me? Are you suggesting that I was not perfect? Did I not make them cry? Did I not make them sad that I killed myself? I could hear them weeping! Even over the music, I could hear them."

Erik disregarded the obvious exaggeration. He took a deep breath and spoke, "You were wonderful. But tonight is one performance. Will you be able to repeat it tomorrow and the next and the next? That is what you will need to do."

"Of course."

"If you intend to be in top form, you must continue to work at it, Carlotta. That means rehearsals, continued training. Are you willing to do that?"

She didn't want to think of the drudgery. She was dazed by the applause, drunk on the lights of the theater, and wanted to drink and laugh and listen to the after-theater jubilation and then sneak off with Rinaldo and make love violently and long into the morning. She did not want to think of rehearsals and training.

"Yes, yes, yes, of course, it is work, work, work with you! You are a tyrant! But tonight we celebrate! And tomorrow or the day after we get back to work. And I want to know the next opera you plan for me."

"Carlotta, we made a bargain. I've fulfilled my part."

The diva had begun to walk away from Erik, but his words stopped her cold.

"What? What? What? What? What are you saying? You have trained me. I am a star. You will find a new opera for me."

"Carlotta, stop! I demand that you fulfill your part of the bargain."

Carlotta's heart plummeted to the depths of her stomach. She swallowed a twisted knot in her throat. He meant to abandon her! He had done all this and now he would simply wash his hands of her! "But I was good. I was wonderful!"

"Yes, you were."

"I have promised that I will not harass you or Mag."

"Meg."

"Meg! I will keep my promise."

Erik sighed deeply. The weight of the past weeks lifted, and he thought perhaps he might hope again.

"But I won't go. I am the diva of the company."

Yet again the tension gripped his muscles. Erik strove to keep the anger from his voice. "You are not the diva of this company. My wife, Meg Giry Costanzi, is the diva. She will star in the next opera we perform."

Carlotta's face dropped. She picked up a prop chair and threw it across the space narrowly missing Erik who stood unflinching, determined to withstand

Carlotta's tantrum. Then she screamed and stomped and looked for something else, anything else, to throw. Meg rushed forward to Erik's side, but he quickly pushed her out of the possible path of any other object Carlotta could get her hands on.

"Carlotta! Stop it!" The voice was deep and loud. Carlotta, startled by it, twisted to see Rinaldo coming fast up the aisle. "You're acting like a child!"

Carlotta let the young man take her in his arms. She quieted almost immediately, but Erik could see her shaking. He was mildly shocked to realize she was crying. Rinaldo patted her absently on the back. "Don Erik? May I have a word with you about Signorina Giudicelli's career?"

Erik scowled at this renewed evidence of Rinaldo's partnership with Carlotta. "In my office, in ten minutes." He took Meg by the elbow and escorted her off to the dressing rooms.

Within the ten minutes, Erik heard the knock at the door.

"Come."

Rinaldo did not come alone. He escorted a curiously quiet Carlotta to the divan and left her there. He himself took the chair across the desk from Erik.

"Signorina Giudicelli would like me to negotiate a contract with you. She is willing to continue working for the company."

"Willing?" Erik stood in disgust at the woman's blatant self-importance.

"Please, Don Erik, hear us out. She has much yet to give. She doesn't want to leave the company. She concedes that Signora Costanzi is the diva and will, therefore, be playing the lead in most productions. She would like to have some role…"

Carlotta rose to her feet, unable to let Rinaldo continue negotiating for her. "I want a role befitting my talent! I will not be a servant or an old lady! Or ugly! No, no, no, no!"

Erik sat down heavily in his seat. How could he stand having Carlotta continually under foot in the Teatro dell'Opera? She would constantly nag him. She would make life hell for Meg. No, he couldn't.

"I will continue singing!" she insisted.

"You promised you would leave us in peace, Carlotta. Can I not trust your word?"

"This has nothing to do with that. I have already left you in peace. Have I done anything to harm you or your family?"

Erik couldn't help but think of the times she berated both Meg and him during the long process of training and rehearsing for this opening night. The pranks had stopped, yes. But her mere presence was a guarantee of no peace for any of them. "I can't," he muttered under his breath as he fixed his eyes on the clutter of papers on the desk. "Oh God."

The silence in the room was oppressive. Rinaldo was the first to break it.

"Don Erik, she would like to be a part of this. She is grateful to you for what you've done."

Carlotta made some unintelligible sound but otherwise let Rinaldo speak.

Erik glanced up at Carlotta, considering his options. Did he have any? If he said no, what would the woman do? He must resolve this. He must not antagonize her, or she might take up her original plan. He studied her. She sat ramrod straight in the chair. She looked every inch the queen Lady Macbeth might have wished to be. Then his eyes fell upon her hands. She rubbed the fingers of one obsessively over those of the other. Otherwise she was impassive. His own former agitation disappeared, replaced by a curious ache of commiseration somewhere behind his breastbone.

"I will do the following." He ignored Rinaldo and addressed Carlotta directly. "I will allow you to take some secondary role in the next several operas of the season. In the meantime, I will try to arrange for you to join another company."

"Why? Why cannot I stay here?"

"Because you and I are like oil and water!"

"No, this is not true! We are oil and vinegar. You are the sour one!"

"What?"

"If you shake us up enough, we make a good dressing! We are like that, you and I. It is exciting. We work together very well. You don't let me…You…You tell me when I have made a…little mistake. You help me to be the best opera singer that I can be. Sometimes we fight, but it is all good." Carlotta's usual confidence seemed to desert her momentarily. Her body turned slightly away, and the color rose in her cheeks.

"Very well." Erik cleared his voice and gritted his teeth. "I surrender. I will allow you to work for the company as long as you continue to work hard and do a good job. I will find something suitable for you in most of the productions."

Before Carlotta could clap her hands together in triumph, Erik spoke again in a firm, serious tone. "But I will not have you berating my wife or causing problems. You will be cooperative and try to be even-tempered and generous. I know it's not in your nature, but you will not defy or contradict me or speak ill of anyone else in the company. You will also not act as if you are the most important person in the cast. Is that agreed?"

Carlotta pouted her lips for a moment, but secretly she was delighted. This would go on and on and on! She loved it. She wanted to be part of the company. "Yes," she finally answered. She could not repress her glee. Her radiant smile burst forth. "Yes, it is agreed!"

CHAPTER 16

Leviathan

*Such as sit in darkness and in the shadow
of death, being bound in affliction and
iron;…He brought them out of darkness
and the shadow of death, and brake their
bands in sunder.*

Psalm 107:10, 14

Leroux stretched his arm out and flexed the muscle several times to relieve the stiffness, the only lingering consequence of the wound he had suffered over two months ago.

He watched them step out of the seamstress's shop. The boy was almost as tall as he was. If he struggled, Leroux might have to hurt him. The woman would be no problem. Mme. Giry was slight of build, a delicate creature made for dancing, not for fighting.

"Sig. Costanzi! Don Erik!"

Two men burst into the hall. Behind them Angelo came swiftly in with a bundle of cloth in his arms. Erik and Marcelo entered the hall from the parlor. The bundle was not bolts of fabric from the shopping excursion Madeleine and François had taken. It was Madeleine herself.

"In here," directed Marcelo.

Angelo gently laid Mme. Giry on the sofa near the fireplace.

"What happened?" Erik grabbed one of Raoul's menservants by the sleeve.

"She sent us down the road for the staff paper you wanted. When we returned to the seamstress's shop, she wasn't there. We found her in the park near the bridge." The man nervously looked to and fro between Erik and the prostrate woman on the couch.

Erik looked behind the man into the hall.

"Where's my son?" he insisted, a dark intuition chilling him to the bone.

Madeleine's groans interrupted them.

Both Marcelo and Erik could see that she had been brutally beaten. Her lip was bleeding, the bluing around her eye was already evident, and her nose looked as if it had been broken. And these were but the visible evidence of the other's crime.

"Erik," she called out to him. He came immediately to her side. She pushed herself up and tried to sit even though Marcelo urged her to lie still.

"François! He's taken him! Oh, my God, Erik, I'm so sorry. He's taken the boy!" Near to hysteria, she took hold of Erik's coat with a demented cry.

"Who?" Erik asked. But he already knew. He hoped against hope that it wasn't whom he thought.

"Leroux. He came out of nowhere and put a gun to François's head and forced him into the park. He told me to stay, but I wouldn't. When I followed, he struck me."

Marcelo rose and paced furiously in front of the divan.

"He took him! I'm sorry, Erik! I couldn't stop him."

Erik patted her shoulder blindly. He tried to put his thoughts in order, to wipe away the blood that was flowing freely across his vision, to think, to think what he needed to do, to kill Leroux, no, not to kill Leroux, to save his son, the anger, the fury, the bare and unforgiving terror, to wipe these away to see the steps he must take.

The next second he was on his feet. "Meg!" he screamed through the opened door toward the staircase. Next he swung toward Marcelo. "I have to go. He wants me!"

Madeleine dabbed at the bleeding lip with Marcelo's handkerchief. "Erik, he went off in the direction of the plaza. It was but a short while ago, perhaps an hour by now."

Raoul, hearing the commotion, came into the parlor. Angelo quietly apprised him of the situation. "What can I do, Erik?"

Erik stared at him in wild fury. "He's got my son! What can you do? Nothing! There's nothing that anyone can do. Except me. If there's time. If there's time, perhaps." He paced the room, his hand raked through his hair as he tried to beat down the rising panic, the fury. He stopped and picked up a glass vase and threw it at the ghost-like image of a demented man he saw reflected in the large veranda window. Shards of glass split the silence and fell to the floor.

Raoul was about to go to Erik when Meg came inside. "What is it?" she demanded, shocked and fearful when her eyes lit on Erik.

He immediately stilled in his tracks and turned toward his wife. In one brief moment, he thought he saw her dressed in black! He recalled Christine's dead eyes as she mourned the loss of her and Raoul's first born child in a watery grave. He went to Meg and drew her to a corner of the room.

Madeleine tearfully watched as Erik bent his head and quietly spoke to Meg. Then a scream rent the false calm that had descended on them all. Meg's knees buckled, and Erik picked her up in his arms and carried her to their room.

"Was Leroux alone?" Raoul asked Madeleine. He winced as he thought of the man striking the woman with his fists. The brutality was shocking. What would he do to Erik's son? What if François struggled or tried to escape?

"No, two other men were in the park waiting. One of them took François off in the direction of the plaza. I tried…I tried…" Madeleine's voice broke into sobs.

"Madeleine, you were very brave, but Leroux is a dangerous man. He might have killed you." For the first time, the monstrosity of Leroux's plan for vengeance struck Raoul. It was one thing for Leroux to labor under a false sense of duty and to come in search of Erik, but it was now clear to Raoul that the inspector would harm anyone who got in his way. He was out of control. Justice had nothing to do with this.

Erik laid Meg on the bed, but she held on to him and wouldn't let him rise.

"Meg, let me go. I have to go and get our son," he explained as calmly as he could.

"But he'll kill you!"

"And what of François?"

"Oh God! Oh God! Erik! Bring him back to me!"

He beckoned to the maid just outside in the passageway to come stay with her. He pulled Meg's fingers from his coat, kissed her lightly on the forehead, and left the room. He had much to do.

Raoul met him halfway down the stairs, an envelope in his hand.

"What is it?" Erik asked as he took it from Raoul and examined it briefly. There was nothing written on the exterior.

"It was in Madeleine's pocket. He must have placed it there."

Erik tore the paper open. He tried to hide the fact that his fingers were trembling. Inside the message was brief and deadly clear. It was from Leroux.

Phantom,

I have your son. I will kill him if you do not turn yourself over to me by the end of next week. I will keep him safe until that point, but if you do not meet me in Paris at the side entrance of the Opera National, March 22 at eleven in the evening, I will cut his throat and watch him bleed to death.

"Oh God!" Erik paled and dropped the note on the stairs. He collapsed on the step. Raoul picked up the paper and continued reading.

Tell no one and come alone or I will kill him. If you are late, I will kill him. If you do not submit yourself to me completely, I will kill him. Since he is innocent as yet of any crime, I don't wish to harm him. I am convinced that he will eventually turn out to be as evil as you, but for now he is safe unless you do not comply with my demands.

Once you have come, I will let your son go free and unharmed. But you must submit yourself to justice at my hands.

The right arm of Justice

"Don't let Meg see this! Promise me!"
"You have my word."
"I leave tonight."

Raoul had insisted on accompanying Erik to Paris. He promised that he would stay far from the opera house and allow Erik to meet Leroux's demands alone as the madman had stipulated. He wouldn't risk François's life. The two men sat silently in Raoul's private carriage. They were proceeding as quickly as they could toward Paris.

"Do you think he'll release François at the Opera National?" asked Raoul.

"No, I don't. I think he'll have François locked away somewhere in the area. The meeting at the Opera National is not the final destination, I'm sure. It's very public. He'll expect to take me somewhere private."

"Do you think you can trust him to let François go once he has you?"

Erik covered his eyes with his hand and did not speak for a long time. The rocking of the coach lulled Raoul who was on the verge of falling asleep. Erik's voice woke him.

"I think I will have to make some demands of my own once we meet at the opera house. I will need some kind of guarantee that my son is safe."

Like a bad penny, the thought of the little girl surfaced in Raoul's mind. He had put aside the report of her cruel death, unwilling to attribute it to Erik. Leroux was mad. Having taken on gigantic proportions in the inspector's imagination, the Phantom had become the incarnation of evil itself. Raoul wondered if Erik had even known about the child. Would it help Erik to know that her brutal murder was in part fueling Leroux's mad vendetta?

"Erik, I found something out about Leroux just before I left to come to Rome. I actually went to the authorities to complain about his harassment. The current chief inspector was more than happy to discuss Leroux's past. Did you know he had a young niece, a child really, who was raped and murdered?"

"No."

Raoul could feel the air thicken between them.

"It happened a long time ago. They found her body at one of the entrances to your tunnels under the Opera Populaire. She evidently held something that Leroux was convinced belonged to you. He was sure that you had killed her."

"And do you think that I kill children, Raoul?"

Raoul blew out a deep exhalation as if seriously considering the question. "No, of course not. But he believes you murdered her. She was fair, small for her age."

Erik's eyes shifted away for a moment from Raoul's. In a cautious voice, he barely answered, "I remember."

Raoul felt a sharp bolt of anxiety course through his chest. He sat still, trying to restrain his reaction to the unexpected confession.

"Oh, I didn't kill her," he said when he saw Raoul's obvious discomfort. "It was before Christine came. I hadn't been hiding in the opera house for long when it happened. I heard things. At first I wasn't sure the sounds were real. Buquet had taken her to one of the lower floors, still far above mine, but deep enough that no one above in the opera house would come upon them. I caught a glimpse of him skulking away. He had raped her, savagely, and then fearing she'd tell, he…had cut her deeply." Without thinking, Erik's hand sliced across his own body, a diagonal slash from the lower rib cage to the groin. "He left her…alone…in the dark. I could see death sitting next to her, just waiting for her to take that last breath. I…stayed with her until she passed over."

He remembered coming upon the child and feeling frightened himself. He might have fled except she had called out to him. She thought he was something else. She must have seen the whiteness of the mask gleaming bodiless in the dark. She wasn't afraid of him; she thought he had come to protect her. There was no one to go to. Madeleine had gone. She had married. So he straightened the child's torn dress and sat with her gently in his arms. Even he could tell that it would be soon. He sang to her well past the moment when he saw the dimming of her eyes. He held her until all her warmth drained away. Erik stared at her quiet face for a long time, trying to reconcile this death of an innocent to the one he had given Abel, the man who had kept him like an animal in a cage. Then he carried her to his rooms, pausing only a moment to pick up a doll that he could never remember not having. It was a crudely sewn monkey made of burlap. He carried her and the doll through the passageways to one of the entrances to the underground tunnels.

"I carried her to the entrance where I knew she'd be found." He had laid the girl where the night patrol would catch sight of her. On her chest, he left his only possession, the sole thing that he knew was really his. He hid in the shadows, unable to abandon her, until the patrol discovered her. Then he slipped quietly away. "I tried to forget about the child until years later when I decided Buquet had to die."

Raoul heard the coldness in his voice. He wasn't sure he wanted Erik to speak of his crimes. Raoul had tried to look beyond them, had managed to put them aside, but it was difficult to forgive Erik the deaths he had caused. There was a side to Raoul that was uncomfortable with the fact that Erik had escaped the court's sentence. All his life he had thought of right and wrong as clearly separate spheres. The Phantom had forever blurred the boundaries between such absolutes.

Erik watched Raoul carefully, perhaps sensing his ambivalence. But he wanted Raoul to know how much Buquet had deserved to die. "I was young when I found the child. I couldn't go to the police and testify against Buquet. I was a fugitive myself. But I kept my eye on him. There were other incidents, but I don't believe Buquet killed again. He became cautious. Once in the stables, I happened upon him and a young chorine. She was struggling to get free of him. Curiously, a rather large bucket of water fell from above, narrowly missing his head. The distraction allowed the girl to extricate herself. I don't believe the incident was unique or isolated."

"Why didn't you kill him then?" Raoul asked innocently.

"You ask me that as if it were easy for me to kill."

Raoul shifted uncomfortably in his seat. He realized his question had suggested that Erik had no qualms against cold-blooded murder. "I see your point. What finally pushed you over the edge?"

"Buquet was watching Christine. He followed her. He was waiting for an opportunity to get her alone."

Raoul went seriously pale. "I didn't realize."

"No, you didn't. No one did. Not even Christine. That was why he was dangerous. He was also intent on hunting me down. The night I strangled him, he caught sight of me in the flies. He was tracking me. Everything came together in that moment. The managers were not taking me seriously. They had given Carlotta the plum role in *Il Muto*. I could feel Buquet's breath on the back of my neck. I had been wanting to find a way to protect Christine. I managed to do that, protect myself, and make a point." Erik smiled cynically at Raoul's expression of disgust. "Oh, I know I sound cold. I'm perfectly capable of murder…when the stakes are high."

Raoul imagined Buquet dragging Christine off into the shadows. The muscles in his gut clenched. *Would he not have done the same had he known the danger Christine was in?*

"I am trying to be honest." Erik stared at Raoul as if trying to gauge his reaction.

"Yes, I can see that." Raoul smiled crookedly. "Unfortunately M. Leroux doesn't realize how painfully honest you can be. He won't believe you if you tell him Buquet killed his niece."

"I know." Erik relaxed, leaning back against the seat, relieved to know that Raoul had not withdrawn his friendship.

"And then again, I don't know if it would make any difference if he did believe you innocent of her death. He's sentenced you for the other crimes." Raoul wondered how one balanced a life for a life. Although it was selfish, he was grateful to Erik that he had protected Christine from Buquet.

"Yes, just so," answered Erik. He stared out onto the passing landscape.

After several moments of silence, Raoul's thoughts strayed to his last conversation with his wife. When he told her to stay in Rome and await his return, she had argued vehemently that she wanted to be with him. He had insisted that she obey and refused to hear more on the matter. Now he had the uncomfortable feeling that she had been too quiet when they parted.

"Do you think the women will do what they've been told?" he found himself asking Erik.

"I have my doubts."

Paris, home, he walked the narrow streets, the streets down which Madeleine had led him that night he escaped from the cage, the lights in the cafés, the laughter, the blessed and joyful sounds of his own language, the voices of strangers alive and gay like bands of sparrows, the words, the lilt, the deep nasal vowels, the liquid sounds of his native tongue, the city was alive, painfully alive, he remembered living here, but not really here, not above ground, not among these loud and friendly faces, not brushed and pushed by bustling crowds of opera buffs pouring from the theaters, spreading across the streets, he remembered them from the amphitheater of the Opera Populaire, all furs and diamonds, tiaras and silks, in their plush seats, the murmur of them not unlike the crowds in Rome, but this *was Paris,* this *was home,* this *was where he had escaped and found sanctuary in the temple of the opera house, down underneath this seething humanity, down below these lights, hidden away from this cool brisk air, in the tunnels on the shore of an underground lake, but he was home, this was home, Paris*

…and here he had learned of passion and betrayal and he had glimpsed madness and he had sought redemption and he had died, he had died and was buried, and here the eyes of those loud and friendly faces had turned hard and cold and had pointed long boney claws at him and sent him to die and here he had known pain and here he had suffered and here he had…cried and had hoped for death a merciful speedy death and such mercy had been denied him and he had despaired that he had been thrown down into the darkness alone so alone but he had also been given a light in this darkness, she had come for him even in the darkness, even though he was a fierce and evil monster, she had stepped through the mirror and found him, a poor lonely creature

Outside the Opera National Erik waited. He stayed hidden in the shadows, a hood covering his face. He wasn't sure if anyone might recognize the infamous Phantom by the sight of his mask. Surely, after all this time, he could walk the streets unnoticed? Yet he knew that his story had passed from mouth to mouth and remained in the imagination. It was forever tied to the shell of the Opera Populaire, a building that still stood. It had been minimally refurbished and was used by traveling troupes of actors and for social and charity benefits and auctions.

It was just minutes before eleven when he felt the sharp knife come up just under his rib cage. The point broke through his cape, his vest and shirt, and pierced just under the skin, enough to guarantee his stillness.

"You will come with me! Now!" came the harsh sound of Leroux's voice.

"Not until I have some…" Leroux drove the point of the blade in a fraction of an inch. Erik bit his tongue against the sharp pain, but he insisted through clenched teeth, "You can kill me here! But I won't go until I know that my son is safe. I want him released."

"You do not set the terms, Phantom. I do. If you delay any longer, I will guarantee that your son's body be sent back to your wife, piece by piece."

"How do you expect me to comply without some assurance?"

"You have my word, the word of an officer of the law, that your son is unharmed and will be unharmed as long as you surrender your life to me!"

Seeing no way out, Erik nodded his agreement.

Leroux removed the tip of the blade from Erik's side, wiped the bead of blood from its tip, and pushed his prisoner forward away from the Opera National and down the darkened alleyway. Within moments, Erik saw her loom amid the squat buildings, dark against a moonlit night. A wounded leviathan, the Opera Populaire, sat silent waiting for him to come home.

Christine had actually tried to dissuade Meg from following after Erik. She wanted with all her heart to be with Raoul. Both of them were pregnant. Christine was entering her sixth month, and Meg was in her fourth. It would be risky to travel. Meg had argued that Christine should remain at the estate; she would go alone. But Christine would not sit by and allow Meg to go on her own to Paris in search of Erik. So finally, Christine had made Meg promise to wait several days so that Raoul and Erik would have no time to send them back again. They readied Mario and Laurette for the journey, and then they set off for the Chagny mansion that lay just outside Paris.

When Christine walked up the steps to the Chagny estate, she was greeted with surprise by Dupré. It was painfully obvious to her that Raoul had not returned home. Dupré knew nothing of his master's return and had not expected her either. The Chagny children were thrilled to see their mother and Aunt Meg and questioned the latter endlessly about François, Mario, and Laurette. Only two of Meg's children were downstairs, being served a light dinner. Christine had to scold Victor and Elise to desist when they repeatedly asked after François. She could tell that Meg was on the verge of tears.

François was in the hands of a madman. What if Erik couldn't save him? Meg was beside herself with worry about her first born. She was haunted by the feeling that she might never see him or Erik ever again.

"Dupré, where would my husband go if he wanted to be in the area unbeknownst to you or anyone else at the estate?"

"Well, madame, I believe he still has the deed to several town properties. There's the small villa in the country, too."

"No, he'd want to be in the city if at all possible."

"Then I would suggest the apartment near the Louvre would be the more comfortable."

"Anything else?"

"I'm not sure, madame, of the exact location, but I do recall he had rented some rooms above the Café du théatre, near the river and the old opera house."

"Thank you, Dupré. That will be all for the evening."

Christine confided to Meg, after the children had retired, that she would not doubt that Raoul and Erik had rented rooms in the area of the Opera National, the rendezvous point dictated by Leroux.

"There's not much we can do, Meg. I'm sure they'll come here when it's over."

Meg nodded. Her throat had squeezed tight, and she couldn't trust her voice.

When it's over. Those words seemed prophetic in nature, and Meg was afraid to imagine what they actually meant. *After Erik is dead? After Erik and François are dead? After Leroux drags Erik to the police station to prove to all his doubters that he was correct all along? After I see my husband hanged again in the public square?* Was it already over for her and Erik? And what of François? Even if he returned unharmed to Meg, what burden might the child be forced to carry, knowing that his safety was purchased at the cost of his father's life? He'd never forgive himself!

Erik's heart leapt with joy the moment his eyes discerned the shape of his son in the damp gloom. But in the next moment, a rage overwhelmed him as he noticed the chain fastened to François's ankle and saw the dirty and frightened face of his young son. He reined in the fury, knowing he must control himself at least until the child was safe.

"François, are you all right?" he called out as he ran toward the boy.

"Stop where you are!" shouted Leroux.

"Papa! He told me you'd not come!" François's veneer of bravery threatened to crack and crumble.

Erik turned and stared uncomprehendingly at the man. "Why would you say that to him? He's just a boy! He's not a part of this!"

"Stay right where you are!" To make his point, Leroux aimed the firearm he had leveled at Erik at the boy instead.

Erik's face was ashen under his mask. He immediately drew back a step so that Leroux would understand that he was obeying his orders.

"You will let him go now." Erik tried to keep his voice calm and level, but he could not restrain the impulse to demand.

Leroux considered the situation for a moment. He could tell how desperate the Phantom was to have his son released. He allowed the moment to stretch out, enjoying the agony he could see in the Phantom's eyes.

"Take off the mask!"

When the Phantom glared at him, rigid in his refusal to comply, Leroux motioned with his firearm significantly in the direction of the boy.

Erik eased his bound hands up toward his face, slipped his fingers under the edge of the mask, and lifted it. It fell to the uneven stone floor, two hollow eyes, a blind witness to madness.

"Age has not improved you," Leroux sneered. He liked the fact that he could tell just how vulnerable Erik was without the mask to hide behind. "I intend to keep my promise to let the boy go. But first he needs to know why we are here, why *you* are here. As well as what I plan to do to you."

"Let him go, Leroux. He has nothing to do with this."

"Just as I assumed, he knows nothing about who you really are, does he? You've lied to everyone, even to your own children. He must be told. He needs to understand why you are to be imprisoned and executed."

"No, please," cried François. "You can't! You can't hurt my father!"

"François, you must be quiet. Inspector Leroux will let you go in a few minutes." Before the child could cry out again, Erik went on in a stern voice, "You are to go to the streets above. You are to find your way to the Chagny estate. They'll take care of you." Raoul was somewhere above, searching for them. But Erik had no illusions that Raoul would save them. Even if it occurred to him to search the opera house, Raoul didn't know the tunnels. He'd never find his way. He might even get lost or fall into one of Erik's old traps.

"François, were you aware that your father used to live here?" Leroux's hand swept the circumference of the stone chamber. He knew how afraid the child had been to be left alone in this underground prison.

François scanned the hollowed gaping mouth of the earth, the jagged stone walls of the vault pressing inward, the darkness that clung in the uneven surfaces. He listened to the sound of dripping water, felt the damp cold clutch at his ankles, his neck and face. He shivered. Cold and fear sat on either side of him.

Erik took the moment to observe his son closely. "Leroux, what have you done to him?" he interrupted.

"I was speaking of your past, M. Phantom. You will not interrupt me."

"Did you drag him down here, chain him in this dank hole, and abandon him?" The thought of his child left alone in this world filled him with rage. It was small consolation to recall that he himself had been merely a child when Madeleine brought him to hide in the underground rooms. But for him, it had been a necessity and a refuge.

"If you do not remain quiet, M. Phantom, I will have to demonstrate my resolve. Do you wish to force my hand?"

Erik tensed at the madness in Leroux's eyes. To stop from speaking, Erik clenched his teeth and welcomed the pain.

"This was where the Phantom lived. Not for a couple of days like you have, my boy, but for years and years. He grew up here in this dark, damp world. He stole for a living. He robbed the theater above. He snuck out of these foul tunnels and attacked people on the street."

Again the lies! Erik could not stifle the groan. He looked at François whose eyes were fixed on him. There he saw disbelief and fear. Oh, but God help them, it was not all lies!

Leroux continued, "Did you know that he lusted after your Aunt Christine? That he dragged her down to these cellars and…"

"Leroux! He's just a boy!"

"And he raped her like he had many other innocent creatures in the past. You're old enough to understand rape, aren't you boy?" In his eagerness, Leroux stepped forward to speak more intimately with the child.

François nodded his head slightly. But Erik could see the confusion on his son's face.

"He murdered Joseph Buquet, a scene-shifter, in the middle of a performance. He strangled him and dropped his body at the end of a rope to the stage while the ballet corps danced before an entire auditorium of witnesses. But this didn't satisfy his bloodlust. Oh, no."

As Leroux spoke to François, Erik backed away, sliding his feet silently, until he stood to the side and just an inch behind the officer. He bit the inside of his mouth to stifle his need to defend himself, to silence the cruel litany of his offenses.

"Your Aunt Christine was appalled by him, frightened and repulsed. She tried to flee from him." Leroux's voice thundered in the cavernous room. "Then one night he sang on the stage, taking the tenor's spot, and when she refused to come away with him, he dropped the chandelier into the auditorium filled with innocent people, setting the fire that destroyed this house."

The officer once more stepped forward, oblivious that Erik was now beyond the periphery of his vision. "He killed eleven people that night. Your father is a monster, my boy." Leroux paused, waiting for the words to take their full effect on the child, a child who was the spawn of the Phantom. "And *you* have his blood in you. I will have to keep my eye on you, François."

Erik lunged at Leroux. "I'll kill you!" he shouted, the cry vicious and raw with the desire to destroy his tormentor. Erik struck Leroux with the full weight of his body, crashing the man against the rocky surface. The firearm went off wildly, its blast reverberating against the stone walls, and then slipped from Leroux's fingers. Leroux pushed impotently against the beast he'd awoken. Erik lifted his arms, his hands still bound, to encircle Leroux's neck. Erik stepped to the side and rotated his arms, scissoring across Leroux's throat and cutting off his airway. The smaller man searched frantically for his knife as the vice tightened.

The sounds erupting from the grimace that had been Erik's mouth were not human as he twisted and crushed the life out of Leroux. The man struggled frantically. Finding the knife in his pocket, Leroux brought the blade up and sliced at Erik's arm. Erik shook the man like a wolf would its prey. Leroux lost his grip on the knife; it clattered noisily to the ground. The inspector's face turned red, then purple, finally black, his hands clawed uselessly at Erik's arm, Erik could smell the man's bowels and bladder loosen, and then his body went slack like a dirty rag. Yet Erik still pressed his arms tightly across the man's neck. Slowly, reluctantly, he released the pressure. Then he felt Leroux's dead body slip to the ground, his limbs collapsing in an unnatural way beneath him. The gash in Erik's arm was bleeding, and he watched, fascinated, as steady drops of blood landed on the inspector's blood-darkened face. Curiously, he stared at the bulging eyes and the extended and swollen tongue. He waited.

Only dimly aware of the cold, Erik heard the drops of blood, nothing else for the longest time. Gradually he understood that he was not alone. François was huddled in the corner; he had been calling to his father over and over. The words had been drowned out by the drops of blood and the silent cry in the gaping maw of the dead man. Erik shivered, his teeth rattling convulsively. His hands were still bound by leather straps that bit into his flesh. He made his way clumsily to the knife that Leroux had dropped and turned the sharp edge onto the straps. His hands free, he rifled through Leroux's pockets. The stink was nauseating, but he continued searching the body until he found the key.

Even as Erik drew near, François remained huddled on the floor, his knees wedged tightly under his chin. He had stopped calling to his father long before he saw him approach.

Erik couldn't look at his son's eyes. He found the lock and released it. He dragged the chains from François's leg. The boy threw himself roughly onto Erik's neck and buried his face against his father's shoulder. Erik couldn't move or think. A moment of sheer pain was followed by a cold resolve. He returned his son's embrace until the child's trembling calmed.

"François, did he hurt you?" he whispered, dreading to find out that perhaps the man had tortured the child.

His son shook his head and sniffled. "No, Papa. He was rough, but he didn't hurt me."

At least that small mercy had been granted. He would cling to that.

"Is it true that you lived down here all those years? Was that before you met Maman?"

Erik stared at the child. He was so beautiful. But Leroux's words were already boring their way into his soul. Erik answered with a quiet, reluctant voice that it was true.

"Did you kill him, Papa?"

Erik glanced over at the monstrous cadaver that had been a man.

"He lied about you, didn't he?" There was such a plea in the child's voice to know that it had all been madness, that none of it had been real.

"No. Yes. No, François, some of what he said is true."

"The part about you living here. Is that the true part, then?" He could hear his son's desperate insistence, his need to be reassured that his father was not a monster.

Blood, he tasted blood. He pulled François to his feet and half carried him through the long tunnel. The trembling weakness in his body had been replaced by an urgent need to get his son away from this tomb, away from the blood, away from himself. The shell of the Opera Populaire, his entire world, had become a graveyard, and he would not have his son mired in it. He ascended the great stone stairs, rising, reaching for the surface, struggling away from a leaden weight that dragged at him, demanding that he sink down beside the body of his victims and wait for death.

When Erik saw the last corridor along which they would go to reach the street beyond the opera house, he hesitated. He released his hold on his son and stooped before him so that their faces were close. François's eyes were his!

"I have killed, but I have not done all the things he said. I am a bad person, and I can't be with you anymore. You must go now. You must take care of your mother. She will be very sad. She is with child. Be kind to her. Take care of Laurette and be a loving brother to Mario." To hide his tears, he pulled François tightly to his chest in a fierce hug. Slowly he managed to quell his emotions and steady his voice. "Go now. Don't argue. Tell them not to come in search of me. The tunnels are dangerous. Tell them! Tell Meg…Tell her…Go now!"

"No! You're coming with me!" The child grabbed Erik's shirt and shouted at him. "I won't leave without you."

Erik shook him angrily. "Yes, you will! You will do as I say! Your mother is waiting for you. She needs you."

François quieted, but he didn't move.

Erik grabbed him roughly by the arm and dragged him to the doorway. He pushed François out into the night air. "Go now! You will do as I say, François! Obey me in this! Do not come after me!" He closed the door and fastened the latch so that the child could not get back inside. He leaned against the door and listened to François's pleas, to the banging of his fists on the heavy wooden door, to the tears. It went on and on. From one moment to the next, Erik thought to relent, but he couldn't. He was the contagion. He was the violence. He would not return to his family.

In time, the child's attempts lessened, and then Erik realized that he was gone. He felt it in the gaping fissure that opened in his chest. The pain of emptiness brought a howl from his throat and sent him to his knees.

CHAPTER 17

Madness

I am but mad north-north-west: when the wind is southerly I know a hawk from a handsaw.

Shakespeare, Hamlet

He sat humming to himself the aria Carlotta had sung. He chuckled as he remembered her flailing her arms about her head during one of the rehearsals.

"She learned. She did. You would have been amazed, Leroux."

The cadaver sat twisted strangely but balanced against the wall in a sitting position. His eyes were open, and Erik glanced away as an insect crawled across the dulled whitened surface.

"I couldn't believe my own eyes and ears on opening night. She will be very, very angry with me that I haven't returned to keep my end of the bargain. She won't fare as well with another director. They will be cowed by her hysterics. They will coddle her and let her fall into decadence as before. She'll revert to her old ways."

Leroux chuckled softly. "You think you're so talented! You talk of her as if she were *your* triumph. Wasn't it *she* who stood on the stage and sang? Wasn't it *she* for whom they applauded?"

"Yes, yes, yes," Erik admitted. "You're right, as always, my dear enemy. You were forever in search of the truth, were you not?"

Erik had found his old sanctuary. The officers had destroyed nearly everything. But there were a few bottles of wine hidden in one of the recessed alcoves. He lounged on the dirty scraps of cloth that lay across his old bed and drank deeply of the red vintage.

"Want some?" He offered the corpse the bottle, but Leroux wisely passed on the offer.

"I did deserve to hang, Leroux. I did indeed. Whatever possessed Raoul to save me? He seemed such a reasonable man." The thought of Raoul brought the thought of Christine, which in turn evoked the image of Meg.

For a moment he allowed himself the exquisite pain of remembering her softness, her hair unbraided across her shoulders, the rise of her bosom, her long sleek neck, large fawn-colored eyes, cherries and cream, and taut muscles under velvet skin, graceful lines, ten sweet tapered fingers that stroked his face.

He rose and bellowed a cry of anger at himself. He threw the bottle against the stone wall. He couldn't think about them—those soft, warm temptations calling him back. They did not belong in his world. They were…they were… they were what he could not have, what must not be thought of!

He forced his mind into a blank. He would not even allow himself the music. The notes kept creeping back on him. Melodies, scales, chords played again and again in his mind. That life was over, he had shouted. He struck his temples with his fists and screamed until his throat was ragged. Only then did the music retreat, but it had not stopped. He still heard it softly calling to him.

He had searched the many secret rooms of his former home, rounding up bottles of wine that had not been broken or sacked by the Parisian police. There was no food, all of it had long decayed or been carried off by the rodents. He had opened the first dusty bottle and upended it over his mouth. The liquid had burned his throat and flooded the hollow of his stomach. He drank as long and as deeply as he could. He intended to drain each bottle until nothing was left.

He could not kill himself! He had tried. He could not tell why. But he had sat next to Leroux's body with the knife blade pressed hard against his vein and yet he could not slice his flesh and let himself bleed to death. Why? Why had his hand shaken so violently that he dropped the knife?

So he had decided to wait for death to come to him. Soon he would go off down one of the many corridors to a recess unknown to Meg, unknown to anyone but himself. And there he would die—there in a cold dark place where the music would cease its pull, where silence and blackness would claim him.

"Leroux, you really should try some of this. It's quite good."

Yes, it was fitting that Leroux be present. Although Erik wasn't sure that he could stomach carrying the body any farther along the labyrinth than he had already.

After he sent François away—how long ago had it been?—he had returned to Leroux's side. The body was twisted and lying in its own bodily filth. The stench was revolting, hanging on the damp air, permeating the very stone. But it was not for that reason that Erik stripped the body and washed out the soiled garments in the deep waters of the lake. It was not why he took scraps of cloth and washed Leroux's body clean. He couldn't explain it; he didn't even question himself. He took the still damp clothing and dressed the stiffened corpse again, and then he lifted him and flung him over his shoulder and carried him to these chambers.

Was it that he didn't want to be alone? Or was it that he needed those dead cold eyes to remind him of the punishment he must suffer?

"Well, we can spend a bit more time together, can't we, Leroux? I never did know your first name, and mine was all you knew of me." He stumbled and caught himself. The wine had addled his wits; the room was in constant motion. He stared at his hands, the bent fingers. "I used to have beautiful hands. You took them from me. Why? Why did you hate me so?" In the back of his mind he remembered Raoul telling him about the girl. "Oh, yes. You thought it was I who had done that. I remember now. Was I that evil?"

Leroux had chosen that moment to be uncharacteristically silent.

"Rat got your tongue?" Erik smiled ruefully. He wouldn't be able to shoo them all away, the vermin that slithered and ran in the darkness. Soon Leroux would be crawling with them, but then again so would Erik. Erik would lie dead, his warmth fast dissipating, and then they would all come, his silent companions of the night to gnaw and chew, to burrow deep under the skin and lay their eggs, to claw at his eyes and strip his flesh, to pull off his toes and fingers, and carry them to a nearby nest for their young.

"Well, we will yet be of some service, won't we, Leroux?" Meg would not find his body. No one would wash him and lay him out. But there would be tears! He couldn't lie to himself about that. His canary, his light, his golden love, even now bearing his child in her womb, Meg would cry until all her tears were spent. She would mourn him, perhaps curse him, too. So would others.

"I just wanted," he whispered, "to touch the sun." He slumped down, resting his back against the cold stone. "I just wanted…to feel…the warmth."

He woke with a start. There were noises, not the filthy rats fighting for the choicest bit of his companion, but those of large animals, the human ones, the ones capable of cruelty and mayhem, the ones that raped and pillaged the earth, those like him!

Quickly he dragged the now loose-jointed body of Leroux, holding his breath against the stench, looking away from the effect of the rodents and insects, and laid the body on the bed. It was the last courtesy he could do his tormentor and judge as well as final victim. Then he ran down the passageway toward a dark ledge jutting out of the natural rock surface. He bent and crept underneath it into the dark. There, in between two rocks, he forced his way through a narrow opening, invisible to everyone but the one who knew of its existence.

François had been desperate for his father to open the door. His fists were sore and bloody from pounding. Someone shouted for him to be quiet from one of the nearby apartments, but he continued to whimper and beg his father to open the door, to come out with him so that they could go home. He didn't give a bloody damn what that man had said about his father. He knew who his father was! He was the man who taught him, who sang to him at night, whose scowl alone could keep him from doing something naughty, the man who loved his mother and from whom he would know how to love another when it came his time. He might have done bad things, but he was not a bad man!

But the door remained firmly locked.

He knew that there was a café nearby. He had seen it when the inspector had brought him to the opera house. He remembered looking into the window and seeing the actors and artists celebrating. They were like those he knew at the Teatro dell'Opera. It was a familiar world. They would surely help him.

He heard footsteps in the dark street coming in his direction. He could tell there were several men. He ran without thinking. The sounds echoed off the walls of the buildings, and François became momentarily confused. They seemed to be coming from two distinct directions. He darted into an alleyway and ran frantically away from the sounds. At the end of the passageway, under the street lamp, he looked about, not recognizing the street. He turned again to his right and ran down that road hoping to find something familiar. He wanted to make his way back toward the plaza, back to the café. They would help him find the Count de Chagny! The count would come back and force the door open. They would find his father and bring him home, even if he didn't want to come. He ran and ran, winding his way farther and farther into the labyrinth of the city. A sharp whistle from a passing carriage startled him, and he fell. In the moment before he lost consciousness, he heard the frightened neighing and saw the hoof of the animal hover and come down.

"He's going to be all right, Meg. The horse merely clipped him, but he has a hard head. He's bruised." Raoul squeezed Meg's hand to comfort her.

She had been so relieved to have François back in her arms that she had momentarily forgotten all else. He was injured, but the doctor said it was not serious. He'd come around soon.

As they carried the boy to a room and settled him in the bed, she asked Raoul, "Where's Erik? Is there no word of him? No sign?"

Raoul shook his head grimly. "Meg, Erik did what he had to do."

"Oh, no, please, God, no! I can't have lost him. If we go to Leroux, surely we can convince him to let Erik go?"

"I don't know where Leroux took him, Meg," Raoul confessed. "It might have been anywhere. He may even have taken him outside the city. We were watching, and then the performance let out. Everyone poured from the theater, and we lost him in the crowd. We searched everywhere we could think of. There were so many coaches and carriages coming and going, he might have been in any of them. I'm sorry."

Meg sank down beside François. Although Erik had not returned, he had given her back her son. That had been the only thing that had mattered to him.

The child slept through the night and late into the next day. By evening, he woke and sat up in a wild panic. It took Meg several moments to calm him down.

"No, Maman, listen, you must listen. We have to go back for him!"

Meg held him closely and rocked him back and forth. He pushed away from her, annoyed. "Stop! You must listen to me. That man. The man who took me was mad. He said horrible things about Papa. He was supposed to let me go, Papa said. But the man kept talking, and then Papa put his arms around the man's neck and strangled him."

Raoul dropped to his knee beside the bed and questioned the boy before Meg could react. "You say that Leroux is dead? Erik is alive?"

"Yes, but…" François grabbed his mother's shoulders roughly in his hands and spoke to her. "But Papa says he's bad. He took me to the street and told me I was to take care of you and to tell you something, but he couldn't finish it. And then he barred the door and wouldn't come out with me. That's when I ran. I heard someone coming down the street. I was frightened, so I ran. But Papa is down there still. Maman, I think Papa's going to do something very foolish. He spoke to me as if he were never coming home. You have to go for him." The boy suddenly seemed much older than his years. He turned to Raoul.

"He won't ever come back, unless you go and find him. Uncle Raoul, he might listen to you."

"He's alive. Leroux is…Raoul, call for the carriage. I'll be down in ten minutes." Meg kissed François roughly on his bruised forehead without thinking, "Oh, my sweet, I love you."

"Wait, Meg, we don't have a clue as to where he is."

"What? Weren't you listening? He's down in the underground tunnels. He's planning on burying himself again under the Opera Populaire."

"We've been here already three times, Meg. There's no way out. All the tunnels lead us back here."

"He was here!"

That was undisputable. They had smelled the corpse well before they reached the rooms. Here was where Erik had given Meg her lessons so long ago. These were the rooms where he had gone to die when he was heartbroken and in despair after he set Christine free and she left him to go away with Raoul. Meg had managed to find her way to the rooms, expecting to find Erik as she had before.

They had not spoken of why he had not returned with his son. Raoul was dumbfounded. Meg understood all too well how Erik's mind worked. She imagined his overwhelming sense of guilt. His son had been placed in danger because of his past, a past that Erik and Meg had kept hidden from the children. Leroux then listed and described Erik's crimes to the child. And while his son looked on, Erik had fought with Leroux and killed him. To Meg, this was a clear case of self-preservation, but to Erik it would be confirmation of his violent, brutal nature. Without Leroux, Erik would be forced to punish himself!

But as they approached the chambers, the stench of death accosted them. Meg rushed forward, her heart in her mouth, fearing to have found Erik too late. Instead, the curious scene of a funereal wake was laid out before them. Around the room several tapers still burned casting a fluttering glow across the blanketed figure on Erik's bed. It was not her love. She could tell that immediately, for someone had laid this corpse out and covered it. Someone had taken care to respect it, to perform certain rites. Raoul kept Meg back as he pulled the cover down. He quickly came away, rushed to the far edge of the chamber where he failed to calm the spasms in his stomach. Meg looked away discreetly until Raoul was able to control the violent waves of nausea. He spoke quietly with Angelo and Roger, giving them instructions to take the body to one of the far rooms and burn it. Inspector Leroux had disappeared months ago when he quit the force and set off for Rome. No one would ever find him now.

Meg had insisted on searching and calling for Erik throughout the tunnels. She even forced the men to accompany her to the theater above and to trace the hidden staircase to Erik's original chambers, long abandoned. There she showed Raoul the passage through the mirror and cautioned him to watch for trip wires. They found the well into which Meg had fallen and from which Erik had rescued her. They found evidence of other traps, but these had been dismantled. Raoul could tell from the marks and the displaced dust and dirt that it had been done recently. Erik must have feared that they would search for him, and he didn't want them to be harmed. With more confidence, they proceeded until they came upon this same chamber a second time from which there were no new trails to be searched.

It was a dead end. But Meg refused to accept this fact.

So the next two days they returned. It had been nearly five days since Erik disappeared. Raoul kept his tongue, but he confided to Christine that he thought Erik was dead, somewhere in one of the tunnels. That was the only way he could explain the fact that Erik never answered as they called for him.

"Meg, this is useless," Raoul repeated softly as yet again Meg inspected the chambers.

She must find him. François told her to bring his father back, and that is what she meant to do. He was hers. He belonged to her! Yet for the first time she was terrified that she had come too late. She couldn't feel him. Before, when she thought she had lost him, when everyone around her insisted he had died in the fire Giovanni set in the Teatro dell'Opera, she had sensed that it was not true. She had checked her heart, and he was still there, alive. Now she searched for him, and a horrible emptiness, a painful wound was all she could find. Even so she would have his body. She would perform the same rites he had performed for his worst enemy. She would hold him and wash him and anoint him with oils and perfumes and dress him in smooth silk and cotton. She would be there to say goodbye to him. Please, she must see him once more!

Raoul gently took her by the arm to lead her away. She wrenched roughly out of his grasp with a snarl. "No!"

Exasperated, Raoul leaned against the wall and remembered the day Leroux and his men had cornered the Phantom in this very spot and had taken him away to prison.

"Roger! Turn out the lamp," Raoul ordered, standing away from the cold stone surface.

"I need the light!" Meg complained.

Despite her protest, the light was snuffed out. Blackness spread around them. Raoul had taken his position next to Meg and lightly held her arm. Within a few moments, Raoul's eyes strained to see varying shades of black and gray about him. And then he saw it, a strange luminescence down the tunnel, along the wall. It was as if a faint light were coming through the stones themselves. They approached and felt along the face of the stone. Raoul hit his forehead painfully on an invisible rock shelf before he bent and brought Meg down with him. By feel he found the opening, and they slipped through. Silently Raoul motioned in the dim light to Roger to hand him the lantern. He lit it to find a narrow passageway that they had not seen before. At the end of it they would find the light they were seeking.

...don't listen to them...Mario...you're...a good...boy...generous...you have no gift for the piano...listen...come sit beside François you mustn't worry...Meg... she does love you, don't cry and I...look, Meg, how Mario fawns on Laurette... she'll bear watching...willful like you, Meg...Listen, listen to him, he's playing the Chopin...will he play for me now?...my...my...my son...they will say he's like... no...he's...not...like...what?...yes, François...you played...like an angel...please, Meg, please, please, I...so softly I can't hear...you...please sing to...oh, Meg, your hand...is so...I held my baby girl...her first breath...frightening, it's frightening to have children...so small...so...tender...why?...oh Meg...I will watch over you...I wish I could...kiss...his forehead when he is born...don't put this sadness on him, Meg, I beg you...in sunlight, with joy...the child of your mourning...don't cry, don't...what?...I will...I promise...lie here, let me...I will not have gone, leaving no trace...children...my children...yes, I hear you...but...soon...soon... it will be...soon...stay awhile...will they be there waiting for me?...the dead ones?...no...no...nonononononono...I...I'm...oh, God, I'm...sorry...for...my faults...protect me...won't think of that...what were the words?...Hail Mother of Mercy...our sweetness, our...hope...to thee do we cry, poor banished...children of Eve, to thee do we send...oh I can't remember...Mother Superior, what were the words?...our sighs...yes...our sighs...weeping in this valley...in this...in this valley of tears...I liked that part...Mother...give us mercy...oh, Holy Mother, give me mercy...O loving, O sweet...Virgin Mary, pray for me...pray for...pray for... pray for my loved ones...pray for my Meg...my...our children...have pity...O Holy Mother have pity...on this...on this monster...have pity...on me

As they drew closer, they could hear him. He was speaking in halting fashion, speaking to himself, it would seem. The words were unclear, garbled, then slowly Meg could pick out names, her own. She wanted to rush quickly forward to him, now that she knew he was alive and where he was, but something in the sounds he was making made her hesitate. Raoul, too, felt it. He stopped and pulled her close to him, making a sign of quiet with his finger against his lip. They listened.

It was as if he were speaking to the children. His voice was faint, coming in and out of audible range. Weakened by the fast, crippled by surrender, he had given up and was languishing in the hidden womb of this graveyard!

Was he praying? The sounds grew urgent. A plea, a rending of the soul? She heard the Virgin's name. How often she had encouraged him to pray! He had always ignored her suggestions. But he never interfered with her faith. She still attended mass, insisted that the children be baptized and attend regularly with her, but Erik refused to accompany them. Whenever she prayed and he was present, he grew very still as if fearing to interrupt her. Now she wondered if he might have prayed silently with her in those moments. Strangely it frightened her to hear him pray out loud. He wouldn't do this unless he…unless…

She pulled away from Raoul's fierce grip and ran to the end of the corridor. As she turned the corner, she saw Erik scramble to rise from the floor. He had his back to the wall as far from the entrance as he could be. He seemed poised to attack. His hair was wild and loose, falling over his face. His mask was gone! He was dirty, his face darkly smudged, streaked from tears and sweat, his shirt open to the waist, his chest darkened from dust and grease. The dark stains of blood covered one arm, dripped across the side of his once white shirt and down onto the tawny fabric of his trousers.

"Are you wounded?" she cried.

He was panting like a wild beast, his eyes locked onto her as if she might strike at him or he at her, his arms raised, the hands softly fisted, but prepared. She could see his teeth gritted through his slightly parted lips. Why didn't he respond to her?

She took another step toward him, but Raoul pulled her back at the same moment that Erik jerked perceptibly as if to avoid her. They were several paces away from the wild man that stood in the shallow alcove. Around him were scores of candles, but only a few were lit. He would save the rest, unwilling to be trapped here in the dark. As one would burn down, he would light the next. About him were signs that he had sat and waited here for quite some time. His coat lay wadded at his feet, both bed and cover to him.

Erik couldn't believe they were here. He had gotten beyond the hunger, no longer aware of the nagging emptiness in his gut. He was pleasantly weak, no longer nauseous, just softly drowsy. He had been talking with them. He had visited each of them in turn and given them his blessing. Then the words of the prayer, he had recalled them, some of them, most of them, those that he liked, those that spoke to him and flowed sincerely from his mouth. His mouth was dry. That was his only discomfort.

What were they doing here?

"Go away," his voice surprised him, coarse and dry like dust on the stones. His face was screwed up into an angry grimace, he was momentarily aware that he must look frightening. He had not expected to be seen, to be found, ever. It hadn't mattered that he was dirty, that he was ragged and torn and bleeding. What did it signify if he lay down here and died? The candles would burn down, and his body would be lost to the darkness.

Raoul pulled Meg back, but she resisted him. "Don't! He's hurt!"

"He's more than hurt, Meg. He's not himself. Stand back," he insisted. He forced her behind him.

They think I'm mad! He thinks I'd harm her! Oh God! He lost his fierceness at the thought. Couldn't Raoul hear him? Then he realized he was not speaking out loud. His voice was locked inside his head. Raoul had not heard him say that he would never harm Meg.

"Erik? We've come to take you home."

Finally, Erik found his mouth twisting up into a smile. Could that be a laugh, that sound he just made? "I am home." His throat hurt to work. He hadn't had anything to drink for the past several days, since he took refuge here in his grave.

Meg pushed at Raoul roughly and stepped out from behind him. She spoke with a desperate fury to Erik. "You have no choice! You are coming with me. Don't you dare resist."

Erik studied the small blond woman. There was a light around her as if she shimmered. Her hair melted into the light, and he saw the sounds of her voice rise like notes in the air. He followed them and laughed delighted at their playfulness, but then they fell dead to the stone floor. He felt sad to see them in the dirt. Her voice startled him again, and he looked at her.

"No," he answered.

Meg stared at him in astonishment. His response was simply not in keeping with the circumstances. It was spoken without the least emotion. She had watched his eyes lose focus and wander round the ceiling and floor of the room.

She was frightened, more frightened than she remembered being for a long time. She had found Erik, but it was not he!

"I want Erik." She called to him. She whispered his name as she came forward.

His eyes turned dark. Raoul grabbed Meg and pulled her back just as Erik stiffened and threatened to launch himself at them. "Go away!" This was a voice Meg recognized, angry and rough, brittle from the dryness, but it was his voice. "I am not who I was!"

Raoul had watched Erik the entire time. He was weak from his ordeal. He had lost some blood, not enough to kill him but enough to matter. He was not going to come of his own free will, that was clear.

"Erik, I've come to take you back." Raoul knew that Angelo and Roger would be in the passageway listening. If he needed to, he could call them in. "I intend to take you back, whether you want to come or not."

Erik studied Raoul curiously. "Leave me. I'm dead. You're talking to a ghost!"

Without allowing Erik time to prepare, Raoul threw himself forward onto him and grappled with his arms. He tried to twist him round to hold his arms behind his back, to subdue him. But Erik was anxious to die and beyond pain. Meg screamed as Raoul jabbed Erik in the face, a powerful blow meant to knock him out. Erik stumbled and shook his head, but he didn't go down. Hearing her cry, Angelo rushed forward and latched onto Erik's arm while Raoul restrained the other. Erik tried to unbalance them by hurling his body against one and then the other.

They had not seen Meg approach. Suddenly her hands were on Erik's face.

"Meg, stand back! He's dangerous!" Raoul shouted at her as he saw her come within striking distance.

But Erik felt her hands on his face and opened his eyes to stare at her in wide-eyed amazement. All the fight, all the strength flowed out of him, and he crumpled to his knees. The two men released his arms, sensing immediately that he was no threat. Erik wrapped himself about Meg's legs and hid his face in her lap, against his unborn child.

Muffled against her skirts, Meg could hear his voice. "I'm dead. Leave me, Meg. I'm dead. Don't take me out there again."

In and out of light he passed, heavy, incapable of resistance. They carried him. They picked him up among the three of them and ripped him once more from his grave. He had been so close. He had felt the chasm opening below his feet, felt the sinking rise of his stomach as he began to fall, and felt the fire below searing his flesh. Had he cried for her? He didn't know. She had come, the blond one, the coolness of her milky touch, the glowing light, without fire, round her head.

Meg, his Meg, had come to save him, but he had not wished to be saved. Leroux had told him he must suffer. It was time to die. His little death for all the death he had caused. He had peopled his life with dead ones, and there was no room for him anymore. Leroux had told him: This is the Law. You shall die. You shall die.

They wrapped him in warm blankets and placed him in a large bed. He wanted to tell them not to leave him. The bed was too wide. He was in a room he didn't recognize. He feared they would put out the light. He didn't like the darkness. He wanted the candles lit so he could see Death when He came for him. He didn't want to be startled.

Meg brought him cups of water and held his head until his lips sensed the fresh moisture and he began to drink. She held him against her lap, sitting with her back against the headboard of the bed. The servants brought her broth to spoon feed him. At first he couldn't keep anything down. The first sips of water came explosively from his mouth and nose as he retched. But the next time he drank, the water stayed down. Then shortly after that, Meg managed to feed him several spoonfuls of rich, fatty broth. He rested better.

She spoke to him, but he couldn't hear her.

"Mario, you must go to bed." This was the second night that Meg had found the boy sitting vigil outside their bedroom door.

"Is he better?"

Meg knew he still found it strange to call her 'maman.' She nodded and smiled, the lie transparent to Mario.

"You don't need to protect me...Maman...I saw them carry him in." It had been frightening, even perhaps more to him than to François, who was still in a state of shock, grateful to be safe and to have his father with them. But Mario knew that the man they brought back to the Chagny estate wasn't Erik.

Meg let the reassuring smile drop from her face, relieved to give up the pretense. No, he wasn't better. She pulled Mario to the study and ushered him into the room. She sat him on the sofa and sat down beside him. She held his hand in hers for several moments, quietly composing her thoughts.

"You knew him before, Mario, during difficult times. When he was with Signora Fiortino." He fidgeted uncomfortably at the reference to those tragic days. He would keep his master's secrets even from Meg. "I'm not asking you to talk about that," she said as if she could read his mind. "He's told me himself. I just mean that you're not as…" She was going to say "innocent" when the idea stuck like a sharp bone in her throat. God knew what Mario had experienced while living on the streets by his wits. She'd not drag him back to those memories. Instead, she said, "You are older than François, and I can be frank with you."

Mario smiled at the unexpected confidence his master's wife had in him. "Signora, I know he's not himself. He's very cruel to himself."

Meg couldn't restrain the sudden explosion of tears. She grabbed Mario and squeezed him very hard. "You must call me maman, Mario. We love you. I love you. You're my son."

Mario tried to fight the trembling of his lower lip and let her hold him. The harder she squeezed him, the easier it was for him to keep from crying with her.

Eventually she let him go. "Have you spoken with your brother?"

"Yes, Maman. He wanted to keep vigil with me, but I told him he must rest. He wants to see Papa as do I."

"I'm afraid that's not a good idea."

"No, Maman, you're wrong. It's a very good idea. He has to remember who he is. We won't let him forget. You should not leave him alone. Not ever. That's when…"

"What?"

"That's when the ghosts come for him. And if you aren't there, we must be there for him."

Perhaps he was right. But at the moment, she wanted him to do something else.

"François. Has he spoken to you about what happened?"

Mario knew he'd need to tread softly here. He would not contribute to her problems. Besides, he was perfectly able to deal with François. In truth all François needed was to be with Erik. But she was watching him, and he realized he couldn't lie to her.

"The man said awful things about Papa. I don't think François understood all of it. He was rough with him, but he only struck him once."

Meg's eyes flashed with anger, but she held her tongue.

"The man left him alone in the underground. That was the worst part of it. He said he couldn't understand how Papa had managed to survive down there. Was what he said about Papa true?"

How could she sift through the lies to find a truth that wouldn't endanger Erik? "Mario, Erik has led a violent life. But since he and I have been together, he has tried to live differently. Leroux knew him before…when he did things for which he is very sorry. François saw him kill Leroux, didn't he?"

"Yes, Maman."

"Has he said anything about it to you?"

"He was very frightened until Papa killed Leroux. He said Papa did it to protect him." Mario had listened intently to François describe the encounter. François had been terrified when his father had offered to take his place, when Erik asked Leroux to let François go and promised to stay behind. Leroux had told François that he meant to kill his father. "Maman, he was scared Papa wouldn't fight Leroux. He was relieved when Papa killed the man. If he hadn't, François would have always feared the man might come for him again. How would Papa stop Leroux if he let the man kill him? He wouldn't be here to protect us."

"We have to make sure Papa knows that, don't we?" Meg pulled the boy to his feet and walked him to the room he shared with François.

He felt her slide between the blankets. Her feet were cold, and she placed them between his calves as she was wont to do. He swallowed the urge to complain. The rest of her was warm and soft, and he felt himself move to press against her as if her body were a blanket. Her hands, cool, caressed his face.

How long had it been? He was weary of sleep, weary of closing his eyes only to see Leroux's face in the dark tunnels of the underground.

"Erik?"

…

"Erik? Please."

…

He shifted to wrap his arms around her. She was shivering. Was she cold? He tried to hold her closer. The damp saturated the collar of his night shirt where she nestled her face against him. He scowled. Who had caused her to cry? Then the thought came to him, painful, but certain. He had. But to comfort her, he'd have to speak, and to speak, he'd have to come to life, and if he came to life, if he came away from the tunnels where he meant to endure his sentence, he'd bring the monster with him. The only way to keep the monster away from them was to sink down further into the silent darkness. Leroux had shown him where to go and waited for him there. Each time Erik closed his eyes, Leroux came to guide him away from them.

But Meg was crying…

…

He turned in the bed. His arms felt light as if they'd float away. They held nothing. She had left him.

Someone was prodding him to drink, to sip. The smell of onion, cabbage, a rich meat broth opened his eyes. Madeleine sat on the edge of the bed and fed him. She spoke, but his ears were wrapped in cotton and he was miles away in the dark. He stared at her eyes, watched them. Meg had her eyes! The broth was warm and thick on his tongue. He forced his throat to swallow.

…

"Erik…Erik…"

…

Leroux laughed at his doubts. Behind him the voice—her voice—called.

"You can't leave. You're my prisoner," Leroux growled at him. And Erik saw the heavy chains around his ankles and wrists. "Unclean. Unclean," Leroux repeated over and over.

Erik's hands were stained red. Blood in great oozing clouts dripped between his fingers to the stone floor. He wiped his hands against his thighs, but they were still wet and dripping.

"You've killed innocents. You enjoy killing. You killed your first when you were but a child! It's in your nature."

He heard Meg speak. She told him he could come home.

"Will she want you to touch her with those hands?"

Erik froze unable to decide. He wanted to go to her, but Leroux was right. He must clean his hands. She'd be disgusted, frightened, appalled at him if he touched her with these bloody weapons.

He went to the edge of the underground lake and bent to wash his hands in its dark waters. As he bent over the smooth surface, he saw aghast his reflection. His face—his entire face—had rotted. The flesh, red and purple and sickly gray, lay loose falling away from the white bone beneath. He opened his mouth to scream!

…

"Papa…Papa…"

The bed shifted, a solid weight draped itself across his chest. His arms encircled the slim body of his son. "Papa, I want you to wake up! I'm afraid!"

The room was dark. The child was in his bed shirt. He trembled convulsively. Erik held him closer. François's voice, once many miles away, broke loud and urgent in his ear. The words fell into order, and Erik understood them. François had dreamed of Leroux.

"I'm scared!" he cried. François was such a mature boy. Like him, François prided himself on his reserve. When punished, he refused to cry. He was brave. François, his strong and brave son, François, his first-born, François, on the cusp of adolescence, François clung to him in fear and dread.

Erik patted his back and whispered the first words he'd said in many days. "It's all right, François. I'm here. I won't let anyone harm you, ever."

When Meg slipped back into their room, she was amazed to find François huddled in Erik's arms. On the other side of him, in a bundle, like a wayward puppy, lay Laurette. Next to her, his hand casually flung across the pillows and entangled in Erik's hair, lay Mario.

They had risen and gotten into the bed while she fought insomnia with a glass of warm milk in the kitchen below. She could see they were all, in one way or another, pressed against their father's sleeping body as if to keep him from escaping. She bent to extricate Laurette from between Mario and Erik, thinking to take the little girl back to her room without waking her. Mario and François she'd rouse afterwards. The moment she tugged at Laurette, she felt Erik stir.

"Leave her, Meg." Erik raised his head, and Mario's hand fell to the pillow.

He sounded so calm. He whispered as if reluctant to wake them. His voice was clear, strong, even though it was quiet.

"Are you sure, Erik?" she asked as if it were a normal evening and as if he hadn't slept for the past three days, as if she hadn't feared that he had forever gotten lost in the labyrinth of those underground tunnels.

"Come to bed, Meg," he whispered.

CHAPTER 18

Thou Art Fair

By night on my bed I sought him whom my soul loveth: I sought him, but I found him not.
I will rise now, and go about the city in the streets, and in the broad ways I will seek him whom my soul loveth: I sought him, but I found him not.
The watchmen that go about the city found me: to whom I said, Saw ye him whom my soul loveth?
It was but a little that I passed from them, but I found him whom my soul loveth: I held him, and would not let him go,...
I charge you, O ye daughters of Jerusalem, by the roes, and by the hinds of the field, that ye stir not up, nor awake my love, till he please.

Song of Solomon, 3.1-5

Hunger drove Erik from the warm press of bodies in his bed. It had clawed at him in the cold early morning. The gray light just before dawn spread through the room. He rolled François carefully toward his sister's warm, bundled body. He silently walked to the other side where Meg lay, partially uncovered in the chill. Her shift had twisted up exposing her thigh. Erik brushed his palm gently across the creamy surface before he took the hem of her shift and pulled it down to her knee. He straightened the coverlet to loosen the tangles and covered his wife's sleeping body. She moaned lightly, shifted, and fell back into a deep sleep nestled against Mario.

He watched them sleep until the hunger became unendurable. Broth was all he had had for he knew not how many days.

In the adjoining dressing room, he found clean, pressed clothes laid out for him. On a nearby table rested a mask. He ran his fingers over the smooth white surface. For a moment he wondered what might have happened to the one he had worn. But the thought of the grime and filth, the dried blood—his and Leroux's—that would have stained it made him queasy. He dressed quickly in the essentials. Just before he slipped out into the unfamiliar hallway, he pulled the mask down over his features and adjusted it so that it fit the contours of his face.

He had been in the Chagny estate, uninvited and unwanted, on only a few occasions. Once during the masked ball, later when he came to Christine's bedside to assure himself that she was safe, and the last time when he carried her off to the underground rooms in an effort to save her from the madness of grief when she had lost her child. Strange to be in this home now as a carefully tended guest.

The moment he rounded on the stairs he heard her singing. It seemed a lifetime since he had heard that voice. The hunger slipped to the background as a new sensation overwhelmed him. It was a excruciating joy. The sounds led him, drew him toward a room at the far end of the hall. The door had been left slightly ajar. There he found her—Christine. He stopped on the threshold, half hidden, peering into the dimly lit room. If she were to turn and see him now, would she imagine those days when he watched over her, guided her, cared for her, always in the shadows, a phantom?

Christine played and sang a melody he recognized from a long forgotten opera, one he had written for her. He had thought *The Phoenix* lost, but she had saved it, kept it, learned its delicate strains.

"What, may I ask, do you think you're doing?"

Startled by the quiet voice behind him, Erik turned his head to see Raoul.

The count glanced past Erik's shoulder at his wife, who oblivious to the men, continued to play. "You know," he teased, "we really must stop this, Erik."

"I thought the music had been lost," Erik said.

For one moment, Raoul was puzzled. Then he realized that Christine was playing the music that she had rescued from the underground lair where the Phantom had taken her and where the police had eventually captured him. She had insisted on remaining behind and gathering the scattered sheets as if she would save them if she could not save their composer.

"She kept it," added Erik, affected by gratitude and wonder.

"Yes, she plays it often," answered Raoul, a strange smile on his face. "Sometimes she wakes early and comes down to play. I forgot this song was yours."

"It's hers now. It was always meant to be hers."

Raoul thought it best not to comment. The two men were quiet for a few moments, content to stand outside the room and listen to Christine sing.

"Her voice. It's as beautiful as it ever was." Erik leaned his forehead hard against the doorjamb. He tilted to the side. Raoul grabbed him by the shoulders to steady him as it seemed that Erik might fall. "I'm…dizzy."

"I shouldn't wonder."

"I'm hungry." Erik took a deep breath.

"That's to be expected. Come with me. I know where Cook keeps the cheeses."

Erik waved Raoul's offer of assistance away and stepped reluctantly back from the door. Raoul stole a last glance at Christine before slipping the door closed. He set off toward the back of the house, consciously slowing his step so as not to tire Erik needlessly.

In the kitchen, he invited Erik to sit at the large wooden work surface while he rummaged around in a space that was evidently largely unfamiliar to him. It was still early. On Sunday, the staff assembled late in the morning, so none of the servants were about. Erik watched silently and a bit wickedly while Raoul searched through the different cupboards for something simple that he might serve his guest.

"Here we go," Raoul crowed in triumph, bringing forth a large round wedge of yellow cheese to set beside the day old loaf of bread. Then he scanned the counters for something to drink. Uncorking and sniffing at one bottle after another, he discarded several concoctions—including vinegar and various oils—until he found what Erik was sure must be a cooking wine. Erik couldn't help but smile to see Raoul crinkle his nose at the unpleasant "bouquet" of the dark bottle's contents.

"Well, it wasn't evidently a very good year," he said in apology as he brought it to the table and looked about for a glass.

Erik took the bottle and drank directly from it, suppressed his grimace at the sourness, and wiped the opening. Then he handed the bottle in challenge to Raoul.

For one moment Raoul balked at the unnecessary barbarity of his guest's table manners, but the hard glint to Erik's eye urged him on. He took a huge swig of the liquid, determined not to shrink from the dare. The instant it touched his palate, he cursed himself. Even though his first impulse was to spit it out, he wouldn't give Erik the satisfaction. He blinked back tears and cleared his throat to disguise the sputter of coughing that attacked him.

A tremendous clap of laughter erupted across the wooden table followed by several waves of hilarity.

"Damn you!" Raoul cursed. "You must have a cast iron gullet! What the hell is this?" He held the bottle up to the dim light from the window as if he might be able to read its contents through the glass.

Erik reached for it, and to Raoul's shock, upended it, taking another deep drink. "I'd say it's a basic cooking wine. Tart, but full bodied."

"I see success has not improved your taste."

While Raoul searched for something more palatable, Erik cut huge chunks of cheese, and ate them with handfuls of the crusty bread.

They ate in silence. Raoul was suddenly aware of how seriously dangerous Erik's ordeal had been as he watched him eat ravenously.

"So are you done wallowing in self-pity?"

Erik finished the mouthful of grapes Raoul had placed in front of him before responding. "Always the soul of compassion aren't you, my dear Count?" Then changing his tone, he nodded at Raoul's scarred cheek. "Are you growing used to your new friend?"

"Well, it's the devil to shave around, but yes, I suppose you might say that."

"What doesn't kill us…," Erik whispered, his eyes averted.

"Scars us forever?" Raoul finished.

"Seriously, you shouldn't have let her."

Raoul had grown used to Erik's impetuous jumps. Strangely, he understood exactly to whom he was alluding.

"You can't be serious. I thought you at least understood Meg if not women in general. Seems I was mistaken on both counts. You see how well they obey us. We'd barely left Rome when the two of them set off for Paris."

"She had no business traipsing around those tunnels."

"I would have had to break both her legs to stop her from coming with us to search for you."

"But the baby. You should have…"

"Let you die? Erik, I tried to stop her. Even Christine spoke against her joining the search. And to be quite blunt, if she'd obeyed us, you'd be dead now."

As Erik lifted his eyes to scowl at him, Raoul continued, "François told us Leroux was dead. He also told us what you said to him. Meg was adamant. None of us knew those tunnels nearly as well as she did. Long past the moment the rest of us gave up any hope of finding you alive, she insisted on continuing the search. She was like a…"

"An irascible badger?" Erik's gaze had skirted past Raoul to a point somewhere over the count's shoulder toward the doorway. "A cantankerous mule? An itchy porcupine?"

"I don't particularly like the comparisons," said the person in question. Meg approached the men at the table. "And Raoul is not to blame. You should thank him, Erik."

"For what? He has just admitted that he would have left me there to die but for your unreasonable nagging."

"Wait one moment," protested the count. "I didn't exactly say that!"

The sun had crested over the horizon. A sharp, bright ray of light burst through the window and spread along the wooden surface of the table, eventually stealing across Meg's hand as it closed on Erik's.

"I suppose you'll eventually head back to Rome?" Raoul asked as he saw the look that passed between Erik and Meg.

Erik nodded.

"You'll stay until you're both rested and well. I insist."

"I agree, but only if you open the cellars and bring up some of the wine that's worth drinking."

The first several days of Erik's recovery, the children hung on him, dogging his steps, vying for his attention, rehearsing new and old tricks for his approval. Meg feared their constant demand would exhaust Erik, but it seemed to have the opposite effect. His strength returned steadily with each passing day. He read stories and sang songs to the delight of Laurette and Erica. He assisted Victor, Elise, Mario, and François in designing a complicated fort and supervised their determined efforts to build it on the bank of the pond. When he drew pictures to illustrate the children's favorite stories, Elise and Victor pleaded with him to draw pictures of them, too. The caricatures Erik sketched were so funny that soon he was enlisted to draw everyone on the estate, including Raoul, who pretended to be offended when a particularly satiric caricature of him dressed like Louis XV was left pinned to the wall just outside his study door.

Eventually the children realized that Erik was not going to disappear if they lost sight of him. They began to wander off, content to spend a few hours, instead of every waking moment, with him. Only Laurette persisted in clinging to her father's side, but even she relaxed her vigil on occasion, especially when she found herself distracted by the bushy tail of Robespierre, the Chagny children's gentle golden retriever.

Once Erik showed signs of renewed vigor, Raoul invited him to regular practice in the fencing hall. An hour sometimes stretched into two or more, but the men were obviously content to keep each other's company. Meg and Christine stole away to walk the park or to spend their time together in the garden or the parlor, sewing or reading, but always reminiscing about their childhood in the Opera Populaire.

One rainy afternoon found Christine and Meg trapped inside. The men had abandoned the ladies and taken refuge in the fencing hall to shake off the lethargy of the gloomy weather. Meg sat in a large overstuffed chair, trying to read a slim volume of essays by Montesquieu. Christine had been writing in her diary when she drifted away into memories, staring out into the gray curtain of rain, the pen lax in her hand.

"Meg," asked Christine, "when did you realize that you loved him?"

Meg lowered the book to her lap. She drew her feet up onto the cushion of the chair and wedged them under her skirts. Perhaps she was trying to compose her answer or perhaps she was enjoying having been drawn back to a pleasant memory.

"It's hard to say," she said, the hint of a smile playing at the corner of her lips and eyes.

Christine was intrigued by the wistful expression that Meg could not hide. She sensed that Meg had found herself warmed by private memories too intimate to share.

"You had seen him. Why didn't you ever tell me?" There was no accusation in the question. Christine was simply curious.

"Tell you what?" laughed Meg. "That I had seen a man hiding in the walls, stepping out of wardrobes, staring from the flies? You would have thought I was mad."

"But when I told you…when I mentioned my tutor, did you know it was Erik?"

"I realized that the man I saw slipping in and out of rooms was the Phantom, the Opera Ghost. I had seen him on several occasions coming from the manager's office, after which all hell would break loose. But I wasn't afraid of him. Maman knew about him. She told me there was nothing to fear. So in spite of what everyone said about the ghost that haunted the opera house, I reasoned that he couldn't be dangerous or evil. I didn't realize at first that he was the one whose voice we often heard at night, the one that you thought of as your father's ghost. But I caught a glimpse of him one night. It was the night that you had a bad fever. Remember? We were very afraid for you. Maman sat up with you most of the night, but when you seemed to fall into a deep sleep she went to rest herself. He must have been worried about you because that time he came into the room and he knelt beside your bed and…"

"Yes! I remember. He stroked my forehead as he sang."

Meg smiled at Christine's sudden excitement. "Had you forgotten?"

"No, not really, but I couldn't actually remember it clearly. I wasn't sure whether it had happened or I had dreamed it."

"It was awfully late. I pretended to be asleep. I lay in my bed watching him hover over you for quite a while."

"So you saw him there, by the bed. He watched over me." Christine seemed to be speaking to herself, not to Meg. "But there were several years when I barely remember feeling his presence."

Meg nodded, waiting for Christine to continue if she meant to.

"Not until much later. I was trying to sing one of the arias that Carlotta had sung. I was in the chapel. I loved the song, and I thought that…" Christine blushed and hesitated. With a self-deprecating smile, she blurted, "I thought I could certainly sing it better than Carlotta had."

Meg and Christine both burst out laughing. They took turns recalling certain moments in those years of their adolescence when Carlotta had exasperated M. Reyer practically to the point of apoplexy.

"So you were obviously already thinking of replacing Carlotta as the diva of the Opera Populaire, weren't you?" Meg teased.

"Perhaps. It did cross my mind. But I would never have had the nerve had I not heard his voice that day in the chapel."

"What did he say?"

"Louder, Mlle. Daaé. If you expect those in the back to hear you, you must learn to project." Christine imitated Erik's stern voice, lowering hers to an absurd pitch and speaking as if she were in a large amphitheater.

"That sounds like something he'd say!"

"Then he began to sing the aria to me. I couldn't imagine that voice to be of this earth. I remember telling him that my father had made me believe in angels, that I had hoped my angel of music might come and teach me to sing."

"What did he say?"

"He didn't say anything. Not for the longest time. I thought he had gone so I called out to him. I called him my Angel of Music and asked him not to leave me."

"And he answered," whispered Meg.

"Yes. Yes. My Angel of Music answered."

Shortly afterwards Meg had taken Erik apart to speak with him. She had noticed him scribbling notes on stray bits of paper. Often in the evening while the others chatted or played cards, Erik would spend his time at the piano. The conversation Meg had had with Christine stayed with her. She imagined how strange it must have been for Erik to come upon the young woman in the chapel. Had he recognized her talent? Had he also known that she was the young girl that he had befriended and comforted several years before? Yes, Meg was sure that he had. After all that time he had risked revealing himself to Christine. He had spoken to her. But no sooner had he approached than Christine had christened him her Angel of Music, imposing upon him yet another mask behind which to hide. There was something sad about Christine's memory of that encounter. It was the silence. He had not known what to say to the beautiful young woman. He had thought to reveal himself, but she had not recognized him. When she called him up from her own imagination and desire, he had come. The Angel of Music had come.

"Why don't you join Christine in the parlor while she practices?" suggested Meg.

Erik narrowed his brow and waited.

"Go on, then. I know you'd like to play for her. It's all right." Before she could change her mind, regret her decision, she walked off to the garden ostensibly to read.

Erik stood in the hallway and listened to the deep beating of his heart as it drowned out all other sounds. Only after he felt the surprise dull did he hear the soft notes of a song drifting from the opposite end of the hallway. He stared out in the direction that Meg had taken, but he didn't follow after her. Instead he let the music pull him.

He had been Christine's teacher. For months he had basked in the glow of her adoration. She had believed him to be infallible, an angel, the spirit of music itself. The perfect student she had taken his instructions and understood them as if they were already written upon her soul. For the first time in his life, he had felt that he was part of something beautiful. He had thought that he was loved.

He found himself outside the chamber. He waited for Christine to come to the end of the melody before he silently opened the door. She looked up at him from the piano.

"May I come in?" he asked.

"Brava," cheered Raoul as Christine took an exaggeratedly deep bow. Meg giggled and clapped her hands. Erik tried to disguise the smile that twitched at the corners of his mouth as he shuffled the sheets together, unnecessarily tidying the score.

The performance had been for a small, select audience comprised of Raoul, Meg, and the children. François had stood beside his father, intently scanning the notes while Erik played. Elise had stood at François's elbow, imitating *his* studious air. The other children had been content to sprawl before the fire or to rest on the comfortable cushions on the divan or nearby chairs.

Knowing that the children would be present, Erik had suggested a light aria from the opera that Christine and he had been practicing for days.

The hour being late, the performance at an end, the children were sent off to their rooms. The younger ones, Laurette and Erica, were already asleep and had to be carried. After the children had gone, the room was silent except for a particular string of notes from the aria that Erik lightly played. The melody would not be silenced. In the middle of the cadence, he stopped.

"Meg, come," he said. "There's a duet. It's perfect for the two of you."

Christine had taken her seat next to Raoul. She caught Meg's eye and nodded in encouragement. When Meg didn't rise, Christine went and pulled her from her chair. The two women took their places on either side of Erik. As if to lay claim, Meg rested her hand on Erik's shoulder. For a moment Erik felt their awkwardness, but he pretended not to. He cleared his throat to get both women's attention.

"Meg, you sing this part. Christine knows the other. Watch this change here. It comes again just before the end."

Erik's fingers played the score through once for Meg, then he began in all seriousness again at the beginning. Suddenly time fell away, and Meg and Christine were girls again at the Opera Populaire. The women's voices blended, each setting off the other's, each taking and giving, until the woven sounds seemed to belong to the same fabric.

As the piece ended, Erik sighed. It was a pleasant sound of regret and contentment. He had not wanted the moment to end. Still he could hear the notes, echoes and memories converging from long ago.

"I don't think I've heard anything more lovely than your voices." His hand reached out and gathered Meg to his side. With that one gesture he wiped away any of Meg's lingering doubts. She couldn't resist brushing his lips with her fingers. His eyes searched hers, finding the answer there to all the questions in his soul.

Yes, always.

It was hard to release her. It was even harder to drag his eyes from hers, but Christine was watching. Raoul joined them at the piano and congratulated all three on their performance.

"Now how about something light?" asked Raoul.

"Any recommendations?" Erik sounded skeptical but game.

"Well there is this little song I remember fondly from my sojourn in the Italian inns." Christine laughed as if she must have already heard the ditty. Raoul gave her a wink and continued, "It's about this young barmaid and twelve strapping youths from the country. And it goes something like this…"

A month had drawn to its end, and thoughts had turned to farewells. Raoul suggested that with Leroux's death perhaps Paris was no longer as dangerous as it had been for Erik. Surprisingly Erik disagreed. Paris was no longer home. His children had been born in Italy. Marcelo and Madeleine, probably married by now, were in Rome as was Erik's work. Except for the Chagnys, Paris held only bad memories.

The children could not decide whether to be morose or excited. Mario and François had reluctantly taken their leave of Victor just moments before, reaffirming secret pacts and future plans. And although both boys had wanted to linger over their farewell to Elise, neither wished the other to see how much he was going to miss her. So instead they muttered something incomprehensible. At the last minute Elise kissed each boy on the cheek and ran away to hide, inconsolable, with only her tears for company. Laurette had squealed in anger when she was told that the beautiful golden retriever Robespierre could not come with them. The nurse did what she could to console and distract the disappointed child.

As last minute preparations were completed, Raoul and Erik stood by, impatient and uncomfortable with a sadness each one tried to mask in his own way. The modest assembly of boxes and trunks had been secured on the two carriages that were to make the journey to Rome. Children's voices rose and fell as they argued over who would sit where and for how long.

"Our home is always open to you," said Raoul. He had accepted defeat. He would not be able to convince Erik to begin life over in Paris.

The two men embraced briefly, then separated. Christine and Meg approached, hand in hand, reluctant to be parted until the very last moment. Hands and lips and cheeks touched and bade farewell. Unwilling to linger, Erik handed Meg up to the carriage and was about to climb in after her when Christine touched his sleeve and asked him to wait.

Without a word, she motioned to a servant who stepped forward and handed her a tightly rolled scroll bound in oxblood leather. She smiled shyly as she handed it to Erik. His hand reacted on its own volition and accepted the scroll, but his eyes bore down into hers, unsettled and intensely apprehensive.

"*The Phoenix*," she said in answer to his unspoken question.

"No. No, I can't. It's yours. You rescued it."

Her hand closed hard over his. She would not take it back.

"I memorized it long ago. No one can take it away from me. The music is inside."

"It's incomplete," he said, his voice husky and deep.

"Finish it," she urged. Then she reached up on tip toe and kissed him, a soft kiss on the lips. "Promise me." She stepped back into Raoul's arms.

Erik clutched the leather bound scroll against his chest. Silent, his thoughts lost in the past, he stepped into the carriage. He knocked hard on the outside panel of the door, and they sped off down the avenue toward home.

Later, in the coach, as the gentle rocking lulled them both into quiet contemplation, Meg reminded Erik that not all their memories of Paris had been bad.

Just the day before, Meg had happened upon a secret door, the same secret door that Christine had playfully shown Meg so many years ago. Meg had tricked a disguised Phantom to pass through that very door, intoxicated by carnival, to an alcove within. And there in sadness and joy, they had made love. The Phantom had thought he made love to Christine, but Meg had made love to Erik.

Casually strolling through the various rooms of Christine's home, thoughts of their imminent departure weighing heavily on her mind, Meg had been struck by a sudden flash of memory. The room was familiar. Meg felt as if she had stepped back in time. Along one wall, beside the mantel piece, she traced a nearly seamless opening—a door. It was cleverly disguised by the elaborate design of the wallpaper. Such memories seethed to the surface that she could not resist going in search of her husband. Or perhaps she had gone to find the Phantom. Without explanation, she led Erik down the hallway through the gallery of rooms to stand before the wall. And there she tapped the hidden release. The door clicked open.

Erik peered inside. Recalling the hidden room and the events that had taken place that night of the masked ball, he grew rigid, resisting Meg's insistence that they enter. For him, the memory was fraught with complex and contradictory feelings. It had been a bitter sweet lie and had once tormented him.

"Come," Meg urged, suddenly wicked.

He scowled at her and shook his head. He could tell what was on her mind by the curve of her smile, the way her eyes had grown lustrous and sly. Such a devilish expression could mean that only one thing was on her mind.

"What if someone comes upon us?" he warned, although he knew that he would follow her inside, just as he had that night so many years ago.

"They won't!" she promised, her fingers playing seductively with the fastenings of his shirt.

He placed his broad, firm hand over hers to still its seductive work. Large, moist doe eyes looked into his, and he could not turn away. Suddenly the memory of her dressed in an elaborate costume as Marie Antoinette came to mind. She and Christine had worn the same disguise, a trick played for Raoul's benefit. They had meant to confuse the count and tease him. But it had been the Phantom who had fallen into their trap. How could he have fooled himself into believing that Meg was anyone other than herself? Her dancer's body had swirled before him; her small hand had pulled him through the veranda doors and had brought him inexorably to that moment. Only later had he thought back to that night and realized that he must have known that she was not Christine.

The bright light of day—one window at an angle invisible from any of the nearby rooms afforded the only natural light—revealed an intimate room of blue and burgundy. It had seemed larger in his memory. It held a small brazier, an old, comfortable wing chair, two narrow bookcases along one shortened wall, and the large daybed on which he had lain with his impulsive and tragic queen.

As she remembered the night that she had tricked the Phantom and stolen his love, Meg's pulse quickened. Willfully, she slipped out of her gown and underclothes to stand naked before him. There would be no disguises this time, no misunderstandings, no tricks. While he watched, his eyes hungry and intense, she lay back on the blue and burgundy cushions. Then she held her arms out to Erik, beckoning him to lie with her again, this time in the bright light of day.

"You are wicked, Meg Giry!" he said as he slowly unfastened the buttons on his shirt, determined to linger until well into the afternoon.

"Let me show you how wicked I can be, M. Phantom."

Indeed they were pleased to find that Erik's intuition had proven correct. Madeleine and Marcelo had stolen away to be quietly wed the moment they received word from Raoul that both François and Erik were safe. Madeleine blushed a deep scarlet at Erik's unforgiving stare. Meg had to squeeze his hand to make him stop. It was unintentional on his part. He simply couldn't take his eyes away from Madeleine's face. She was transformed, as if after a long drought the rain had gently fallen on a bed of roses. She had blossomed, and Erik was admiring the effect. Marcelo, also mildly embarrassed, accepted his son's congratulations with modest pleasure.

"Rinaldo has done a wonderful job keeping the company on its toes, but he's nothing as demanding as you. Even so, all in all, the performances have been good, if not stellar, and he's managed Carlotta incredibly well."

"Oh?" asked Erik with mild misgiving. The thought of dealing with Carlotta had been the only blight on an otherwise joyful return.

"I think you'll be pleased, Erik. She has actually been quite concerned about your welfare."

Erik thought to himself that he'd believe that when hell froze over. If she worried, it was because she was concerned that he come back to fulfill his promises to her. "I suppose she's anxious to start a new opera?"

"I won't lie. She's mentioned it on a number of occasions. But, really, Rinaldo has a way with her. I find it rather strange to believe, but I think they have become…intimate."

Erik raised one eyebrow, less shocked than Marcelo. "Let's hope that you're right."

She had waited for three days, patiently. She dared Rinaldo to contradict her! Yes, patiently. She had not screamed at the maestro, Signore Bianchi. She had rehearsed her part, even though it was minor and hardly worth practicing more than a couple of times. She was reasonably sure of the words, and the melody was like that one in the other opera from last season, she thought. She hummed a few bars as the carriage approached the theater and thought she recalled it more or less well. It wasn't as if she would be singing unaccompanied! Yes, damn it, she'd waited patiently.

Rinaldo would have to admit that she hadn't acted on her first impulse to take the coach to the Costanzis' and demand to see Erik the very day of their arrival. "Tired?" she had huffed. "You say they will be tired? And am I not tired? I am tired to death of waiting for him. He goes off and he leaves me when he knows that I am sensitive! I cannot work in an environment that is unsteady."

Lulled by the constant sway of the carriage, she ignored the fact that Rinaldo was clenching and unclenching his jaw muscles at her litany of recent complaints. She pursed her lips into a pout and snuggled up against the tall, young man.

"If it hadn't been for you, Nano, I don't know what I would have done!" she teased. Rinaldo rolled his eyes at her tone, but he couldn't resist looking down and smiling at her.

Men, she thought, they had such fragile egos. It was so easy to wrap them around one's little finger.

As their carriage slowed to a stop near the grand entrance of the Teatro dell'Opera, Carlotta waited impatiently for Rinaldo to hand her down to the sidewalk. She never used the stage door, preferring to mount the stairs and enter the glorious vestibule of the building where there were always aficionados of the opera glad to catch a glimpse of a diva. She smiled and waved her lavender glove at the workmen in the hall and made her way toward the house. As she passed a small crowd of girls from the ballet corps, huddled with tutus jauntily pointing like chicken feathers toward the ceiling, she overheard them whispering. She distinctly heard Erik's name!

So she rushed onto the stage, looking for him, expecting to see him, to hear that voice making his unreasonable demands!

"Where? Where? Where?" She stomped.

"Why do you persist in using that voice of yours as if it were a weapon?"

"Ah hah!" Carlotta twirled toward the sound. There he was, as self important as ever, wearing a beautiful, new alabaster mask that covered, curiously, only the right side of his face. She arched both her eyebrows at how handsome he was! With only the disfigurement hidden, she could finally admire his unblemished features, imagine what he might have looked like had he been born without flaw. She remembered that she had meant to scowl and berate him. She tried to look angry.

"Why is it that you don't come and you don't come for so long? You are irresponsible, a bad director. You have a theater to run."

Erik knew that Carlotta was not ignorant of what had sent him to Paris. But then, too, she must also have learned that everything had been resolved well over a month ago. He waited for her to carry on, as she was wont to do, but strangely she simply stood and looked at him. Her scowl had given way to a slightly stupid expression, as if she didn't quite know what she was supposed to do with his silence.

"I hear that Rinaldo has been doing a competent job of managing the theater. Meg's stand-in has been received with modest praise. You yourself finished the run of *Macbeth* with glowing reports." Erik took out a piece of newsprint from a portmanteau that he carried and handed it to Carlotta.

It was a piece of newsprint carefully cut from an important daily in Paris. Clearly in one column Carlotta saw in bold characters her name. The article, albeit small, reported on the long awaited return of the prima donna, Carlotta Giudicelli, in an acclaimed production of the opera, *Macbeth*, on the stage of the Teatro dell'Opera. The woman read the article, her lips moving silently, looked up at Erik, read the article yet again, and flung it into Rinaldo's hands. The moment the young man accepted the clipping, Carlotta whirled on Erik, grabbed him round the neck, and kissed him forcefully on the lips. Rinaldo stood, his mouth agape, but he was not the most shocked.

Carlotta had barely finished her assault when she felt a hand grab her collar roughly from behind and force her to turn about.

"Signorina Giudicelli, you may not!" Meg sternly reprimanded the former diva.

"Meg, it's all right," said Erik as he discreetly wiped the corner of his mouth with his handkerchief.

"The hell it is!" Meg didn't take her eyes off Carlotta.

"She was just showing her enthusiastic appreciation for the article from the Paris gazette."

"I don't know why you are so nervous, Mag. You don't trust him, your husband? Has he the roving eye?" Carlotta's smile was broad and sardonic.

Meg balled up her fist, but Erik easily slid between the two women and cast a meaningful glance toward Rinaldo.

"Carlotta, you promised me you'd behave," Rinaldo scolded as he grabbed hold of her arm to pull her out of range.

"You are always picking at me! And you!" Carlotta stabbed a pointed finger at the air in the general direction of Erik. "What is the opera you have written next? What is my part?"

"I'm working on it, signorina." Erik took his wife gently by the elbow and guided her back toward the curtains. "Is there a passable opera version of *The Taming of the Shrew*, you think?" he asked Meg in a whisper.

"Eh, you, Signore Costanzi. You," came Carlotta's voice like cannon fire along the corridor. "Erik? M. Phan…M. Costanzi, I have some suggestions for you, for the next opera."

Erik ignored Carlotta's insistent voice. Instead, he bent and kissed Meg lightly on the lips. "Well, my canary, you're the diva of this company and the sole prima donna of my heart. What do *you* wish to sing next, my love?"

Epilogue

My Dearest Friends,

It was with great joy that we read of the birth of your son, Roland. Meg posted our congratulations, as well as our modest gift, more than a month ago. She was at that time anxious in her own confinement and truly relieved, as was I, that Christine was safely delivered of a son and was resting in good health as was the child. We wondered whether the father could boast as much for his own health! I speak only from my own experience, since I believe I suffered far more distress and care than my wife as she approached the birth.

You may wonder why it is I who write this letter since I have so infrequently picked up pen to do anything more than jot the notes and verse to my music. Indeed I fear this letter will not please for I have no talent at crafting clever discourse. Yet I stray, as usual, from my point. Meg is resting contentedly. I hear her breathing at my back with relief at the unusual quiet. My news, if you have not already guessed it, is that I am again a father.

We were quite surprised when Meg complained of her sons' importunate demands. We had come to the theater to watch the last minute rehearsal of "Medea." What a fortunate choice of opera for Carlotta for it involved little or no conceit on her part! There has never been a woman more comfortable with horror than our "prima donna." Among us, we have adopted that endearment for her since she lives the fantasy from hour to hour, whether or not it is true. Rinaldo, I am happy to say, has managed to find a way to soften Carlotta's worst impulses. Although I still arrive home on occasion with bleeding wounds, they are far less deep than they would have been without the intervention of my assistant. Indeed, I have come to trust him again. He has expiated his crimes against us although I believe his affection for Carlotta is surprisingly genuine.

To return to Meg's unexpected pains, she grabbed my hand so forcefully that I knew she was in earnest. We had no time to send for the physician or even to return to the estate. In point of fact, Box 5 will always have a special meaning for us after the rapid delivery of our twin boys. The details are fuzzy to me. I was present, but I can honestly say that I was completely unnerved. I remember a lot of petticoats and skirts, and then I saw one and then another dark-haired head come from amid the jumble of fabric and female limbs. I thought I was seeing double, hallucinating, a bad habit I have always had as you may remember. But fortunately, it was not the return of madness but the sight of the birth of my two sons, Etienne and Raoul. I beg you forgive our not consulting you about the name in this matter. It was a decision shared equally by Meg and myself.

The two boys are as alike as two blooms on the same briar. Mario and François are very happy to have two little brothers, but Laurette is sorely disappointed that one of them is not a sister. She asked us to exchange one of them for a little girl, and we are still trying to convince her that this is not easily done. So she insists we work on bringing her a sister the next time. I pale to think of it.

I am exhausted and delighted. I find myself surrounded by life, amazed that I have been blessed in this way. Surely it must mean something.

I am writing again, a comedy, and I will expect you to come when it is ready to be staged. By that time, Roland should be old enough to travel and Christine fully recovered. We long to see you again, for you and Christine will always be inextricably linked to our good fortune. Meg sends her love, and I remain

Your ever humble servant and sincerest friend,

Erik

978-0-595-48568-0
0-595-48568-5